The School at
Thrush Green

Friends at
Thrush Green

Miss Read, or in real life Dora Saint, was a school teacher by profession who started writing after the Second World War, beginning with light essays written for *Punch* and other journals. She then wrote on educational and country matters and worked as a scriptwriter for the BBC. Miss Read was married to a schoolmaster for sixty-four years until his death in 2004, and they have one daughter.

In the 1998 New Year Honours list Miss Read was awarded an MBE for her services to literature. She is the author of many immensely popular books, including two autobiographical works, but it is her novels of English rural life for which she is best known. The first of these, *Village School*, was published in 1955, and Miss Read continued to write about the fictitious villages of Fairacre and Thrush Green until her retirement in 1996. She lives in Berkshire.

Miss Read

The School at
Thrush Green

Friends at
Thrush Green

The School at Thrush Green
First published in Great Britain by Michael Joseph in 1987

Friends at Thrush Green
First published in Great Britain by Michael Joseph in 1990

This omnibus edition published in 2010
by Orion Books Ltd
Orion House, 5 Upper St Martin's Lane
London WC2H 9EA

An Hachette UK company

A CIP catalogue record for this book is available
from the British Library.

ISBN 9781407230238

Printed in Great Britain by Clays Ltd, St Ives plc

www.orionbooks.co.uk

The School at
Thrush Green

To
Betty and Vic
With Love

CONTENTS

* * *

PART THREE

Journey's End

PART ONE

Time To Go

* * *

1. ROUGH WEATHER

'January,' said Miss Watson, 'gives me the jim-jams!'

She jerked the sitting-room curtains together, shutting out the view of Thrush Green. Firelight danced on the walls of the snug room, and shone upon the face of her friend Agnes Fogerty as she placed a log carefully at the top of the blazing coals.

The two ladies had lived in the school house at Thrush Green for several years, and had been colleagues for even longer. It was a happy relationship, for each middle-aged teacher felt respect and affection for the other.

In most matters Dorothy Watson, as headmistress, took command. She was a forthright and outspoken woman whose energy and enthusiasm had enriched the standing of Thrush Green school. As mistress of the school house, she also took precedence over her companion when it came to any domestic decisions, and Agnes Fogerty was content that it should be so.

It was not that she always agreed with her headmistress's actions. Beneath her mouse-like appearance and timid ways, Agnes held strong views, but at this moment, with Dorothy's opinion of January, she entirely agreed.

'At its worst today,' she said. 'And the children are always so restless in a strong wind.'

A violent gust threw a spattering of rain against the window at this point, and Miss Watson sat down in her armchair.

'Must blow itself out before morning,' she said, taking up her knitting.

All day Thrush Green had been buffeted by a howling gale

and lashing rain. Rivulets rushed along the gutters and cascaded down the steep hill that led to the nearby town of Lulling. The windows of the stone Cotswold houses shuddered in the onslaught. Doors were wrenched from people's grasp, umbrellas blew inside out, and the chestnut trees along one side of the green groaned and tossed their dripping branches in this wild weather.

It had made life particularly exhausting for the two school-teachers. Every time the classroom door opened, a score of papers fluttered to the floor pursued by delighted children. A vase of chestnut twigs which little Miss Fogerty was nurturing in order to show her children one day the fan-shaped young leaves and the interesting horseshoe-shaped scars where the old leaves had once been, was capsized by a sturdy infant intent on rescuing his drawing.

The ensuing chaos included a broken vase, a miniature Niagara down the front of the stationery cupboard, a sodden copy of *The Tale of Squirrel Nutkin* from Agnes's own library, and a great deal of unnecessary mayhem which was difficult to suppress.

Through the streaming windows the two teachers, in their respective classrooms, had watched the inhabitants of Thrush Green struggling to go about their daily affairs.

Mr Jones, landlord of The Two Pheasants hard by, had lost his hat when he was staggering outside with a heavy crate of beer cans. He pursued it, with a surprising turn of speed, across the grass, where it came to rest against the plinth of Nathaniel Patten's statue.

Molly Curdle, who lived in a cottage in the garden of the finest house on Thrush Green, home of the Youngs, wheeled out her bicycle, and little Miss Fogerty was anxious on her behalf as she wobbled away townwards. Surely it was highly dangerous to cycle in such wicked weather! But then Agnes remembered that she had heard that Molly's father, Albert Piggott, the surly sexton who lived only yards from the school, was in bed with bronchitis and perhaps Molly was off to get him some medicine. No doubt his wife Nelly could have fetched it, but perhaps she too was ailing? With such conjectures are village folk made happy.

It was certainly a relief to be in the comfort of the school house at the end of such an exhausting day, and the fire was burning comfortingly.

Agnes opened a crack in a large piece of coal with an exploratory poker. A splendid yellow flame leapt out and she surveyed it with pleasure.

'I often think,' she mused aloud, 'that it must be trapped sunshine.'

'What is?' enquired Dorothy, lowering her knitting.

'Flames from the coal. After all, coal comes from very ancient forests, and it stands to reason that the trees must have seen sunshine. And when, after all these millions of years, we crack the coal – why, there it is!'

Dorothy, who was not given to such flights of fancy, considered Agnes's theory for some moments. It might not be scientifically feasible, but it was really rather poetic.

She smiled indulgently upon her friend. 'It's a nice idea, dear. Now, what about scrambled eggs for supper?'

Molly Curdle, tacking along Lulling High Street in the teeth of the gale, was indeed going to fetch some medicine for her father.

What a problem he was, thought Molly! Every winter now, it seemed, he had these spells of bronchial coughing. His second wife Nelly could not be said to neglect him. Her cooking was as splendid as ever. Albert was offered luscious soups, casseroles, roasts, pies and puddings in abundance.

Nevertheless, thought Molly, swerving to dodge a roving Sealyham, it was a pity she was not at home more often. Nelly was now a partner in The Fuchsia Bush, a flourishing tea-room in Lulling High Street, and her duties took her out from the house soon after eight in the morning, and her arrival home varied from five to seven o'clock.

Not that you could blame Nelly, Molly commented to herself. She could never really take to this step-mother, far too fat and vulgar for Molly's taste, but at least she took good care of Albert and not many would do that for someone as pig-headed as her father. This job at The Fuchsia Bush gave her some respite from Albert's constant moaning, and her salary was now the mainstay of the Piggott household.

By now she had reached the chemist's shop, and tried to lodge her bicycle against the kerb, but the wind made it impossible. She wheeled it across the pavement and leant it against the shop window.

'Not against the glass, please,' said a young woman peremptorily, and Molly pushed it wearily a few paces along to a brick pillar.

The chemist's assistant, resplendent in a white coat, watched smugly from the shelter of the door. When she caught sight of Molly, whose face was almost hidden in a sodden headscarf, her mood changed.

'Why, Moll, I never knew it was you! Come on in. You're fair soaked.'

Molly recognised a schoolfellow, Gertie, who had shared her desk at one time at Thrush Green school.

'I've come to get Dad's cough mixture. Dr Lovell's given me a chit.'

She followed the snowy coat towards the back of the shop. It was marvellous to get out of the raging wind, and she was glad to sit down on a high stool by the counter.

'I'd have thought your ma could have come in for this,' observed the girl. 'She's only a few doors down the street.'

'She has to be at The Fuchsia Bush dead early. Long before Dr Lovell's surgery opens. Anyway, he's my old dad. I don't really mind.'

The girl handed the prescription through a hatch behind her, and settled down for a few minutes' gossip.

'And how's Thrush Green then? I'm in one of them new houses behind the vicarage here. Don't get up your way often.'

'Much the same. The Two Pheasants is doing well. My Ben likes his job, Anne, my youngest, goes to play school, and our George is doing well with Miss Fogerty.'

'She still there? I heard as she and Miss Watson were thinking of retiring.'

'Well, that's been on the cards for some time, but they're both still at the school.'

'Proper bossy-boots that Miss Watson,' said Gertie, blowing some dust from a row of first-aid tins.

The hatch opened behind her, and a disembodied hairy hand passed out a large bottle. Gertie took it, the hatch slammed shut, and Molly looked in her purse for money.

'Hope it does the trick,' said Gertie. 'I'm not saying it will cheer him up, Moll. We all know him too well for that, don't we?'

Molly smiled. As a loyal daughter she had no intention of agreeing with this barbed remark, but nevertheless she knew it had the ring of truth.

People in Lulling and Thrush Green knew each other too well to be deceived, and there could be no hidden secrets in such a small community. Whether this was a good thing or not, Molly could not say, but she pondered on the problem as she set out again through the twig-littered street to her home at Thrush Green.

Meanwhile, Albert Piggott looked gloomily about his bedroom. Beside him on a small table stood a glass of water, a medicine bottle containing the last dose of cough mixture, a tin of cough lozenges, so strong that even Albert's beer-pickled tongue rebelled at their potency, and an egg-cup containing his wife's cure-all for ailing throats and chests – butter, sugar and lemon juice mixed together. At least, thought Albert grudgingly, Nelly's stuff tasted better than the rest.

He could hear the familiar sounds of pub activity going on beyond the window. The clattering of crates, Bob Jones's hearty voice and the occasional crash of the bar door made themselves heard above the roaring of the wind in the trees surrounding the churchyard opposite his cottage.

If only he were that much fitter he would damn well get out of this damn bed, and have a pint with the rest of them! But what was the use? Any minute now Molly would be in to fuss over him, and that dratted doctor had said he'd call. Trust him to come if he ever tried to go next door! He'd read the riot act if he even found his patient out of bed, let alone abroad!

Albert remembered his old mother had always maintained that doctors waited around the corner until a hot meal was dished up, and then they knocked at the door to create the maximum confusion within.

It was a hard life, sighed Albert. Here he was, for at least another week, living on slops, and not the right sort either. And then, he supposed gloomily, he would not be fit for cleaning the church or tidying the churchyard for weeks after that.

It was a good thing Nelly brought home a decent pay packet at the end of each week. His own earnings had halved over the last year, and if he felt as wobbly as he did now, what hopes of work in the future?

He pondered on his wife. True, she was no oil-painting, and had a temper like old Nick himself at times, but she still cooked a good meal, and brought in the money.

And heaven alone knew how important that was these days, with the price of a pint going up so alarmingly.

Dr Lovell finished his surgery stint, and battled his way to his car, case in hand. January was always a beast of a month, he mused, setting the windscreen wipers going, but this year it seemed more detestable than ever.

He decided to visit a family at Nidden before coping with the Thrush Green round. Chickenpox was rife, and he was concerned about the year-old baby of the house who had seemed unusually listless when he had called the day before.

He planned to get back about midday to see Albert Piggott and one of his patients in the recently built old people's home, known as Rectory Cottages, on Thrush Green. With any luck he should be in time to have lunch at home with Ruth his wife.

The lane to Nidden was awash. Sheets of water flowed across its surface, and the ditches each side of the road were full. Heaven help us if it freezes, thought John Lovell.

The gale had brought down scores of small branches, and one large one which lay more than halfway across the road. It could cause an accident, and the good doctor drew into the side of the road, and emerged into the howling wind.

The branch was sodden and heavy. His gloves were soon soaked and covered with slime, and it was hard work lugging the awkward object to a safer place on the grass verge. By the time it had been dragged out of everyone's path, John was thoroughly out of breath, and glad to return to the shelter of his car.

'Too much flab,' he said aloud, fastening his seat belt across the offending flesh. He would have to cut down on the helpings of delectable puddings Ruth made so well.

The hamlet of Nidden seemed to have suffered even more severely than Thrush Green. A chicken house lay on its side in one of the gardens. A bird-table was askew in another, and a plastic bucket rolled about in the road. Somebody's tea towel was fluttering in a hedge, and the wind screamed alarmingly in the trees above.

He wondered if the mother of his patients would hear his knocking above the bedlam around him, but she must have seen him arrive for the door soon opened, admitting a swirl of dead leaves into the hall.

'Come in, doctor. I'll be glad to see the back of January, I can tell you!'

'Won't we all,' responded John Lovell.

It was later than he had hoped when at last he returned to look in on Albert Piggott. Molly had just taken up a tray with a bowl of soup, a slice of bread, and some stewed apple for her father when they heard the doctor's tread on the stairs.

'Just like my old ma always said,' grumbled Albert, putting the tray to one side. 'Waits till the grub's ready, then the blighters come.'

'And how's the patient today?' asked John entering.

'None the better for seeing you,' replied Albert. 'I was just goin' to have me bit of dinner.'

'Well, I shan't keep you two minutes,' said the doctor. 'Just want to listen to those wheezy tubes again.'

'I'll go and keep the soup hot,' said Molly, vanishing with the bowl.

Albert bared his chest reluctantly.

'You're a lucky chap to have two good women looking after you,' said John, adjusting his stethoscope.

'No more'n they should do,' growled Albert. 'I've done enough for them in me time.'

The doctor applied his instrument to Albert's skinny chest.

'Cor! That's perishing cold!' gasped his patient. 'Enough to give a chap the pneumonics.'

The doctor smiled as he went about his business. How long now, he wondered, since he first encountered this most irascible of his patients? A fair number of years, before he had married Ruth and settled so happily at Thrush Green.

'You'll do,' he said at length, buttoning the old man's pyjama jacket. 'You could do with a shawl or cardigan round your shoulders. There's a fine old draught from that window when the wind's in that quarter.'

'Can I get up then?'

'Not for a day or two. Tell me where to find you a woolly.'

He made his way towards a chest of drawers.

'I'll tell Molly to look one out. Don't want you scrabbling through my stuff.'

The doctor laughed. 'I'll tell her myself on the way down. Now you can stay there, take your medicine, drink plenty of warm liquid – *and not any alcohol* – and don't make a damn nuisance of yourself, or I'll put you in hospital.'

He was pleased to see that this awful threat seemed to subdue his recalcitrant patient and he made his way downstairs.

Molly was standing by the stove watching the soup. He mentioned the shawl, and then added, 'You and Nelly do a fine job between you, and I know you get little thanks for it. He's coming along all right. We'll let him out when the weather changes.'

'If it ever does,' responded Molly, letting him out into the elements.

Some of the newest inhabitants of Thrush Green were the oldest, for recently a row of old people's homes, designed by the doctor's architect brother-in-law Edward Young, had been built on the site of the old rectory after fire had razed it to the ground. The new homes were called Rectory Cottages in remembrance of the former building. The seven little houses and their inhabitants were looked after by Jane and Bill Cartwright, the wardens, who lived in the last house of the eight.

Jane had been brought up in Thrush Green, had been a nurse at Lulling Cottage Hospital and then a sister at a Yorkshire hospital where she had met and married Bill. They were both pleased to be appointed to the post at Thrush Green and were doing a fine job among their charges.

While Dr Lovell was speeding home to a late lunch, Jane Cartwright was sitting with one of the old people. Miss Muriel Fuller had been a headmistress at the little school at Nidden for many years, and was now thoroughly enjoying her retirement in this small house.

Unfortunately, a septic throat was causing her acute pain and loss of voice, which is why Jane, although a trained nurse, had thought it wise to get the doctor's opinion.

'I was sure I saw his car outside the Piggotts' house,' whispered Miss Fuller. 'I can't think why he didn't come over here. Perhaps he's forgotten.' She looked alarmed.

'I'm sure he hasn't,' said Jane sturdily. 'Perhaps he had an urgent call. An accident, you know. Something that couldn't wait.'

How all these professional people hang together, thought Miss Fuller wearily! 'The point is,' she whispered, 'I'm due to take my remedial class tomorrow morning at the school, and I ought to let Miss Watson know.'

'Now don't you worry about that,' replied Jane, patting the patient's hand. 'As soon as the doctor's been I shall telephone Miss Watson. In any case, they won't be home until four at the earliest, and I'm sure he will have called long before that.'

Miss Fuller nodded, and reached for a very nasty throat lozenge. The more unpleasant the taste, the more good it does, she remembered her grandmother saying. But then her grandmother had always been one of the fire-and-brimstone school, and thoroughly enjoyed being miserable.

Jane rose to go. 'I'm just going to see the others, and I'll come along as soon as Dr Lovell arrives.'

Miss Fuller nodded. What with her throat and the lozenge, speech was quite impossible.

'Now who can that be!' exclaimed Dorothy Watson when the telephone rang.

She heaved herself from the armchair and made her way to the hall. A freezing draught blew in as she opened the sitting-room door, and sparks flew up the chimney from a burning log.

Agnes closed the door quietly and hoped that the call would not be a lengthy one. She would have liked to spare dear Dorothy the bother of answering the call, but as headmistress and the true householder it was only right that she should take precedence.

Within a few minutes her friend returned, and held out her hands to the blaze.

'That hall is like an ice-well,' she shuddered. 'Of course, the wind is full on the front porch, and fairly whistling under the door. I fear that this house is getting too old for comfort.'

'Anything important?' queried Agnes. It was so like Dorothy to omit to tell one the main message.

'Only Jane Cartwright. Muriel Fuller has laryngitis and won't be able to come along tomorrow.'

'Poor Miss Fuller!' cried Agnes. 'It can be so painful! Has the doctor been?'

'So I gather. Anyway, it need not make much difference to the timetable. After all, Muriel's visits are very much a fringe benefit.' She picked up her knitting and began to count the stitches.

Agnes considered this last remark. It seemed rather callous, she thought. Her own soft heart was much perturbed at the thought of Miss Fuller's suffering, but Dorothy, of course, had to think of the school's affairs first, and it was only natural that she saw things from the practical point of view.

'Eighty-four!' pronounced Miss Watson, and gazed into the fire. 'You know, Agnes,' she said at length, 'I really think it is time we retired.'

'To bed, do you mean? It's surely much too early!'

'No, no, Agnes!' tutted Dorothy. 'I mean retired properly. We've been talking of it for years now, and the Office knows full well that we have only stayed on to oblige the folk there.'

'But we've nowhere to go,' exclaimed Agnes. 'It was one of the reasons we gave for staying on.'

'Yes, yes, I know we couldn't get what we wanted at Barton-on-Sea, but I think we should redouble our efforts. I really don't think I could stand another winter at Thrush Green. Sitting in the hall just now brought it home to me.'

'So what should we do?'

'First of all, I shall write to those estate agents, Better & Better, at Barton, and chivvy them up. They know perfectly well that we want a two-bedroomed bungalow with a small garden, handy for the church and post office and shops. Why they keep sending particulars of top floor flats and converted lighthouses, heaven alone knows, but they will have to pull their socks up.'

'Yes, I'm sure that's the first step,' agreed Agnes. 'I will write if it's any help.'

'You'd be much too kind,' said her headmistress. 'I think I could manage something sharper.'

'You may be right,' murmured Agnes. 'But when should we give in our notice?'

'The sooner the better,' said Dorothy firmly. 'We'll arrange to go at the end of the summer term. That gives everyone plenty of time to make new appointments.'

'We shall miss Thrush Green,' said Agnes.

'We shall miss it even more if we succumb to pneumonia in this house,' replied Dorothy tartly. 'We can always visit here from Barton. We shall have all the time in the world, and there is an excellent coach service in the summer.'

She caught sight of her friend's woebegone face. 'Cheer up, Agnes! It will be something to look forward to while we endure this winter weather. What about a warming drink?'

'I'll go and heat some milk,' said Agnes. 'Or would you like coffee?'

'I think a glass of sherry apiece would do the trick,' replied Dorothy, 'and then we shan't have to leave the fire.'

She rose herself and went to fetch their comfort from a corner cupboard.

2. DOROTHY WATSON TAKES STEPS

The rumbustious January weather continued for the rest of the week, and the inhabitants of Lulling and Thrush Green were as tired of its buffeting as the rest of the Cotswold villages were. But on Saturday morning the wind had dropped, and a wintry sun occasionally cast a gleam upon a thankful world.

Miss Watson and Miss Fogerty agreed that the weekly wash would benefit from a spell in the fresh air, and Agnes was busy pegging out petticoats, nightgowns and other garments, when she was hailed by a well-known voice on the other side of the hedge. It was her old friend Isobel, wife of Harold Shoosmith, who lived next door.

When Agnes had heard that her old college friend of many years was going to be her neighbour, her joy was unbounded. The two students had soon discovered that they both hailed from the Cotswolds, and this drew them together.

Isobel's father was a bank manager at Stow-on-the-Wold, and Agnes's a shoemaker in Lulling. It meant that they could visit each other during the holidays, and the friendship grew stronger over the years.

Marriage took Isobel to Sussex and family affairs prevented her from visiting Thrush Green as often as she would have liked. But on the death of her husband she had renewed her close association with Agnes and her other Cotswold friends and, now that her children were out in the world, she had decided to find a small house in the neighbourhood.

But marriage to Harold Shoosmith, who had retired to Thrush Green some years earlier, had provided a home and a great deal of mutual contentment, and everyone agreed that the Shoo-smiths were an asset to any community.

'Isn't it wonderful to have no wretched wind?' called Isobel, advancing to a gap in the hedge, the better to see her neighbour. 'How are you both?'

'Very well. And you?'

'Fed up with being stuck indoors. Harold has battled out now and again, but I really couldn't face it. One thing though, I've caught up with no end of letters, so I suppose that's a bonus.'

Agnes wondered whether she should say anything about their proposed retirement but, cautious as ever, decided that dear Dorothy might not approve at this early stage of the project. She remained silent on this point, but joined her friend by the gap.

'Not snowdrops already?' she cried with pleasure. 'Now isn't that cheering!'

'And aconites too at the end of the garden,' Isobel told her. 'And my indoor hyacinths are at their best. Come round, Agnes, when you have a minute and see them.'

Agnes promised to do so, and the two ladies chatted for five minutes, glad to see each other again after their enforced incarceration.

'Well, I must go and see about lunch,' said Isobel at length.

'And I must finish my pegging out,' agreed Agnes, and the two women parted company.

What a warming thing friendship was, thought Agnes, fastening two pairs of respectable Vedonis knickers on the line. Even such a brief glimpse of dear Isobel enlivened the day. She would miss her sorely when the time came to move to Barton.

While little Miss Fogerty was busy with the washing, Nelly Piggott was in The Fuchsia Bush's kitchen in Lulling High Street. Here she was engaged in supervising the decoration of two large slabs of sponge cake ready to be cut into neat squares for the afternoon teas for which The Fuchsia Bush was renowned.

The new recruit was a nervous sixteen-year-old whose hand shook as she spread coffee-flavoured water icing over the first of the sponges.

Lord love old Ireland, thought Nelly! Would the girl never learn? She had come with a glowing report from her school's domestic science teacher, and another, equally fulsome, from her last post. Glad to see the back of her no doubt, thought Nelly grimly.

'If you dip your knife into the warm water more often,' said Nelly, striving to be patient, 'it won't drag the icing.'

The girl flopped the palette knife into the jug and transferred a small rivulet of water on to her handiwork.

Unable to bear it any longer, Nelly took over and began to create order out of chaos. To give her her due she bit back the caustic remarks trembling on her tongue.

'You fetch the walnut halves,' she commanded, 'and I'll leave you to space them out when this has begun to set.'

The girl fled, and at that moment Nelly's employer and partner at The Fuchsia Bush entered the kitchen from the restaurant.

'Can you leave that a moment? Bertha Lovelock is in the shop and wants to know if we can send in lunch – an *inexpensive* lunch – for three today.'

Nelly gave a snort, drew one final steady blade across her masterpiece, and followed Mrs Peters.

The Misses Lovelock were three ancient spinsters who lived next door to The Fuchsia Bush in a splendid Georgian house in which all three had been born and which they had inhabited all their lives. Although quite comfortably off, and the possessors of many valuable antiques, the sisters were renowned for their parsimony. No one knew this better than Nelly Piggott, who had 'helped out' for a time before finding permanent work at The Fuchsia Bush.

Nelly still remembered, with a shudder, the appalling meals she had been expected to cook from inferior scraps which she would not have offered to a starving cat. The memory too of a tablespoonful of metal polish, intended for a score of brass and copper articles, still rankled, and the meagre dab of furniture polish with which the dining-room table and chairs were meant to be brought to mirror-like condition.

Nowadays, she rejoiced in catering and cooking amidst the plenty of The Fuchsia Bush. She had grown confident in the knowledge that her work was appreciated and that, as a partner, she was enjoying the fruits of her expertise.

She approached her former employer secure in the knowledge that here she had the upper hand.

'Good morning, Miss Lovelock. Lunch for three, I gather? You'll take it here, I imagine, so I'll book a table, shall I?'

Nelly felt pretty sure that this was not what Miss Bertha really wanted. For a time, when the three old ladies had been quite seriously ill, the doctor had suggested that their midday meal might be sent in from next door. It had not been easy to find someone free at exactly the right moment to take in a hot meal, but Nelly and Mrs Peters had felt sorry for the Lovelocks and had been obliging.

They were glad though when the arrangement ended. The Lovelock sisters, anxious to stop the expense, had cancelled the lunches as soon as possible, to the relief of all. But now, it seemed, they were attempting to use the staff of The Fuchsia Bush as if it were their own, and Nelly was determined to nip this plan in the bud.

'No, Nelly, that is not quite what I meant. Miss Violet is in bed with her chest—'

Not that she would be in bed without it, thought Nelly reasonably.

'And neither Miss Ada nor I really feel up to coping with the cooking and shopping,' continued Miss Bertha. 'It would be a great help if you could send in a hot meal each day as you did before.'

Nelly assumed an expression of doubt and regret. 'It can't be done, Miss Lovelock,' she said. 'We haven't enough staff to make a regular arrangement like that. As you know, we're run off our feet here at lunch time.'

'But you did it before!'

'That was an emergency. We did it to oblige the doctor as well as you, but it couldn't be a permanent arrangement.'

'Well, that's very provoking,' said Miss Bertha, turning pink. The Lovelock sisters almost always got their own way.

'If I might suggest,' said Nelly, 'that you was to advertise for a cook-general in the paper, you might get suited quite quickly. Or the Labour might help.'

'The Labour?' echoed the old lady, looking mystified.

'Exchange,' added Nelly.

'Exchange?' echoed Miss Bertha.

'Job Centre like,' amplified Nelly. 'Up near the Corn Exchange.'

Miss Bertha picked up her gloves from the counter and began to put them on with extreme care, smoothing each finger. Her mouth was trembling and Nelly's kind heart was moved.

'Tell you what,' she said. 'You let me know if you'd like me to look out for someone when you've had a talk with Miss Ada and Miss Violet.'

'Thank you, Nelly,' said Miss Bertha. 'Most kind. We shouldn't want a great deal of cooking done. Just something light.'

'I know that,' said Nelly, with feeling, as she opened the door for her.

It was dark when Nelly toiled up the hill to Thrush Green, but it was a relief to find the air so still and the stars already twinkling from a clear sky.

Albert, still in his dressing gown and slippers, was sitting by the fire, but he had put on the kettle Nelly noted with approval.

'Well, and how have you been getting on today?' she enquired, sitting down heavily on a kitchen chair.

'Had a look at the paper. Took me medicine. Took a dekko out of the winder. This sunshine's brought 'em all out. Even old Tom Hardy, over at the Home, took out Polly for a walk on the green.'

'That dog must be on its last legs,' commented Nelly. 'Nearly as shaky as old Tom.'

The kettle set up a piercing whistle, and she rose to attend to it.

'I near enough went next door for a drink,' said Albert, 'but our Molly came in and put a stop to it.'

'So I should hope! What'll I say to the doctor if you catch your death?'

'Won't matter much what you say,' rejoined Albert morosely, 'if I'm a corpse, will it? Molly says he's coming on Monday, and may let me get out again, if I don't go too far.'

'Well, next door's about as far as you'll want to go anyway,' replied Nelly, stirring the teapot vigorously.

'There was a car stopped over by Mrs Bailey's,' observed Albert changing the subject. 'Some young chap got out.'

'Meter man, most like.'

'No. I knows him. Looked like that nephew of hers, Richard.'

'He'll be about as welcome as a sick headache,' pronounced Nelly. 'What's he come badgering his poor aunt for, I wonder?'

It would not be long before Nelly, Albert and the rest of Thrush Green knew the purpose of Richard's visit to Dr Bailey's widow. Meanwhile, there could only be the pleasurable conjecture of diverse opinions on the subject.

That weekend, there was considerable literary activity at the school house as Dorothy Watson took up her pen to write to the estate agents at Barton-on-Sea, who had the honour to be dealing with her affairs. She had chosen them from many in the area as she thought their name, Better & Better, sounded hopeful.

Agnes was busy sewing together the pieces of a baby's matinée jacket, in between bobbing in and out of the kitchen to keep an eye on a cake in the oven.

As she stitched she listened, in some alarm, to Dorothy's occasional snort as her pen hurried over the paper. She did so hope that the letter was *courteous*. After all, civility cost nothing, as her old father had so often said, and really one did not want to antagonise the estate agents at Barton on whom they were relying for their future comfort. Dear Dorothy could be so *downright* at times, and not everyone realised how kind her heart really was.

She was about to rise and go into the kitchen to stab the cake with a skewer, when Dorothy threw down her pen, leant back and said proudly, 'Now listen to this, Agnes.'

I write on behalf of my friend Miss Agnes Fogerty and myself. For some time now we have had our names on your books, and, to be frank, have had very poor service.

Although all the particulars of our needs are with you, let me repeat them. We need a two-bedroomed bungalow, on a level site, with a small garden. It must be within walking distance, i.e. no further than half a mile from shops, post office and church (C of E).

It must be in a good state of repair, as we hope to move in this summer, preferably in July.

Please do not waste your time and ours by sending particulars of outrageously useless properties such as the converted windmill, the granary with outside staircase and the underground flat made from a wine cellar, which were enclosed in your last communication.

I expect to hear from you by return.

Yours sincerely.

She turned to smile at Agnes. 'How's that? Can you think of anything else, Agnes dear?'

Agnes looked hunted. Her hands were shaking with agitation as she put the baby's coat aside.

'Well, I do think it was wise to repeat what we need, Dorothy, but I just wonder if that last paragraph isn't the tiniest bit – er—'

'Strong? That's what I wanted! It's about time they were jerked up.'

'Yes, I know, dear, but we don't want them to think us *unreasonable.*'

'Unreasonable? They're the ones that are unreasonable! Fancy sending two middle-aged ladies those absurd properties! We told them about my hip and that we are retiring. We're not a couple of mountain goats to go skipping up an outside staircase in a howling gale, and *with no handrail*, as far as one could see from that inadequate photograph. Or to go burrowing down a flight of steps into the black hole of Calcutta like that idiotic wine cellar!'

Dorothy's neck was becoming red, a sure sign of danger, and little Miss Fogerty knew from experience that it was time to prevaricate.

'My cake!' she exclaimed, hurrying out.

She busied herself for some minutes with her creation, allowing Dorothy to calm down before returning to the sitting-room. A delicious scent of almond cake followed her into the room.

'Something smells good,' said Dorothy smiling. 'Well, Agnes dear, let's go through the last paragraph and perhaps temper it a little before I make a fair copy.'

She picked up the letter and began to read. Agnes resumed her sewing, trying to hide her agitation.

It was not until the next day that she realised that she had sewn in the sleeves inside out, and would have to face a good deal of tedious unpicking. But at least, she told herself, it was really a small price to pay in the face of making enemies of a reputable estate agent.

The young man, whom Albert Piggott and various other observers had noticed calling on Winnie Bailey, was indeed her nephew Richard, and his visit occasioned her some alarm. She discussed this with Dr Lovell the next day when he paid his customary morning visit after surgery next door.

Winnie's husband Donald Bailey had been the much-loved doctor at Thrush Green for many years, and John Lovell had become his junior partner when the older man's health began to fail. It had been a happy relationship, and John deeply appreciated his partner's wife's kindness. When Donald died, he kept on the same surgery which the two men had shared and made sure that he did all he could for Donald's widow.

He knew a good deal about Richard. He was a brilliant young scientist and mathematician, completely selfish and inclined to batten on Winnie whenever he was in difficulties. His marriage had collapsed a year or two previously, and his young child was with his wife Fenella and her current paramour Roger. John Lovell, who liked a tidy life himself, had little time for Richard's vagaries, but he knew that Winnie loved her nephew, despite his gross selfishness.

'You see,' Winnie told him, 'he is absolutely set on buying a little house here or in Lulling. In some ways I can see that it would be a good thing. He really needs a base to keep his things and to prepare his lectures and so on. And of course, I should enjoy seeing him now and again, but—'

'But?' prompted John.

'Well, he wants to stay here until he finds something, and I simply can't have him here for any length of time. Jenny and I have all we can do to cope with our own little chores, and Richard would be in and out at all hours, needing meals and so on.'

'Surely you told him that? He knows well enough how you are placed.'

'Of course I told him, but you know Richard. He doesn't want to hear. I said I'd see if I could find lodgings somewhere handy, and would let him know.'

'Give me his number,' said John, 'and I'll ring him myself today. He can hear your doctor's honest opinion that neither you nor Jenny is fit enough to cope with him.'

Winnie looked perturbed. 'Oh, John! I don't know if I should let you. After all, he is my nephew, and it seems so awful to turn the poor boy away from my doorstep.'

'He can easily find another doorstep,' replied John firmly. 'He's rolling in money. What's wrong with a hotel room? Leave this to me, Winnie. I promise to be quite civil to him, but you need some support over this little problem.'

'It's at times like this,' confessed Winnie, 'that I miss Donald.'

'You're not the only one,' the young doctor assured her, setting off on his rounds.

3 · News Travels Fast

Nelly Piggott did not forget her promise to Bertha Lovelock, made in a weak moment and much regretted. It soon became apparent, however, that there would be no ugly rush for the proposed post of cook-general at the Lovelocks' establishment.

'No fear!' said the first woman approached by Nelly.

'Not Pygmalion likely!' said the second.

Nelly put her problem to her friend Mrs Jenner, as they walked to Bingo one evening. Mrs Jenner was the mother of Jane Cartwright, warden of the old people's homes, and a much respected character locally.

Unlike Nelly, she had known Lulling, Nidden and Thrush Green all her life, and the doings of the Misses Lovelock were old history to her.

'My dear,' she told Nelly, 'don't waste your time and energy. No one is going to take on a job like that these days. Those old things are still living in the past when they could get some poor little fourteen-year-old to skivvy for them for five shillings a week. You know yourself how mean they are, and the rest of Lulling knows, too.'

'That's true enough,' agreed Nelly.

'They'll just have to face facts,' went on Mrs Jenner. 'After all, they're lucky enough to live next door to The Fuchsia Bush, and have enough money to eat there daily without breaking the bank. And if things get really tough for them they will have to apply for a home help.'

'Well, I just felt I should make an attempt, as I'd promised,' said Nelly.

'And so you have,' replied Mrs Jenner. 'Now let them do their own worrying. From what I know of those old dears, they really don't deserve a great deal of sympathy.'

The two friends entered the Bingo hall in Lulling High Street, content to shelve the problem in the face of an evening's pleasure.

Dr Lovell too had been keeping a promise, and had rung Winnie Bailey's nephew. It had not been easy to get hold of Richard, but he tracked him down one evening.

Richard sounded suspicious and uncommonly haughty.

'I'm not sure why you are telling me this,' he exclaimed, when John began his tale. 'After all, she is my aunt, and I know how she's placed quite as well as you do. If I may say so, I find your interference somewhat offensive.'

Dr Lovell, no coward, was firm in his reply.

'I don't think you do know as much as I do. Winnie is now in her seventies, and Jenny not much younger. They are neither of them in the best of health and they have quite enough to do coping with everyday living. A visit, no matter how short, would be too much for them.'

There was a snort from the other end of the line. 'What rubbish! She said she would be delighted to have me there for a few days.'

'Naturally she would. She is fond of you and would do all she could to fall in with your requests. My point is that you should not make any. She is my patient, and so is Jenny. I won't see their health put at risk.'

There was another snort.

'If you must stay in the area,' went on John remorselessly, 'I'm sure you could get a room at The Fleece. I can give you the telephone number.'

'I *know* the telephone number, thank you very much,' replied Richard stuffily, and rang off.

'Well, I hope that's choked him off,' said John, replacing the receiver. 'And if it hasn't, I'll have the greatest pleasure in knocking his block off.'

News of Richard's visit and his intention to find somewhere to live locally was soon common knowledge at Thrush Green. How this came about was the usual mystery, for Winnie had only mentioned the matter to Jenny and her old friend and neighbour Ella Bembridge, and John Lovell had said nothing, not even to Ruth, his wife. Nevertheless, speculation was rife, and sympathy for Winnie Bailey's predicament was general.

Betty Bell, who kept the school clean and rushed round the Shoosmiths' house next door twice a week, told Isobel all about it as she wound the vacuum cleaner cord into the tight figure-of-eight which Harold so detested.

'Too soft by half Mrs Bailey is,' she pronounced. 'That nephew of hers gets away with murder over there.'

'Oh come!' protested Isobel.

'Well, near enough,' conceded Betty, crashing the vacuum cleaner into a cupboard and capsising two tins of polish, a basket full of clothes pegs and half a dozen bottling jars. 'Luckily, Dr Lovell's given him a piece of his mind, so maybe he'll stop bothering his poor auntie.' She sat back on her haunches and began to repair the damage. 'And anyway,' she continued, 'what's he want coming to live here? He's all over the place, from what I hear. America, China, Bristol, Oxford, lecturing or something. Waste of money, I'd say, to have a home.'

'He needs somewhere to keep his things,' Isobel pointed out.

'But why here? It's all coming and going, isn't it? You heard as they're giving up next door?'

Isobel felt shocked. 'Are you sure?'

'Positive. Miss Watson said so. In the summer, she said.'

Isobel could not help wondering if this were true. Surely, Agnes would have told her if this were so.

'Awful lot of clobber you keep in here,' commented Betty, rising from her task. 'You really want it all?'

'It has to go somewhere, Betty,' said her employer. 'Like Richard, you know.'

The house was remarkably peaceful after Betty Bell had departed on her bicycle and Isobel, still a little perturbed by her news, went in search of Harold.

She found him in his study with his old friend Charles Henstock, rector of Thrush Green and vicar of Lulling.

'What a nice surprise! Is Dimity around?'

'No, she's busy shopping in the town and calling at the Lovelocks.'

'Not for lunch, I hope,' said Harold.

Charles laughed. 'No, no. Nothing like that. I have to be home at twelve-thirty for lunch, Dimity told me.'

Harold glanced at his watch. 'Well, far be it from me to speed a parting guest, particularly such a welcome one as you, Charles, but it's nearly ten to one now.'

'Good heavens!' exclaimed the vicar, much flustered. 'I must run for it. Can I leave the upkeep account with you then?'

'Of course you can, and don't worry about it. I'm sure there's some simple explanation about the discrepancy.'

Charles was busy collecting his gloves, scarf, hat and a brown paper bag bulging dangerously with over-ripe bananas.

'Well, thank you, thank you, my dear fellow. I don't know how I'd get on without you.'

He hastened to the door, and made for his car. Isobel and Harold waved him off.

'What's worrying the dear old boy?' asked Isobel.

'He has just over fifty pounds in the tobacco tin he keeps the Thrush Green church upkeep money in, and his accounts say he should have just over five hundred.'

'That's worrying!'

'Not with Charles's arithmetic. He never has been any good with noughts. I'll soon sort it out.'

Over lunch, Isobel told him about Betty's disclosure.

'It seems so odd. Not that I've seen a great deal of Agnes and Dorothy, but I did have a natter over the hedge recently and I'm sure Agnes would have told me.'

'Probably forgot,' said Harold equably. 'You'll know soon enough.'

It seemed that almost everyone knew about the ladies' retirement plans, other than Isobel. Not that Agnes had told anyone, for she still felt obliged to keep silent about things until Dorothy deemed otherwise.

It was some shock to her, therefore, when three of her young charges, four mothers, Betty Bell, the milkman and Mr Jones the publican brought up the subject all in the course of one day.

She mentioned the matter to Dorothy that evening.

'Oh yes!' said that lady carelessly. 'I did tell the Office, of course, and I believe I mentioned it to Betty Bell a day or two ago. No harm done, is there?'

'Well, no, I suppose not,' said Agnes doubtfully, 'but I have been particularly careful to say nothing. Not even to Isobel,' she added.

It was plain that she was upset, and Dorothy was quick to apologise.

'It was thoughtless of me, and I should have realised how the news goes through this place like a bush fire. I really am deeply sorry, Agnes dear. I had no idea that it was putting you into an awkward position. Anyway, it's now common knowledge that we are retiring in the summer, so we can be quite open about it.'

Agnes smiled her forgiveness. 'I will have a word with Isobel when I see her,' she said. 'I shouldn't like her to hear our news from somebody else first.'

'Why not telephone now?' suggested her friend. 'The sooner the better. After all, she may well be told by someone else very soon.'

If not already, she said to herself, watching Agnes roll up her knitting before going to the telephone.

Really, it was exasperating! Was *anything* private in a village? And would Barton-on-Sea be equally enthralled by its neighbours' affairs?

Time alone would tell.

Luckily for Charles Henstock, Dimity too had been delayed, so that he was not late for his meal.

'And how are the Lovelock girls?' he enquired, using the usual Lulling euphemism for the three ancient sisters.

'Worried about help in the house,' answered Dimity. 'Well, perhaps not so much *the help* as having to pay for it.'

'Have they advertised?'

'No, I don't think so. But they've asked Nelly Piggott and they are wondering if The Fuchsia Bush would put a postcard in the window.'

Charles, who could not help thinking that both these aids would cost nothing, dismissed the thought as unworthy and uncharitable, and forbore to comment.

'They told me, by the way,' went on his wife, 'that Miss Watson and Miss Fogerty are retiring at the end of the school year.'

'Then we must start thinking about some little celebration to mark the occasion. I mean,' he added, feeling that this could have been better expressed, 'they have both been so much respected and admired all these years, that I'm sure Thrush Green will want to honour them in some way.'

'A sort of bunfight and presentation of a clock?'

'Well, something like that,' agreed Charles, feeling that perhaps dear Dimity had over-simplified the matter to the point of banality. 'We shall have to consult various people and come up with something suitable.'

'I should ask them what they would like,' said Dimity, always practical. 'You know how difficult it is to find houseroom for some of those presents you've been given over the years. I mean, who wants a silver inkstand with cut-glass inkwells these days? And that black marble clock like the Parthenon has to be kept in the spare bedroom. And as for those silver-plated fish servers the Scouts gave you, well, I don't think they've been used more than twice in twenty years. No, Charles, I should see that Agnes and Dorothy get something they really need. Like money, say.'

'I'll bear it in mind,' the rector assured her.

February, everyone agreed, was much more cheerful than January at Thrush Green. It was true that the first few days had been dark and foggy, but the relief from the battering winds of the first month of the year had made even the gloomy days quite welcome.

But by St Valentine's day there were a few signs of spring. Clumps of brave snowdrops, first espied by Agnes across the Shoosmiths' hedge, were to be seen in many cottage gardens. Aconites, their golden faces circled with green ruffs, responded to the sunlight and good gardeners were already making plans to put in new potatoes, broad beans and peas as soon as the ground was warm enough.

Winnie Bailey thought how hopeful everything seemed as she had one of her first walks of the year.

She set off up the road to Nidden, noting the activity of the little birds, chaffinches, sparrows, starlings and an occasional robin, darting from hedge to hedge or pecking busily at the grit on the edge of the road. Soon there would be nests and young birds, butterflies and bees to  add to all the joys of early summer. Winnie felt a surge of happiness at the thought.

It had been a long hard winter and the older she grew the more she dreaded the bitter cold of the Cotswolds in winter. She half-envied the two schoolteachers planning to move to the south coast, but she knew that she would never emulate them. Her whole married life had been spent at Thrush Green. The house held many memories and every mile around her home was crowded with remembered incidents. The cottages she passed were the homes of old friends. The shepherd, to whom she waved across the field on her right, had brought Donald from his bed one snowy night. It was a breech birth and Mrs Jenner, the midwife, had sent an urgent message for help. That waving figure, knee-deep in his flock, must now be forty years old.

She turned along a bridlepath on her left. It was very quiet between the trees. The small leaves of the honeysuckle were a vivid green. The buds on the pewter-grey ash twigs were black as jet. A few celandines had opened on a sunny bank.

Before long she was skirting Lulling Woods and beginning to feel tired. There was no doubt about it, she could not walk the distances she once had done. She resolved to call on her old and eccentric friend, Dotty Harmer, whose cottage was now in sight. She had much to talk about, and she might even mention this worrying business of Richard's move. Sometimes Dotty was uncommonly shrewd, despite her odd ways.

The door was opened by Connie, Dotty's niece. Her husband, Kit Armitage, stood beside her.

'What a lovely surprise!'

'I'm having the first stroll of the year,' said Winnie. 'How's Dotty?'

'Waiting for her coffee,' said Connie. 'Go into the sitting-room and I'll bring it in.'

Dotty was sitting on the sofa looking remarkably like the scarecrow Winnie had just passed in a neighbouring field, but her eyes were bright and her voice welcoming.

'Winnie! I've just been talking about you and dear Donald.'

For one dreadful moment Winnie wondered if Dotty still thought that Donald was alive. She had these lapses of memory which could be most disconcerting for those trying to carry on a conversation. This time, luckily, all was well.

'I remember how good he was to old Mrs Curdle. Is her grandson still with the Youngs?'

This was splendid, thought Winnie relaxing. Dotty was definitely on the ball this morning. She accepted the cup of coffee which Connie offered and sat back to enjoy it.

'We hear Agnes and Dorothy are off,' said Kit. 'They'll be missed.'

'Betty Bell told us,' added Dotty. She moved some crochet work from her lap and stuck the hook behind her ear like a pencil. It gave her an even more rakish appearance than usual.

'What's more to the point,' she said, 'how is Albert Piggott? I've got all sorts of jobs waiting here for him to do, and I suppose he's still ill, as we don't see him.'

Winnie said that as far as she knew Dr Lovell was still attending him.

'A nice boy,' conceded Dotty, pulling up her skirt and exposing stick-like legs festooned in wrinkled stockings. She scrabbled in the leg of her knickers, which at a cursory glance appeared to be constructed of whipcord, and produced a man's khaki handkerchief.

'But not a patch on your Donald, of course,' She blew her nose with a loud trumpeting sound, replaced the handkerchief and covered her legs again.

'Kit's made a lovely little pond for the ducks, Winnie. You must see it. I want Albert to put in some irises and other water plants.'

'You know I can do that,' said Kit. 'No bother.'

'No, I want Albert to do it. He's good with such things and I want the angle right when the sun's overhead. Ducks like shade, you know. Albert understands their needs.'

Kit smiled at Winnie and shook his head. How patient he and Connie were, thought Winnie, with this lovable but infuriating old aunt.

'Now, I want to hear all about Richard's new house. Where is it?'

'Nowhere, as far as I know,' replied Winnie. 'Obviously you

know that he hopes to find something in these parts. He asked me to put him up while he looked around.'

'And is he going to do that?' asked Connie.

'No. I don't think so. John was rather firm about it and, to tell the truth, I can't face Richard for an indefinite time, fond of him as I am. But I should like to see him settled somewhere near by, so if you hear of anything do tell me.'

'I hear Nod Hall is on the market,' said Dotty, picking up her crochet again and looking about wildly for the hook. Connie rose without a word, removed it from her aunt's hair and handed it to her.

'But surely,' said Kit, 'that's got about twelve bedrooms, a lake and eighty acres!'

'He could always marry again,' said Dotty, 'and have a large family. I think it's such a pity that people don't have more children these days. Leave it too late, I suppose. I mean, gals got married at eighteen or so when I was young and had about six by the time they were thirty. Much healthier, I'm sure.'

'Nowadays, Dotty, the girls have to go out to work before they can make a home. And large families need large incomes.'

'Perhaps we could have him here,' said Dotty brightly. 'As a lodger.'

'No!' said Kit and Connie in unison. 'He wouldn't want that!'

'And neither should we,' Kit added. 'But we'll keep our ears open, Winnie, in case we hear of anything. Now come and see the pond.'

Farewells were made, and Winnie followed her friend into the garden, much refreshed by her rest, the coffee and the encounter with the resilient Dotty.

The mild weather meant that the children of Thrush Green school could play outside, much to the relief of the staff.

Miss Watson and Miss Fogerty paced the playground together, smiling indulgently upon their charges.

'I had a brainwave in bed last night, Agnes. I think I shall take driving lessons.'

Agnes could not believe that she had heard aright, which was more than possible as two little boys were being Harrier jets and making almost as much noise as the real thing, not three yards from her.

'I'm sorry, I didn't catch what you said.'

'*Driving lessons*!' shouted Dorothy fortissimo. 'It would be so useful to have a little car at Barton. We could have trips here and there.'

She broke off and bent to face one of the Harrier jets. 'Go away!' she bellowed. Looking pained, the child shuffled off with his fellow.

'But don't you have to have a test?' queried Agnes. She felt some alarm at this idea of Dorothy's.

'I shan't,' said her friend, with some satisfaction. 'I learnt, you know, when I first started teaching, and have kept up my licence luckily.'

She looked at her watch and raised a whistle to her lips. At the first blast the children stood still, with a few exceptions. Two of them were the disgruntled Harrier jets, but a quelling glance from their headmistress soon brought them to a standstill.

The second blast sent them all running to lines and the third set them walking into school. Really, thought Agnes, watching these manoeuvres, Dorothy is a wonderful organiser! Of course, one was bound to get one or two naughty little things, like John Todd who *pushed*, but on the whole Thrush Green children were very well disciplined. How she would miss them!

She shelved the troublesome problem of Dorothy's latest brainwave, and followed her class indoors.

4. SPRING PLANS

If little Miss Fogerty had hoped that Dorothy's wild idea of taking driving lessons would pass, then she was to be disappointed. Her headmistress brought up the subject again with great enthusiasm that evening.

'I could brush up my driving skills while we are still here, you see, and get some advice about the most suitable car to buy.'

'But won't that cost a great deal of money? And there is the insurance and licensing and so on.' Agnes was becoming agitated.

'I've thought of all that. I have quite a nice little nest egg, and an insurance policy that matured last Christmas. And then think of the money we should save in fares!'

Agnes nodded doubtfully.

'We could actually drive down to Barton to look at properties,' went on Dorothy. 'Every weekend, if need be. And it would mean that we have more scope in choosing a place down there, if we don't have to rely completely on buses or our two feet. Don't you like the idea, Agnes?' She spoke kindly, knowing her old friend's timid ways and her dislike of anything new.

'If you are quite happy about it, Dorothy,' she said slowly. 'But I was thinking not only of the *expense*, and of course I should like to pay my share, but whether you would feel up to facing all the dreadful traffic about these days. After all, it was some thirty years ago that you started to drive. Things were much more peaceful.'

'Now, Agnes, just listen to me! This car will be *mine*, and I can well afford to run it, so don't worry about that side of things. As for the traffic, well, one sees plenty of people driving who are far older than we are. I'm quite sure that I can cope with *that*.'

Agnes remembered, with a shudder, seeing Dotty Harmer tacking to and fro across the hill from Lulling, when that lady owned a car for a mercifully short time. And Dorothy's own brother, Ray, had spent some time in hospital as the result of a car accident.

But there it was. If Dorothy was set upon having a car then who was she to try and stop her? And surely she would have guidance and advice from whoever would be teaching her?

'Who would you ask to give you lessons?' she enquired.

'Well, I know Reg Bull has taught a number of people, and of course he knows a great deal about cars as a garage owner, but I'm not too sure about him.'

'He is getting rather old,' agreed Agnes. 'And sometimes the worse for liquor, I hear.'

'Quite. Also he might try to sell us a car that is not quite suitable. One that he has had in stock for some time, say, and can't get rid of. We have to face the fact, Agnes dear, that some men are inclined to take advantage of ladies if they think that they are gullible.'

Agnes nodded her agreement. 'Would it be a good idea to have a word with the rector?'

Dorothy gave one of her famous snorts. 'Charles Henstock is a living saint, my dear, and if I had any spiritual doubts he would be the first person I should turn to. But he doesn't know a carburettor from a sparking plug, and I doubt if he has even *looked* under the bonnet of his car.'

'What about Harold?'

'Ah now!' said Dorothy speculatively. 'That's a different kettle of fish altogether! Harold really knows about cars, and what's more, he may know of someone really reliable to give driving lessons. What a brilliant idea of yours, Agnes!'

Little Miss Fogerty basked in her friend's approbation. Now that she was getting used to this novel idea, she realised how much dear Dorothy was looking forward to owning a car again.

In any case, there was nothing that she could do to stop her. Far better to agree with good grace. And Harold Shoosmith, she felt sure, would be a tower of strength and wisdom in this new adventure.

While the two schoolteachers were considering the question of driving lessons, the three Miss Lovelocks at Lulling were making a momentous decision. This was really the result of Dimity Henstock's morning visit. The sisters had told her of their domestic problems and Dimity had been unusually forthright in giving her advice.

'For a start,' she said, 'book a table regularly for lunch next door.'

'What! Every day?' exclaimed Miss Ada.

'The *expense*!' echoed Miss Bertha.

'Not every day,' conceded Dimity. 'Say once or twice a week. And then shut up the attics here and the bedrooms that are not in use. That will save fuel and cleaning.'

She looked about the vast chilly drawing-room, littered with occasional tables, unnecessary chairs and a never-used grand piano.

'I'd be inclined to close this too,' she said decisively. 'Your kitchen and dining-room are much the pleasantest places in the house.'

'But one can't live in the *kitchen*!' protested Ada.

'And we should miss the view of the street,' added Bertha.

Miss Violet spoke at last. She was the youngest of the three, and less hidebound in her ways. 'I think Dimity's ideas are right. We ought to use The Fuchsia Bush more. After all, we aren't exactly short of money.'

Miss Ada drew in her breath sharply. 'You know mother always said that it was vulgar to mention *money*, Violet. In any case, there is such a thing as *thrift*, though one doesn't hear a great deal about it these days.' She inclined herself towards

Dimity. 'Thank you, my dear, for your advice. We will consider it most carefully.'

'Yes, indeed,' echoed Bertha.

Violet gave a conspiratorial smile, as she showed Dimity to the door.

Later, the matter had been discussed with great earnestness.

'I think,' said Ada, 'that we might go to The Fuchsia Bush on Wednesdays – and perhaps Thursdays – for our luncheon. The Sunday roast usually lasts through Monday and Tuesday.'

The Sunday roast at the Lovelocks' establishment was never anything so splendid as a round of beef or leg of lamb. Often it was breast of lamb stuffed and rolled or, as a treat, half a shoulder of that animal. Occasionally in the summer, a small piece of forehock of bacon was eaten cold with an uninspiring salad from the garden. How any of these meagre joints afforded meals for three days for the three sisters was one of the wonders of Lulling.

'What about Fridays and Saturdays?' queried Bertha.

'We can do as we normally do,' responded Ada. 'Something on toast, such as a poached egg. And the herrings are looking very good at the moment. To think we once called them "penny herrings", girls!'

The three sisters nodded sadly, mentally visualising the dear dead days of long ago.

'Then shall we settle for Wednesday and Thursday?' said Violet briskly, the first to return to the present day. 'I will go to see Mrs Peters tomorrow morning, if you agree, and give a standing order.'

Her two sisters nodded.

'But I certainly shan't dream of doing as Dimity suggested about shutting up the drawing-room! The very idea! There's no room to sit in the dining-room, and in any case all our best pieces are in the drawing-room.'

'And the window looking over the street,' said Bertha. 'One must keep in touch with what's afoot.'

'Absolutely!' said Violet. 'But I think shutting the attics and the second spare bedroom is a good idea.'

'Well,' replied Ada doubtfully, 'we must bear it in mind. I'm sure Dimity's suggestions were made with the highest motives, but one doesn't want to *rush* things.'

'Perhaps,' said Violet, beginning to wonder if matters were not slipping back into general apathy, 'it would be a good idea to bob into The Fuchsia Bush now before Mrs Peters closes.'

'Very well,' said Ada. 'But make it quite clear that we shall need only a *light luncheon*. Our digestions won't stand a great deal.'

'Nor our purses,' added Bertha, as Violet made her way into the hall to fetch her coat, hat and gloves.

The Fuchsia Bush might only be next door, but a lady did not walk in the High Street at Lulling improperly dressed.

Albert Piggott's first venture outside after his illness did not involve a long journey. He simply took a few paces northward from his own front door to the shelter of The Two Pheasants.

Mr Jones, a kindly man, greeted him cheerfully. 'Well, this is more like it, Albert! How are you then? And what can I get you?'

'I'm pickin' up,' growled Albert. 'Slowly, mind you. I bin real bad this time.'

'Well, we're none of us getting any younger. Takes us longer to get back on an even keel. Half a pint?'

'Make it a pint. I needs buildin' up, Doctor says.'

'Well, your Nelly'll do that for you,' said the landlord heartily, setting a foaming glass mug before his visitor. 'I hear she's doing wonders down at Lulling.'

'That ain't here though, is it?' responded Albert nastily. He wiped the froth from his mouth with the back of his hand, and then transferred it to the side of his trousers.

'You going to get back to work?' enquired Mr Jones, changing the subject diplomatically.

'Not yet. Still under the doctor, see. Young Cooke can pull his weight for a bit. Won't hurt him.'

At that moment Percy Hodge entered and Mr Jones was glad to have another customer to lighten the gloom.

'Wotcher, Albie! You better then?' said Percy.

'No,' said Albert.

'Don't look too bad, do he?' said Percy, appealing to the landlord.

'Ah!' said he non-committally. If he agreed it would only give Albert a chance to refute such an outrageous suggestion, and maybe lead to the disclosure of various symptoms of his illness, some downright revolting, and all distasteful.

On the other hand, if he appeared sympathetic to Albert claiming that he still looked peaky and should take great care during his convalescence, the results might still be the same, and Albert's descriptions of his ills were not the sort of thing one wished to hear about in a public place.

Mr Jones, used to this kind of situation, betook himself to the other end of the room, dusted a few high shelves and listened to his two clients.

Percy Hodge had a small farm along the road to Nidden. He was related to Mrs Jenner, but had nowhere near the resourcefulness and energy of that worthy lady.

His first wife Gertie had died some years earlier. For a time he had attempted to court Jenny, at Winnie Bailey's, but was repulsed. He then married again, but his second wife had left him. Since then, he had been paying attention to one of the Cooke family, sister to the young Cooke who looked after the church at Thrush Green and its churchyard.

'Still on your own?' asked Albert, dying to know how Percy's amorous affairs were progressing.

'That's right,' said Percy. 'And better off, I reckon. Women are kittle-cattle.'

From this, Albert surmised that the Cooke girl was not being co-operative.

'Here I am,' went on Percy morosely, 'sound in wind and limb. Got a nice house, and a good bit of land, and a tidy bit in Lulling Building Society. You'd think any girl'd jump at the chance.'

'Girls want more than that,' Albert told him.

'How d'you mean?'

'They want more fussing like. Take her some flowers.'

'I've took her some flowers.'

'Chocolates then.'

'I've took her chocolates.'

'Well, I don't know,' said Albert, sounding flummoxed. 'Something out of the garden, say.'

'I've took her onions, turnips, leeks and a ridge cucumber last summer. Didn't do a ha'p'orth of good.'

'Maybe you're not *loving* enough. Girls read about such stuff in books. Gives 'em silly ideas. Makes them want looking after. They wants attention. They wants—'

He broke off searching for the right word.

'*Wooing*!' shouted Mr Jones, who could bear it no longer.

'Ah! That's right! *Wooing*, Perce.'

Percy looked scandalised. 'I'm not acting *soppy* for any girl and that's flat. If they turns down flowers and chocolates and all the rest, then I don't reckon they're worth bothering about. If they don't like me, they can leave me!'

'That's just what they are doing,' pointed out Albert. 'I take it you're still hanging around that Cooke piece as is no better'n she should be.'

Percy's face turned from scarlet to puce. 'You mind your own business!' he bellowed, slamming down his mug and making for the door.

'There was no call for that,' said Mr Jones reproachfully, when the glasses had stopped quivering from the slammed door.

'I likes to stir things up a bit, now and again,' said Albert smugly. 'I'll have a half to top up.'

The mild spell of weather which had brought out the first spring flowers and those people, like Albert, recovering from their winter ills, now changed to a bitter session of hard frosts and a wicked east wind.

The good folk of Thrush Green pointed out to each other that after all, it was still February, a long way to go before counting the winter over, and February and March were often the worst months of the winter.

It was cold comfort, and Jane Cartwright took extra care of

the old people in her charge. The health of old Tom Hardy, in particular, caused her some concern. She mentioned her worries to Charles Henstock one afternoon when he paid a visit to his old friends at the home.

'It isn't anything I can pin down,' she said. 'His chest is no worse. He eats very little, but then he always did. He goes for a walk every day with Polly, but something's worrying him. See if you can get it out of him. He'll tell you more than he will me.'

The rector promised to do his best, and made his way to Tom's little house, bending against the vicious wind which whipped his chubby cheeks.

He found the old man sitting by a cheerful fire, fondling the head of his much-loved dog. To Charles's eye old Tom seemed much as usual as he greeted his visitor warmly.

'Come you in, sir, out of this wind. I took Poll out this morning, just across the green, but I reckon that's going to be enough for today.'

'Very wise, Tom. And how are you keeping?'

'Pretty fair, pretty fair. I never cease to be thankful as I'm here, and not down at the old cottage. Jane Cartwright looks after us all a treat.'

Polly came to the rector and put her head trustingly upon his knee. The rector stroked her gently. She was an old friend, and had stayed at Lulling vicarage when her master had a spell in hospital.

Charles wondered whether to mention Jane's concern, and decided that it could do no harm.

'She's a marvellous woman. I think she worries rather too much about you all. She certainly said just now that she hoped that everything was right for you.'

Tom did not reply.

'She said you seemed pretty healthy, which was good news, but she had the feeling that something was troubling you. Is it anything I can help with?'

Tom sighed. 'It's Polly. I frets about her.'

'But let's get the vet then.'

'It's not that. It's nought as the vet can do. She's got the same trouble as I have, sir. We be too old.'

'We're all getting old,' replied Charles, 'and have to face going some time. But what's wrong otherwise with Polly?'

He looked at the dog fondly, and felt her tail tap against his legs as she responded to her name.

'It's what happens to her when she goes,' said Tom earnestly. 'All the dogs I've had has been buried by me in my garden. There's two graves now down at my old place by the river.'

'So what's the difficulty?'

'There's no place here to bury poor old Poll when her time comes. It grieves me.'

The old man's eyes were full of tears, much to Charles's distress.

'Then you can stop grieving straightaway,' he said robustly, leaning across Polly to pat his old friend's knee. 'If it makes you happier, let Polly be buried in the vicarage garden at Lulling. There are several pets buried there and Polly was well content when she stayed with us.'

Tom's face lit up. 'That's right good of you, sir. It'd be a weight off my mind.'

'And if you go ahead of her, Tom,' said the rector smiling, 'she can come to the vicarage anyway and be among friends. So now stop fretting.'

Tom drew in his breath gustily. 'I wish I could do something to repay you,' he said.

'You can, Tom. What about a cup of tea?'

He watched the old man go with a spring in his step to fill the kettle. He was humming to himself as he went about setting a tray.

If only all his parishioners' troubles could be settled so simply, thought Charles!

As Agnes Fogerty had guessed, Harold Shoosmith was proving most helpful on the subject of Dorothy's driving tuition and the buying of a small car.

The two ladies had been invited next door for a drink to discuss matters and Harold was waxing enthusiastic.

It was strange, thought Agnes, how animated most men became when discussing machinery. Her dear father, she recalled, could read a book without any sort of reaction to its contents. It was the same with a play or a concert. He was quite unmoved by these products of the arts, but his joy in his old tricycle, upon which he rode when delivering the shoes he repaired, was immense.

Later, he had taken to driving a three-wheeled Morgan and the same fanatical light had gleamed in his eyes. To Agnes any form of locomotion was simply the means of getting from one place to another and she looked upon this male fever as just one more incomprehensible facet of man's nature.

'I've thought a good deal about driving lessons,' Harold was saying. 'I shouldn't get Reg Bull if I were you. I'd offer myself, but I don't know that friends make the best instructors. Worse still are spouses, of course, but you are spared those.'

'I certainly shouldn't have allowed you to teach me,' said Isobel. 'As it is, you gasp whenever I let in the clutch.'

'Do I? I never realised that!'

'Well, you do. And very trying it is,' said his wife briskly. 'But go on. Tell Dorothy your bright idea.'

'It occurred to us both that perhaps Ben Curdle would be willing to give you lessons. He's a marvellous driver, very steady and calm. I'm sure he'd be first-class. If he's willing, of course, to let you learn on his Ford. It's a good gearbox. You could do worse than buy a little Ford when the time comes.'

'Ben Curdle would be just the man,' agreed Miss Watson. 'But would he do it? He doesn't seem to have much spare time.'

'If you like, I will have a word with him and let you know the result. One thing I do know – he would be glad to earn some money in his spare time.'

'That would be very kind of you. I have the greatest respect for Ben, so like his dear grandmother. If he will take me on, I shall be delighted.'

'And, of course,' added Harold, 'I can take you out occasionally for a run in my car, just to get the hang of things.'

'How lovely! I should appreciate that. And I hope you will advise me when it comes to buying a car.'

Harold's eyes sparkled at the prospect. 'What was the car you drove earlier?' he enquired.

Dorothy frowned with concentration. 'Now, what was it? I know it was a red one, with rather pretty upholstery, but I can't think what make it was.'

Harold looked flabbergasted.

'I'm sure the name will come back to you when you are not thinking about it,' said Isobel soothingly. 'Like throwing out the newspaper and knowing immediately what ten down was in the crossword. Harold, Agnes's glass is empty.'

Recalled to his duties as host, Harold crossed to the side-table, but he still appeared numb with shock at the abysmal ignorance of the female mind.

5 . PERSONAL PROBLEMS

'I've just had a letter,' said Miss Watson at breakfast one morning, 'from Better & Better.'

'From who?'

'From whom,' corrected Dorothy automatically. 'From Better & Better, dear. The estate agents. My sharp note to them seems to have done some good. They've sent particulars of two bungalows and a ground-floor flat. Mind you, I suspect that the ground-floor flat is really the *basement*, but at least it's an improvement on that converted oast house with five bedrooms, and that attic flat in some terrible old castle, which they sent last time.'

Agnes Fogerty nodded, looking bewildered. She was perusing the Appointments pages of that week's *Times Educational Supplement*.

'Our advertisement's in,' she said, 'But no house.'

Dorothy put down her letter. 'Not a *house*, Agnes. Two bungalows and a flat.'

'I know, Dorothy, about the Barton properties. I'm talking about *our* house, this one.'

'What about it?'

'Well, last time our posts were advertised, it said something about a school house. It doesn't this time.'

Miss Watson held out an imperious hand. 'Here, let me look!'

Agnes handed over the paper meekly, noticing, with a wince, that one corner had been dragged across the marmalade on Dorothy's toast.

'Well, how extraordinary!' said that lady. 'What can it mean? Perhaps they just forgot to mention it.'

'Or perhaps the printers made a muddle of it,' suggested Agnes.

'I shall be ringing the Office this morning,' replied her friend, 'and I'll see if I can find out about this. Not that I shall learn much if that fiddle-faddling secretary fellow answers,'

'What's wrong with him?'

'Terrified of his own shadow! Never gives a straightforward answer to any question,' said Dorothy trenchantly. 'I asked him only the other day about those desks which have been ordered for two years, and he gets flustered and waffles on about things being *at the committee stage*, whatever that means, and he has no power to tell me.'

Secretly, Agnes felt rather sorry for the man. Dorothy, at her most demanding, could instil great terror.

'Still, never fear, Agnes! I shall do my best to see what lies behind this omission.'

She handed back the paper, catching another corner on the marmalade in transit, and poured herself a second cup of tea.

The bitter east wind did not show any signs of abating, and the old people at Rectory Cottages were once more housebound, and particularly glad of Jane and Bill Cartwright's daily visits.

Tom Hardy seemed much more cheerful after the rector had called. Jane had not had an opportunity of finding out the reason for this improvement, but was glad when the old man volunteered the information.

'Mr Henstock says he'll have my old Polly in his garden.'

Jane was somewhat bewildered. 'Which day is this to be?'

'Why, for ever!'

'You mean that you are letting him have Polly? Can you bear to part with her, Tom?'

'No, no, no!' exclaimed the old man testily. 'Why should I want to give Poll away?'

Jane waited for enlightenment.

'When she's dead,' continued Tom. 'I've been fretting about what would happen to her when she's gone. No decent garden here to bury her, see? All my other dogs was buried proper. Dug their graves myself, and wrapped their poor bodies in their own dog blanket for comfort like.'

Jane was touched by the old man's concern. 'I'm sure we could have found a corner for her somewhere, Tom.'

'Well, now there's no need,' said Tom, with great dignity. 'She'll be comfortable in the vicarage garden, when the time comes.'

Jane looked from the frail old fellow to his equally aged pet lying at his feet.

As if reading her thoughts, Tom spoke again. 'And if I goes first, then Mr Henstock's having Poll,' he said, 'A good man is the rector, and a fine gentleman.'

And with that Jane heartily agreed.

At Winnie Bailey's, Jenny had just come in from the garden where she had been hanging out the tea towels.

'My goodness!' she gasped, crashing the kitchen door behind her. 'Don't you go out today, Mrs Bailey. Enough to catch your death in this wind. I shan't be surprised to find the tea towels in Mrs Hurst's garden when we go to fetch them.'

'I've nothing to go out for, I'm thankful to say,' said Winnie. 'Ella's coming along later, probably early afternoon.'

'Will she stay to tea?' asked Jenny hopefully. She loved an excuse to make scones or hot buttered toast.

'No, Jenny. She's only dropping in the magazines. She won't stop.'

At that moment the telephone rang. It was her nephew Richard.

'Aunt Win, can I pop in?'

'Of course. When?'

'About twelve?'

'Fine, We'll put another two sausages in the oven.'

'Splendid! And another thing!'

'Yes?'

'I'll have Timothy with me. In fact, I wondered if you could have him for an hour or two, while I go along to Cirencester to pick up some books waiting there.'

'Of course. I haven't met Timothy yet. I shall look forward to it.'

'Good!' said Richard, sounding much relieved. 'See you soon then.'

Winnie conveyed the news to Jenny.

'How old is this Timothy?' she enquired.

'Four, I think.'

'Well, if he doesn't like sausages he can have an egg,' replied Jenny decisively. 'And don't let him wear you out. Didn't we hear he was a bit of a handful?'

'Good heavens! We surely can cope with a four-year-old for an hour or so!'

'Let's hope so,' said Jenny, 'but children today aren't what they were in our young days.'

'They never were,' responded Winnie.

The arrival of Richard's car was first noted by Albert Piggott who was standing at his kitchen window.

He had just returned from a visit to The Two Pheasants, and was watching the dead leaves eddying round and round in the church porch opposite his cottage.

The wind seemed more formidable than ever. The branches of the chestnut trees outside the Youngs' house were tossing vigorously. The grass on the green flattened in its path, and no one seemed to be stirring at Rectory Cottages.

The advent of a car outside Winnie Bailey's was a welcome diversion in the waste of Thrush Green. Albert recognised Richard and was intrigued to see a small boy being helped from the car. The child appeared to be reluctant to get out, but at last the two figures set off for the front door.

Albert watched avidly. Jenny opened the door, and Richard and the boy vanished inside.

'Now, whose can that be?' pondered Albert. 'One of Richard's by-blows maybe?'

But he did Winnie's nephew a disservice. Timothy, had he known it, was the child of an earlier marriage of Fenella, his wife, so that Richard was the boy's stepfather. To all appearances, he seemed to be taking his responsibilities seriously.

'Must ask Nelly about this,' said Albert to his cat. 'Women always knows about such things.'

The cat, who was engrossed in washing his face, ignored his master's remarks.

'So this is Timothy,' smiled Winnie, surveying the newcomer.

The child was dark-haired and skinny. He looked sulky, and tugged at Richard's hand.

'Say "How do you do",' prompted his stepfather.

'No,' said the child. 'Let's go home.'

The two grown-ups sensibly ignored this, and Winnie poured two glasses of sherry. Timothy sidled to the chair where Richard sat and hoisted himself on the arm.

Winnie noticed that his knees were dirty, and his jersey stained with food droppings of some antiquity. Why, she wondered, was Richard taking charge of the child? The last she had heard about the marriage was that there was talk of a divorce. Obviously, Richard had a responsibility towards his own child of the marriage, but Timothy really had little claim on him.

As if reading her thoughts, Richard spoke. 'Fenella suddenly remembered, when she woke this morning, that she had to take Imogen to the clinic for an injection. Timmy always screams the place down, so I said I'd keep him out of the way.'

Winnie noticed that the child gave a satisfied smirk at hearing of his behaviour at the clinic, and wished that Richard would have more sense than to mention such things before the boy.

'And what time will Fenella be home again?'

'Well, you know what these places are,' Richard replied, shifting in his chair so that Timothy could squash down beside him. 'Every one there wants to be done first, and there seems to be a lot of muddle one way and another. I don't suppose she'll be back until the afternoon.'

'I want my mummy,' whined Timothy.

Luckily, Jenny put her head round the door and summoned them to lunch.

'You'd better wash his hands in the kitchen,' said Winnie.

'I *never* have my hands washed,' announced Timothy.

'You do here,' said Winnie, leading the way.

A lordly dish of sausages, bacon, eggs and tomatoes graced the kitchen table, and Timothy surveyed it as Richard tried to wash the child's hands.

'I don't like sausages,' he said.

'What a pity,' said Winnie, settling herself at the table.

'And I don't like eggs.'

'Oh dear!'

'Nor bacon, nor none of what's for dinner.'

'You will be hungry,' said Winnie matter-of-factly.

She began to serve out. Richard took his seat, and Timothy was hoisted by Jenny on to a cushion in the chair beside him.

Winnie served the three adults and then looked enquiringly at Timothy.

'Are you going to try any of this?'

'No.'

'Very well, we won't worry you.'

Conversation flowed while Richard enquired about his old friends at Thrush Green, and Winnie tried to find out discreetly about Richard's domestic plans. Was the marriage still on or not? What had happened about the proposed divorce? Was Fenella's paramour, Roger Something, still living at the art gallery which was her home? If so, where did Richard fit in? It was all rather bewildering, thought Winnie, who was used to a tidy life.

Timothy, who disliked being ignored, now began to kick the table leg and was restrained by Jenny.

'Would you like to get down?' said Winnie.

'No. I want something to eat.'

Winnie lifted the servers.

'Not that old stuff!'

Winnie replaced the servers.

'So tell me about Imogen,' she said politely to Richard. 'Any teeth yet?'

Timothy began to tug furiously at Richard's arm, and a piece of sausage fell to the floor.

'I hardly know,' said Richard. 'Should she have teeth by now? I don't see much of her.'

By the time the first course had been demolished, Timothy had sunk down in his chair and was sucking a thumb disconsolately.

Jenny cleared away and returned with a steaming dish of baked apples.

'Shan't eat that,' said Timothy.

'Then you may get down,' said Winnie, serving the three adults imperturbably.

The child slid to the floor, and remained seated under the table.

Winnie looked enquiringly at Richard. 'What does he have at home?' she asked in a low voice.

'Oh, he eats when he feels like it. Bananas or peanuts, anything he fancies really. He doesn't have meals with us. He fits in very well with Fenella's work, you see. She has to be in the gallery quite a bit. We don't stop for regular meals as you do.'

When the meal was over, Jenny offered to take the child to play on the green, where there were some swings and a slide. Amazingly enough, the boy went with her, smiling.

'Now Richard,' said Winnie, when they were settled with their coffee, 'I want to know how things are with you. Are you and Fenella making a fresh start? What's happened to Roger? And are you still determined to find a home down here?'

Richard stirred his coffee thoughtfully. 'Well, first of all, Roger's gone back to his wife, but I can't see it lasting long.

That's partly why I want to get Fenella away. We might make a go of it without Roger looming over us all the time.'

'Very sensible. So the divorce is off?'

'Oh yes. So far, at any rate. I think we should consider the children.'

Better and better, thought Winnie. Richard seemed to be growing up at last.

'Mind you,' continued Richard, 'it's not going to be easy to pry Fenella from the gallery. It's her whole life really. Besides, she hates the country.'

Not so good after all, thought Winnie.

'And, of course,' went on her nephew, 'we do live rent free there. We should have to find a pretty hefty amount for a house round here. It needs thinking about.'

'I should imagine it's worth it to save your marriage,' said Winnie. 'And surely, if Fenella sold the gallery it would fetch a substantial sum, in such a good part of London.'

'I suppose so,' said Richard, but he sounded doubtful.

'Well, you must work out your own salvation,' replied Winnie briskly. 'And now you will want to get along to Cirencester. We'll see you about five, I suppose? No doubt you will want to get Timothy home again for his bedtime.'

'Oh, he doesn't have a set time for going to bed. He just has a nap when he feels like it.'

He set off to his car, followed by Winnie. Across the green she could see Timothy on a swing, with the gallant Jenny pushing him lustily. At least he was happy at the moment, thought Winnie, waving goodbye to Richard, and noticing that Ella was emerging from her gate.

As it happened, it was half-past eight when Richard returned, and by that time Timothy had eaten an apple, a banana sandwich, and had had two short naps on the hearth-rug. He was in excellent spirits when he drove off with Richard, and looked fit for several hours of activity.

But Winnie and Jenny went to bed early, with an aspirin apiece.

Harold Shoosmith kept his word and spoke to Ben Curdle about driving lessons for Miss Watson.

That young man considered the suggestion for some minutes.

'Don't make up your mind now,' Harold urged him. 'Just let me know when you've talked it over with Molly. You may not feel like letting a learner-driver loose on your Fiesta.'

Ben smiled. 'I don't need to think it over,' he said at last. 'I think Miss Watson would be pretty steady, and she's driven before.'

'But donkey's years ago!'

'Never quite leaves you, you know. And I'd be glad to help.'

'Shall I let her know, or will you?'

'You have a word with her. She can come over to see me and the car any evening. I take it she's got a licence?'

'Yes, she was wise enough to keep it up. I'll tell her, Ben, and I'm sure she will be most grateful.'

The two men parted, and Harold returned to his gardening

pondering on the remarkable fortitude of Ben Curdle, He himself would rather face a mad bull than give a woman driving lessons. Still, he told himself, Dorothy Watson should prove less horrifying than Dotty Harmer at the wheel.

'By the way,' said Dorothy to Agnes that evening, 'I found out a little more about that advertisement.'

'Which one, dear?'

'About the posts, of course,' said Dorothy.

'The posts?'

'In the *Times Educational Supplement*,' said Dorothy impatiently, 'with no house.'

Agnes seemed to make sense of this garbled explanation and nodded.

'I understand that the present policy is to get rid of the school house when a new appointment is made.'

'But surely,' said Agnes, 'the new head teacher might want it.'

'Not according to the Office. Their attitude is that nine out of ten heads want to live well away from the school, and as almost all of them now have cars they can live where they like.'

'Yes, I can see that,' agreed Agnes, 'but it was so nice to live close to the school. And after all, that was why the house was built – to go with the job.'

'Those days have gone, my dear, and you must admit that this house wants a lot doing to it. The education authority can make a nice little sum in selling off these old school houses for others to renovate. It seems to make sense.'

'So when will it be on the market? I don't like the idea of having to get out.'

'I gather that nothing will happen until later in the year. There is no need for us to hurry our plans, they told me.'

At that moment, Harold entered with the message from Ben.

'Well, well!' said Dorothy, her face alight with excitement. 'What marvellous news!' She glanced at the clock. 'I think I may slip over now, Agnes, to see Ben and make arrangements.

So very kind of you, Harold. Won't you sit down and have a drink with Agnes?'

Harold excused himself, and he and the would-be driver left Agnes alone, in a state of some agitation.

Their home to be sold! Driving lessons! Really, thought poor little Miss Fogerty, life sometimes seemed to go too fast for comfort!

6. WHAT SHALL WE GIVE THEM?

The news of Agnes and Dorothy's retirement created a great deal of activity among such bodies as the Parent-Teacher Association, St Andrew's church where the two ladies worshipped, the local Women's Institute, as well as individual friends.

Respect and affection for the two hard-working spinsters united all these bodies, and it was generally agreed that some appropriate tribute should be paid. Dimity's suggestion of 'a bunfight and a clock' rather summed up the general feeling but it was expressed more elegantly, and at much greater length, when the various committees gathered together to come to a decision.

Charles Henstock, as chairman of the school managers – or *governors*, as he tried to remember they were now designated – consulted his old friend Harold Shoosmith before approaching his fellow managers.

'Have you any ideas, Harold? Dimity suggests money – but somehow I feel that might not be acceptable. I rather favour a nice piece of silver. Perhaps a salver?'

'Does anyone ever use a salver?'

'I suppose not,' replied Charles doubtfully. 'And Dimity says silver would need cleaning.'

'What about a piece of glass?' suggested Isobel who was sitting in the window-seat, doing the crossword.

'Such as?'

'Well, a nice Waterford fruit bowl, or a decanter. Dorothy has a little tipple now and again, and Agnes says she "sometimes indulges", so it would be used.'

59

'I should see how much is contributed,' said Harold sensibly, 'and then decide. You might find that you get a hefty sum and then you could give a cheque as well. I take it that you are combining with the Parent-Teacher Association in this?'

'That was the idea.'

'And the church members, I suppose, will give their own present?'

'That's what we thought. After all, a great many of the parents attend chapel or, sadly, no place of worship at all, so the church's offering will be separate. We thought that perhaps a book token, or something for their new garden, might be appropriate.'

'But they haven't got a house yet,' pointed out Isobel, 'let alone a garden,'

The rector sighed. 'It really is a problem. Of course we must fix our dates for the little parties and the presentations and that alone is fraught with difficulties in the summer months, what with bazaars, and garden parties, and fêtes. Every weekend in July and August seems to get booked up by February, if you follow me.'

'We do indeed,' said Harold.

'If need be,' went on Charles, looking distracted, 'we can have these occasions at Lulling Vicarage, but it's such a truly Thrush Green affair that I feel we should have things arranged here.'

'If you want a garden you are very welcome to this one,' said Harold. 'Otherwise, what's wrong with the school itself?'

'Thank you, my dear fellow. You have been a great help, and I feel that I can make a few suggestions to the managers – I mean, *governors* – when I meet them. We are having a private meeting next week at the vicarage to sort things out.'

Harold accompanied him down the path.

The rector looked at the village school next door. 'I wish they weren't going,' he lamented.

'Don't we all,' responded Harold.

*

A few days later, the committee of the Parent-Teacher Association also met to pool ideas. This was held at a house belonging to the Gibbons along the road to Nod and Nidden.

Mr and Mrs Gibbons were newcomers to village life and, as they were anxious to play their part in Thrush Green affairs, they were heartily welcomed, and very soon found that they were chairmen, secretaries, treasurers and general servants to an alarming number of local activities.

Before moving to Thrush Green, Mrs Gibbons had been a personal assistant in a firm of exporters in the City of London, and retained her drive, industry and, to be frank, her formidable bossiness, in this her new place of abode. Half the residents of Thrush Green were afraid of her. The other half viewed her activities with amused tolerance, and wondered how soon she would tire of all the responsibilities so gladly heaped upon her by the lazier inhabitants of the village.

Her husband's business seemed shrouded in mystery, much to the chagrin of his neighbours. It took him from home early in the day, and often obliged him to spend the best part of the week away from Thrush Green.

Some said that he was one of the directors of that same firm of exporters for whom his wife had worked. Others maintained that he had a top job – very hush-hush – in the Civil Service, the Army, the Admiralty or MI5. A few knew, for a fact, that he was connected with Lloyd's, the Stock Exchange, the Treasury and the Ministry of Transport.

Whatever he did, it was universally agreed that it was something of enormous importance giving him power over a great number of people, so that Harold Shoosmith had been heard to dub him irreverently 'Gauleiter Gibbons', but not, of course, to his face.

The meeting of the PTA committee met in Mrs Gibbons' large upstairs room which she called her office. It was a strange apartment to find in Thrush Green, where local committee members usually found themselves sitting in chintz-covered armchairs in someone's sitting-room, balancing a cup of coffee and an unsullied notebook, whilst discussing the latest gossip.

Mrs Gibbons' office was decidedly functional. There was a large desk made of grey metal and upon it stood two telephones, one red and one blue. There were two matching grey filing cabinets and a shelf along one wall which bore a number of mysterious gadgets, rather like miniature television sets, which had rows of keys, buttons and switches attached.

On a side wall was a chart with red and green lines swooping spectacularly across it, reminding at least one committee member of her own fever chart when confined once to Lulling Cottage Hospital. On another wall was a map of Europe and beneath that, on a shelf of its own, was a splendid globe, lit from within, which rotated majestically and drew all eyes to its movements.

Mrs Gibbons seated herself at the desk and surveyed her companions sitting before her in a semi-circle on rather wispy bedroom chairs. There were, she noted severely, far too few committee members.

The PTA really had eight committee members, but this evening only four were present. Besides Mrs Gibbons there were Molly Curdle, whose son was at the school, unmarried Emily Cooke who also had a boy in the same class, and a quiet father who had three children at Thrush Green school. Mrs Gibbons herself had a boy and a girl there, both remarkably bright, as might be expected from such parentage, but also thoroughly modest and sociable.

'Such a pity so many of the committee members are absent,' commented Mrs Gibbons. 'Never mind, we constitute a quorum so we can go ahead.'

The three nodded resignedly.

'It's just about Miss Watson and Miss Fogerty's presents, isn't it?' asked Miss Cooke. 'Won't take long, I mean? I've left my Nigel with Mum and she's got to go to Bingo later on.

'Oh dear me, no!' replied Mrs Gibbons briskly. She added a particularly sweet smile, for although she secretly felt it highly reprehensible of Emily Cooke to produce a child out of wed-lock, she did not want to appear censorious or hidebound in any way, and after all it might have been a grievous mistake on a young girl's part years ago. But somehow she doubted it. One did not need to live in Thrush Green very long before becoming aware of the sad laxity of the Cooke family.

'Well, let's get down to business,' said Mrs Gibbons. At that moment, the red telephone rang, and she picked up the receiver.

'Indeed?' said Mrs Gibbons. 'You surprise me,' she added. 'Not at all,' she continued. 'I will ring you back.'

She replaced the receiver, and smiled brightly at her companions, who had found the interruption decidedly disappointing, and had been looking forward to seeing their chairman with the receiver tucked between chin and shoulder, whilst taking down notes in efficient shorthand, just as people did on the telly.

'Any ideas?' she enquired.

As one would expect, there was a heavy silence. A blackbird scolded outside. A motorcycle roared past.

'That'll be me brother,' volunteered Miss Cooke, and silence fell again.

'Well,' said Mrs Gibbons at last, 'shall I start the ball rolling? I thought it would be a good idea to present the ladies with something really *personal* connected with Thrush Green.'

'How d'you mean, personal?' asked Molly. 'Like something they could wear, say?'

'No, no! Nothing like that. I was thinking of something on historical lines. Perhaps a short account of all that had happened in Thrush Green during their time here.'

'A sort of *book*?' queried Miss Cooke, sounding shocked. If Mrs Gibbons had suggested a pair of corsets apiece for the ladies, the committee members could not have appeared more affronted.

'I shouldn't think they'd want a *book*,' volunteered the quiet father, who was called Frank Biddle. 'Unless of course, you

63

have come across a contemporary account of Thrush Green which we haven't yet seen.'

'I envisaged *compiling* such a book,' said Mrs Gibbons. 'From people's memories and cuttings from the local paper. And photographs, of course.'

Silence fell again, as all present considered the magnitude of the task and the inadequacy of anyone, Mrs Gibbons included, to undertake it.

Frank Biddle rallied first. 'A nice idea if we had thought of it a year or two ago perhaps,' he began cautiously, 'but we'd never get it done in time.'

Molly Curdle and Emily Cooke hastened to agree.

'Right! Scrub out that one!' said Mrs Gibbons, wielding a large blue pencil and slashing across her notepad.

'Then what about something for their new home to which we all contribute? I thought a large rug – perhaps a runner for their hall – with a few stitches put in by every person in the parish.'

'It'd take a fair old time,' observed Molly.

'And we'd have to cart it about from one house to the next,' pointed out Emily. 'Get it wet most likely, or find people out.'

'Yes, rather a *cumbersome* project,' agreed Frank Biddle.

Mrs Gibbons' blue pencil tapped impatiently on the desk top. 'Well, let's have your ideas,' she said shortly.

Silence fell again, broken only by the tapping of the pencil, and a distant squawk from one of Percy Hodge's chickens.

Molly Curdle was the first to pluck up her courage. 'What about some sort of *thing*? I mean, a nice vase, or set of glasses, or a wooden salad bowl, if you think breakables a bit silly.'

'Not silly at all,' said Frank, relieved to have someone beside him with ideas to offer.

Molly cast him a grateful look.

'I was thinking rather on the same lines,' said Frank, not entirely truthfully, as he had toyed with suggesting a lawn mower or some window-boxes for the new residence.

'Possible,' said Mrs Gibbons with a marked lack of enthusiasm.

Emily Cooke, anxious no doubt to return to Nigel, came out strongly in support of Molly. 'Far the best thing to go to a shop for something nice. See it all ready, I mean, and make a choice, like. A book or a rug, like what you said, Mrs Gibbons, would need no end of time and trouble, and there's plenty could make a muck of their bit and spoil it for the others.'

'That's very true,' agreed Frank Biddle. 'I suggest that we make a list of suggestions ready to forward to the rector.'

'Very well,' said Mrs Gibbons resignedly, 'if that is agreeable to you all.'

There was a murmur of assent.

'I must say,' went on their chairman, ripping off a clean sheet from the notepad, 'that I had envisaged something more *personal*, something more inspired, but there we are.'

She spoke more in sorrow than anger, as though her best students had failed Common Entrance through no fault of her own. Her three companions appeared relieved rather than rebuked, and smiled warmly at each other.

'Ideas again?' prompted Mrs Gibbons, pencil poised.

'Piece of glass. Vase or similar,' repeated Molly.

'Something for the garden,' said Frank, feeling that he should make some contribution as the only man present. 'Perhaps a garden seat?'

'Garden seat,' muttered Mrs Gibbons, pencil flying.

'Wooden salad bowl,' added Emily, conscious that it was really Molly's idea, but unable to think of anything of her own.

'And servers, if the money runs to it,' added Molly, smiling forgivingly at Emily.

'Very good,' said Mrs Gibbons sitting up from her task. 'And I think I shall add a picture of the school. Perhaps a watercolour or a *really good* photograph.'

'Now that *would* be nice,' exclaimed Emily who felt that they could now afford to be generous as the meeting was almost over and the list of suggestions was mainly their own effort.

'I agree,' said Molly. 'They'd treasure that, I'm sure.'

'A really bright idea,' said Frank, collecting his stick ready for departure. 'Thank you for managing things so splendidly, Mrs Gibbons.'

He gave her a polite bow and made for the door, soon followed by the two ladies.

'I don't know that I really approve of the suggestions,' said Mrs Gibbons to the Gauleiter later that evening, 'but they all seemed grateful for my guidance, so I suppose one must be content with that.'

At the school itself, young Miss Robinson who had recently finished her probationary year and was beginning to settle nicely with the lower juniors, was contemplating the same problem. It was she who would have to collect contributions, amidst deadly secrecy, from all the children and then decide what form the present should take.

She confided her worries to the rector when he called one afternoon. As always, he was comforting.

'I should tell the children that we do not want them to give more than say ten pence. It is fairer to the less well-off, and in any case should bring in enough to buy a beautiful bouquet, or a box of chocolates, something welcome but unpretentious, don't you think?'

'And a big card with everyone's name on it, I thought,' said Miss Robinson.

'I'm sure that it would be deeply appreciated by both ladies,' agreed the rector, giving her the gentle smile which mollified even the most militant of his critics.

Later, at the insistence of her own class, Miss Robinson was obliged to outline this plan, stressing the fact that no money should be brought until sometime during the summer term.

However, this did not dissuade one conscientious child from arriving one March morning and offering her a hot tenpenny piece with the words:

'It's for the teachers' wreaths.'

*

It was in March that Miss Watson was given her first driving lesson by Ben Curdle.

He arrived at six o'clock. The Fiesta gleamed with much polishing and not a speck sullied the mats on the floor.

A few children who had been playing on the green came to watch the proceedings, as Miss Watson, pink with excitement, took her place beside Ben.

'I'll take you up the Nidden road,' said Ben, eyeing the interested spectators. 'Be more peaceful, like. Then we'll change places when I've shown you the controls.'

'A good idea,' said his pupil, much relieved.

She decided to ignore the children. If she smiled at them, they might be encouraged to familiarities she did not wish for at the moment. On the other hand, it would not be fair to scold them. After all, they had every right to play on the green. It was just annoying that they appeared so curious. Perhaps a word about *being inquisitive* at tomorrow's assembly? But then, that would be an aspersion on their parents, who were every bit as agog at others' affairs. How difficult life was, thought Dorothy, trying to attend to Ben's explanations.

They drew up a little way beyond Mrs Jenner's house, where there were only a few black and white Friesian cows watching from one of Percy Hodge's fields.

Dorothy and Ben changed places and, with the car stationary, Ben began his lesson.

'First thing is the seat belt. Get that fixed. Then look in both mirrors and see if you can see the road behind in the top one and a view along at an angle in the wing mirror.'

Dorothy nodded vigorously and did as she was told, finding some difficulty in slotting the belt to safety in her excitement.

'Now these three pedals,' went on Ben, pointing floorwards, 'I expect you remember are the clutch, the brake and the accelerator.'

It was some twenty minutes later that Dorothy was allowed to switch on, to put the car into low gear and to let in the clutch. The cows, who had watched with deep interest, now backed away in alarm as the Fiesta jerked forward in kangaroo hops.

'You wants to take it a bit smoother,' said Ben kindly. 'Let's start again.'

Half an hour later, Dorothy Watson reappeared in Thrush Green, driving at approximately twenty miles an hour in second gear, and feeling triumphant but exhausted. She drew up at the gate of the school house and sighed happily.

'I *did* enjoy that, Ben. Thank you for being so patient. How did I do? Be truthful now.'

'All right, miss,' said Ben warmly. 'You'll soon get the hang of it, and everyone muddles the brake and the accelerator to begin with.'

'Will you come in and have a cup of coffee?'

'That's nice of you, but I'd best get back. Molly's expecting me.'

'Then I'll see you on Thursday. And many thanks again.'

Ben smiled at her, and drove his hard-worked car homeward. He could do with something stronger than coffee when he got in, he told himself.

Little Miss Fogerty was all of a twitter when Dorothy arrived.

'And how did it go? Were you nervous? Was Ben pleased with you? Would you like a drink, or are you too tired?'

Dorothy bore the spate of questions with composure. 'It went quite well, and I wasn't nervous. Ben said he was pleased with me, and yes, I should love a drink. Coffee would be perfect.'

The two ladies went into the kitchen. Dorothy set out two cups and saucers, and Agnes poured milk into a saucepan.

'And I've had some excitement too,' said Agnes, as they waited for the milk and the kettle to boil.

'And what was that, dear?'

'A little cat came to the back door – a tabby one. I think it must be a stray, as I'm sure I haven't seen it before.'

'Better not encourage it,' said Dorothy.

'Well, I did give it some milk,' confessed Agnes, 'it seemed so very hungry. And a few scraps of chicken skin from the meat dish.'

'It probably comes from one of those new houses off the Nidden road,' said Dorothy, snatching the milk saucepan from the stove where it was hissing dangerously.

'I do hope it has got a home,' replied Agnes wistfully. 'It had the sweetest little face.'

'I shouldn't think we'll see it again,' said Dorothy with satisfaction, lifting the tray.

Following her friend into the sitting-room, little Miss Fogerty hoped that Dorothy was mistaken. There was something so endearing about that tabby cat. It had backed away when she had attempted to stroke it, eyeing the plate anxiously until Agnes had gone indoors. She watched it return and gulp down the food ravenously, and her tender heart was touched.

Dorothy waxed enthusiastic about her driving lesson, and explained to Agnes how difficult it is to let in the clutch *really smoothly*, and how pleasantly responsive the Fiesta was, and it might well be the right car for them, when the time came to buy.

Agnes smiled and nodded over her coffee cup, but she was not really attending.

Would that little cat have a warm bed tonight? She hoped so. Perhaps it would be possible to make a straw bed in the wood shed? It would mean leaving the door ajar at night, and perhaps Dorothy would object.

'I shall turn in early tonight,' said Dorothy yawning. 'I must say, learning something new is very tiring. I must try and remember that when I'm teaching the children.'

Agnes nodded her agreement. She too was tired with hearing about the mysteries of the combustion engine, in which she had no interest.

Dorothy dreamt that she was driving a large and powerful car of Edwardian design across the grass of Thrush Green. Her right foot twitched in her sleep, as she did her best to distinguish between brake and accelerator.

But next door, Agnes dreamt of a tabby cat, warm and purring, asleep on her lap.

PART TWO

Battling On

* * *

7 · SPRING AT THRUSH GREEN

The long doleful winter seemed to be coming to an end when a welcome warmth crept across the land, the daffodils lengthened their stems, and lambs bleated in the fields near Thrush Green.

Hopeful gardeners itched to put out from their greenhouses the waiting trays of annuals. The vegetable plots were raked over in readiness for early potatoes, peas and broad beans. Older and wiser gardeners did their best to restrain these optimists, and took gloomy pleasure in pointing out the late snowfalls of yester-year and the innumerable frosts which April and May could bring with doom in their wake.

The ladies of Lulling and Thrush Green hastened to the two dress shops in the High Street to replenish their wardrobes with cotton frocks, only to be told, with considerable satisfaction on the part of the assistants, that all summer clothing should have been bought last October, and that now they were showing winter wear only.

'But surely that's rather silly,' commented Winnie Bailey, wondering if she would find a Viyella button-through frock a good investment, and deciding, on looking at the price ticket, that it might be wiser to invest in a few dozen gold bars instead.

'The Trade has always followed this traditional pattern,' said the assistant loftily.

Some rock music was blaring round them making conversation difficult.

'Do you think we could have that switched off?' asked Winnie.

The assistant looked shocked. 'Quite out of the question,' she replied. 'It's *Company Policy* to have background music. The customers like it.'

'Well, here's one who doesn't,' retorted Winnie with spirit, casting the Viyella frock across the counter.

She strode out into Lulling High Street, vowing never to darken the doors of that insufferable shop again, and noticed a fluttering of hands at the windows of the Lovelocks' house.

She responded vigorously, crossed the road, and was welcomed indoors by the three sisters.

'I don't know what's come over that shop,' commiserated Ada. 'Ever since that new woman came and called it "Suzilou" it has gone downhill.'

'We *always* bought our stays there,' volunteered Violet. 'Right from girlhood, but now they say they aren't stocking *foundation garments*! Would you believe it?'

'I believe it readily,' said Winnie. 'Also I am getting heartily tired of asking for a size sixteen or eighteen only to be told that those sizes are so popular that they have sold out.'

'Most trying,' agreed Bertha. 'If that is so, why don't the manufacturers make more of those sizes?'

All four ladies sighed and shook their heads.

'A cup of coffee, Winnie dear?'

'Or a glass of sherry?'

'Or we have some madeira somewhere, if you prefer it?'

'Nothing, thank you. Tell me, how are you faring at The Fuchsia Bush, and have you been able to get help in the house?'

Ada, as the eldest, took it upon herself to answer.

'On the whole,' she began judicially, 'we are being well served at The Fuchsia Bush. We go every Wednesday, and sometimes, when we feel we can afford it, on a Thursday as well.'

Winnie Bailey, who had known the sisters' parsimony for almost half a century, was not affected by the pathos of the Thursday decision.

'Of course, we always let Mrs Peters or Nelly know on the *Wednesday* if we shall be requiring lunch on the *Thursday*,' explained Bertha.

'The food is excellent,' added Violet.

'But expensive,' reproved Ada.

'It's far dearer at The Fleece,' responded Violet, sounding militant. 'I looked at the menu outside when I was passing yesterday, and their set lunch is twice the price of Mrs Peters'.'

'We were not considering The Fleece,' retorted Ada. 'For one thing it is far too far to walk there, particularly if the weather is inclement. I can't think why you troubled to pry into their tariff at all.'

Winnie hastened to break into this family squabble. 'Well, I'm sure you are wise to go next door occasionally. They were so obliging to you when you were all ill. It's a good thing to repay their kindness, by giving them your custom.'

The ladies smiled.

'But to answer your other question,' went on Ada. 'No, we haven't found regular help yet. Nelly Piggott approached one or two people, but they were unable to come.'

'It isn't as though we are asking them to do too much, you know,' said Bertha. 'Just a hand with the silver cleaning.'

Winnie surveyed the occasional tables, laden with silver bric-à-brac, recalled the drawers full of heavy silver cutlery, and the vast tureens and sauce boats in the dining-room, and was not surprised that any cleaner's heart would plummet at the magnitude of the task.

'And scrubbing the kitchen floor, and the back places,' added Violet.

'And taking the gas stove to pieces for a monthly spring clean.'

'And, of course, the windows,' added Violet. 'We do seem to have rather a lot of windows. And Father always liked to see the steps whitened with hearth stone, and we like to keep that up.'

'We *did wonder*,' said Ada meditatively, 'if she would

undertake some decorating as well, now and again. Just simple paper-hanging and gloss-painting for the woodwork. You don't know of anyone who would like a light job, I suppose?'

'Well, no,' said Winnie rising. 'But if I hear of any able-bodied person who might suit you, I will let you know.'

She made her farewells, and walked down the steps to the pavement.

'And an able-bodied person,' thought Winnie to herself, as she traversed the High Street in the warm sunlight, 'is what would be needed in that household.' She approached the steep hill leading to Thrush Green. 'And would they be able-bodied for long?' she wondered aloud, much to the astonishment of a passing collie dog.

The warm spell jolted everyone into activity. The inhabitants of Lulling and Thrush Green, who had been hibernating as thoroughly as the hedgehogs, now stirred themselves to clean windows, wash curtains, throw rugs on to the clothes lines for thorough beating and generally welcome the spring with a spurt of domesticity.

Local telephone lines hummed with invitations to coffee, lunch, tea, a drink, or even a full-blown formal evening dinner. People who could not be bothered to do more than fend for themselves during the bitter winter months, now remembered how much they wanted to see their friends again, particularly as the gardens were at their best, aglow with daffodils, aubrietia and golden alyssum, and mercifully free, so far, from the more noxious weeds which would be rampant in a month's time.

Harold Shoosmith's garden was particularly colourful. Yellow, blue and mauve crocuses like gas flames had burst through the soil beneath the flowering cherry trees and the golden forsythia bushes. His Thrush Green neighbours paused to admire the garden when they passed, and even Albert Piggott had to admit that it was 'a fair picture'.

Harold had kept his word and had taken Dorothy Watson for a trial spin in his own car. He confessed to Isobel, before he called for his pupil, that he was a bundle of nerves, but gained confidence after a mile or so, for Dorothy seemed to be making steady progress, and was careful when changing gear.

Harold's new car was an Audi which Dorothy handled very well, but she gave a sigh of relief when at last they drew up at the Shoosmiths' house.

'Lovely, Harold dear,' she said, 'but I think a *small* car would be more suitable for Agnes and me.'

Harold agreed that there was no need for the two ladies to own a car as large – or as expensive – as the Audi, and that parking would be a lot easier with a vehicle the size of Ben's Fiesta, or even smaller.

'When the time comes,' he offered, 'I should enjoy trying out any that you favour. That is, if you still propose to buy.'

'Yes, indeed. Ben seems to think that I am getting on quite well. I only hope he's right.'

'I'd trust Ben's judgement.'

By this time they were in Harold's house where Agnes and Isobel were comfortably ensconced.

'And what news of the house-hunting?' enquired Isobel.

'Very little news, I fear,' replied Dorothy. 'Except that the particulars from Better & Better have been more plentiful with spring on the way, and rather more realistic.'

'Dorothy wrote to them,' explained Agnes, 'about how silly it was to send us details of top floor flats or bits of castles. Such a waste of everyone's time.'

'Well, we've all been through it,' said Isobel. 'Harold always says that after forty-three viewings he simply settled for forty-four, which was this one, because he had cracked completely.'

'You were let off comparatively lightly,' Harold reminded her. 'Only a dozen or so, and then I persuaded her to marry me. I still don't know if I or the house was the real attraction.'

'Fifty-fifty,' his wife told him, with a smile.

'Well, we don't know any nice single men in Barton,' said Dorothy. 'And certainly not one who would offer us marriage. I think we shall simply have to rely on Better & Better.'

'I'm looking forward to visiting you there when you've settled in,' said Isobel. 'I visited it on a couple of occasions when I took my neighbour in Sussex to visit her aunt there. It was an awkward cross-country journey by train, so I ran her across. We had a splendid picnic on the way, I remember, which she insisted on preparing. Asparagus, strawberries and cream! Delicious!'

'Why don't we have grand picnics like that?' queried Harold.

'Because you prefer thick ham sandwiches, or a ploughman's in a pub,' said Isobel.

She rose and beckoned to the ladies. 'Now come and have a proper look at the garden. Harold's done wonders.'

And the party moved out to enjoy the last of that day's spring sunshine.

On the following Wednesday, Ada, Bertha and Violet Lovelock walked to The Fuchsia Bush. Nelly Piggott herself placed their lunch before the Misses Lovelock.

Miss Ada had ordered fillet of plaice, Miss Bertha lasagne and

Miss Violet braised beef. As the youngest of the three sisters, she was well aware that she would have to face some criticism when she returned home. Braised beef was more expensive than plaice or lasagne. Miss Violet was content to face her sisters' strictures later. In any case, she was not only used to them, but would be fortified by good red meat.

'There you are then,' said Nelly encouragingly, 'and I hope you enjoy it.'

The ladies inclined their heads.

'Not got suited yet, I suppose?' went on Nelly.

'I'm afraid not,' murmured Ada.

'Marvellous, innit? All this unemployment they keep on about, and yet no one wants a day's work.'

'Quite,' said Bertha.

'Could we have some mustard?' asked Violet. 'English, please.'

'Well, I won't forget to look out for someone,' said Nelly, as she departed in search of mustard. 'But it'll be an uphill job, I warn you.'

Through the window of The Fuchsia Bush the life of Lulling High Street pursued its peaceful way. Young Mr Venables, retired solicitor of Lulling, and now in his seventies, was chatting to an equally venerable gentleman beneath the pollarded lime tree immediately outside the restaurant. Several dogs were trotting about on their daily affairs, and young mothers were gossiping over their prams.

On the other side of the road, the greengrocer had put out some boxes of early annuals on the pavement below the rich display of apples, oranges, forced rhubarb and melons.

Velvety pansies, glowing dwarf marigolds and multi-coloured polyanthus plants all tempted the passers-by, particularly those gardening optimists who were dying to get down to some positive work after the months of winter idleness.

Among them was Ella Bembridge, close friend of Dimity, Charles Henstock's wife, and an old friend of the Lovelock sisters.

She was stooping over the boxes, her tweed skirt immodestly high, and a plume of blue smoke from one of her untidy cigarettes wreathing above her head.

Violet, who was facing the window, noticed her first, and wondered idly if their old friend would also be lunching at The Fuchsia Bush. She did not wonder for long. Ella straightened up and plunged across the road towards the restaurant. A startled motorist screeched to a halt, stuck his head out of the window, and presumably rebuked Ella.

Violet saw Ella give him a dismissive flick of her hand as she gained the kerb. Her expression was contemptuous. The motorist, muttering darkly, drove on.

'Well, well! Hello, hello!' she shouted boisterously. 'Got room for one more at your board?'

The two older Misses Lovelock looked up in surprise, and Ada choked delicately on a bone which had no business to be in a fillet of plaice. It was left to Violet to do the honours.

'Of course, Ella dear. Just let me move the water jug and the ashtray. Oh no! You may need that, perhaps.'

'Not for a bit, thanks. How nice to see you here.'

She settled herself with a good deal of puffing and blowing, throwing off her jacket, tugging at her cardigan sleeves, dropping her gloves to the floor, and generally creating as much disturbance as a troop of cavalry.

'Nearly got run down by some fool car driver who wasn't looking where he was going,' she announced. 'Proper menace some of these chaps. I hear Dorothy Watson's learning to drive. Think she'd have more sense.'

Violet, handing the menu to the newcomer, considered this comment. Did Ella mean that she would imagine that Dorothy would have more sense than the male drivers who were menaces? Or did she think that Dorothy ought to have more sense than to have undertaken driving lessons and the probable future ownership of a car? Really, the English language was remarkably ambiguous.

Ella studied the menu briefly and then slapped it down on the table. The salt and pepper pots jumped together.

'What are you lot having?' she said, peering at their plates in turn. 'Don't care for fish in white sauce myself, and that lasagne is no tastier than wet face flannel I always think.'

She studied Violet's half-finished portion. 'Looks good that!'

She caught sight of Nelly hovering by the kitchen door.

'Ah, Nelly!' she roared cheerfully. 'Bring me a plate of Miss Violet's stuff, will you? There's a good girl!' She turned to her companions in the greatest good humour. 'What luck catching you here! I was just about to call to see if you would like to contribute to the Save The Children Fund. Dimity asked me to help.'

Ada and Bertha exchanged looks of horror, speechless at the idea of parting with money.

Violet rose to the occasion.

'Of course, Ella dear. Such a good cause.'

She ignored the glances of her two sisters. If she were to get a wigging anyway for choosing braised beef, then she might just as well be hanged for a sheep as a lamb.

No one relished this amazingly warm spell as keenly as little Miss Fogerty. Her bird-like frame suffered severely in the bitter Cotswold winters despite sturdy underclothes and several hand-knitted garments protecting her shoulders and chest.

The sunshine woke her earlier now in the mornings, and it was a joy to come downstairs early to see that the breakfast table was in good order, and to greet whichever Willie was postman for the week.

Willie Bond, large and lethargic, came one week. He was a cousin of Betty Bell's who cleaned the school and also attended to Harold and Isobel Shoosmith's domestic affairs, and to Dotty Harmer's at Lulling Woods.

His counterpart was Willie Marchant, a lanky and morose individual. Nevertheless, he was always polite to Agnes Fogerty, remembering an occasion when she had personally escorted a nephew of his to his home, when the child had been smitten with a severe bilious attack.

'Not many would've bothered,' he told people. 'She's a kind old party, even if she was behind the door when the looks was given out.'

Agnes enjoyed these few precious minutes of tranquillity before the rigours of the day.

There was another reason too for her pleasure in this early morning privacy, for more often than not these days the little tabby cat approached timidly, and sat by the dustbin waiting for his milk.

Agnes did not fail him. She also added a few scraps which she had garnered during the day before, and had taken to purloining any specially acceptable tit-bits from the school left-overs.

She put this largesse on the flagstones behind the dustbin. The cat always ran away, but she noticed with joy that he fled less far away as the days passed, and he returned to Agnes's bounty very quickly.

She stayed at the window as he ate, hoping that Dorothy would not appear before he had finished his meal. It was not that she was *ashamed* of feeding the poor little thing, she told herself, but there was no reason to upset Dorothy who had seemed to be rather dismissive about their visitor when Agnes had mentioned it.

While she waited she admired the dewy garden. Already the birds were astir, and a pair of collared doves were flutter-ing by the hedge. A young rabbit sat motionless nearby, and Agnes thought how perfectly the pearl-grey of feathers and fur matched.

The cat licked the last delicious drops of milk from the saucer and made off quickly through the hedge. The doves whirred away, and the rabbit vanished.

Whose cat could it be, wondered Agnes? Although it was thin, it seemed to be domesticated and certainly knew how to cope with provender on saucers.

She went out to collect his crockery, and washed it up as Willie Bond dropped the letters through the front door.

Perhaps the children would know about the cat, she thought suddenly, bending to collect the post. She must remember to enquire, but not, perhaps, in dear Dorothy's hearing.

8. CAT TROUBLE

As one might expect in March, the fine spell was of short duration. After about eight days of heart-lifting sunshine, the clouds returned, the temperature dropped, and the winter garments, so joyously discarded for a brief time, were once more resumed.

One chilly morning when Miss Fogerty's infants were struggling with various arithmetical problems, designated Number on the timetable, and involving a great many aids such as coloured counters, rods of varying length, and a good deal of juvenile theft between the children, Agnes was surprised to see the tabby cat sitting on the wooden bench inside the playground shed, sheltering from the drizzle.

She clapped her hands, and the children looked up.

'Can anyone tell me,' she said, 'who owns that nice little cat out there?'

There was a surge of infant bodies towards the window, which Agnes quelled with consummate experience.

'We don't want to frighten it! Just look quietly.'

It was Nigel Cooke, son of Miss Cooke of the PTA committee, who spoke first, hand upraised in quivering excitement.

'Please, miss, it lives next door to us, miss.'

Agnes felt her heart sink. So it had a home after all!

'Well, it used to, sort of,' said another child. 'Them Allens left it behind when they done a moonlight flit.'

'They never paid the rent, see,' explained Nigel. 'They went one night. My dad saw 'em go, as he was on late Shift.'

'Well, where does the cat live now?' enquired Miss Fogerty.

84

'He don't live nowhere like,' said one little girl. Agnes decided that this was not quite the time to point out the result of a double negative. She was too anxious to know the present position of the animal.

'He comes up ours sometimes,' said another Nidden child. 'My mum gives him bits, but he won't come in. My mum says the Allens should be persecuted, and was going to give the cruelty to animals man a ring, but my dad said she was to let well alone, so she never.'

Really, *men*! Agnes felt furious and impatient. Anything for a quiet life, she supposed, was their motto! No thought for the poor starving cat!

She hid her feelings, and spoke calmly. 'Who knows where it sleeps?'

Nigel was again the first to answer. 'If it's fine he sleeps on the step up against his back door.'

Agnes's eyes pricked at this poignant picture. 'And if it rains?'

Nigel looked blank. 'Up the farm sheds at Perce Hodge's, I reckon.'

Agnes determined to find out a little more, by discreet enquiries of Percy himself and any other reliable adult living along the Nidden road.

Meanwhile, work must be resumed.

'Back to your tables now. I want to see who can be first solving these problems.'

Comparative peace enfolded the class and Miss Fogerty, watching the cat washing its paws, made plans for the future.

It was about this time that Charles Henstock had an interesting telephone call from his great friend Anthony Bull.

Anthony had been Charles's predecessor at St John's of Lulling. He was a tall handsome man with a splendid voice which he used to great effect in his rather dramatic sermons. Despite a certain theatricality which a few of the males in his congregation deplored, Anthony Bull was deservedly popular, for he was a conscientious parish priest and a good friend to many.

The ladies adored him, and at Christmas a shower of presents descended upon the vicar, many hand-made, and creating a problem in their discreet disposal. Anthony's wife grew efficient in finding worthy homes for three-quarters of this bounty, all at some distance, so that the givers would not take umbrage. There had been one occasion, however, when one particularly devoted admirer of the vicar's had come across a piece of her handiwork at a cousin's bazaar in Devon. It had taken all Mrs Bull's ingenuity and church diplomacy to explain that unfortunate incident.

When Charles had first taken over the parish at Lulling and its environs, there had been some comparisons made by many of Anthony's more ardent followers. They found Charles's sermons far too simple and low key after Anthony's perorations from the pulpit. Charles, short and chubby, modest and unassuming, ran a poor second to his predecessor in looks and panache.

But gradually his congregation began to admire their new vicar's sincerity. They came to value his advice, to appreciate his unselfish efforts, to recognise the absolute goodness of the man.

The two men, so different in temperament, remained firm friends although they only met occasionally now that Anthony had a busy parish in Kensington.

The telephone call was greeted with joy by Charles, standing in his draughty hall and looking out into the windswept vicarage garden.

After the first greetings, Anthony came to the point. It appeared that he had been approached by a young woman who had been brought up in Lulling and was now in service in his London parish. She wanted to return to be near her mother. Did Charles know if it would be easy for her to get work?

'Domestic work, do you mean?' asked Charles. 'Or something in a shop or office? Has she any particular qualifications?

I know that Venables wants a typist, and there's a new super-market opening soon, and there might be jobs there. I take it she will live with her mother?'

'Well, no! I think she wants cheap digs, or a living-in job. There's a snag. She has a little boy of three or thereabouts. No husband, of course, and I gather the fellow was a bad lot, but I've only heard one side of the affair, naturally. The mother, by the way, is Gladys Lilly. Chapel, I think.'

'I know her slightly. Yes, she does go to the chapel at the end of the town, I believe. A jolly sort of person.'

'Well, she wasn't too jolly about the baby, I gather, but she's willing to mind him while the daughter is at work, so that's a step in the right direction.'

'I'll have a word with Dimity,' promised Charles, 'and keep my ears open. As soon as I have any news I will ring. Now, when are you coming this way? The garden is looking very pretty despite the weather, and you know we'd love a visit.'

Anthony said he would do his best to get to Lulling again, and with mutual messages of affection the old friends rang off.

'Dimity!' called Charles, setting off towards the kitchen. 'We have a problem before us!'

The end of term was now in sight at Thrush Green school, and all three teachers were looking forward to the Easter holidays. Agnes and Dorothy admitted to being even more tired than usual.

'I suppose it's because we've had such a wretchedly long winter,' said Dorothy, who was standing at the sitting-room window, surveying the grey drizzle outside.

'Partly,' agreed Agnes, busy with her knitting. 'And then we've been doing a good deal of clearing up at school. And your driving lessons must be a strain.'

'I enjoy them,' said Dorothy shortly.

'Then, of course, we have the house business hanging over us,' continued Agnes. 'It would be nice to get that settled.'

'Not much point in buying at the moment with a whole term

to get through,' commented Dorothy, 'although I suppose we'd need time to get anything we bought put into order.'

She sounded a little snappy, Agnes thought. Dear Dorothy had been somewhat on edge lately, and to be honest, she had felt irritable herself. Perhaps the approaching break after so many years at the school was beginning to take its toll.

'There's that cat!' exclaimed Dorothy suddenly. 'Do you

know, that's the second time I've seen him this week. I hope he's not coming regularly.'

Agnes made no answer. Dorothy turned round from the window.

'Agnes, are you *feeding* that cat?'

Little Miss Fogerty's hands trembled as she put down the knitting into her lap. She took a deep breath.

'Well, yes, Dorothy dear, I am!'

It was Dorothy's turn to breathe in deeply, and her neck began to flush. This was a bad sign, as Agnes knew very well, but now that the matter had arisen she was determined to stick to her guns.

'Well, really, Agnes,' protested her friend, with commendable restraint, 'you know I think it is wrong to encourage the animal. We can't possibly take on a cat now when we are off to Barton in a few months. And what will happen to it when we have gone?'

'I can't see the poor little thing go hungry,' answered Agnes. 'I've only put down milk, and a few scraps.'

'When, may I ask?'

'First thing in the morning, and as it gets dusk. I don't leave the saucers down in case mice or rats come to investigate.'

'I should hope not. In any case, the mere fact of putting food out in the first place is enough to encourage vermin.'

'It's a very *clean* little cat,' said Agnes, becoming agitated.

'I daresay. Most cats are. But I think you have been very silly, and short-sighted too, to have started this nonsense. It's cruel to encourage the poor animal to expect food when we know we shall not be here to provide for it before long.'

'It would be far more cruel to let it starve to death,' retorted Agnes with spirit.

Dorothy rarely saw her friend in such a militant mood, and resolved to deal gently with her.

'Of course it would, Agnes dear. I'm simply pointing out that we must look to the future. If it becomes dependent upon us it is going to be doubly hard on the animal when it finds we have gone.'

She noticed, with alarm, that Agnes was shaking.

'Perhaps we could find a home for it if it is really a stray,' she continued. 'So often cats go from one house to another for anything they can cadge, when they have a perfectly good home of their own.'

'This one hasn't,' snapped Agnes.

'And how do you know?'

Agnes explained about the Allens' departure, and abandonment of the cat, and its present plight. By now her face was pink, her eyes filled with tears, and her whole body was quivering.

'Then we must certainly try and find a home for it,' said Dorothy. 'Perhaps the RSPCA could help.'

'I don't see why we shouldn't take it on ourselves,' protested Agnes. 'It is getting tamer every day, and *whatever* you say, Dorothy, I intend to go on feeding it. I am very fond of the little thing, and I think – I'm sure – it is fond of me.'

Dorothy gave one of her famous snorts. '*Cupboard love*!' she boomed.

At this the tears began to roll down little Miss Fogerty's papery old cheeks, and splashed upon her knitting.

Dorothy, curbing her impatience with heroic efforts, tried to speak gently. 'Well, carry on as you are, dear, if you think it right. You know my own feelings on the subject.'

Agnes blew her nose, and mopped her eyes. She was too overwrought to speak.

'I think,' said her headmistress, 'that we could both do with an early bed tonight.'

And early to bed both ladies went, much perturbed. Civil goodnights were exchanged on the landing as usual, but both were relieved to enter the peaceful surroundings of their respective bedrooms.

Little Miss Fogerty washed her face and hands, cleaned her teeth and brushed her hair. Normally, she did a few exercises to help her arthritis, as directed by John Lovell, but tonight she was too exhausted to bother.

The night was bright. A full moon was hanging in the branches of the Shoosmiths' plum tree next door. Standing in her sensible nightgown, long-sleeved and high-necked, she noticed the cat's saucer behind the dustbin. She had forgotten to retrieve it in the worry of the evening.

In a strange way the sight calmed her. Well, now Dorothy knew. What was more, Dorothy had accepted the fact that the cat was going to be fed. There was now no need for subterfuge. It was quite a relief to have things out in the open. Tomorrow, she thought rebelliously, she would buy a few tins of cat food and discover the cat's preferences. The tins could be stored on the scullery shelf, and she would buy a new tin-opener to be kept specially for the cat's provender.

These modest plans gave her some comfort. She crept between the sheets and lay watching the shadows of the branches move across the ceiling in the moonlight.

She was truly sorry to have upset dear Dorothy, and she would apologise for that before breakfast. But she was not going to apologise for feeding the cat. It was the right thing to do – the *Christian* thing. The hungry should be fed, and she was determined to do it.

As the warmth of the bedclothes crept around her, Agnes's eyes closed. Yes, an apology first, then a saucer of milk for the cat, and perhaps a little of the minced lamb she had prepared for a shepherd's pie, and then . . .

But that was the last waking thought of little Miss Fogerty before she dropped into the sleep of the utterly exhausted.

Next door, Dorothy was more wakeful. She too regretted the evening's upset. Perhaps she had been too sharp with Agnes. She had not quite realised how deeply Agnes was involved with the little animal. It was extraordinary that she had never noticed that the cat was being fed regularly. Agnes must have been putting the food out in a well-hidden place. It was pathetic really.

She began to feel deeply sorry for her friend. She had always recognised her devotion to animals. It was akin to the strong affection she had for her young children and all defenceless things, and Dorothy heartily approved of such compassion. She supposed that some psychiatrists would dismiss it as 'thwarted motherhood', but Dorothy knew it was far more than that. It was a respect for life in all its forms, and a right-minded desire to protect and cherish it.

Maybe, thought Dorothy with a guilty pang, it was simply that she herself was worried about the extra responsibility of an animal about the place, when there were so many things to consider at this time. Would she normally have been so thoughtless to dear Agnes? Would she have been willing to welcome that cat into the household if they had been staying at Thrush Green indefinitely?

She tossed restlessly in the bed. Really, the moonlight was almost too bright, and yet it would be unpleasant with the curtains drawn.

On impulse she threw off the bedclothes and went to look out of the window. Thrush Green was deserted and beautiful. The bare branches threw black lacy shadows on the dewy grass, and Nathaniel Patten's statue gleamed in the moonlight.

What a world of utter tranquillity, thought Dorothy! Yet

here she was, at its very centre, aquiver with self-torment and unhappiness.

Well, she must make amends tomorrow, she told herself, clambering back into the bed. Probably they were both over-tired with all this wretched end-of-term worry, and the added tension of the final break ahead.

She would tell Agnes, first thing, that she was truly sorry to have upset her, and she would try and say no more about the cat. With any luck, it would adopt someone else well before the move to Barton.

The chief thing was to be reconciled with dear Agnes. She was not going to let a mere cat come between old friends!

At half-past three, as the moon dipped behind Lulling Woods, she fell into a troubled sleep.

Albert Piggott's first real outing was down the footpath at the side of his cottage to visit Dotty Harmer.

He had, of course, visited The Two Pheasants daily, and during the brief spell of warm weather, had shared a seat on the green with Tom Hardy and Polly one bright morning. But this was his first proper walk, and he sniffed the air appreciatively as he made his way towards Dotty's cottage some quarter of a mile away.

It was good to be out and about again after his enforced sojourn indoors. Some young dandelion leaves caught his eye, and he pulled a few as a present for Dotty's rabbits. Bending down caught his breath, and he had to stand still for a while in case a fit of coughing followed, but all was well.

He watched a coral-breasted chaffinch hopping up the stairs of the hawthorn hedge where it had its home. A rook floated down across the field on its black satin wings, and in the distance he could hear the metallic croak of a pheasant, now safe from man's guns.

Albert felt almost happy. He liked being alone. He liked all the country sounds and smells. They reminded him of his boyhood in these parts, when he had run across this same meadow at buttercup time, and gilded his broken boots with their pollen.

He looked forward to seeing Dotty after so long. The two strange people had much in common. Neither cared a button about appearances or other people's opinions of them. Both loved the earth and all that could be grown in it. Both had a way with animals, preferring them to their own kind, and each respected the other.

Dotty was pottering about the garden when he arrived. She was well wrapped up in a man's old duffel coat girded at the waist with orange binder twine. She wore a balaclava helmet, knitted in airforce-blue wool, which was obviously a relic from the days of war.

Wellington boots, much muddied, hid her skinny legs, but her hands were bare and as muddy as her boots.

Her face lit up as Albert approached.

'My dear Albert! This is a lovely surprise. Come and sit on the garden seat, and tell me how you are.'

'Not too bad, considerin',' replied Albert, secretly much touched by the warmth of her welcome. 'You better now?'

'Never had anything wrong,' asserted Dotty roundly. 'But you know what families are.'

'I do that,' agreed Albert. 'Everlastin' worryin'.'

Dotty waved towards a small, freshly constructed pond, around which half a dozen Muscovy ducks were sliding happily.

'You haven't seen that, have you, Albert? Kit dug it out and lined it. So clever. The only thing is, I want your advice about shady plants.'

Albert considered the problem. The ducks were slithering about on the muddy edge of Kit's creation, and it was obvious that nothing much would grow there while the birds disturbed the surroundings.

'If I was you,' he said, 'I'd put some sort of stone edging round it.'

'But it would look *horrible*!' cried Dotty. 'Like those pad-dling pools you see in municipal parks!'

Albert could not recall ever seeing a paddling pool nor, for that matter, a municipal park though he supposed she meant something like the playground at Lulling.

'I never meant concrete,' he explained. 'Some nice flat bits of Cotswold stone. Percy Hodge has got no end of odd slabs lying about where his old pigsties was. Settle in nicely round that pond they would.'

'But the plants? I thought of shrubs. Some sort of willow perhaps.'

'You'd be best off standing a few tubs around with some nice bushy fuchsias or lilies. That way you could shift 'em about where you wanted 'em, and them ducks couldn't flatten the plants. Keep the edges dry, too. Ducks slop enough water about to drown growing stuff.'

Dotty was silent, envisaging the picture sketched by her companion. It could be the answer. It was practical too.

'Albert,' she said, putting her skinny claw upon his sleeve, 'you are quite right! What a comfort you are!'

Albert smirked. He was seldom praised, and had certainly never been told that he was a comfort to anyone.

He cleared his throat awkwardly. He was as pink with pleasure and embarrassment as a young suitor.

'Well, I don't know—' he began deprecatingly.

'Well, I do!' replied Dotty. 'Now when can we get hold of Percy to discuss buying the stone?'

Albert straightened his shoulders. He looked as determined as a military commander.

'You leave it to me, miss! You leave it to me!'

9. SCHOOL HOUSE FOR SALE

The fact that the school house would be for sale sometime after the departure of the ladies was soon common knowledge in Thrush Green. Naturally, it was an absorbing item of news. It seemed that the school authorities might be able to sell the property earlier, as private approaches seemed welcome, but it was understood that the present tenants would not be turned out betimes.

Mr Jones of The Two Pheasants reckoned it would be pulled down and an office block erected on the site. He was already envisaging bar lunches of some sophistication for the staff, who would no doubt patronise the nearest establishment.

Percy Hodge said it was a perfectly good solid house, and his great-uncle Sidney had been one of the bricklayers on the job when it was constructed. It would be a crying shame, in Percy's opinion, to pull it down.

Albert Piggott, pint in hand, agreed with him. 'If it was good enough for Miss Watson and Miss Fogerty, let alone all them earlier schoolteachers, then it should be good enough for anyone.'

Muriel Fuller, who was spending one of her half-days of remedial teaching at the school, lamented the fact that the house was not to be maintained as part of the school premises.

'I've always felt,' she said earnestly as the teachers sat in their minute staffroom that playtime, 'that a head teacher needs to be Part of The Community.'

'Why?' said Dorothy Watson, who found that a little of Muriel Fuller went a long way.

Miss Fuller, who was still savouring her last phrase and trusting that it would be impressing her listeners, was somewhat taken aback by Miss Watson's query.

'Well,' she began, 'after all, a head teacher in evidence should be a Good Thing. An Example, I mean, a pattern of Decent Behaviour.'

'What about Ernest Burton?' enquired Dorothy, naming a local recently-dead headmaster who had been requested to leave the profession because of some unacceptable and peculiar habits.

'There are exceptions to every rule,' pronounced Muriel, glad to be let off further justification of her earlier statement.

But Dorothy Watson, as determined as a bull-terrier when she had her teeth into something, was not to be deflected.

'I really can't see why a head teacher worth his salt can't set enough example during school hours, without needing to live on the premises. After all, who is going to see him anyway, on a winter's night? And anyone who wants to get in touch with him need only lift the phone, and get him wherever he lives.'

'That's not quite what—' began Muriel, but was saved by the whistle. Little Miss Robinson, on playground duty, had just blown a long blast, and the three ladies hastened back to their duties.

Young Miss Robinson's reaction to the news had been one of wistful longing. If only she had enough money, she mourned, she would buy the school house and live happily ever after. Happily, that is, if she could persuade her present boyfriend to marry her, but he seemed remarkably shy about the future, and she had a horrid feeling that the new typist in his office had something to do with it.

So desirous of a home was Miss Robinson, at present in rather dingy digs, that she even sounded out her father one weekend, but got short shrift.

'I might scrape together a thousand,' he told her, 'but you'd want fifty times that, my girl. You save up your pennies while you're in lodgings, and maybe in a year or two you'll be able to think about owning a house.'

Harold and Isobel only hoped that quiet people, who would be unobtrusive neighbours, would take the next-door property when the time came. They were going to miss the two ladies, and Isobel, in particular, felt very sad at Agnes's departure. She determined to keep in touch with her when she moved to Barton.

The news presented Winnie Bailey with a personal problem. She felt that Richard should be told about the coming sale, but did not want him to upset her two old friends by arriving unannounced – a common habit of his – nor did she know if he would consider the house a possibility at all for his needs.

She decided to call at the school house and discuss matters with the ladies before doing anything about informing Richard. To be honest, she felt some qualms about her nephew living at such close quarters. His married life seemed to be remarkably variable and unstable, and Winnie wondered how the sober inhabitants of Thrush Green would view such a bohemian household.

However, she quelled such doubts, for Richard had expressed a desire to find a home nearby, and she had promised to let him know if anything cropped up.

Well, now it had, and she must keep her word. She crossed the green one early evening, timing her visit to fall comfortably between the ladies' teatime and the six o'clock news bulletin from the BBC.

Dorothy answered her knock, and she was soon ensconced in the sitting-room. A fire burned in the grate, and a fine bowl of paper-white narcissi scented the air.

'How snug you are in here!' cried Winnie.

'We like our creature comforts,' said Dorothy. 'We only hope we can find somewhere as agreeable in Barton.'

This gave Winnie her opening, and she explained about Richard's desire to find a home locally.

'It would be lovely to think of Richard living here,' said little

Miss Fogerty. 'I remember him so well as a baby – always very forward. And if he now has two children of his own it would be so convenient for them to walk across the playground to school.'

'Only one is Richard's actually,' explained Winnie. 'His wife was married before, and the little boy is hers.'

'Well, by all means let him know about the house,' said Dorothy, 'and if he likes to come and see it we should be very pleased to let him look over it. Out of school hours, naturally.'

'I will impress that on him,' promised Winnie, 'and I shall tell him that he must telephone first to make an appointment. I'm afraid he is terribly absent-minded, and I don't want him to turn up unexpectedly.'

After a few more minutes' conversation, Winnie took her leave, and retraced her steps, planning to ring Richard later that evening, and to make quite sure that the ladies would be consulted about any visit he might make in the future.

She might have saved her breath, for Richard, true to form, was observed by a sharp-eyed infant in Miss Fogerty's class some ten days later.

'Miss,' said the child, 'there's a man walking about in the playground.'

'Probably someone to see Miss Watson, dear,' replied Agnes, who was delving into the cupboard which held, among dozens of other things, some small garments known as 'the emergency knickers'. A tearful little girl, standing close by, was obviously about to receive a pair.

'It ain't a parent,' said the boy. 'I knows all them.'

'Isn't,' corrected Agnes automatically, 'and "I know", not "knows".'

She emerged, shaking out a pair of blue gingham knickers.

'There, dear, just run along and change. Put the others into this polythene bag.'

'And it ain't a policeman, and it ain't the gas man, and it ain't the water man 'cos it ain't got no uniform on.'

'*Isn't*,' repeated Agnes, shutting the cupboard door, and making her way to the window.

'Perhaps it's a loony,' said the boy brightening.

Sure enough, the stranger appeared to be delightfully vague, weaving about the playground, and occasionally bending to study something in the hedge dividing playground from the Shoosmiths' property next door. Luckily, Agnes recognised their visitor as Richard, opened the window, and called him over.

'Oh, hallo, Miss Fogerty,' said Richard, giving her the winning smile which disarmed so many people who had dealings with the young man, and who had determined to give him 'a piece of their minds' until the smile melted their fury. 'Are you busy?'

'I'm afraid so. You wanted to see the house I expect.'

'What house?' said the boy, who still stood by Agnes's feet.

'Go to your desk,' said Miss Fogerty sternly. 'This has nothing to do with you, Robert.'

'Well, I saw him first,' muttered the child resentfully, making his way towards his desk. Agnes was a little flustered.

'Do call at Miss Watson's classroom,' she said. 'Perhaps we could take you round the house at playtime.'

The class by this time was open-mouthed, and all work had ceased.

'Emily,' said Agnes, choosing a sensible-looking six-year-old, 'take this gentleman to Miss Watson's room, and don't forget to knock on the door first.'

The child bounced out importantly, and Agnes watched her take Richard by the hand to lead him across the playground to the headmistress.

What, she wondered with some apprehension, would Dorothy's reaction be?

Playtime had been somewhat protracted that morning as the ladies took Richard round the house.

Miss Robinson had nobly offered to do playground duty in

place of Miss Watson, and watched the departure of her two colleagues and Richard with a sore heart. To think that only lack of money stood between her and a delightful home of her own! She supposed that this Richard, despite his scruffy appearance, had the wherewithal to contemplate buying the school house. Envy filled her youthful heart, but she did her duty resolutely despite an extra ten minutes added to the usual span of playtime.

She watched Richard crossing the green towards his aunt's house. Miss Watson and Miss Fogerty hurried back to their duties.

'Many apologies, my dear,' said her headmistress. 'I shall do your turn myself tomorrow to make up for your kindness. I'm afraid that young man arrived without warning. An expensive education seems to have had no effect on his manners, I'm sorry to say.'

Winnie Bailey was as surprised to see Richard as the two schoolteachers had been.

'Well, I was just passing,' said Richard when rebuked by his aunt, 'and it seemed a pity not to call in. They didn't mind a bit, you know. I don't know why you fuss so.'

'Because you are so selfish,' said Winnie. 'They are busy people, and you obviously didn't think of them at all, but simply pleased yourself.'

'In any case, I don't think it would suit us,' said Richard, ignoring his aunt's criticism of his behaviour. 'The rooms are rather poky, and there really isn't enough room to build on. On the other hand, I might bring Fenella down one day to have a look at it. She's awfully clever at seeing possibilities in a place.'

'Then you think she might contemplate leaving the gallery?'

'I don't know, Aunt Win. All I know is that we ought to get away together before things crack up again.'

He sounded despondent and Winnie's soft heart was touched.

'Well, you must sort things out between you,' she said more

gently. 'Now Jenny and I are off to Lulling to do some shopping, so I shall say "Goodbye". Help yourself to coffee if you are staying for a while.'

'No, no. I'm off too. I have to look up something at the Bodleian, and then I thought I'd get a haircut. There's a good chap in the Turl.'

He waved his farewells, and the ladies collected their shopping baskets.

On the way down the hill, Winnie told Jenny about Richard's reactions to the school house.

'Good thing,' said Jenny. 'He'd never do at Thrush Green, and you'd be everlasting minding those children. Or I would!'

'Well, there are only two of them,' pointed out Winnie reasonably.

'So far,' replied Jenny. 'But I bet there'll be more. I always thought Richard looked the sort to have a big family. Profuse, like.'

'Prolific, I think you mean,' said Winnie. 'And I must say, that I hope you are wrong.'

The following Wednesday Thrush Green school broke up for the Easter holidays, much to the relief of the children and staff, and the dismay of some of the parents.

'Can't do nothing with 'im in holiday time,' announced Miss Cooke when she came to collect Nigel on the last afternoon.

'Give him plenty to do,' advised Miss Watson. 'He's an active child.'

'You're telling me,' retorted his mother, 'but he's active the wrong way. Last Christmas the little devil painted my Mum's fireplace with pink enamel paint. Said he was making it nice for Father Christmas. It ponged something awful when we lit the fire.'

Dorothy smiled vaguely and watched her lead the budding decorator away. They were the last to leave the premises, and she and Agnes returned to the school house wearily.

'Only one more term,' sighed Dorothy, 'and frankly it's a great relief to contemplate retirement.'

'I do agree,' said Agnes, easing off her shoes. 'Thank goodness we haven't too many things arranged for this holiday. It will do us good to have a real rest.'

'I must concentrate on my driving lessons though,' said Dorothy. 'Ideally, I'd like to have a day in Barton, just to chivvy the estate agent, and generally have a look round. We could stay the night at our usual place.'

'That would be lovely,' said Agnes. But she sounded half-hearted. Weariness was not all that depressed her. Somehow she had not yet found complete confidence in dear Dorothy's driving.

Besides, who would feed the little cat?

As Agnes was the first to admit, Dorothy had behaved with outstanding magnanimity over the affair of the cat. Apologies accepted on both sides, the business of feeding the animal went ahead, Agnes delighting in the cat's growing confidence and affection, and Dorothy gallantly refraining from expressing her disfavour of the whole affair.

She had even turned a blind eye to the wooden box filled with straw which appeared in the garden shed, and was obviously used by the cat at night. Agnes had timidly expressed the hope that Dorothy did not object to the shed door being left ajar.

'I can't see anyone stealing our ancient lawn mower and all our gardening tools are in a deplorable condition. No, it won't worry me to leave the shed open,' Dorothy had replied, much to Agnes's relief.

By now, the cat allowed Agnes to stroke its tabby fur, but leapt away when she tried to lift it in her arms. To Agnes's pleasure, it purred when she put down its food, and occasionally rubbed round her legs.

But it always beat a hasty retreat if Dorothy appeared. It seemed to know that its presence was not welcomed by that lady.

When she thought about it, Dorothy was still perturbed at

the idea of the animal being left high and dry when they departed in the summer. However, she told herself, Agnes had been warned, and there was still time for a good home to be found for it or, with any luck, it would depart of its own accord to a cat-lover as fond and foolish as Agnes herself.

The Easter weekend was as bright and beautiful as it should be, 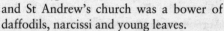 and St Andrew's church was a bower of daffodils, narcissi and young leaves.

Round the steps of the font the children had put vases of primroses from Lulling Woods, and two magnificent pots of arum lilies from the Youngs' greenhouse flanked the chancel steps.

Mrs Bates from Rectory Cottages had surpassed herself with the cleaning of the church silver and brass, and even Albert Piggott had stirred himself enough to tidy up the porch and the gravel drive.

Everyone agreed, as they gossiped after church, that Easter was one of the loveliest of church festivals, and that St Andrew's had never looked so magnificent.

Young Cooke had mown the grass of the churchyard, and Thrush Green's inhabitants admired its striped neatness. All opposition to the moving of ancient tombstones had now vanished. It was difficult to remember the battle which had raged, some years earlier, about the levelling of the site and the shifting of the gravestones to the outer wall. Poor Charles Henstock had endured many sleepless nights worrying about the hostility of some of his parishioners to the scheme, but time seemed to have healed the wounds very successfully.

As Dorothy and Agnes crossed the green to the school house Ben Curdle appeared trundling a wheelbarrow.

'Ah, Ben!' called Dorothy, hastening towards him. 'Would it be convenient to have a lesson tomorrow evening? I really want to have an intensive course in the next week or so. Would you be free?'

'Any time you like,' said Ben. 'I'll come round about six, shall I?'

'Perfect!' replied Dorothy. 'I always enjoy my driving lessons.'

But she was not to know, when she spoke so enthusiastically, just what was in store for her.

Meanwhile, Charles Henstock did his best to assist his friend Anthony to find a suitable post for the young woman, daughter of Mrs Lilly, about whom they had spoken on the telephone.

The manager of the new supermarket about to be opened in Lulling High Street was of no help.

'Sorry, padre,' he said, 'but I've got all the girls I need. Tell you what, I'll write down the young lady's name, and if I get a vacancy she can come for an interview.'

The typist's post at Twitter & Venables was satisfactorily filled, and very few people needed, or could afford, domestic help in the house.

'Of course,' said Dimity doubtfully, 'the Lovelocks want help, but they are such hard taskmasters one hesitates to send anyone there.'

'I suppose we could make it clear,' said Charles, 'that she is quite a young woman, and has this small child to care for. You wouldn't care to put the matter to Ada? Suggest that she goes for a trial period, and that not too much is demanded of her?'

'I should dislike the job intensely,' said Dimity with spirit.

Charles sighed. 'Well, we'll go on with our enquiries, dear, but if nothing turns up, I'd better tackle the Lovelock girls myself.'

His woebegone face turned Dimity's heart over, but she did not offer to face the task herself.

Who knows? Something suitable might turn up very soon.

Promptly, at six o'clock, Ben Curdle arrived with his Fiesta at the gate of the school house, and Dorothy hastened to climb in.

It was a warm April evening. The daffodils were nodding in the gardens, and the lilac was already in bud. There was a stillness in the air, and a gentle radiance, which moved Dorothy to quote poetry.

' "It is a beauteous evening, calm and free", ' said Dorothy, fastening her seat belt.

'Yes, it is that,' agreed Ben, looking a little startled. 'Beautiful, I mean.'

'Which way?' asked Dorothy, abandoning poetry and getting down to business.

'I thought we'd take her up the main road, and then come back by way of Nidden. Then, perhaps, go up the High Street for a bit of traffic practice.'

'Right,' said his pupil, scanning both mirrors, and letting the clutch in gently.

She turned down the chestnut avenue in front of Edward Young's splendid house, and then left along the main road.

'I really love driving,' said Dorothy. 'Am I doing all right, Ben?'

'You're doing fine,' said he sturdily. 'But keep the pace down a bit. Lots of kids on bikes now the evenings are light.'

They drove in companionable silence for two or three miles, then turned left into Nidden, and the lane which would return them to Thrush Green and Lulling.

This was a much quieter road, and involuntarily Dorothy's pace increased. They were bowling along between the hedges which bounded Percy Hodge's fields, when the worst happened.

Out from the farmyard gate burst Percy's young collie dog, barking furiously. There was a sickening thump as the near front wheel hit it, and the barking changed to a bloodcurdling squealing.

With commendable speed and control, Dorothy pulled into the side of the lane, and was out of the car in a flash. Just as she approached the pathetic black and white bundle, Percy appeared, rake in hand.

'What you bin and done to my dog?' he yelled menacingly. 'Women drivers!'

He spat in an unlovely fashion, as Ben came up to his pupil's support.

10. The Accident

With considerable authority Ben Curdle went into the attack.

'Pity you can't keep your animals under control,' he said. 'There's a couple of cows of yours pushing at the hedge half a mile up the road. And now this!'

He squatted down beside the dog and felt its legs and ribs with expert fingers. Dorothy, much shaken, watched him with admiration, and with thoughts of Ben's indomitable old grandmother, Mrs Curdle, who had met every disaster with the same supreme courage and calm that Ben was now showing.

'We should get the vet,' she said to Percy. 'Can I use your phone?'

She was much alarmed at the condition of the animal. Its eyes were closed, its breathing heavy, but there did not appear to be much blood, except for a cut on its side.

'I'll look after my own dog, thank you,' replied Percy nastily. 'You stay here with Gyp and I'll ring young Bailey.'

He departed, leaving Ben and Dorothy eyeing the dog.

'Do you think we should lift him on to the verge?' asked Dorothy.

'Best not move him. He may have something wrong inside. We'll stay with him till the vet comes.'

'Will he die, Ben?'

Ben looked up at his distraught pupil and gave his slow reassuring smile.

'I'll take my oath, he don't,' he said. 'My guess is he's

concussed, just knocked out. This 'ere graze and cut is nothing much. He'll be all right this time next week.'

'I should have seen him.'

'You had no chance. He run into you at the side. Don't you fret, miss. You've nothing to blame yourself for.'

At that moment, Percy reappeared.

'We're lucky. Surgery girl just caught the vet leaving Bill Bottomley's at Nidden. He's coming straight here.'

Dorothy strove to behave calmly. 'I'm extremely sorry to have hurt your dog, Mr Hodge, but it was entirely its fault. Ben here saw exactly what happened.'

'I don't care who saw what or whose fault it was,' declared Percy, now down on his knees beside the recumbent animal, 'but I paid good money for that dog and I'll need compensation and the vet's fees too.'

Dorothy was about to say that she would be pleased to do so, when she caught Ben's eye, saw the almost imperceptible shake of his head, and remained silent.

The dog now gave a little whimper and opened his eyes. At that moment David Bailey's Land Rover arrived on the scene, and the three stood up with relief.

'My old friend Gyp in trouble, eh?' he said, squatting down beside him. The dog began to thump his tail.

The vet ran expert fingers over the animal's body, while the others watched anxiously.

'As far as I can see he's had a bit of concussion, and this cut could do with a couple of stitches and cleaning up. If you give me a hand, Percy, I'll take him back with me to the surgery for a proper check-up. No bones broken luckily.'

'What a relief!' cried Dorothy.

'No thanks to you,' exclaimed Percy, rounding on her. 'Proper careless driving caused this, Mr Bailey. I reckon it's a case for the police.'

'If you take my advice,' said the vet who had heard all this before, 'you won't get involved with the law. The dog's not badly injured, and should have been under control in any event.

Now, you lift his legs gently, Percy, and we'll get him into the back.'

'I'm coming too,' said Percy.

'So I should hope,' replied David Bailey shortly. 'Get in the front.'

'I'll telephone in an hour or two,' promised Dorothy, 'to see how he's got on.'

Percy gazed stonily ahead of him, making no reply, as the Land Rover drove slowly away.

'Oh, Ben,' quavered Dorothy, 'what a terrible thing to happen! What shall I do?' There were tears on her cheeks, and Ben's kind heart was stirred.

'You get in the car, and I'll drive us home. Remember you've nothing to blame yourself for, and don't give old Percy Hodge money for nothing. It only puts you in the wrong.'

'Well, I do see that,' admitted Dorothy, busy with her hand-kerchief, 'but I truthfully would feel so much better if I could have the vet's bill.'

'That's up to you,' said Ben. 'I'd probably do the same. But don't you have no truck with Percy's threats about the law. That dog had no right to be loose like that, and Perce knows it. I bet them cows is all over the road up Nidden by now,' he added with considerable satisfaction. 'Give him something to think about.'

By now they had arrived at the school house, and Dorothy's tears had dried.

'I can't thank you enough, Ben,' she said shakily. 'You were a tower of strength. I was reminded of your grandmother who was such a wonderful woman, I've been told, and a great help in trouble.'

'It was nothing, miss. Don't go worrying about it, and don't forget I'm coming to take you out again tomorrow evening. You mustn't look upon this as a set-back. It could have hap-pened to anyone. Why, I once ran into one of my gran's fair ponies!'

'Really? What happened?'

'Nothing to the pony. But it dented the front of my motor-bike something horrible.'

Charles and Dimity Henstock had no need to brace themselves to approach the Misses Lovelock, for Nelly Piggott had also heard about Doreen Lilly, from Gladys her mother, after a Bingo session one evening.

'I know some old ladies who want some help,' said Nelly hesitantly, 'But I'm not sure whether the job would suit her.'

'She can but try,' responded Mrs Lilly. 'She knows she'll have to knuckle down to a bit of hard work to keep herself and the boy. But she's certainly not living with me! For one thing I've no room, and after two days we'd be fighting like Kilkenny cats.'

'I'll do what I can,' promised Nelly, feeling some sympathy for the daughter and her problems.

The Misses Lovelock were duly informed at their next Wednesday lunch at The Fuchsia Bush, and word was sent to Gladys Lilly that they would be pleased to interview Doreen as soon as possible.

'Not that I am altogether happy about the idea of employing an unmarried mother,' observed Ada, when the sisters were back in their cluttered drawing-room.

'Oh, really, Ada,' exclaimed Violet, 'what difference will it make to her housework?' She was struggling with that day's crossword puzzle, and finding an anagram of 'grenadine' particularly elusive.

'It's not her *housework* that is in question, but her *morals*,' pointed out Bertha.

'Well, we can't do much about that,' said Violet flatly. 'It sounds to me as though she has had a hard time. Nelly said the father has vanished completely, and left this poor girl in the lurch.'

'It is very unwise,' pronounced Ada, 'to try and pre-judge the girl, and to let our hearts rule our heads. All we can do is to sum up her abilities when she comes for interview, and to show her what will be required of her. I gather from Nelly that the girl has first to find lodgings, as Mrs Lilly has no room for the daughter and child.'

'What about our top floor?' said Violet. 'There's our old nursery and the maid's bedroom.'

'Out of the question,' said Ada, rolling up her knitting. 'This house is *quite* unsuitable for a young child.'

Violet was about to say that all three of them had been born and reared in this same house, but Ada had on the look which brooked no arguing, and in any case Violet had just realized that 'endearing' fitted her clue, and so busied herself in filling it in.

It was unfortunate that the very morning after Dorothy's accident, Agnes had found the little cat unusually affectionate towards her.

It had allowed her to stroke its ears, and to pat its back very gently near the tail, and in return had patted Agnes's shoelace in a remarkably playful manner. Little Miss Fogerty was entranced, and prattled happily at the breakfast table upon such agreeable progress.

Dorothy, still shaken by her ordeal, and awaiting further news from Percy Hodge with some trepidation, found Agnes's enthusiasm hard to bear. Kindly though she was in disposition, on this particular morning Dorothy found the animal kingdom decidedly irritating.

'Don't make too much fuss of it,' she said crossly. 'It will be coming into the house next.'

Agnes curbed her tongue. It was plain that poor Dorothy was still upset about Percy Hodge's dog, and who could wonder at that? A truly dreadful experience, and Percy could be a formidable opponent if it came to warfare.

At that moment the telephone rang and Dorothy hurried to answer it. Agnes listened anxiously, and for once did not close the hall door.

'I am greatly relieved to hear it,' said Dorothy.

There was a pause.

'It was good of you to ring so promptly. I have been very worried.'

There was a second pause. Agnes debated whether to put a saucer over Dorothy's coffee.

'By all means send Mr Bailey's account to me. I should like to pay it, although as Ben pointed out, it was really the dog that was at fault.'

The third pause seemed longer than ever, and Agnes could hear Dorothy's fingernail tapping on the telephone rest – a bad sign. It might be as well to put the coffee back in the saucepan, at this rate.

'Well, we're not going to discuss that now, Mr Hodge,' said Dorothy, in her most headmistressy voice. 'The main thing is that Gyp has recovered, and I'm sure you will see that he is under control in the future.'

She put down the receiver briskly, and returned to the breakfast table. Apart from unusually flushed cheeks, she seemed calm.

'Thank heaven that dog is all right,' she sighed. 'Now Agnes, you were telling me about the cat.'

'Another time will do,' said Agnes with dignity.

The Misses Lovelock interviewed Miss Lilly in their diningroom. They sat in a row at one side of the immense mahogany table, and Doreen on the other, facing them.

She was a wispy little thing with fluffy fair hair, and a permanently open mouth, indicative of adenoids. But she was soberly dressed and was clean and polite.

Miss Violet's kind heart warmed to her. She looked so young to be the mother of a three-year-old.

The girl confessed that she had no written references from her previous post, but said that she knew her employer's name and address and the number of her telephone.

'I was there nearly two years,' she said. 'She'll speak for me, I know. It was after that row with my boyfriend I decided I'd be better off nearer my mum.'

'A row?' queried Bertha.

'That's when he lit off,' explained Doreen.

'Lit off?' said Ada.

'Cleared out,' said Doreen.

'Cleared out?' echoed Bertha.

'Slung his hook,' agreed Doreen.

'Slung—' began Violet. 'You mean he left you?'

'S'right,' acknowledged the girl.

'And you do not expect to see him again?' asked Ada.

'Hope not. About as much use as a sick headache he is. Better off without him.'

'Well, in that case,' said Ada, 'you had better come and see the kitchen first.'

The three old ladies shepherded the girl all over the house.

She made no comment as she was led from the kitchen's archaic grandeur, to the drawing-room, study, and then up the lofty staircase to the over-furnished bedrooms above.

After twenty minutes all four returned to their seats in the dining-room. Violet thought that the girl looked somewhat over-awed at the prospect before her.

Miss Ada produced a paper and pencil. 'Perhaps you would write down the name, address and telephone number of your last employer. That is, of course, if you feel that you want the post.'

'What wages would you be offering, miss?'

Ada told her.

'But I was getting twice that before,' she protested, 'and only half the work as you've got here.'

'My sisters and I will consider an increase, and let you know,' said Ada.

She pushed the paper and pencil towards the girl, and with some hesitation the prospective maid began to write.

'I'm not putting my name to it,' she said, looking bewildered.

'There's no need,' Ada assured her. 'I simply want to speak to this Mrs Miller – or is it Mitter?' She squinted at the paper, holding it at arm's length.

'Mrs Miller.'

'If all is satisfactory, could you start next Monday?'

'Well, I could, I suppose. Nine till twelve, my mum said.'

'That is correct. Three mornings a week. Definitely Mondays, and we can arrange the other mornings to suit you. I think a week's notice either way would be best. If you call again on Friday morning I can let you know what we have decided would be a fair remuneration, and you can give us your decision then.'

The three ladies rose, and ushered Doreen to the door.

When she had vanished round the bend of Lulling High Street, the three sisters discussed the affair.

'I do think,' said Violet, suddenly emboldened, 'that you

were rather high-handed, Ada. Why couldn't we have had a word together and raised her wages then and there?'

'One doesn't want to rush into these things,' replied Ada. 'I still have to discover from Mrs Miller what sort of person she is.'

'She didn't look very *strong*,' observed Bertha.

'And one must check her *truthfulness*,' continued Ada. 'How do we know that she was getting twice the amount we offered? We'll be in a better position to discuss terms when I have telephoned Mrs Miller this evening. Do the cheap rates start at six or six-thirty? I can never remember.'

It was at the next Bingo session that Gladys Lilly told Nelly about the job which Doreen had accepted after a good deal of thought, and some prodding from her mother.

'Well now,' said Nelly, 'she's a brave girl, and I only hope she knows what she's let herself in for. You tell her to pop round to the kitchen at The Fuchsia Bush before she takes up the job on Monday. I can give her a few tips about them old ladies, and the best way to manage 'em. And if she wants my advice, tell her to make sure she never agrees to do the cooking.'

'I'll tell her to look in,' promised Mrs Lilly. 'And she asked me to thank you for finding her the place.'

'Time enough to thank me,' said Nelly darkly, 'when she's had a couple of weeks with them stairs, and that half a ton of silver as needs cleaning once a fortnight. She won't be idle, I can tell you!'

'Hard work,' said Doreen's mother virtuously, 'never hurt no one!'

11. DECISIONS

It was during the Easter holidays that Dorothy Watson decided that the time had come to buy her car. The sitting-room at the school house was littered with glossy brochures from local garages extolling the virtues of innumerable vehicles. Such a plethora of literature bewildered little Miss Fogerty, but Dorothy was made of sterner stuff.

'We know what we want,' she said firmly, when Agnes confessed her perplexity in the face of so much richness. 'The car must be small, so that it will fit into any existing garage, and be easy to park. Also a small car will be more economical to run.'

'Quite right,' approved Agnes.

'Then it must be *new*, so that any defects are dealt with under guarantee. I don't propose to dabble in the secondhand market. We are not knowledgeable enough.'

'Indeed we're not,' agreed Agnes, with feeling.

'And it must be a well-known brand,' continued Dorothy, rather as if she were talking of fish-paste. 'Spares, you know.'

Agnes looked bewildered.

'I gather from Ben and Harold that it is very difficult to get spare parts for some cars. One might have to wait weeks, they tell me, for some vital bit.'

'Oh dear!' commented Agnes. 'But if it were a really new car would it need spare parts?'

'Some cars,' responded Dorothy grimly, 'have been known to be sold with several things missing completely.'

Agnes, already timid about the entire project, felt her spirits quail yet further, but she remained stoically silent.

'So after tea, dear,' said Dorothy, shuffling the jewel-bright brochures into a pile, 'we will pick out three or four possibles, and then get Harold and Ben to give us their expert advice.'

'I'm sure that would be best,' agreed Agnes bravely.

Doreen Lilly began her duties at the Misses Lovelock at nine o'clock on Monday morning.

She arrived punctually, which put all three sisters in a good mood, and Miss Violet undertook to show her the tasks allotted.

'I think it would be best to concentrate on the first-floor bedrooms today,' she said, mounting the stairs before Doreen. Violet's speckled lisle stockings, garments never before seen by the young girl, strode briskly ahead as she opened three bedroom doors to display a daunting amount of heavy mahogany furniture, curtains from floor to ceiling, and a massive washstand in each room, bearing a vast china bowl and matching ewer, soap dish and tooth mug. Such equipment was unknown to Doreen, used as she was to a modern, if scruffy, bathroom at her mother's home.

'We make our own beds,' said Violet kindly, 'so you won't have to bother with those. The curtains will have to come down before long and have a really good shaking in the garden, but today I think a thorough cleaning of the furniture and washing things will keep you busy.'

Not half, thought Doreen, but nodded silently.

'We have a vacuum cleaner for the floors,' said Violet, as one might say: 'We have a helicopter for the shopping.'

'We'd best get it then,' said Doreen.

'Of course,' replied Violet. 'We will get everything together, and I will show you where we keep all the cleaning materials. I'm sure I have no need to tell you that we expect you to use *everything* very economically. No waste in this house!'

They finished the tour of the bedrooms, and returned down the long staircase to the kitchen where Violet displayed the cupboard housing the cleaning aids. They appeared sparse and archaic to Doreen's eye, even by her modest standards.

The brushes and brooms must have been bought many years earlier, and some were almost without bristles. A pile of folded pieces of material, which were obviously squares cut from outworn petticoats and the like, appeared to be the only dusters available. Three long bars of yellow soap and a large bag labelled SODA seemed to constitute the major part of the washing department, but Doreen was relieved to see some canisters of Vim. It was like meeting an old friend amidst ancient aliens.

A mammoth tin of furniture polish, the size which Doreen had once encountered in a hospital, was handed up to her, with two of the deplorable dusters, and then Violet indicated the rest of the store with a vague wave of the hand.

'Well, there you are, Doreen, and if you find you need anything else this morning, just come and find me. You are here until twelve, I believe.'

'That's right, miss,' replied Doreen. 'Well, I'll go and make a start.'

She was half-way up the stairs, struggling with the heavy furniture polish tin, when she remembered the basins and their matching accessories.

'I'd best take up the Vim,' she said to Violet standing below.

'Ah yes! I'll shake a little into a saucer for you,' said Violet, hurrying back to the cupboard.

Doreen deposited her burden on the stairs, cast her eyes to heaven for much-needed help, and followed her new employer into the kitchen.

Percy's dog and its adventure was still a topic of conversation at Thrush Green. Blame for the accident was largely on Percy's shoulders in the bar of The Two Pheasants.

Albert Piggott took great pleasure in recounting this piece of news to Percy while they were busy selecting fragments of Percy's tumble-down wall for future use round Dotty's garden pool.

'A lot of ignorant tittle-tattle,' grunted Percy, heaving a lump of stone into his battered van. 'They wasn't there, was they? Never saw what I see. That Miss Watson was rushing along like a bat out of hell.'

Albert, who was taking care to select pieces of stone less than half the size of his workmate's, tossed his contribution into the van.

'Ben Curdle wouldn't let her go fast. And no one ain't ever seen the old girl do more than twenty-five mile an hour. It was your job to keep old Gyp out of the road. Why, that car might have mounted the bank and tipped over! You might've been had up for murder, mate.'

'Don't talk so daft,' snapped Percy.

He changed the subject abruptly.

'How much more of this stuff do you want? I reckon this little lot will cost the old girl a tenner already.'

Albert eyed his drinking companion with dislike.

'You'll be settlin' with me, Perce, so don't you start any profiteering lark. I'm not goin' to see old Dotty fleeced, that's flat.'

'Have it your own way,' growled Percy. 'But it'll cost you a pint or two.'

Although public opinion was on her side in this much-discussed affair, Dorothy herself was more upset than she would admit.

She had put a brave face upon the matter, and Percy had certainly not gone any further with the threats he had made in the heat of the moment, but she had been shattered by his violence.

As a headmistress of some standing in the village she was unused to enmity and invective. She was also plagued, in the still of the night, by the horrors of the might-have-been, common to all.

Supposing it had been a child? Supposing she had killed not just Percy's Gyp but one of her own pupils? Or, for that matter, an adult, a friend, a neighbour? How devastatingly quick the whole incident had been! How right Ben was to point out that a car could be a weapon as lethal as a gun!

Naturally, as the days passed, her agitation grew less, and reason told her to put aside her fears and enjoy the practical advantages of having a car of her own. She envisaged the pleasure of driving with dear Agnes to various seaside places not far from Barton. There were several beautiful old houses to visit well within driving distance, and shopping could be transported with the minimum of effort.

It had been a sharp lesson, she told herself, and she must learn from it. In future she would keep a wary eye open for such dangers, but she did not intend to spoil the delight of choosing and driving her new car.

Nevertheless, the incident had left one particularly unfortunate scar. It was plain that dogs, cats, birds, and even cattle, could be a hazard, and Agnes's growing pleasure in the visiting cat worried Dorothy greatly. She really wanted nothing to do with animals at the moment, and she certainly did not want to have one permanently in the household.

What would happen, for instance, if she and Agnes decided to go away for a holiday? When they had a car they would be free to go anywhere when they had retired. An animal would be a perfect nuisance, especially a cat which would probably hate to go to a boarding establishment.

Really, thought Dorothy with exasperation, life could be very trying, particularly when one was hoping to simplify it and to make sensible plans for the future.

Well, one thing at a time, she told herself.

She went into the garden to find Agnes, and found her digging up a gigantic dandelion plant.

'Don't forget we're due next door in half an hour,' she said. 'I've collected all the car literature together, and we'll see what Harold thinks of our choice. I shall let you choose the colour, Agnes. I'm afraid you haven't had much say in the rest of the discussions.'

'I really couldn't begin,' confessed Agnes, 'but I should be delighted to choose the colour. In fact, I rather liked Alpine Snow, or perhaps Moonlight Silver. That is, of course, if you like the idea.'

'I shall like whatever you choose,' said Dorothy handsomely, and they went indoors to get ready.

Winnie Bailey, across the green, observed the two ladies making their way to Harold and Isobel's front door, and guessed correctly that the meeting had something to do with Dorothy's purchase of a car.

The ringing of the telephone interrupted her surmises, and she was pleased to hear Richard's voice.

'Fenella wants to have a look at the school house. We thought we would come down for the weekend.'

'With the children?' asked Winnie, mentally putting up a cot in the spare room, and ordering an extra quart of milk.

'Oh yes! We shall have to bring them. Our help's on holiday. I've rung The Fleece.'

Winnie dismissed the cot and milk with relief. 'And they can put you up?'

'Yes. Friday and Saturday night. Roger is going to call in to feed the animals. The dog can be rather a nuisance in the car. Gets sick.'

'Well, I hope that you will bring Fenella and the children to see me. Tea perhaps, on Saturday?'

'I'll give you a ring when we're in Lulling, after I've sorted out our plans.'

'That will be nice. By the way, you have told Agnes and Dorothy you are coming?'

'Not yet. I was going to give them a call now.'

'Make it later this evening,' advised Winnie. She suddenly recalled the erratic hours kept by her nephew. 'But before nine, dear. They go to bed soon after.'

'*Soon after nine?*' gasped Richard. He sounded shocked.

'Yes, Richard. We keep early hours at Thrush Green. I shall look forward to seeing you all during the weekend.'

For once, Richard seemed incapable of speech, and Winnie put down the receiver.

The Shoosmiths' sitting-room was littered with Dorothy's bro-chures. At first sight, it appeared that all was chaos, but in fact much had been accomplished in the first half-hour, and the choice had been whittled down to three suitable vehicles.

'There's not a lot of difference in price and size and perform-ance between the Polo or the Fiesta or the Metro,' Harold assured them. 'It's really a personal matter. Comfort in the seating, for instance, and how you can handle her.'

Agnes, of necessity taking a minor role in this weighty dis-cussion, wondered why cars and ships always seemed to be of the female gender.

'Well, I must say I've enjoyed driving Ben's Fiesta,' said Dorothy, 'but is it *British*?'

'I think so,' said Harold.

'Ben said he thought so too, until he opened the lid—'

'The *bonnet*,' corrected Harold automatically. Agnes thought how fitting it was for a female vehicle to have a bonnet.

'Of course, *bonnet*,' agreed Dorothy, 'and he found it was made in Spain.'

'Really?'

'Not that I have anything against *Spain*,' continued Dorothy magnanimously, 'except the bullfights, but I should like to buy a British car ideally.'

'Then it will have to be the Metro,' said Harold. 'The Polo is German, as you know. Personally, I would plump for the Polo. It's a well-made job, and nicely finished.'

Dorothy looked doubtful, and Isobel rose to refill the sherry glasses to fortify all those present. This final decision was obviously going to be taxing.

'That impresses me, Harold. It really does. I value your opinion as you know.'

She sighed heavily, and took a refreshing sip from her glass. 'And of course I have nothing against Germany *now*,' she added, turning over the Polo brochure and studying the bird's eye view of its interior seating arrangements.

'However,' she resumed, putting it aside and reaching for the Metro's contribution to the temporary decor of the sitting-room. 'I still like the idea of a *British* car, supporting home industry and all that.'

'Right,' agreed Harold. 'We'll go down to the garage in Lulling and have a good look at the Metro and a drive around.'

It was a quarter-past ten when the two ladies said goodnight and retired to their bedrooms.

Dorothy was excited but exhausted. It really was dreadfully tiring making such a decision. After all, a great deal of money was involved, and the car would have to last them for several years. Perhaps the Polo would have been the right choice?

She was just removing her stockings when the telephone rang in the hall.

'Now who on earth is ringing at this time of night?' she said testily, making her way downstairs, clad only in her petticoat.

'Richard here.'

'Who? Richard Who?'

'Winnie's nephew Richard.'

'Ah yes! What can I do for you?'

He explained at some length, and Dorothy did her best to keep her feet warm by rubbing one against the other, with small success.

Filled, as her mind was, with such things as car seats, two- or four-doors, gear levers and what the trade euphemistically called 'optional extras', Dorothy hardly took in all that Richard was saying, but absorbed the salient point that he and his wife wanted to see the house.

'What about Saturday afternoon? Shall we say at two-thirty?' she said, catching sight of something which looked distressingly like a dead mouse under the nearby radiator. She hitched her cold feet on to the chair rail, in case life still pulsed in that small body.

'Goodbye,' she said civilly, replacing the receiver, and bravely went to investigate.

Luckily, the object was nothing more terrifying than a small ball of wool which must have escaped from Agnes's knitting bag.

Dorothy returned to her bedroom and the comfort of her warm bed.

What a day it had been!

Charles Henstock decided to call at the Misses Lovelocks' house one morning. He was rather anxious about Anthony Bull's protégée, and wondered how she was faring with her new employers. Prudently, he carried with him a copy of the monthly church magazine, so that he had a legitimate excuse for his morning call.

It was a blustery April morning, and little eddies of dust whirled about the High Street. The striped awning over the window of The Fuchsia Bush flapped in the breeze, and the young leaves of the pollarded limes which lined the street were being tossed this way and that.

Charles took off his hat, and held it in safety with the church magazine as he waited for the front door to be opened.

It was Doreen herself who performed the operation. She was looking, Charles was relieved to see, quite healthy and well fed.

'Ah, Doreen, I believe? You know my old friend Anthony Bull.'

'Yes. Want to come in?'

Charles entered, somewhat disconcerted by this laconic greeting. He was saved by the arrival of the three sisters from the kitchen quarters. They greeted him with little flutters of excitement, and ushered him into the drawing-room.

'So you've now met Doreen,' said Ada. 'She's settling in very well, considering.'

Charles wondered what doubts were covered by this last word.

'Good. And you find her a real help?'

'Rather slow,' said Bertha.

'And refuses to take on any cooking,' added Violet. 'But works quite hard.'

'Well, of course, it's early days yet,' said Charles soothingly. 'No doubt she will get quicker as she gets used to the work.'

He surveyed the laden occasional tables. Dozens of small silver ornaments gleamed as brightly as ever, and the two massive trumpet-shaped silver vases which occupied each end of the mantelpiece appeared to be equally immaculate. It must make an enormous amount of work, he thought, with a pang of pity for the new maid.

'I have to ring Anthony this evening,' he said, 'about a diocesan matter. I'm sure he will want to know how the girl has settled.'

'Dear Anthony,' sighed Ada.

'What sermons he gave us!' sighed Bertha.

'And always looked so handsome!' sighed Violet.

Not for the first time, poor Charles realised what a lowly figure he cut beside his distinguished predecessor. It was a good thing that he was so devoted to Anthony himself, or common jealousy might have soured his outlook.

'Some coffee, Charles dear?' said Bertha, suddenly recalled from fond memories of Anthony Bull to the duties of a hostess.

'Yes, do,' urged Ada. 'We have some left over from yesterday.'

'Most kind, most kind,' murmured Charles rising, 'but I have one or two things to get for Dimity, so I mustn't delay.'

They accompanied him to the door. Doreen was nowhere in sight, but the sound of a vacuum cleaner hummed from above.

'I meant to ask you about her living arrangements. Is she living here?'

'Good heavens, no!' replied Ada. 'Where would we put her?'

'And the boy,' pointed out Violet.

Charles, knowing full well the plentiful accommodation in the house, refrained from comment.

'It so happens,' explained Bertha, 'that her younger brother has found a job in Shropshire—'

'Somerset,' interjected Violet.

'With an uncle,' went on Bertha, giving her sister a sharp look.

'Cousin,' said Violet.

'So that there is now a spare bedroom at Mrs Lilly's and she has let Doreen and the child stay there.'

'Good. I'm glad to hear it,' said Charles, descending the steps to the pavement. 'I will let Anthony know how things are.'

'And give him our love,' called Violet to Charles's departing figure.

'I think "our love",' said Ada reprovingly, 'is rather forward. "Kind regards" would have been much more suitable for a man of the cloth.'

12. VIEWING THE SCHOOL HOUSE

As Winnie Bailey expected, Richard's telephone call came just before noon on the Saturday, when he announced that they would call about three-thirty. Miss Watson had arranged for them to see the house at half-past two.

'Jenny and I will look forward to seeing you,' said Winnie. She wondered if she should offer to have the two children whilst Richard and Fenella paid their visit to the school house, decided that Richard was more than capable of asking this favour, and put down the receiver with some relief.

What was Fenella like? Somehow she envisaged her as a wispy girl, dressed in unbecoming dark garments from an Oxfam shop, and with a vague expression. No doubt she would be entirely subservient to Richard, she decided. Richard, after all, was a very dominant person. It couldn't be much fun being married to someone quite so ruthlessly selfish.

She helped Jenny to set the tea in the dining-room. If Timothy were to be one of the party it was simpler to have him on a chair, at least for part of the meal time. As for Imogen, it was to be hoped that such a young child would be content with a rusk in her pram.

It was striking three by the grandfather clock in the hall when Winnie saw Richard's car parked outside the gates of Thrush Green school. There was no sign of life in or around it, so Winnie surmised that the tour of the house was taking place.

Some twenty minutes later she saw the car driving round the green, beneath the budding chestnut trees, making for her own home. She went out into the spring sunshine to greet them.

Contrary to expectation, Fenella turned out to be a large woman, quite as tall as Richard, and built on statuesque lines. She had a mop of auburn hair which cascaded over her shoulders, and clashed disastrously with the scarlet of her coat.

'Fenella, Aunt Win,' said Richard.

'How do you do? I'm so glad that you decided to have a look at Thrush Green,' said Winnie.

'I know Aunt Win,' said Timothy, appearing from the other side of the car. 'She gave me a banana.'

'What about the baby?' queried Winnie.

'Oh, she's fast asleep on the back seat,' replied her mother, in a deep contralto voice. 'Far better to leave her to it.'

Winnie was a little perturbed at the thought of the child abandoned in the car, but as the rest of the family were making purposefully towards the open front door, Winnie went ahead and ushered them in.

'Well, what did you think of the school house?' asked Winnie, when coats had been removed, and Timothy had departed to see Jenny in the kitchen.

Richard and Fenella exchanged glances.

'Well,' began Richard, 'I like it, of course, although it's really rather small. But then I've always wanted to live at Thrush Green.'

Fenella made an impatient gesture. 'He has this *thing* about Thrush Green. A *fixation*, I suppose you'd call it. Frankly, I prefer town life, but of course one could get to London fairly quickly, I imagine.'

'Would you want to?'

'Naturally. I have the gallery to run.'

Winnie was somewhat nonplussed. She had envisaged a straightforward choice. Either the family moved from town, firstly to remove Fenella from Roger's attentions, and secondly to raise the money for the new abode by the sale of the gallery, or else they did not move at all.

'I think,' said Richard, 'that we might build a large room at the back of the school house, and have a good-sized bedroom above with a bathroom and so on over the new room.'

'It would look clumsy,' said Fenella. 'Far better to knock down that grotty little kitchen, and make a really big living-room there.'

Winnie was glad that neither Dorothy nor Agnes were at hand to hear their immaculate kitchen so summarily dismissed.

'So you think it might be altered?' she said diplomatically. 'I mean, it looks possible for your needs?'

'Richard seems to think so,' said Fenella off-handedly. 'Where he's getting the money from, I really don't know.'

'Fenella,' began Richard, 'you know we've discussed this time and time again! If you sell the gallery—'

'I've no intention of selling my only means of livelihood,' replied Fenella, her voice rising dangerously. 'So you can put that idea out of your mind at once.'

Luckily, Timothy burst into the room at this juncture, and waved a fistful of finely cut bread crusts in his father's face.

'Jenny's making sandwiches for tea. Tomato. She said I was to throw these out for the birds, but I'm not going to. I'm hungry.'

He shook his burden fiercely, scattering crumbs upon the carpet. Richard and Fenella, glowering at each other, appeared to be oblivious of the child's presence, and it was Winnie who took him into the garden, and directed his attention to the bird-table, with some relief.

Whilst the boy deposited some of the crusts there, and three or four into his mouth, Winnie considered the recent conversation. Either Richard had not told her the whole story on his earlier visit, or Fenella had suddenly decided to hold out and remain at the gallery. Without its sale, Winnie had gathered, they could not consider a move, even into something as relatively modest as Thrush Green school house.

Well, it was their affair, she told herself, returning to her duties as hostess.

'Come along, Timothy. We'll ask Jenny to put on the kettle. If you are so hungry we'd better have an early tea.'

Richard was standing by the sitting-room window, gazing across the green, and jingling coins in his trouser pocket. He looked extremely irritable.

Fenella had put her feet up on the çouch and was immersed in a copy of *Country Life*. The air was heavy with unspoken acrimony.

'I think we'll have tea early,' said Winnie. 'Timothy seems hungry after his journey, and I'm sure you can both manage a cup.'

Fenella dropped the magazine to the floor, and removed her feet from the couch.

'I never take tea,' she said. 'And, do you know, this is the first house I've been in which takes *Country Life*.'

'I'm having tea,' said Richard.

'So am I,' said Timothy.

'Oh well,' said Fenella, flouncing to her feet. 'I suppose I'd better have some too.'

Winnie would like to have retorted with: 'Don't strain yourself!' but common civility restrained her, and she led the way into the dining-room.

This, she feared, was going to be one of the stickiest tea parties she had ever had to direct.

Whilst Winnie and Jenny were entertaining their guests, Albert Piggott and Dotty Harmer were surveying the ornamental pond site.

At the moment it was far from ornamental. The pile of Cotswold stone from Percy's farmyard was stacked to one side, and six inches of slimy water filled the shallow crater which was to be metamorphosed in days to come. Most people would have found it a depressing sight, but Dotty and Albert, with future beauty in their inner eyes, were beaming upon it as if irises, goldfish, lilies, dragonflies and all the delights of water were already before them.

The ducks were huddled together beneath a nearby gooseberry bush. There was disenchantment in their beady eyes and their only hope, it seemed, was a nice bran mash before darkness set in.

'Won't they just love it,' cried Dotty, pulling her shabby cardigan round her with such force that a button flew into the depths of the pool.

'Ah, they will that!' agreed Albert. 'I've bin thinking. Once we've set these 'ere stones around flat, what about a little stone path for them to walk down into the water?'

'An excellent idea, Albert,' exclaimed Dotty. 'How soon can you start?'

Albert pushed back his cap and scratched his lank locks. Years of procrastination made him cautious when confronted by such a direct request.

'I might manage a couple of days later in the week,' he said grudgingly. 'But I'd need a hand shifting some of these bigger slabs. Too much for you, miss.'

'Never fear,' cried Dotty. 'Kit will help, I know, and I could direct things.'

The prospect of Dotty supervising the laying of the pond's surround, with numerous agitated and contradictory directions, was not one which Albert cared to dwell upon, but having committed himself so far there was nothing much which could be done about it.

He replaced his cap, and sighed. 'Well, see you Wednesday then, if that suits Mr Armitage.'

'He will fit in with you, Albert,' said Dotty firmly.

Poor devil, thought Albert! A rare pang of pity for a fellow-creature stirred his stony heart. There was a good deal of Dotty's rugged old father in her, and a wicked tyrant he had been, as any past pupil of Lulling Grammar School would affirm.

Albert, as a reluctant scholar, had always counted himself lucky to be in the dunces' class at his much more kindly elementary establishment at the other end of Lulling.

'I'll leave all that to you, miss,' he said, shuffling off towards Thrush Green.

Harold Shoosmith took Dorothy and Agnes to view the three cars which they had selected from the brochures, but it was quite apparent to Harold that Dorothy was already determined to have the Metro.

Luckily, there was a demonstration model waiting at the garage, and the manager took out his prospective customer with Harold sitting in the back. Agnes excused herself, saying that she had some Vedonis underwear to collect from the draper's, and four currant buns from The Fuchsia Bush. She would meet them again at the garage.

Dorothy managed the car very well, and Harold felt very proud of his minor part in her tuition. Ben Curdle had done a good job, and if she had needed to pass a driving test, thought Harold, she would have been perfectly competent.

She coped with the traffic in Lulling's busy High Street, and then drove a few miles out into the Cotswold countryside. Harold was relaxed enough to notice the signs of spring, the lambs in the fields, the warm breeze blowing through the window, and the freshness of young leaves. It was a good time to buy one's first car, he thought, and how much the two friends would enjoy it!

They had certainly earned their leisure after so many years of devoted teaching. He hoped that they had many years of health and retirement before them at Barton.

When they turned into the forecourt of the garage, Agnes was already waiting for them. She looked at Dorothy's face, pink with pleasurable excitement. There was no doubt about it. This was the car she wanted. Left to herself, she would have signed, there and then, any papers put before her by the delighted manager, but Harold felt a few minutes to calm down might be a wise thing.

'I suggest that we have a cup of coffee,' he said, 'and we will let you know after that.'

'Good idea,' said the manager. 'I have one or two telephone calls to make, so I shall be on hand if you need me.'

Harold ushered the two ladies into The Fuchsia Bush, and ordered a pot of coffee from the languid Rosa who seemed reluctant to leave the job of painting her nails.

'Definitely the right car,' announced Dorothy when Rosa had ambled away. 'What do you think?'

'It will suit you very well,' said Harold. 'The Metro's got a good name, and it is a British car which is what you want. You handled her beautifully, my dear.'

Dorothy flushed with pleasure at such praise.

'But the colour?' faltered Agnes.

'I was coming to that,' said Dorothy. 'You still like the idea of a white one?'

'Well,' said Agnes, 'it's just that I think a *white* car shows up so much better than a dark one. Coming out of turnings, or driving under trees, you know, one always seems to *take notice* of a light-coloured car. But, of course, Dorothy, if you prefer *another* colour, you know that—'

'White it shall be,' said Dorothy firmly. 'Now, Harold, tell me about any particular points that you think we should consider before we return.'

Over coffee the two discussed such matters as petrol consumption, maintenance, the advisability of having mud flaps fixed, a wiper for the rear window and a host of financial queries, so that Agnes let her mind drift happily on the peculiar names given to car colours. Quite as odd, she thought, as the names on the stockings she had inspected when going to collect her underwear at Lulling's foremost draper's. Who would know what colours to expect from 'Wild Mink', 'Desert Rose', or 'Spring Smoke', if they were ordering by post?

Dorothy and Harold had finished their coffee long before Agnes had got half-way through hers, and as Dorothy had now reverted to her usual sensible self, after her bout of euphoria, she and Harold departed to the garage, leaving Agnes to finish her coffee in peace.

It was while she was savouring the last few drops, that the door of The Fuchsia Bush was pushed open by a young man who was a stranger to little Miss Fogerty. He was exceptionally tall, with close-cropped auburn hair, and wore one gold earring. He was clad in the usual blue denim trousers and a leather jacket, much decorated with studs and fringe.

Rosa, whose nails were now finished to her satisfaction, sauntered over to this visitor, and exchanged a few words, which Agnes was unable to hear.

Rosa accompanied him to the door, and appeared to be directing him along Lulling High Street towards the church. He vanished from sight for some minutes, and then appeared on the other side of the road, where he stood, partly concealed by one of the High Street's lime trees. He was taking a great interest in one or more of the buildings close to The Fuchsia Bush, and Agnes wondered if he were, perhaps, an architectural student of some sort. Certainly, there were several fine examples of Georgian buildings close by, which many people came to admire.

He was still there when Agnes emerged to make her way to the garage. He was now making a sketch, it seemed, of the front of one of the houses.

Without doubt, a student, thought Agnes kindly, with great plans and ambitions.

If she had known the plans already fermenting in the young man's mind, little Miss Fogerty would have been severely shocked.

The end of the Easter holidays was now approaching and, much to Dorothy's disappointment, the eagerly awaited new car had not arrived.

A *white* Metro, she was told, would have to be ordered. If she would be content to have a blue, a red, a black or a green one then, of course, it could be supplied immediately.

'It really is ridiculous,' fumed Dorothy. 'I'm sure there must be dozens of people asking for a *white* car. So frustrating! I was so looking forward to a trip to Barton during the holidays.'

Agnes was much agitated. 'Oh dear! I feel that it is all my fault, Dorothy, for suggesting that we settled for a white model. Are you sure you wouldn't like to change your mind? You know that I shall be perfectly happy with any colour you choose.'

'I shouldn't dream of it,' said Dorothy firmly. 'White it shall be, even if we wait until the cows come home.'

They spent the rest of the morning tidying the school house garden. The daffodils were now dying, and Agnes felt how sad it was that this would be the last time that she snapped off the dead heads in this much-loved garden.

She said as much to Dorothy who was attacking the garden bed beneath the kitchen window with a small hand fork.

'And the last time, I hope, although I very much doubt it, when I shall be digging out this fiddling bindweed. These wretched roots travel miles underground, and keep snapping off just when I think I've conquered them.'

She sat back on her heels and pushed the wisps of hair from her perspiring forehead. Agnes was standing, holding the bucket brimming with dead daffodil heads. She was gazing intently at the hedge between their garden and the school play-ground, and very soon Dorothy saw what had caught her attention.

The tabby cat was emerging into the spring sunlight. It paused for a moment, as if to assess any perils in the offing, and then came steadily forward to greet Agnes with little chirruping sounds, half-mew half-purr.

Agnes put down the bucket very gently, and held out her hand. Her face was suffused with pleasure, Dorothy noticed. Without any hesitation the cat came to rub round Agnes's legs and to respond to the rubbing of its striped head.

Dorothy, sitting very quietly, watched this display of mutual affection with mixed feelings. It was touching to see the joy with which Agnes greeted her friend, and certainly the cat was a fine creature, far more handsome now than some months earlier when she had caught sight of the bedraggled animal in the garden. Agnes's succour had certainly been rewarded.

On the other hand, how difficult it was going to be to part these two friends when the time came to leave Thrush Green. Dorothy gave a gusty sigh, and the cat suddenly became aware of her presence.

It darted away to the shelter of the hedge again, and Agnes, still bemused with joy, picked up her bucket.

'Isn't that wonderful?' she cried. 'It's the first time he has come up to me of his own accord! And I haven't even got his saucer with me! It shows how confident he is getting, doesn't it?'

Dorothy scrambled inelegantly to her feet, and sat down on the nearby garden seat with relief. For once, she was speechless. Much troubled, she watched her friend as she carried her load to the distant compost heap. Agnes was singing quietly to herself. Her step was light. She was a girl again.

Oh dear, oh dear, thought Dorothy! How would it all end?

13. BINGO GOSSIP

One bright morning, Betty Bell burst into Harold Shoo-smith's study bearing two dusters and a tin of polish in one hand, and lugging the vacuum cleaner behind her with the other.

'All right to do you now?' she cried.

'Well—' began Harold, folding the newspaper resignedly.

'Good. I always like to get you settled first,' said Betty, dropping the polish, and untangling the flex of the cleaner.

'As a matter of fact—' said Harold. The whirring of the cleaner drowned his words.

'Where's Mrs Shoosmith then?' shouted Betty, above the racket.

'Shopping.'

'What say? Can't hear a word with this contraption going.' She switched it off.

'I said that she was shopping.'

'Ah!' Betty bent again as if to switch on, thought better of it, and stood up, hands on hips.

'You seen Dotty's – Miss Harmer's pond?'

'Not yet.'

'It's a real treat. She called me in to see it as I was passing Monday. No – I tell a lie! It must have been Tuesday, because it was Bright Hour, Monday. Or was it Tuesday now?'

'Does it matter?'

'What, Bright Hour?' cried Betty indignantly. 'Of course it matters! Why, we have lovely talks about what to do after being in prison or hospital – *after-care* it's called – and how to keep your husband off the booze, and that!'

137

'I'm sorry,' said Harold humbly. 'I meant, does it matter if you saw the pond on Monday or Tuesday?'

Betty looked baffled. 'Well, I never saw it *both* days. Now I come to think of it, it was definitely Tuesday because my book come.'

The book, as Harold knew, was her weekly magazine. Occasionally she had pressed a copy upon him, recommending one of the stories whose illustrations had been enough to quell any desire to read the text. However, he had kept it for a day or two, out of politeness, before returning it.

'So, go on,' he said.

'What about?'

By now Betty was on her knees retrieving the tin of polish which had rolled under a chair.

'The pond.'

She sat back on her haunches.

'It looks a bit of all right. Percy Hodge took the stones there, out of one of his old buildings what fell down. I bet he charged poor old Dot – Miss Harmer – more'n he should. He's that sharp, is Perce, must have been born in the knife drawer.' She stood up, puffing heavily. 'And Albert Piggott and Mr Kit laid 'em round. Mind you, Miss Harmer stood by and told 'em how she wanted it, but between them all it looks lovely.'

Harold could well envisage the operation, and particularly the part of overseer played by the redoubtable Dotty.

'Well, can't stop here all day chatting to you,' said Betty cheerfully. 'Best get on.'

She switched on the cleaner again and Harold made good his escape into the peace of the garden.

Here all was cool and calm. The schoolchildren were safely in their classrooms. The playground lay empty in the sunlight, and Betty's activities were muted by distance to a low humming noise.

Harold seated himself on the garden bench, and looked about him with approval.

The tulips were making a brave show, stretching up to meet the budding lilac. The gnarled old red hawthorn was breaking into rosy bloom, and the irises were in bud close by. There was no doubt about it, Thrush Green was the right place to live!

He thought of the years he had spent abroad, of the dust, the heat, the appalling smells of tropical lands where he had been obliged to spend his working life, and he sighed with pleasure at his present surroundings. He still came across old friends who had shared his life abroad, who bemoaned the fact that they had so little help with their domestic duties, who bewailed the fact that it was they who now had to shop and cook, to clean and mend, where once the ubiquitous 'boys' obliged.

Harold had no time for such self-pity. Left alone, he had managed pretty well and enjoyed the change of occupation. His happy marriage had added to his well-being, and the advent of the boisterous Betty into the household had certainly helped with the everyday chores. He was a lucky man!

He could hear her now, voice uplifted in song.

> *See what the boys*
> *In the back room will have,*
> *And tell them*
> *I'm having the same!*

carolled Betty. Her fresh country voice was in complete contrast to the husky tones of Marlene Dietrich's rendering which Harold recalled from years ago.

'I bet she didn't learn that at the Bright Hour,' observed Harold to a gaggle of chaffinches nearby, and went in to find his newspaper.

Dotty's pond was now a topic of discussion generally at Thrush Green. Albert Piggott was flattered to find several people congratulating him on his efforts. In such a beneficent atmosphere he almost smiled, and certainly Nelly found him a relatively cheerful companion when she returned from her labours at The Fuchsia Bush.

'It's the exercise,' she told him, as she sizzled liver and bacon for their supper. 'That's what you need. You're always on about your diet, but good food never hurt no one, and I don't care what Dr Lovell says. A good bustle about in the fresh air is all you need.'

'In moderation! In moderation!' growled Albert who did not want to abandon his role as a martyred invalid too readily. It came in useful when unwelcome jobs such as tidying the church cropped up. 'That's what my old dad always said,' he continued. 'So don't think you can go on everlasting with that frying pan, just because me ulcer's a bit better.'

Nelly snorted, and slapped a heaped plate before her husband. It gave her some satisfaction to see that it was cleared in ten minutes.

'It's my Bingo tonight,' she informed him. 'So don't go swilling beer next door while I'm out.'

She cleared the table, bustling briskly about the kitchen despite her bulk, and was ready within half an hour to accompany her friend Mrs Jenner to the Corn Exchange at Lulling, for her weekly treat.

Halfway through the evening's proceedings there was always a welcome break for coffee and biscuits. On this occasion, Nelly found herself sharing a small table with Gladys Lilly, and asked how Doreen was faring at the Lovelocks.

'It's pretty hard going,' admitted Mrs Lilly, 'as you said it would be, but I tell her she's lucky to have a job at all.'

'That's right,' agreed Nelly comfortably.

'But between ourselves,' continued Gladys, lowering her voice, 'she's proper unsettled. Keeps wanting to go out of an evening instead of stopping in with the baby. After all, I have him all day. It's only fair she takes over when she's home.'

'Well, she's young, of course,' said Nelly indulgently. 'Probably misses her husband.'

'He never was her husband,' said Gladys shortly.

'Sorry. I never thought.'

'To tell you the truth, that's another worry.'

'What is?'

'That chap of hers. I don't mind telling you, because I know it won't go any further—'

'Of *course* not,' said Nelly, now agog.

'But he was sent down for a twelvemonth for stealing, and I reckon he's just about out now.'

'In prison?' breathed Nelly.

'It wasn't all his fault,' said Gladys. 'Mind you, I'm not making excuses for him. I'm chapel and proud of it, and stealing's stealing, no matter what these social workers tell you. But all I'm saying is that the lad got into bad company soon after he left school, and they led him on. You know how it is. A bit of threatening, and a bit of jeering, and some of these tough boys can get the weaker ones to do the dirty work.'

'Well, I never!' gasped Nelly, suitably impressed with these disclosures. 'So where is he now, do you think?'

'That's what I don't know, but I hope he doesn't come worrying our Doreen to go back to him. She's that soft, she might well give in.'

'Surely not, if he left her in the first place?'

'Well, I hope not, but girls these days are soppier than we were, for all their dressing tough in denims and that. I blame this pill for a lot of it. In my young days we just said "No", and that was that.'

'You're quite right,' agreed Nelly virtuously.

At this moment the master of ceremonies called the company to the second half of the proceedings.

'Mind, not a word to anybody,' warned Mrs Lilly, as the two made their way back to their seats.

'Trust me,' Nelly assured her.

Of course, she told Mrs Jenner this delicious morsel of gossip as they returned home after Bingo, and her friend was suitably impressed.

'I don't like to speak ill of anybody,' said Mrs Jenner, who was obviously about to do just that, with every appearance of enjoyment, 'but Doreen Lilly was always a fast hussy, and Gladys Lilly was too soft with her by half.'

'Is that so?'

'There was talk of a baby on the way when she was in her last year at school. I never knew the rights of the affair, but there's no smoke without fire, I always say.'

'Very true. Some of these young girls get very headstrong.'

'They bring their troubles sometimes,' agreed Mrs Jenner. 'And I'm always so thankful that my Jane never gave us cause for concern. A thoroughly good girl she always was.'

'Properly brought up, that's why,' said Nelly, as they puffed up the hill to Thrush Green.

'Well, maybe that had *something* to do with it,' conceded her friend.

They said goodnight with affection, and made for their own abodes with the comfort of this new nugget of news to warm them.

Within a week or so, as might be expected, it was generally known that the father of Doreen Lilly's child had been in prison.

Probably the only two people unaware of this interesting fact were Dorothy Watson and Agnes Fogerty. They had more than enough to do to cope with their own affairs at the moment. This last term at Thrush Green school seemed to be packed with out-of-classroom activities. Already the ladies had been asked to keep the final afternoon of the school term free, for what Charles Henstock called 'a little celebration.'

He was considerably agitated when Dimity pointed out that 'a tribute' might have been a better way of putting things.

' "A celebration" might sound as though you are celebrating their departure,' explained Dimity.

'Well, we are,' protested Charles.

'Yes, but you are not *pleased* that they are going! It's like those notices in the "Deaths" column about a service of thanks-giving. If only people would fork out the extra money to add: "For the life and work of etc.", all would be clear, but it does look sometimes as if the bereaved were thankful to see the back of the dear departed.'

'Really,' exclaimed Charles, 'you horrify me! I had *never* in all my life, looked at it that way!'

'That's because you are a thoroughly good man,' said Dimity affectionately. 'Now stop worrying about it.'

The two teachers had also been asked to 'a meeting (venue to be arranged)' on the last Sunday of term, and to the July meeting of the Parent-Teacher Association when 'a presenta-tion to two well-loved ladies' was planned.

The engagement diary, kept beside the telephone in the school house, was getting uncommonly full although it was only May, and already Dorothy and Agnes were beginning to feel somewhat harried.

'I know it is all meant so *kindly*,' said Dorothy after school one day, when the two were restoring themselves with a cup of tea in the sitting-room, 'but I must say I shall be quite relieved when it is all over.'

'I feel exactly the same,' confessed Agnes.

The telephone rang, and Dorothy padded out in her stock-inged feet to answer it.

She was some time in the hall, and Agnes sipped her tea and studied Dorothy's abandoned shoes lying askew on the carpet.

'Not another party?' she asked when her friend returned.

'Worse,' said Dorothy. 'Ray and Kathleen are calling in on their way back from Dorset next week.'

'How nice!' exclaimed Agnes. Dorothy's brother Ray and his wife were always more welcome to Agnes than to Dorothy who had little time for Ray and even less for his self-pitying hypo-chondriac of a wife.

'Well, at least they won't stop long,' said Dorothy, thrusting her feet into the shoes. 'They're stopping for tea before they get here, so a glass of sherry should foot the bill, and make less washing up.'

'Do you think they will bring their dog? What's-his-name?'

'Harrison? Heaven forbid!' Dorothy shuddered at the remembrance of the havoc caused by the exuberant animal in the house.

But Agnes was anxious about the well-being of her dear little cat, who might be scared away from the garden by the boisterous visitor. With commendable restraint she forbore from mentioning her fears to Dorothy, but she hoped that Ray and Kathleen would have the sense to leave their pet safely in the car.

One of the first people to visit and admire Dotty's new plaything was Winnie Bailey, who took advantage of a fine May afternoon to cross the green and take the footpath to Dotty's cottage.

The air was soft and balmy. Rooks wheeled above the lime trees in the gardens behind The Two Pheasants, bearing food for their vociferous nestlings.

In the Youngs' garden a sea of forget-me-nots surged around some splendid pink tulips lined up against the Cotswold stone of the fine house. A waft of warm air brought the scent of a bed of wallflowers, hidden from Winnie's sight by a mellow wall, and already the chestnut trees were showing embryo flower spikes.

Nothing, thought Winnie, could touch the month of May for sheer natural beauty. There were many devotees of autumn, praising the blazing trees, the joys of harvest and the like, but May was a time of hope, of youth, of splendours to come. It renewed her strength every year with its promise of summer joys.

She found her old friend in the chicken run, clutching an armful of wet weeds to her cardigan.

'Ah, Winnie!' cried Dotty. 'How nice to see you! Just let

me scatter this nourishing salad for the girls, and I'll be with you. Such richness! Chickweed, hogweed, dandelions, shepherd's purse, groundsel, and lots more – all *teeming* with natural goodness. I can't persuade Connie to use such things for us unfortunately, but I suppose we get the nourishment, at second-hand as it were, in the hens' eggs.'

She cast her burden from her among the cackling birds, wiped her muddy hands down her skirt, and emerged from the run. Her bedraggled appearance somewhat shocked Winnie.

'Don't you think you should change your cardigan, Dotty? It's soaking wet, and you know how easily you catch cold.'

'Nonsense!' said Dotty, slapping her skinny chest. 'It'll soon dry. You're as bad as Connie.'

Winnie did not like to point out that it was Connie who had to do any nursing of this rebellious patient, and she followed Dotty across the garden to the new pond.

It certainly looked a fine piece of work, although still rather raw in appearance. No doubt, thought Winnie, once the stones had weathered and Dotty's tubs of plants were in place, it would be very attractive. The ducks seemed to be enjoying themselves, half of them diving with their feet waving happily, and the rest preening themselves on the surrounding stones in the sunshine.

'Dear things,' said Dotty fondly. 'It's such a treat for them, and I've had four eggs already.'

She waved her friend towards a garden seat, and they took their ease.

'And you are keeping well?' asked Winnie, trying to ignore Dotty's damp bosom.

'Just a touch of the jim-jams in my back, but Connie's taking me to see Tom Porter tomorrow, and he'll put me right.'

'You still go to him?'

Tom Porter was the local osteopath, used by a great many Lulling people, but Winnie had never had need, or desire, to take advantage of his gifts. Donald had never countenanced osteopathy and Winnie remained loyal to his beliefs.

'I never liked to tell your dear Donald,' said Dotty, as if she could read Winnie's thoughts. 'I know he didn't approve, but I always felt that Tom had such a sound working knowledge of the *skeleton*!'

'So have doctors,' replied Winnie defensively.

'Not to the same extent. I'm sure that Donald was very good on muscles and skin and the fleshy bits. And, of course, all those inner tubes – so alarmingly complicated – but the *framework* seems to be somewhat ignored by general practitioners.'

'Well, I shan't argue with you,' said Winnie. 'But what does he do?'

'He makes me lie flat on his rather hard couch, and crosses one leg over the other for a start.'

Here Dotty thrust out her skinny legs in their wrinkled lisle stockings for Winnie's approval.

'Then he presses on one knee, *quite gently*, and keeps measuring the lengths.'

'Of your knees?'

'No, no, dear! My legs! One seems to get shorter than the other which makes my back hurt.'

Winnie was about to say that surely the displacement of the back did the leg-shortening, but Dotty's grasshopper mind had already leapt to other topics.

'Tell me about Dorothy and Agnes. Have they got their car yet? And have they found a house at Barton? I hear from Betty Bell that Ray and Kathleen Watson are going to visit them soon. I wonder if they might take the school house eventually? Ray must be almost at retirement age, and I'm sure that country air would be good for Kathleen's health.'

'I don't know much about Ray and Kathleen's plans,' began Winnie, 'but I know that Dorothy is still waiting for a *white* car, and I don't know if a house at Barton has cropped up yet.'

She paused, while Dotty leapt to her feet, entered the nearby garden shed and reappeared with a hunk of stale bread which she began to tear into pieces and throw to the ducks.

A frenzied quacking and splashing ensued, while Dotty beamed upon her charges and scattered her largesse.

She really grows scattier every month, thought Winnie, but when it came to keeping an eye and ear open to local gossip then Dotty was as sharp as the rest of Thrush Green.

PART THREE

Journey's End

* * *

14. TRYING TIMES

Affairs at Thrush Green school seemed to grow more hectic as the weeks passed. As well as the interminable tidying up, wondering what to reject completely, what to pass on to Miss Robinson for future school use, and what to keep 'just in case', the two retiring ladies had had several visits from would-be future teachers at the school.

To give them their due, these aspirants were careful to make an appointment and were sensible enough to make their visits brief, but nevertheless Dorothy found the interruptions to routine excessively wearing.

'I suppose it is only right that they should want to see where they might be spending the rest of their lives,' said Dorothy, 'and these are all on the short list.'

'I wonder how many have been invited?' pondered Agnes.

'Five or six for each post, I presume,' replied Dorothy. 'I imagine they'll appoint to both posts on the same day. What do you think?'

'I've no idea,' said Agnes, secretly hoping that none of them would be as nervous as she had been when she applied for her present post so many years ago.

'Quite a few men among the applicants, I noticed,' went on Dorothy. 'For the headship, of course. Naturally, a woman will take on your place.'

'I don't see why a nice man couldn't do the job,' said Agnes, with some spirit. 'I particularly liked that young fellow in the National Trust tie you brought in.'

'I can't see him coping with young children,' said Dorothy

grimly. 'He talked of nothing but racing cars and rugby football.'

'No news, I suppose, from Better & Better?' asked Agnes, steering the conversation into different, if not less controversial, waters.

'A small house and two flats,' replied Dorothy, fishing in her handbag. 'I meant to show you at breakfast but you were out feeding that cat.'

'Any hope?' said Agnes, ignoring the slight on her pet.

'The small house,' said Dorothy, adjusting her glasses, 'is reached "by a long drive". That means we'd have to keep it up, dear, unless it's a cart track, in which case it would probably be impassable for part of the year.'

'And the flats?'

'In the same garden, and four miles from Barton.'

'So we are no nearer?'

'As you say. Sometimes I think our estate agent should be called "Worse & Worse". If only we had the car, we could run down and visit the estate agent and try and get some sense out of him.'

'Perhaps another letter—'

'I sometimes wonder if they ever read letters,' replied Dorothy with despair. 'Ah well! There's the bell. Better get back to our classrooms.'

Some of the applicants had asked to see the school house, although they knew that it did not now automatically go with the post, and Dorothy and Agnes had readily invited them to view the property in case they wished to buy.

Otherwise, only Richard and Fenella, and a local couple who had heard about the future disposal of the building, had visited the ladies, and for this Dorothy was grateful.

She admitted to herself that these last few months were a great strain. After so many years of well-organised living she found the unknown a little daunting. Impatient by nature, she suffered far more from the frustration of waiting for the new car and from the interminable delay of finding suitable living places in the Barton area, than did Agnes.

Agnes, however, was equally agitated about the change of circumstances. Devoted as she was to Dorothy, would it be difficult to live for the whole of the day, every day, with her? She had found her extremely short-tempered of late, and although she knew only too well that they were both living under extra pressure, she was secretly hurt by one or two wounding remarks, and had had to curb her own tongue.

Then, too, she was beginning to get very anxious about the cat. It was now remarkably tame and affectionate, and Agnes felt quite sure that it could be introduced into the school house, and later transported to Barton, without much trouble.

Alone, of course, there would have been no difficulty, but Dorothy still appeared adamant, and showed no sign of relenting, or even being willing to discuss the matter. With so much else to occupy their minds, Agnes had shelved the problem, and simply enjoyed the growing companionship of her new friend.

She was the one, she realised, who would miss severely the children and all their old friends in Thrush Green. Dorothy was more out-going and would soon make friends at Barton. Agnes, less bold, knew full well that it would take her longer.

However, there was not much one could do about it at this stage, and apart from deciding to keep up with such dear neighbours as Isobel and Harold, Winnie Bailey, Muriel Fuller and the like, by letter writing, or the occasional telephone call, Agnes pursued her gentle way from day to day, and dealt with the problems as they turned up.

It was about this time that Isobel received a letter from her old friend in Sussex. It was several pages long, and seemed to engross Isobel all through breakfast time.

'Your post seems more interesting than mine,' observed Harold. 'I've only got one offering me a loan, another asking me to support a family in Africa, and a demand for the rates.'

'This is from Ursula,' said Isobel.

'The one who gave you splendid picnics on the way to see some aged relative? Strawberries and cream, wasn't it?'

'And cold asparagus wrapped in brown bread,' agreed Isobel, smiling at him. 'How greedy you are!'

'What does she want?'

'Nothing. Just the other way about in fact. She has a rather splendid tea set to give me.'

'How's that?'

'The aunt at Barton has evidently left it to me. Ursula said I admired it, and her aunt made a note of it. Very sweet of the old lady, I must say. I remember it well – Wedgwood, white with a gold band, very elegant. We must keep it "for best", Harold.'

'Does she want us to fetch it?'

'That's the idea. She's at Barton clearing up the place. I imagine she will live there eventually.'

'Well, it won't take us long to run down. Does she give her telephone number?'

'She does indeed. I will ring this evening. Isn't it a lovely surprise?'

'A much nicer one than my rates demand,' agreed Harold.

Ray and Kathleen's visit coincided with a particularly trying day at Thrush Green school.

For a start, one of Agnes's children fell in the playground before school began. The boy grazed both knees, and understandably yelled the place down, which upset Agnes considerably. Furthermore, he resisted any attempts at first aid with such violence that Agnes was obliged to scribble a note to his mother, luckily at home nearby, and dispatch note and child in the care of the oldest and most responsible girl in Miss Watson's class.

In her classroom, after assembly, Dorothy noticed a girl weeping. Her face was flushed, her forehead afire, and on examination Miss Watson discovered a fine bright rash on the girl's chest, which she readily recognised as chickenpox.

As the child had twin sisters in Miss Robinson's class, it

seemed sensible to send all three home, but both parents were at work, and there seemed to be no obliging aunts, grannies or neighbours to take charge. Dorothy took them over to the school house, put the sufferer on to the spare bed with a doll and two books, and ensconced the twins in the kitchen with lemonade and drawing paper.

At playtime it was discovered that all the milk was decidedly off-colour, and none of the children would touch it. The staff's coffee had to be black which none of them liked.

By midday, the mother of the three invalids had arrived in answer to the message sent to her place of work. She seemed to blame Miss Watson for allowing her child to catch chickenpox, and gave no word of thanks for the care which the children had been given.

School dinner consisted of fatty minced meat and boiled potatoes with the eyes left in. Jam tart, normally greeted ecstatically, was burnt round the edges and refused by a number of pupils.

The nurse who came to look at heads arrived unannounced in the middle of the afternoon, and when Dorothy, interrupted in her reading of *Tom's Midnight Garden*, remonstrated, Nurse told her that she knew for a fact that notice had been sent a fortnight before, and it was probably that Willie Merchant's fault for not delivering it.

It did not improve Dorothy's temper to discover the letter later, unopened, tucked inside a stern missive from the Office about 'Economy and School Stationery'.

After school, Agnes had felt obliged to call at her wounded boy's home to see how he was faring, and found him, catapult in hand, doing his best to hit a nearby sparrow, luckily without success. His mother was perfunctory in her thanks, and Agnes tottered back to the school house ready for tea.

'I could well do without a visitation from Ray and Kathleen,' commented Dorothy, as they cleared away their teacups, 'but there it is. I only hope they don't stay long. What a day it has been!'

The ladies went upstairs to change from their workaday clothes, and Agnes was just trying to decide whether the occasion warranted the addition of her seed pearls to the general ensemble, when the car arrived.

Dorothy admitted her brother, his wife and the boisterous Labrador, Harrison, who luckily was on a lead.

'Is he going to stay indoors?' queried Dorothy, in a far from welcoming tone.

'He'll soon calm down,' Ray was assuring her as Agnes entered the sitting-room. 'He's very obedient these days.'

Harrison leapt upon Agnes and nearly felled her to the Axminster carpet. She sat down abruptly on the couch.

'Down, sir!' shouted Ray in a voice which set the sherry glasses tinkling. 'D'you hear me? Down, I say!'

Dorothy put her hands over her ears, Kathleen bridled, and Agnes attempted a polite smile.

'It's just that he's excited,' bawled Ray, tugging at the lead. 'So pleased to see everyone. Awfully affectionate animal!'

The affectionate animal now attempted to clamber on to Agnes's lap. As it was twice her size and weight, she was immediately engulfed.

'Take him out!' screamed Kathleen. 'He's obviously upset. He's extremely highly-strung,' she explained fortissimo to the dishevelled Agnes.

Reluctantly, Ray tugged the dog outside, and to the relief of the two hostesses Harrison was deposited back in the car.

'Well!' exclaimed Dorothy. 'I should think you could do with a restorative after all that. Sherry, Kathleen?'

'Thank you, but no,' said Kathleen primly. 'I have to keep off all alcohol, my doctor says.'

'Tomato juice, orange juice?'

'Too acid, dear.'

'Perrier?'

'I simply can't digest it,' said Kathleen, with great satisfaction.

'A cup of tea? Or coffee?'

Dorothy was starting to sound desperate, and Agnes noticed that her neck was beginning to flush.

'If I might have a little milk,' said Kathleen, 'I should be grateful.'

'I will fetch it,' said Agnes, anxious to have a moment's peace in the kitchen.

It would be today, she thought, examining the dubious milk, that Kathleen wanted this commodity. For safety's sake she took the precaution of pouring the liquid through the strainer into a glass, and hoped for the best.

Without Harrison the sitting-room was comparatively tranquil. There was general conversation about the Dorset holiday, the state of their respective gardens, Ray's health, soon disposed of, and Kathleen's, which threatened to dominate the conversation for at least two hours, if not checked.

Over the years, Dorothy had developed considerable expertise in cutting short the recital of her sister-in-law's complaints and their treatment. At times, Agnes had felt that she was perhaps a shade ruthless in her methods, but today, exhausted as she was with the vicissitudes it had brought, she was glad to have the conversation turned in the direction of their own future plans.

'It surprises me,' said Kathleen, 'to know that you haven't found a house yet.'

'It surprises us too,' replied Dorothy tartly. 'It's not for want of trying, I can assure you.'

'Time's getting on,' observed Ray. 'You ought to make up your mind. Prices seem to rise every week.'

Agnes trembled in case Dorothy responded with a typical outburst, but for once her friend remained silent.

'Once we have the car,' Agnes said timidly, 'Dorothy and I intend to have a thorough look at houses.'

'I imagine that you will be getting rid of a good deal of furniture,' remarked Kathleen. 'What do you propose to do about it?'

'Nothing, until we've seen what we need in the new place,' said Dorothy.

Kathleen drew in her breath. Agnes noticed that she cast a quick glance at her husband.

'I only ask,' she continued, 'because we wondered if we could help at all by taking it off your hands.'

'What had you in mind?' enquired Dorothy, with dangerous calm.

'Well, this nest of tables, for instance,' said Kathleen, putting down the glass of milk, 'and dear mother's kitchen dresser, and any china which might be too much for the new home.'

'Anything else?' asked Dorothy, her neck now scarlet.

Ray, ill at ease, had now gone to the window, removing himself, man-fashion, from the source of trouble.

'There were one or two items that Ray was always so fond of,' said Kathleen, looking somewhat sharply at her husband's back. 'He often talks of that silver rosebowl his mother always cherished, and her silver dressing-table set.'

'I cherish those too,' said Dorothy.

'And I don't suppose that any of the carpets or curtains will fit the new place,' continued Kathleen happily. 'So do bear us in mind if you are throwing anything away.'

At this point, a desperate howling from Harrison pierced the air, and Ray leapt at the excuse to hurry outside.

'He's probably seen a cat,' said Kathleen. 'Hateful creatures!'

Agnes, full of fears, betook herself to the window. There certainly was a cat in sight, but to her relief it was only Albert Piggott's, an animal which could well take care of itself, and was now sitting smugly on the garden wall, gloating over its imprisoned enemy.

'We must be on our way,' announced Kathleen. She drained her glass, much to Agnes's relief, and began to fidget with her gloves and handbag. 'Who would have thought it was half-past six?'

Ray returned, and seemed glad to see preparations for departure.

'Is he all right?' asked Kathleen anxiously. 'We don't want him unsettled with a journey before him.'

'Just a cat,' replied Ray, in what Agnes felt was an extremely callous manner. Just a cat, indeed!

'It was good of you to break your journey,' said Dorothy, her feelings now under control. 'We'll keep you in touch with our plans. I can't see us moving from here much before the late summer.'

'But won't the new head want it?' queried Ray.

Dorothy explained about the sale of the house.

'I wonder,' began Kathleen, making her way to the front door, 'if it would suit us, Ray?'

'We are quite happy where we are, dear,' Ray said firmly. 'Besides, it would be a terrible upheaval for Harrison. He's so used to his present daily walkies, and no one could be better with him than our local vet.'

'Of course,' said Dorothy, as she kissed them in farewell, 'it would save us taking up the carpets and curtains if you took over, and we might even come to some arrangement about the kitchen dresser. Mother's silver, of course, means too much to me to part with.'

Deafening barking put a stop to all further conversation, and the two drove off with much waving and hooting.

'Well,' said Dorothy, with infinite satisfaction, 'I think I had the last word there!'

Half an hour later, the two ladies were sitting with their feet up, going over all the problems of the day.

'One thing after another,' said Dorothy, 'and then Ray and Kathleen on top of everything. Really, it's as much as I can do to be civil to her. If I weren't so devoted to Ray, I could say a great deal more than I do.'

'She is rather trying,' agreed Agnes. 'I suppose it's partly because she is delicate.'

Dorothy snorted. 'Delicate my foot! She's as strong as an ox, and always was. A great pity they didn't have half a dozen children to take her mind off herself. As it is, they make a fool of that awful animal.'

'Not a very tractable dog,' said Agnes, with considerable understatement.

The telephone rang, and Dorothy padded out to answer it.

'Probably some irate parent,' she commented on her way out. 'Just to add the final straw to the camel's back.'

Agnes could not hear much of Dorothy's side of the conversation, but at least she sounded pleased. Agnes closed her eyes, and promised herself an early night after the hazards of the day.

'The car's arrived!' cried Dorothy, returning. Her eyes sparkled, her cheeks glowed.

'How splendid!' said Agnes, sitting up.

'I can fetch it tomorrow after school,' went on Dorothy. 'Isn't it marvellous? And it's a *white* one!'

Agnes did not like to dampen her friend's high spirits by pointing out that it was exactly why they had waited so long, but smiled kindly at her.

'I think I shall ask Harold to accompany me,' said Dorothy. 'Do you mind if I slip round now and have a word?'

'Of course not,' said Agnes, deciding that this would be just the time to feed the little cat. 'And don't be surprised if I have gone up to bed. I'm terribly tired.'

'No wonder,' said Dorothy. 'Me too, but this last bit of news has made up for all the day's annoyances. Now we can really start to make plans.'

And the two ladies parted to pursue their errands.

15. AGNES IS UPSET

The choice of presents for the departing teachers was now becoming a pressing problem for those responsible.

Miss Robinson's task was probably the simplest. The ten-penny pieces came in apace, and were stored in a small biscuit tin which was decorated with illustrations from *The Country Diary of an Edwardian Lady*. So often had it been opened that the hinge had given way, but it still shut firmly, and Miss Robinson was proud of the number of coins it enclosed.

The children much enjoyed the secrecy surrounding this project, and had all sorts of suggestions ranging from a puppy to keep their teachers company, to two electric blankets. Miss Robinson still thought that two bouquets and two boxes of chocolates would fit the bill far better, as the rector had suggested.

Charles Henstock, as chairman of the governors, had been surprised to find how determined his fellows were to present the ladies with a clock.

'Always have given a clock,' said the oldest member of the governors. 'Useful too.'

'Excellent idea,' said another.

The good Charles, remembering Harold and Isobel's suggestions, was somewhat taken aback by this solid attack.

'I wondered if a piece of china or glass might be acceptable.'

'Such as?'

'Well, a nice decanter, say.'

There was a sharp indrawing of breath from the only tee-totaller on the committee.

'Or a fruit bowl,' added the rector hastily.

'I still think a clock would be best,' said the first speaker. 'What do the PTA people suggest?'

Charles remembered, with relief, that the Parent-Teacher Association were combining with the governors in this matter, and put in a word.

'We must consult them, of course. Now I have your suggestions here, and have noted that the general feeling is that a clock of some kind would be your choice.'

'A decent-sized one,' said the oldest member firmly. 'None of those fiddle-faddling things you can't see without your glasses. Something with a good big face. We're none of us getting any younger.'

Hearty agreement broke out, leading to discussions of arthritis, the afflictions of themselves and aged relatives, and general denigration of the National Health Service.

'Well, ladies and gentlemen,' said Charles, patting his papers together. 'I think we've done very well for this evening, and with your permission I will get in touch with Mrs Gibbons and then report back to you.'

The meeting dispersed slowly, and as the rector crossed the green to his car, he overheard the oldest governor explaining to his companion about the efficacious properties of a potato, carried in the pocket, for warding off the pains of rheumatism.

'Better than the Health Service any day!' he assured his friend.

Mrs Gibbons, on behalf of the PTA, had already gone ahead with her plans to get a suitable picture of the school for the unsuspecting teachers.

She had first approached Ella Bembridge, who had lived at Thrush Green for many years, and was recognised as the most artistic resident there.

But Ella was not much in favour of the idea, and said so in her usual gruff way.

'I was quite taken aback,' said Mrs Gibbons, reporting on the interview to the Gauleiter that evening. 'She said she gave up "finicking about" with watercolours thirty years ago. She's now besotted with stitched rugs evidently.'

'I should get a decent photograph,' advised her husband, whose practical approach to all problems had led him to his present position of eminence. 'That chap at Lulling, by the butcher's, seems to know his stuff. He did a good job at the Rotary Club dinner.'

'I suppose that would be best,' said his wife doubtfully. 'Not very *imaginative*, of course.'

'The two ladies won't want anything *imaginative*. A nicely-composed photo, by a local chap, should be very acceptable.'

'I'll put it in hand straightaway,' promised Mrs Gibbons, and did so.

There were times when she found the Gauleiter's down-to-earth advice a great comfort.

It was about this time that Dorothy and Agnes heard about their successors.

To Agnes's delight the young man with the National Trust tie had been appointed as headmaster.

'Such a cheerful young fellow,' she said, 'with short hair too.'

'Short hair is back in fashion,' Dorothy told her.

Agnes suddenly remembered the cropped red hair of the stranger who had been so interested in the architecture of Lulling High Street. Who could he have been, she wondered?

'And I think the young woman who will take your place,' went on Dorothy, 'should do very well. Mind you, *no one* can really take your place, Agnes.'

'And *no one*,' Agnes replied loyally, 'can take yours.'

They smiled fondly at each other.

'Ah well,' said Dorothy, 'we've had a good run for our money, as they say, and now it's time for a change. What about a little spin in the car, as the evening is so lovely?'

'A good idea,' replied Agnes, trying to look enthusiastic.

'Somewhere quiet, I think, don't you? What about the road to Nod and Nidden?'

'As long as Percy Hodge has his dog under control,' said Dorothy. That disastrous encounter still rankled, but there was no point in raking up old memories, she told herself, as she collected the car keys.

It so happened that Isobel Shoosmith made the journey to Barton alone, as the only day that fitted in with Ursula's plans was the day which Harold had fixed with a local tree-feller to take down an ancient plum tree at the end of the garden.

This hoary monster had produced no plums for years, but still had enough life in it to send out dozens of healthy plum suckers which sprang up from the grass for yards around.

It was a cloudless morning towards the end of May, and Isobel enjoyed her journey. The New Forest was fluttering with young leaves, the roaming ponies and cattle were as endearing as ever, and Isobel's spirits were high.

She had always been fond of Ursula, and secretly missed her company now that she lived at Thrush Green. One thing, she told herself as she peered at a signpost, Ursula would be much more accessible at Barton than at her old home in Sussex, and the New Forest was a joy at any time of the year. Next time she would bring Harold down to meet her old friend.

She remembered the aunt's road as soon as she saw it, and the white bungalow seemed little changed outside. Ursula was at the gate to meet her, and they embraced warmly.

'So little changed,' said Isobel, eyeing the house.

'Wait till you come inside,' warned Ursula, and sure enough chaos greeted the eye.

There were tea-chests everywhere, the dining-room chairs were upturned on the table, and the sitting-room was shrouded in dust sheets. A man in a boiler suit, spanner in hand, was doing something to the pipes in the kitchen, and Ursula led the way into the garden at the back.

Here there was a seat in the sun, and the two friends found a little peace.

They went out to a nearby pub for lunch, and Isobel gratefully packed her inheritance in the boot of the car, well-wrapped up in a car rug. Both women were hoarse with exchanging news.

'I shall ring you about half-past six,' she told Ursula. 'It's been a lovely day, and I'll tell you more then.'

Isobel had plenty to think about as she drove home. There the plum tree was down, the tree-feller had vanished, and Harold was ready for all the news.

'She's selling the place, and I really think it might suit Agnes and Dorothy. To be honest, I don't know why she doesn't settle there herself. It's so convenient and easily managed.'

'Probably prefers her own home,' responded Harold. 'People do, you know.'

'I think she likes being near the daughters and the grandchildren,' said Isobel, 'and I must say moving is the most appalling upheaval.'

'So did you say anything about our neighbours?'

'Rather tentatively, but I did say that they were looking for something that way. Now I'm beginning to wonder if I should have done. Perhaps I shouldn't interfere?'

'Nonsense!' said Harold robustly. 'You pop round and have a word with the girls, before you ring Ursula.'

'I feel like Meddlesome Mattie,' she said, setting off reluctantly next door.

She found the two friends busy weeding.

'Must try and keep the place decent,' cried Dorothy, removing her gardening gloves. 'I see the plum tree has gone.'

'Well, it was more of a nuisance than anything else,' said Isobel apologetically, 'and not a plum to be seen.'

'Harold told us you had gone to see a friend,' said Agnes.

'Yes, at Barton, strangely enough,' replied Isobel and launched into her tale. The ladies listened attentively.

'And you say that she has just put it into the hands of Better & Better?'

'I think that was the name. She said it was an excellent firm.'

Agnes waited for Dorothy's snort, but none came.

'You don't think me too interfering, I hope,' pleaded Isobel. 'It just seemed a marvellous possibility, and of course you need not take it – or even go and see it.' She was horrified to hear her voice babbling on apologetically.

Dorothy cut her short. 'It was a great kindness, and Agnes and I would love to drive down to see it whenever your friend—'

'Ursula.'

'Ursula can show us round. Or, of course, the estate agent can do his duty at last.'

Isobel explained about the telephone call she was about to make, thanked the two for being so understanding, received thanks for being so thoughtful, and returned to her own home in a state of extreme agitation.

'What you need,' said Harold looking at her kindly, 'is a nice little snifter before you ring Barton.'

And he went to pour out two of them.

Naturally, before the week was out, it was common knowledge in Thrush Green and Lulling that Miss Watson and Miss Fogerty had found a home at Barton.

Some said an aunt of Isobel's had left her the property. Others maintained that it was a relative of Harold's who was selling the house. One or two actually got it right, and said that a friend of Isobel's was the vendor. All trusted that the good ladies would be very happy in their new abode.

'And we haven't even seen it yet,' cried Dorothy, when she heard the gossip. 'Really, one despairs of trying to keep anything private in this place.'

'It is aggravating,' agreed Agnes.

Both ladies were tired after a day at school. Dorothy's legs were aching, and Agnes's head throbbed. It was at times like this that they longed for the end of term, to have the various leaving parties behind them, and to set off to a quiet life of retirement. Would it ever come?

At that moment, Agnes's sharp ears heard a small mewing sound. She hurried to the french window and saw the tabby cat looking hopefully at her.

'Ah! The dear thing's here,' she cried, turning sharply to go and fetch its supper. She caught her foot in the hearth rug and fell sprawling.

'Oh, Agnes!' cried Dorothy. 'Are you hurt?'

Agnes struggled up. 'No, no,' she said, somewhat shakily. 'How clumsy of me.'

'You shouldn't rush about so after that animal,' exclaimed Dorothy, her anxiety on Agnes's behalf showing as irritation. 'It's a perfect pest. And anyway, how do you think it will manage when you have abandoned it?'

At these appalling words Agnes felt her eyes fill with tears, and hurried from the room. In the privacy of the scullery she prepared the cat's food, and a few salt drops mingled with the tinned meat in the enamel dish.

It was that word 'abandoned' which hurt most. There was something so cruel and callous about it, and of course Agnes had tortured herself quite enough already thinking about the cat's future. And to call her tabby friend 'a perfect pest'! It was more than flesh and blood could endure.

She put the plate outside in its usual position, and the cat came trustingly towards it. But this evening Agnes could not bring herself to stand and watch this normally happy sight. Conscious of her tear-stained face, and complete inability to control her emotion, she rushed down the garden, and betook herself to the privacy of the field beyond.

Here she sat down on the grass behind the hawthorn hedge, and abandoned herself to the grief which engulfed her. It was insufferable of Dorothy to behave in this way! For two pins she would tell her that the idea of sharing a retirement home was now absolutely repugnant to her. A vista of long grey years giving in to Dorothy's bullying suddenly assailed her mind's eye. Could she bear it?

Why should she part from her dear new friend? If she stayed at Thrush Green she could keep it. After all, she had lived very happily for many years in digs at Mrs White's. There must be other lodgings where a well-behaved cat would be welcome.

Agnes's sobs grew more violent as she grew more rebellious. Her small handkerchief was drenched, and her head throbbed more painfully than ever.

It was at this stage that Isobel, who had been depositing vegetable peelings on her compost heap, came through the wicket gate at the end of the garden to see what the strange noise was about.

She was appalled to see her old friend in such a state of despair, and dropped to the grass beside her.

'But what is it? What has happened?'

She put her arm around Agnes, and felt hot tears dampening her shoulder. The colander, which had held the peelings, rolled away unnoticed, as Agnes's distress increased in the face of her friend's sympathy.

From an incoherent jumble of sobs, hiccups and comments about Dorothy's remarks and the cat's pathos, Isobel began to understand the real nature of Agnes's anguish, and was seriously perturbed. It was even more alarming to hear Agnes's ramblings about her future, and the possibility of refusing to leave Thrush Green if it meant parting from the cat.

'If only Mrs White were here,' cried Agnes, shoulders still heaving. 'I know she would take me back again, and the cat, too. She adored cats.'

At the thought of Mrs White's affection for the feline world, Agnes's tears broke out afresh.

There was little that Isobel could do apart from patting her friend's back and uttering words of comfort.

At last, the paroxysm passed, and Agnes was able to mop her eyes and control her breathing again.

'Oh, Isobel!' she wailed. 'What a comfort you are! What am I going to do?'

'You are coming home with me,' Isobel told her. 'And you are going to have a rest until you feel better. Does Dorothy know you are out?'

A look of panic crossed Agnes's tear-stained face. 'No, I'm sure she doesn't. Oh, please don't say anything to her! I shouldn't want to upset her.'

'Don't worry,' said Isobel. 'The first thing to do is to get you to my house for a little drink.'

'But Harold—' quavered Agnes.

'Out at a meeting,' replied Isobel. 'We shall be quite alone.'

The two friends made their way through the evening sunshine to the house next door.

There, feet up on the sofa, and a restorative cup of coffee to hand, Agnes recovered her composure, regretted her outburst, and thought, yet again, how much she loved Isobel.

Dorothy meanwhile, ignorant of all the upset her words had produced, was engrossed in a television programme about education. Those taking part were obviously more theorists than practitioners, and Dorothy's disgusted snorts accompanied many of the panel's remarks.

The programme which followed was about birds, and Dorothy found this equally absorbing and far less irritating. It did occur to her, half-way through, when a humming-bird was extracting honey from a trumpet-shaped exotic bloom, how much Agnes would enjoy it, and where could she be, but she guessed – correctly, as it happened – that she was probably next door visiting Isobel.

So that when the sitting-room door opened a chink, and Agnes said that she proposed to have an early night as her head ached, Dorothy replied that it was a sensible idea and she would come up later, and kept her eyes glued to the television screen, quite unconscious of all that had devastated her friend's evening.

True to her word, at ten o'clock she switched off the set, and made her way upstairs. She knocked gently on Agnes's door, but there was no response. She eased it open and listened. There was no sound at all. Presumably, Agnes was asleep, and she closed the door, with infinite care, and crept across to her own room.

She was asleep within half an hour, but next door Agnes lay awake, too agitated to settle, until she fell asleep at five o'clock, completely exhausted.

When Harold Shoosmith returned from his meeting, Isobel told him what had happened.

'Poor old dear,' was his response, 'but not much we can do about it. After all, this cat business is their affair.'

'I agree. But I feel rather responsible for Agnes.'

'Good heavens! Why?'

'She has no family. She talked wildly of staying on at Thrush Green in digs – somewhere where she could have the cat.'

'You mean she's thinking of ditching Dorothy, and Barton, and all the rest of it?'

'At one stage this evening, she certainly was. And how would she manage? Her pension won't be much. She'll be horribly lonely. I'm quite willing to have her here for a few weeks until she finds lodgings, if that's what she really wants, but the long-term outlook is so dismal.'

'She can't possibly intend to leave Dorothy!'

'No, I don't think she will when it comes to it. But it does show how desperate she is. I don't think Dorothy has any idea how much she wants that cat. I think I shall have to tell her.'

Harold sighed. 'Well, watch your step, my dear. It's really such a storm in a teacup.'

'Not to Agnes. I've never seen her like this, and I'm appalled to think she may be jettisoning her future – and Dorothy's too, for that matter. If I get the chance, I shall let Dorothy know how things are, and what's more I shall try and persuade her to accept the cat into the household.'

'You're a brave woman,' said Harold.

16. A Trip to Barton-on-Sea

While little Miss Fogerty was weeping in the shelter of the hedge, attended by Isobel, two more old friends were enjoying each other's company on the other side of Thrush Green.

Dimity had called to see Ella Bembridge. She looked with affection at the cottage which they had shared for several happy years before Charles had proposed and she had gone to live at the bleak rectory across the road, now replaced by Rectory Cottages, the pleasant homes for old people.

Ella appeared to be wrapped in a brightly stitched garment reminiscent of those worn by Peruvian peasants. Actually, it was one of the stitched rugs which so engrossed her at the moment, and after she had disengaged herself from its folds, she showed her work to Dimity with some pride.

'It's wonderfully colourful,' said Dimity politely. Secretly she thought it downright garish and quite unsuitable for the cottage. A nice plain beige Wilton now, thought Dimity, would look tasteful anywhere.

'It's a runner for the hall,' explained Ella, looking fondly at her handiwork. 'Nice cheerful welcome it'll make, won't it?'

'Very colourful,' repeated Dimity, trying to be truthful without giving offence, a common predicament among well-mannered people.

'Let's have a cup of something,' suggested Ella, 'or a glass. Which, Dim?'

'Nothing for me,' said Dimity.

'Well, I must have a gasper. I'm cutting down but it's killing work, I can tell you.'

She rooted among the clutter of bright wools, magazines, ashtrays and two apples on the table, and found the battered tin which constituted her cigarette-making factory. As she rolled a very thin, and very untidy, cigarette, she asked Dimity about any news from Lulling.

'Charles is getting rather agitated about the Lilly girl at the Lovelocks.'

'What's the trouble? Slave driving?'

'Pretty well. They are adamant about how little they ask of her, but I gather she's already talking of giving in her notice. Gladys Lilly is pretty cross about it.'

'So why does Charles worry?'

'He feels he's letting down Anthony, you see. It was his idea to see if the Lovelocks would take on the girl. I don't think he realises how demanding they are.'

'Tell him from me to forget it. Half the time these things blow over. In any case, he acted in good faith and if things have gone wrong I don't see that it's any fault of his.'

Dimity took some comfort from these stout words.

'And now your news. I heard about the house at Barton. Have they seen it yet?'

'Next weekend, I believe. I hope something comes of it. This hanging about would drive me up the wall.'

Patience, Dimity knew, was not one of her old friend's strongest virtues, and was not surprised when she changed the subject to Muriel Fuller who had evidently called earlier in the day.

'What's known as "an excellent woman",' said Ella, shaking ash in the vague direction of the ashtray. 'She came here at eleven o'clock just when I was counting twenty-five holes on my canvas, and stayed until twenty-past twelve.'

'Was she collecting for something?'

'Yes, she always is. Something to do with an African mission. I gave her fifty pence and hoped she'd go, but I had to listen to the history, customs, marriage rites – and very unpleasant they were, I can tell you – not to mention how much they needed my money. She really is the most outstanding bore.'

'Oh, come!' protested gentle Dimity. 'She's only trying to do good.'

'All I can say,' said Ella forthrightly, 'is that doing good always seems to bring out the worst in people.'

Charles Henstock's concern about Doreen Lilly's position at the Misses Lovelock was shared by the ladies themselves. They certainly expected too much of the girl, and Violet at least recognised this.

All three sisters had been used to first-class resident help until the last ten or twelve years. They still expected the house to look immaculate, the meals punctually on the table, the laundry snowy and the prodigious array of silver in sparkling condition.

While their parents were alive, a cook, a general maid and a parlour maid had occupied the two attic bedrooms, and served the family devotedly from seven-thirty in the morning until ten-thirty at night.

It was hardly surprising that, with the sketchy domestic help now available, the house and its contents had lost their pristine look, and that the mingled fragrance of beeswax polish and home-baked bread had been superseded by a general fustiness.

The three old ladies did their best in the circumstances, but they were untrained in the art of housekeeping themselves, and had no knowledge of the effort needed to keep such an establishment as theirs in perfect order. They found Doreen's ministrations deplorably inadequate, and became more and more querulous.

'Surely she knows that the *bedroom* furniture needs polish on it,' protested Ada. 'Why just do the dining-table?'

'Because she sees it gets marked,' explained Violet. 'So she gets out the polish and tackles it.'

'And she hoovers for hours,' added Bertha, 'but never thinks to dust the skirting boards.'

'I have told her,' said Violet, 'but I don't think she takes in anything very readily.'

'And she's getting a little impertinent,' added Ada. 'Tossed her head at me when I pointed out the smears on the landing window, and said she had no head for heights. Why, dear old Hannah thought nothing of balancing a plank across the stairwell when she did the high parts of the landing and stairs.'

'Dear old Hannahs have gone,' said Violet shortly.

There was a heavy silence, broken at last by Ada. 'Well, what's to be done? Do we give her notice or not?'

'Who could we get in her place?' queried Bertha. 'You know how difficult it was to find Doreen.'

'Carry on as we are,' advised Violet. 'It wouldn't surprise me to find that *we* get given notice, not Doreen.'

And so the unsatisfactory state of affairs was left.

Gladys Lilly was equally worried about her daughter. She confided her fears to Nelly Piggott one evening before the Bingo session began.

'She's proper unsettled. Back to biting her nails, like she used to do as a little mite. Always was secretive. I tell you, I'm real worried about her.'

'I can't say I'm surprised,' said Nelly. 'That house of the Lovelock ladies would get anybody down. Can't she find some other place?'

'I doubt it. And to tell the truth, I'm not so sure the work is the real trouble.'

She looked around the hall, dropped her voice, and spoke conspiratorially to Nelly. 'I think she's fretting for that useless chap of hers. He's out again, we do know that. One of his pals told us. I've told Doreen time and time again to keep clear of him, but you know what girls are!'

Nelly and Gladys sighed heavily together over the short-comings of susceptible females.

'Things were different in our young days,' agreed Nelly. 'We took heed of what our parents said. And I was always told to bring home any young man who was being attentive.'

'Quite right,' approved Gladys.

But there were quite a few attentive young men in the youthful past of both ladies who had certainly not been presented to their parents. And these they dwelt on, secretly and fondly, as they settled down to Bingo.

Isobel had been busy on her neighbours' behalf and had arranged for the ladies to visit Ursula's house at the weekend.

She had offered to take them down in her car, but Dorothy was looking forward to her first long drive in the Metro, and turned down Isobel's invitation politely but firmly.

However, on Friday evening she spoke to Isobel over the hedge. She sounded somewhat agitated.

'Oh, Isobel! So glad to catch you. Poor Agnes is not too fit. In fact, she's been very much off-colour all this week, and I'm afraid she won't be able to face the journey tomorrow.'

'Oh dear! Well, shall I take you? I think we ought to go as Ursula has planned everything.'

'No, no! But if you don't mind coming with me, I should be most grateful. I feel quite competent about the *driving*, but should anything happen to the *engine*, I must admit total ignorance, although Ben did explain how it worked.'

'Well, I shan't be much better,' confessed Isobel, 'but I could always go for help. And of course I should love to keep you company, and introduce you to Ursula.'

It was Harold who pointed out later that this was the heaven-sent opportunity to broach the delicate subject of the tabby cat.

'I suppose so,' said Isobel doubtfully. 'On a straight piece of road where she won't get too agitated.'

And so, soon after ten o'clock on a glorious June morning the two ladies set out, leaving Agnes to enjoy the peace of the school house and a possible visit from the cat.

It was true that she had been remarkably quiet, even by her standards, since her outburst. The headache had never really departed. She was sleeping badly, and occasionally found her-self trembling violently.

She did not intend to bother Dr John Lovell with these minor ailments, recognising only too well that they were the result of all the worry over the cat, the future, the extra labours involved in clearing out the debris of many years' teaching, and general anxiety about her relationship with Dorothy, as retirement drew ever closer.

But she was relieved not to have to make the journey. She was quite sure that Dorothy was a good driver, but then there were so many people on the roads who were not. She did not mind admitting that she was most unhappy in the passenger seat, and foresaw all sorts of appalling situations involving hospitals, firemen cutting one out of the wreckage, bodies and blood strewn over the road, followed by interminable court cases about two years later, when one could not reasonably be expected to remember a thing, not to mention permanent injury with possibly one or more limbs missing.

While Agnes was quietly pottering about with the duster, hoping for a few minutes with the cat, Dorothy and Isobel were enjoying the countryside on their way south, and the latter was trying to pluck up courage to approach the subject of Agnes's unhappiness.

Luckily, it was Dorothy who brought up the matter.

'She's too conscientious,' said Dorothy. 'Everything has to be done perfectly, and of course she gets over-tired. I shall be mightily glad when we've finished at the school. Of course, we shall find it all a great change, and I think Agnes worries more than I do about missing the children. She needs something to love. More than I do, I must admit.'

Isobel took a deep breath. The road was straight, and there was very little traffic.

'That's why she is so devoted to the stray cat,' she began.

'I know she is fond of it—' said Dorothy.

'But I don't think you realise *how* fond,' broke in Isobel, and began to tell her about the sad scene she had encountered behind the garden hedge.

Dorothy listened in silence, and then drew in quietly at the next lay-by.

'Tell me more,' she said, her expression very grave. She shifted sideways in her seat so that she could study Isobel's face as she unfolded the tale.

Isobel, taking the bull by the horns, spared her nothing, even recounting Agnes's anguished doubts about their future happiness together.

'It's so little to ask,' went on Isobel, 'and there is so much to lose. She would be most unhappy if she really took this idiotic step of staying behind. From the practical point of view, I don't think she could manage financially. And then she would be so lonely.'

'And so would I,' said Dorothy. 'I can't imagine why I have been so dense, and so thoughtless. I honestly had no idea that she felt like this. It makes me want to turn round straightaway, drive back, and apologise.'

'Well, we can't do that now,' said Isobel practically, 'as Ursula is expecting us. But I felt that you should know how Agnes is feeling. I love her dearly, and have for years. I should hate her to throw away her future with you.'

'And so should I. I've always enjoyed her companionship enormously. The cat will be invited in tonight, and made welcome.'

Isobel gave a great sigh.

'You know,' said Dorothy, looking at her steadily, 'you must have dreaded telling me all this. What a brave woman you are!'

'It's true,' admitted Isobel, 'and I've still to face Agnes's dismay when she finds what I've done. But I can truthfully say I'm glad it's all in the open now.'

'I shall never forgive myself,' said Dorothy, starting the car, and continuing the journey. 'To have been so *cruel* to my most loyal friend!'

'As long as you make it plain that you are truthfully happy to include the cat in the household,' said Isobel, 'I think everything will sort itself out splendidly. And there's no need to abase yourself too much with Agnes. Least said soonest mended. It would only upset her, and if she realises that you have simply had a change of heart about the cat, all should be well.'

'I shall get Ben Curdle to make a cat flap in the back door,' said Dorothy, adjusting to this new situation with her usual common sense. 'And I propose to buy Agnes a splendid cat basket in Barton, and take it back with us this evening. What about that?'

'You couldn't make a more generous gesture,' Isobel assured her.

Meanwhile, at Thrush Green, Winnie Bailey had just welcomed her nephew Richard, who had arrived, as was usual, quite un-announced.

'I had to return some books to Aubrey Hengist-Williams,' he explained. 'He rang up last night and said that he wanted them urgently. Getting some lecture notes ready for next term.'

'Isn't that the great professor? I think I've had a glimpse of him on Open University on television when I've been trying to get the right time.'

'Well, he's on television, I know, but that hardly makes him great,' replied Richard. 'Actually, I've always thought him a very silly fellow, and I never have been able to subscribe to his theory on the side-effects of nuclear fission. Have you?'

Winnie smiled patiently. 'Richard dear, I am completely ignorant of nuclear fission, let alone its side-effects, but tell me all about the family.'

She did not like to add that both Richard and Fenella had left in a black mood on the last occasion, but hoped that things were now amicably settled.

'Oh, they are fine,' said Richard vaguely. 'Fenella seems happier now that Roger has gone.'

'Roger? Gone? Where?'

'Spain, I think. He and his wife have made it up, and gone to live abroad permanently. I think I helped in the decision.'

'I must say it seems all for the best,' agreed Winnie. 'Did you persuade him?'

'I punched him on the nose,' said Richard, with evident satisfaction. 'I went into the gallery to get some drawing pins, and he was kissing Fenella's left ear. I didn't like it, so I punched him.'

'Then what?'

'Oh, he bled rather a lot. And all over the gallery carpet which was a nuisance, but Fenella and I sponged it with cold water after he'd gone, and it's not too noticeable.'

'But what did Fenella say?'

'She said we could stand a stool over it, and no one would notice.'

'No. I mean about Roger going?'

'She hasn't said anything about it. I think she was getting rather fed up with him drooping about in the gallery all the time. He was an awful drip, you know. I should have punched him years ago.'

'Yes, well, I can see your point,' said Winnie reasonably, 'but has this made any difference to your future plans? No chance, I suppose, of persuading Fenella to come to Thrush Green to live?'

'Fenella,' replied Richard, 'does not respond to persuasion. I do not propose to punch my wife on the nose, but sometimes I think it would be the only way to make her change her mind.'

'So the school house won't be seeing you as its new owners?'

'I'm afraid not. The fact is, Aunt Win, the gallery is Fenella's life, and I'm away such a lot that it would be foolish and silly to deprive her of it. As far as I can see we shall be staying where we are until I retire. And then, too, I expect,' he added resignedly.

'I'm sorry, but not surprised,' said Winnie. 'It was obvious that she did not want to come here, and she would have been resentful about leaving the gallery anyway. I'm sure things have worked out for the best, and now that Roger has gone she may settle down more happily.'

'At the moment she's busy getting an exhibition of abstract art in the seventies and eighties ready for next month.'

He began to fish in his pockets. 'She gave me an invitation for you, but I expect I left it with Aubrey's stuff by mistake. I'll send you one by post.'

'Don't trouble, dear. I find a trip to town rather too much these days, and my knowledge of abstract art, of any date, is on a par with my grasp of nuclear fission. So just give her my thanks and love.'

'I must be getting back,' said Richard, standing up.

'Won't you stop for lunch? Take pot luck?'

'No. I promised to take Timothy to the zoo this afternoon. He's fallen in love with a baby giraffe there.'

'That sounds harmless enough,' observed Winnie.

They went to the front gate together, and Richard paused for a moment to look across the green at the school house.

'It would have been fun,' he commented wistfully. 'But not worth losing a wife for, I suppose.'

'Definitely not,' said Winnie. 'You take care of what you've got, my boy. And don't get too pugnacious. One day you might get punched back!'

'If I started on Fenella,' replied Richard, 'I certainly should!'

He climbed into the car, grinned cheerfully, and drove away.

It was half-past nine when the two ladies arrived back from Barton-on-Sea. Dorothy had insisted on taking Isobel to have a remarkably delicious dinner on the way home, after telephoning Agnes to explain the delay, and over it they had discussed the pros and cons of putting in an offer for Ursula's property.

'Do come in,' pressed Dorothy. 'I know Agnes would love to see you.'

But Isobel declined, saying that Harold would be expecting her, and secretly feeling that she would like to have a night's sleep before facing any recriminations which might come from gentle Agnes after her own exposures.

Agnes heard the garage doors slam, and hastened to the window. She saw her friend coming up the path, and carrying an awkward circular object. It appeared to be made of wicker-work, and was giving Dorothy some difficulty, tucked as it was under one arm.

Agnes hurried to open the door for her, and met her on the threshold.

Dorothy smiled and held out the basket in silence.

'For me?' quavered Agnes, deeply perplexed.

'For our cat,' said Dorothy.

17. Summer Heat

July brought a spell of welcome sunshine. The first week was greeted by all in Lulling and Thrush Green with immense pleasure.

The flower borders burst into colour. Oriental poppies, pink and red, flaunted their papery petals above marigolds, godetia, penstemon and pansies, vying only in height with the pink and purple spires of lupins and larkspur.

In less than a week, it seemed, summer had arrived in full splendour. Deckchairs were brought out from sheds and garages, rustic seats were brushed clean, bird-baths needed filling daily, and cats stretched themselves luxuriously in the heat.

Prudent housewives took the opportunity of washing winter woollens, blankets, bedspreads and curtains. Window cleaning was much in evidence, cars were hosed clean of past dirt and lawn mowers whirred.

Out in the meadows around Thrush Green the cattle gathered under clumps of trees, welcoming the benison of cool shade. Their tails twitched tirelessly against the constant torment of flies.

In the sparse shade thrown by the dry-stone walls, sheep rested, flanks heaving rhythmically, in the heat of the day. Butterflies hovered above the nettles and thistles, or alighted on the warm stones to flaunt the beauty of their wings. The air was murmurous with insects of all kinds, and bumble bees crawled languorously from one meadow flower to the next.

In the distance, Lulling Woods shimmered in the heat haze. The little river Pleshey moved even more sluggishly than usual, only the trailing willow branches, it seemed, disturbing the glassy mirror of its placid surface.

At Thrush Green, the inhabitants of Rectory Cottages either took to the shade of the chestnut trees or drew their curtains and lay on their sofas.

Tom and Polly were among the former seekers after coolness, and sat contentedly surveying the peaceful scene before them. Both man and dog relished the warmth which comforted their old bones, and Tom hoped that this spell of splendid weather would last a long, long time. He intended to stay there, his head in the shade, and his thin shanks stretched out into the sunshine, until the children came out from school and then he would think about returning slowly to make himself a cup of tea at his home.

It was a good life, he reflected, and much better than he had found it when he lived by the water in the Pleshey valley. He had been happy enough while he was still active, but looking back he realised that the damp cottage had been partly to blame for his increasing rheumatism. Since the move to higher ground and to the warmth of the new house he had felt very much better, and knew that the care he received there from the kindly wardens contributed to his well-being. Any aches and pains now were due, he knew ruefully, to advancing age, and there was little one could do to fight against that.

Meanwhile, he drowsed in the heat, one gnarled hand resting on the glossy head of his beloved Polly beside him.

At the school the children looked expectantly at the wall clock. Would it never be time to go home, to be free, to grab bathing things and rush down to the shallow pool in an arm of the river Pleshey?

The backs of their thighs stuck to their wooden seats. Their sunburnt arms smelt of fresh-cooked biscuits, and sweat moistened their brows.

In Agnes's terrapin classroom it was hotter than ever. The door was propped open with one of the diminutive wooden armchairs, giving a view of the shimmering playground and the Shoosmiths' hedge beyond, but little relief from the heat.

Agnes, clad in a blue checked gingham frock and Clarks sandals worn over lightweight summer stockings, read *The Tale of Jeremy Fisher*, hoping that its background of rain and ponds and water-lilies would give some refreshment on this afternoon of searing heat, but she too was relieved when the hands of the clock reached three-thirty and she could let her young charges go free.

It was very peaceful when at last she was left alone. She locked her desk and the cupboards, brought in the little armchair, and closed the door. She stood there for a moment, looking at the well-loved view towards Lulling Woods in the blue distance.

In this brief pause between activities, she suddenly became conscious of living completely in the present. It came but rarely. One was either looking back anxiously wondering which duties had been left undone, or forward to those duties which lay before one.

Now, in temporary limbo, she felt the sun on her arms, heard a frenzied bee tapping on the window for escape, smelt the dark red roses which stood on the desk, and saw, with unusual clarity, the iridescent feathers of the wood pigeon pecking in the playground. All her senses seemed sharpened. It was a moment of great intensity, never to be forgotten.

The spell was broken by a child opening the classroom door.

'Forgot me book,' he said, retrieving it from the top of the cupboard, and then vanishing.

Little Miss Fogerty sighed. She was going to miss Thrush Green school sorely. She wondered if Dorothy had any real misgivings about the ending of a long and successful career. They had, of course, talked of such things in a general way, but latterly so many day-to-day problems had beset them that little had been said of the deeper emotions.

It was only natural, Agnes supposed. They were both women who abhorred emotional outbursts, and kept their private feelings well under control. Maybe it was a good thing that they had so much to think about from the practical point of view. Time enough to be sentimental when term was over, Agnes told herself robustly.

Meanwhile, she would hurry across to the school house and put on the kettle. Perhaps a few tomato sandwiches would be pleasant? They could have tea in the shade of the apple tree, and look out for the dear little cat, still to be named.

'*Our* cat,' said Agnes aloud, with infinite satisfaction.

She left the classroom and made her way home, happy in remembering Dorothy's generosity of spirit, and looking forward to the future.

To Agnes's delight, the tabby cat pushed its way through the Shoosmiths' hedge and approached the two ladies cautiously, as they sat in the shade relishing their rest and the tomato sandwiches.

When it was within a few yards of the garden seat, it sat down, very upright, very dignified, its eyes fixed upon Agnes.

'It really is a handsome cat,' commented Dorothy in a low voice. The cat was still wary of her, which was understandable, but it was rather hard, she thought, to be so steadily ignored, when Agnes could now call her new friend to her side without much effort.

'It's only to be expected,' said Agnes, reading Dorothy's thoughts. 'After all, I have been feeding it for some time now. Before long, it will come to you just as readily. I feel sure.'

The cat yawned, displaying a healthy pink tongue and sharp teeth.

'It's time it had a name,' said Dorothy. 'What do you think? It's obviously male. We had a very sweet white cat once called Butch.'

Agnes looked pained. 'I don't think this one looks like a Butch. I rather thought of Tim, after Tiger Tim, you know – he was striped like this one.'

Dorothy nodded approval. 'What pleasure we had from that

comic! I was a great devotee of Mrs Bruin. Perhaps that's why I took up teaching?'

'Possibly,' agreed Agnes. She poured some milk into her saucer and put it down gently beside her Clarks sandals.

'Tim! Tim!' she called softly.

Dorothy held her breath.

The cat came fearlessly to the saucer and began to lap quickly.

'Poor thing,' said Dorothy in a whisper. 'This heat has made it terribly thirsty.'

'You see,' said Agnes happily, 'it really did answer to its name.'

'I think,' said Dorothy, with a hint of malice, 'that it would have come if you had simply said: "Milk! Milk!" '

'Possibly,' said Agnes equably. 'And I think we ought to call it *him* now, don't you?'

'Without a doubt,' agreed Dorothy, helping herself to another sandwich.

Later that evening, as the evening air cooled, the two ladies discussed their future housing plans. Things had now got to the interesting stage of dealing with something that they both wanted.

Agnes had found herself charmed by Ursula's aunt's property when Dorothy had taken her to see it one weekend. She liked its sunny aspect, its small neat garden, the mature shrubs, and the fact that there were no exhausting hills in the neighbourhood. She had not admitted to anyone that she was beginning to find the steep hill from Lulling rather more than she could cope with now that her arthritis was taking hold.

Inside, the house was light and warm. There were two good-sized bedrooms, a large sitting-room and kitchen, and what was called by Ursula's estate agent 'a morning room'. This, it was agreed, should be Dorothy's study, though what she intended to study was not stated.

'But it would be handy to keep my desk in there,' said Dorothy, 'with the bills and things. Besides, if someone should call particularly to speak to just one of us, it would be somewhere to take them if the television happened to be on.'

'An excellent idea,' agreed Agnes.

The big kitchen, they decided, was where they would eat.

'At our age,' said Dorothy, 'we don't need a dining-room anyway. Any visitors will be invited to a cup of tea, or a glass of sherry. If we are *retired people*, then we have retired from cooking large meals as well as from school-teaching.'

Agnes admired such masterly forethought.

'But what about Ray and Kathleen?' she ventured.

'We take them out to one of the excellent hotels nearby,' said Dorothy firmly.

They had gone ahead. A Lulling estate agent, used by both Harold and Isobel in their earlier house-hunting, was engaged to make a survey of the property, to negotiate an acceptable price, and young Mr Venables, now well into his seventies, had agreed to deal with the conveyancing and any other legal matters.

'And now,' Dorothy had said, 'they can all get on with it while we concentrate on the end of term. I want to leave everything ship-shape for the next head. The poor young man has never had a headship before. I only hope that he realises what he is taking on.'

From the way she spoke, one would have thought that the new headmaster was about to undertake the running of the United Nations single-handed, instead of a small and efficient country school, but Agnes observed a prudent silence, knowing from experience that Dorothy occasionally enjoyed seeing herself as an unsung heroine overcoming fearful odds.

The date of the move was something which gave the two ladies some concern. There seemed to be so many ifs and buts about the timing. If the survey proved satisfactory. If the legal arrangements went forward smoothly. If the alterations to the new house were finished. If they could stay where they were until everything was ready for the move. All these matters gave the ladies much worry, but two facts also gave them comfort.

The education authority was obliging about the timing of their departure, simply stating that as soon as the house was on the open market would be soon enough, and implying that this contingency was not expected to occur until late in the year.

The other factor was the attitude of the incoming headmaster, who made it clear that he would be making the journey from his present home, some twenty miles away, while he looked for a house in Lulling or Thrush Green, at his leisure.

The two ladies had hoped that he might put in an offer for the school house, but this did not happen. Whether he, or perhaps his wife, just disliked their much-loved abode, no one knew. Perhaps, Agnes surmised, he did not like 'living over the shop?'

'Always been good enough for us!' Dorothy had snorted.

But she agreed that it was a great relief to know that they

would not be thrown out on the last day of term, like orphans in a storm.

The sunny spell of weather continued unabated, and the first rapturous welcome to the heat began to turn to disenchantment. The flaunting poppies dropped their silky petals. The lupin spires turned rusty. Brown patches appeared on lawns, and cracks grew wider on well-trodden earth.

Stern notices appeared in the local press about the use of hoses and sprinklers in the gardens, with dire threats of the fines to be imposed on malefactors.

The river Pleshey dwindled visibly, exposing fast-drying mud banks, and giving forth unpleasant odours in those stretches where the river weed dried in the heat. The cattle took to standing in the water, tails ever-twitching, and heads tossing to scare away the clouds of flies.

Dotty's new plants languished by the pool, and gave her great concern.

Albert, when appealed to, took a strong line. 'We got plenty of rain-water in them butts,' he told her, 'and we be going to use it.'

'But when that has gone, Albert?'

'We use tap.'

'But Albert, you know it is forbidden.'

'Only them hoses and sprinklers the paper say. It don't say nothin' about watering cans.'

'But it is just as wrong, surely?'

'I'll slip down after dark. What the eye don't see, the heart don't grieve over.'

Dotty, brought up on the stern precepts of her father, looked unhappy.

'Think of them poor plants,' urged Albert. 'Ain't hardly got to know the selves before this hits 'em. It's cruel to let 'em die for a drop of water.'

'I do see that,' agreed Dotty doubtfully. 'But I still dislike breaking the law.'

'That ain't the law, that old stuff from the local. Just some jumped-up know-nothin' like Councillor Figgins! You leave it to me.'

'Well, I only hope it rains before the rain-water butts dry up,' said Dotty, seeing that Albert was adamant. 'Otherwise, I can see us both in court.'

In Lulling High Street the sun awnings gave a gay continental look to the Cotswold scene. People kept to the shady side of the road. Cars were too hot to touch. The trees were beginning to turn yellow, and dust eddied in the gutters and veiled the window-sills.

At The Fuchsia Bush a brisk trade in ices and lemonade took the place of the usual tea and coffee, and Nelly Piggott found that the demand for cakes at teatime had much decreased.

'Too hot to eat,' she told her friend Gladys Lilly who had called in for a vanilla ice-cream after her shopping.

'Too hot to sleep too,' said Gladys. 'I don't get off until about two these nights. In fact, I usually go for a walk, just before it gets dark, to cool off.'

'Well, walk up our way sometime,' suggested Nelly. 'It's quite fresh sitting out on the green once the sun's gone down.'

'Thank you, dear. I might do that. Not tonight though, I've got a heap of ironing to do. Doreen is everlasting changing that child's clothes, but don't offer to do the ironing of 'em.'

'She settled down now?'

'Far from it. Seems proper restless, but it's no good my questioning her. She shuts up like a clam. Funny girl, though she is me own flesh and blood.'

She scooped up the last melted spoonful, and stood up. 'Probably pop up tomorrow night, all being well. About nine, say?'

'Suits me,' said Nelly, and the two friends returned to their separate duties.

*

Ben Curdle had made a neat square hole in the back door of the school house, and had fitted a new cat flap for the convenience of Tim. Needless to say, the cat completely ignored this innovation, and continued to wait near the french windows or by the dustbin.

'He doesn't seem to understand it,' said Agnes, much bewildered. 'Ben has been so patient, propping up the flap with a cork in the join so that Tim can see through, but he still won't venture in.'

'He's bound to be over-cautious,' Dorothy said reassuringly, 'having had to look after himself for so long, and exposed to all sorts of dangers.'

'That's true,' agreed Agnes.

'And he's not likely to come in during this heat wave. He seems to prefer that cool patch under the holly bush.'

'Yes. I do see that. It's just that I did so hope to get him used to indoor life before we go away.'

'At the rate we're going,' replied Dorothy grimly, 'he'll have until Christmas to get used to that cat flap. Sometimes I think lawyers and estate agents could do with a squib behind them.'

'They do seem a trifle dilatory,' agreed Agnes, expressing the understatement of the year.

St Andrew's clock was striking nine when Gladys Lilly emerged from her front gate and turned left.

The house stood in a cul-de-sac not far from the hill up to Thrush Green. At one end of the short road were some allotments, the gateway being overshadowed by a large elder tree.

Gladys could smell the sharp scent of its great flat blossoms which glimmered like a hundred moons in the gloaming. She noticed too, a shabby van drawn up in the shadow of the tree, but took little heed of it, imagining that one of the allotment holders might have brought some bulky article such as wire-netting or a sack of manure to his site.

She strode briskly away, and was at Nelly's within ten minutes. Nelly welcomed her with a cup of tea, and the two ladies agreed that it was amazing how refreshing tea was whatever the weather.

'And how's Albert?' enquired Gladys politely.

'Fair enough,' said Nelly. 'He's next door, so he's all right.'

She rose to collect the cups and saucers, and stacked them neatly on the draining board.

'Well, let's have a bit of air, shall we?' she said, leading the way.

They settled themselves on a nearby bench, and admired the remains of a spectacular sunset. Bands of lemon and pink glowed above Lulling Woods, and nearer at hand the lamps shone from the windows of The Two Pheasants and the school house. Across the green, Mrs Bailey's light winked, and nearby the lamplight shone from Ella Bembridge's cottage windows.

It was all very peaceful. There was no one else about. The children's swings hung motionless in the still air. A pigeon roosted on Nathaniel Patten's shoulder, and only a tiny scuffling sound from the nearby churchyard told of some small nocturnal animal about its business.

The scent from a fine bank of tobacco plants in Harold Shoosmith's garden added to the contentment of the two friends who sat in companionable silence, enjoying the rest from their work and the welcome freshness of the cool air, after the heat of the day.

The evening star appeared on the horizon. Gladys gave a satisfied sigh, as St Andrew's clock began to strike ten.

'Well, I suppose it's time I was going, Nelly. I've thoroughly enjoyed it here. Perhaps I could come up again sometimes, while this heat's on?'

'Any time,' said Nelly. 'It's good to have a bit of company. As you can see, our Albert don't give me much of an evening.'

'Ah well!' said Gladys diplomatically. 'We all knows what the men are like, and in any case I hear he's doing a good job down at Miss Harmer's. I expect he needs a break after that.'

She rose to her feet, and Nelly walked with her to the brow of the hill. The lights of Lulling winked below, and the air was beginning to stir with a light breeze.

'Goodnight, my dear,' said Gladys. 'It's been lovely. Now, you pop in and see me one evening. Promise?'

'I'll do that,' said Nelly.

It was during Gladys's hour of absence, as dusk was falling, that Doreen Lilly emerged cautiously from her mother's house.

She stood in the shelter of the front porch looking about her, but all was quiet. The neighbours were by their television sets. The allotment holders had finished their labours, locked their tools in the little sheds dotted about their plots, and had gone home.

Doreen sped across to the shabby van, now hardly discernible in the near-darkness. The scent of the elder flowers, mingling with the cloying sweetness of the privet blooms nearby, was over-powering.

A tall young man emerged from the driver's seat, and the two embraced. They both got into the van, Doreen looking anxiously up to a bedroom window where a nightlight was giving a glow-worm illumination for the comfort of her young child.

All was as quiet as the grave. No one was in sight, and after ten minutes Doreen emerged, and returned to the shelter of the porch.

The van turned and drove off, and Doreen was busy at the kitchen sink, washing her hair, when Gladys Lilly returned.

'Nice to see friends, isn't it?' she said conversationally.

'I suppose so,' said Doreen, groping for a towel. 'By the way, I'm off to London tomorrow to see Jane.'

'Well, you might have said!' protested her mother.

'I forgot. Be back Sunday night anyway. It means catching the nine-thirty tomorrow, but as it's Saturday I don't have to go to them Lovelocks.'

'Maybe it'll do you good,' said her mother. 'You've seemed a bit peaky lately.'

'And so would you if you had to work with them old slave-drivers.'

There was a note of vindictiveness in her daughter's tone which distressed Gladys.

'Well, you'd best get your bit of packing done tonight,' she said. 'Want a hand up to the station tomorrow?'

'No. I've got the pushchair, and I shan't take much.'

'Be nice to see Jane again,' continued Gladys. 'She was good to you when you first went to work with the Reverend Bull. If you should see him, give him my respectful regards. He's a good man, even if he is Church,' said Gladys with commendable magnanimity.

But Doreen made no reply.

18. AN INTRUDER

Gladys Lilly was not the only one to have difficulty in sleeping during the heat wave.

Violet Lovelock, always the lightest sleeper of the three sisters, found herself listening for the chimes of St John's church throughout most of the night.

At two o'clock, on that same night which had seen Gladys Lilly's visit to Thrush Green, Violet became conscious of unusual sounds below. Could she have left the door ajar? But then, on such a still night, would the door have moved?

She crept to the window and looked out. Lulling High Street was deserted except for a white dog, ghostly in the darkness, which was padding by the closed shops on the other side of the road, intent on its own affairs. The lime tree nearby was already beginning to flower, and through the open window its heady fragrance drifted.

There was another bump from below, and Violet froze into rigidity. Could there possibly be a burglar in the house?

Already the Lovelock ladies had experienced this upsetting occurrence. On that occasion they had been in the garden, picking gooseberries, when some opportunist thief had tried the front door, found it open, and whisked much of the silver so generously displayed into a bag, and vanished. Little of that haul had been recovered, but the beautiful rose bowl presented to their father had been replaced on the dining-room sideboard on its return.

It would certainly prove a temptation to any dishonest intruder, thought Violet. And there was so much else in the house. The drawing-room occasional tables were laden with the silver knick-knacks collected over the years, and the Queen Anne coffee set was permanently on display on its exquisite silver tray on the table just outside her door on the landing.

At this horrid thought Violet became thoroughly alarmed. Should she rouse her sisters? They would not be best pleased if there were no real cause for such stern measures. Violet, despite the brave front she put on things when dealing with Ada and Bertha, was secretly still in awe of her older sisters, and hesitated to incur their wrath.

She put on her dressing gown and slippers, listening for every untoward sound, and crept to the door. The trayful of silver on the landing table still glimmered comfortingly, she was relieved to see.

With extreme caution, Violet began to descend the stairs. The fourth one from the top was liable to creak, as she well knew, and she stepped delicately upon it. At the same time, there was a metallic clanging sound from the dining-room, and Violet froze into stillness.

It was suddenly very quiet. Should she go on, or go back, or wake Bertha and Ada after all? If only there were an upstairs telephone she would dial 999 and let the police come, even if it turned out to be a groundless scare.

But, of course, one telephone in the house had seemed gross extravagance to the Lovelocks, and that was kept in the hall where everyone could hear at least half of the conversation, whilst enduring the cross-draught from the front door and the dining-room. There was no help there, thought poor Violet.

After a few minutes, which seemed like hours to Violet, immobile on the stairs, the noises began again, though more quietly.

Violet, who was no coward, descended firmly, intent on confronting the intruder. She traversed the hall, heard an almighty crash, and flung open the dining-room door.

She was just in time to see a figure dashing across the kitchen, which was beyond the dining-room, and clambering out of the window. Within seconds there was the sound of metal jangling, receding footsteps, and a minute or two later, the sound of a car engine revving furiously.

Violet found herself shaking violently. She went into the dining-room, and found the silver on the sideboard had gone, and the two drawers containing the heavy silver cutlery, up-turned and empty on the floor. The kitchen window still swung gently to and fro from the violent exit of the marauder.

Violet, with commendable control, remembered the earlier burglary, and forbore to touch anything. Instead, she went to the telephone, and was about to dial for help, when her two sisters appeared at the head of the stairs. Their skimpy locks were plaited into thin grey braids, and both wrinkled faces looked extremely vexed.

'What on earth, Violet, are you doing at this hour?' said Bertha.

'Are you ill, dear?' enquired Ada. 'You woke us up, you know.'

'We've been burgled,' said Violet flatly. 'I'm just about to ring the police.'

'*Burgled*? Not again!' cried Ada.

'But will there be anyone at the police station at this hour?' cried Bertha.

Violet, telephone to ear, twirled the dial forcefully.

'Yes, *again*,' she replied. 'And naturally the police should be informed immediately, and *of course* there will be someone on duty, Bertha!'

The two old ladies descended the stairs and stood one on each side of Violet.

'Yes,' she was saying. 'Miss Violet Lovelock speaking. I want to inform you of a burglary here. About ten minutes ago. The thief made his getaway in a car or van.'

'I don't like that word "getaway",' complained Ada. 'It sounds American.'

'We shall expect an officer here immediately,' said Violet.

'No, of course nothing has been touched. We know the correct procedure in cases like this.'

She put down the telephone.

'Really, Violet dear,' said Bertha admiringly, 'you coped with that very competently. Shall I make us a hot drink?'

'Better not,' said Violet, much mollified by Bertha's appreciation of her actions. 'Let's wait until the police arrive. But it might be as well to get dressed,' she added. 'It's going to be a long night, I fear.'

Another cloudless day dawned, and the country awoke to banner headlines in the press telling it that THE DROUGHT IS NOW OFFICIAL and that penalties for wasting water would be severe.

It also had some distressing pictures of dried-up water-beds with stranded fish, sheep and cattle dying of thirst, wilted crops and various other horrid sights guaranteed to curdle the blood of breakfast-time readers.

'I can never understand,' remarked Ella Bembridge to Winnie Bailey, when they met on Thrush Green, 'why a nation which is fanatically absorbed with its weather conditions is so bad at organising them.'

'How do you mean?'

'Well, take last spring. There we were, up to our hocks in puddles, the Pleshey water-meadows brimming over, all our water-butts overflowing, and a few months later, here we are, being told we'll be clapped in irons for watering the lettuces.'

'I think it's all right to water lettuces with *used* water,' Winnie began, but was swept aside by Ella's eloquence.

'And look at snow!' declaimed Ella unrealistically. 'The Canadians and Americans, and the Swiss for that matter, get yards of the stuff overnight, and their trains continue to run, and the children get to school, and the milk's delivered. And what happens here?'

'You tell me,' said Winnie equably, knowing that she would anyway.

'Two inches and the country's paralysed! No buses, no trains, no deliveries! Chaos!'

'I thought everyone coped very well last winter,' said Winnie. 'I know we never went short of milk, and the postman never missed once.'

'You've a much nicer nature than I have,' said Ella. 'You look on the bright side. I don't. Sometimes I think I'll write to the papers.'

And with this dark threat she stumped off homewards.

On Sunday evening Gladys Lilly was a little annoyed at the non-appearance of her daughter and grandson. A piece of smoked haddock was simmering gently, awaiting poached eggs on top for the two travellers, but at nine-thirty Gladys ate the fish herself, and became resigned to the fact that Doreen would probably turn up the next morning in time for work.

Nothing happened. Now becoming agitated, Gladys called at the Misses Lovelocks' house to find out more. The gossip about the burglary had not reached Gladys.

She found the ladies in frosty mood, far from pleased at Doreen's dereliction of duties.

'We have had a most upsetting weekend,' Ada told her. 'And we were relying on Doreen to help us clear up after a burglary on Friday night.'

'Oh, my lor', m'm,' gasped Gladys. 'I'm real sorry about that! Did they take much?'

'Far too much,' said Bertha.

'And what's more,' added Ada, 'the police think that *some-one* helped the intruder by leaving the kitchen window ajar.'

The full impact of this last remark did not dawn on poor Gladys until she was next door at The Fuchsia Bush, steadying her nerves with a cup of Darjeeling tea.

Nelly Piggott spared a few minutes from her labours in the kitchen to offer consolation.

'Don't take no notice of them old tabbies,' she told her friend. 'How could your Doreen have been mixed up in it? She was washing her hair when you got home, and then you know she went up to bed. You'll be her alibi, if they make accusations against her.'

'Well, I've no wish to be whatever it is, but I can certainly say she was home when Miss Violet saw that chap.'

'That's right,' agreed Nelly, secretly relishing this drama.

'But where on earth has the girl got to today?' wailed Gladys, setting down her cup. 'Why ain't she turned up? Should I tell the police?'

'I wouldn't get the law in yet,' replied Nelly prudently. 'You wait and see if she turns up today. If she's not home by this evening I'd telephone this Jane friend of hers. Perhaps she's been took bad.'

'In *hospital*, d'you reckon?'

Poor Mrs Lilly went white at the thought of her daughter in one of those dreaded institutions.

'Not necessarily,' said Nelly, feeling she may have gone too far. 'Perhaps just a bilious attack.'

'But I don't know Jane's telephone number, nor where she lives, come to that. She just worked nearby where our Doreen did. For the Reverend Bull, you know.'

'Well, he'd know Jane's address.'

Gladys Lilly was now near to tears, and Nelly's heart was touched.

'Look here, I must get back to the kitchen. Them new girls are making a proper pig's breakfast of the flaky pastry. But if she ain't turned up by closing time, you come in here and I'll get the Reverend's number from our Mr Henstock. Then we'll go on from there. All right?'

She patted her friend's shoulder encouragingly. Gladys mopped up her tears, and tried to smile.

'That's what I'll do, Nelly. And thank you for being a true friend.'

Still sniffing, she went to pay her bill. Rosa, one of the two haughty waitresses, was consumed with curiosity, as Gladys departed.

'What's up then?' she enquired of her colleague who was engrossed in filing her scarlet fingernails rather too close to a tray of meringues.

'Search me,' was the answer. 'But we do see a bit of life here, don't we?'

It was six o'clock before Nelly and Gladys met again. The owner of The Fuchsia Bush, Mrs Peters, had gone home early in the afternoon to totter to bed with a blinding migraine. The rest of the staff had also gone, leaving Nelly to lock up the premises, and this she was doing when a tearful Mrs Lilly appeared.

'No sign of her,' she cried. 'D'you think I could ring Mr Henstock?'

'You come in and sit down,' said Nelly, unlocking the door, 'and I'll get the number.'

Charles Henstock was much perturbed to hear of Doreen's disappearance. He supplied Anthony Bull's telephone number, and expressed the hope that all would be well.

'I feel quite guilty about all this,' he told Dimity. 'I know that Anthony would never blame me for any trouble that has cropped up, but I wish I hadn't suggested her to the Lovelock girls. I fear that they may have overworked her.'

'You did what you thought was right at the time,' Dimity comforted him. 'After all, you were not to know how matters would turn out.'

Meanwhile, Gladys Lilly rang Anthony Bull, who said that he would go down the road immediately to make enquiries of his neighbour, and would ring back.

The two friends sat in the empty restaurant awaiting the call.

'I must pay for these telephone calls,' said Gladys. 'I'd feel better about it, if I could. And what about Albert's tea? You ought to be getting off home by rights. What a nuisance I am!'

Nelly did her best to allay Gladys's fears. By now, she too was imagining the worst – abduction, seduction, incarceration, even murder!

'They say,' said Gladys, 'that Miss Violet said the chap was exceptionally tall and had cropped hair. Head like a bullet, she said, though she never saw much else.'

'Which way did he go, I wonder?'

'Ran off down the garden to that lane as runs along the back of these places here. That's when she had a glimpse of him. Must have left his car out there, I suppose.'

'Well, he'd need a car or something to carry all that stuff from the Lovelocks! Never see so much silver under one roof in all the time I was in service,' said Nelly. 'I used to dread silver-cleaning days in that place, I can tell you.'

At this moment, the telephone rang, and Gladys leapt to answer it.

Nelly watched her face crumple as she listened to the voice at the other end of the line.

'Oh dear, sir! What a terrible thing. Now I really don't know which way to turn.'

There were soothing sounds coming from the other end, while tears began to course down poor Gladys's face.

'Yes, sir. I'm sure you're right. It's just that I'm that upset that she told me a lie.'

She mopped her face with a handkerchief. The other hand quivered as it held the telephone. Nelly's kind heart was touched at this display of motherly concern.

'Well, thank you, sir, for all your help,' sniffed Gladys. 'You've been real kind, and I shan't forget it. I'll do what you say. I'm sure you're right.'

There were a few more murmurs from the other end, and Gladys put down the receiver.

'She never went to Jane's at all,' sobbed Gladys. 'Nothing better than a liar. Me own daughter – and brought up chapel too!'

Nelly gave what comfort she could, but Gladys was almost too distracted to take in Nelly's kind words.

Eventually, Nelly accompanied Gladys to her home, in the hope that the truant had returned but the house was empty.

'Mr Bull said I was to go to the police,' she said. 'What d'you think, Nelly?'

'I think,' said that sensible woman, 'that you need a cup of tea. I'll put the kettle on, pop up and see to Albert, and be back with you within half an hour. Then we'll walk up to the police station together.'

'Oh, Nelly!' cried Gladys, tears starting afresh at such kindness. 'How I ever got on before I met you, I can't think!'

'Well, I'm glad to be of help,' said Nelly, making her departure.

Gladys came with her to the door. The kettle was beginning to sing, promising comfort.

'What I truly fears now,' admitted Gladys, 'is that them Lovelocks was right. I bet our Doreen left that window open, and I bet it was that chap of hers that done it. I wonder if I ought to tell the police?'

'Find the girl first,' advised Nelly, 'and what follows will have to be faced when the time comes. See you in half an hour.'

She set off to puff up the steep hill to Thrush Green.

What a day it had been, one way and another! And not over yet, thought Nelly.

19. The Drought Breaks

Naturally, the news of the Lovelocks' burglary was common knowledge, within twenty-four hours, in Lulling and Thrush Green.

Comment on the incident varied considerably. It was felt at The Two Pheasants that 'them old girls asked for it, showing all that stuff openly for any passer-by to covet'.

Winnie Bailey, and other Thrush Green friends, were profoundly shocked that such a thing should have occurred, and that the three sisters had been robbed again.

Young Cooke, who did most of the caretaking work now at St Andrew's, said that in his view 'nobody should own all that valuable stuff, and the chap as took it was only evening out wealth, like, and good luck to him.'

At this, Albert gave him a hefty swipe on the shin with the broom which had been supporting him, and a string of curses, of Anglo-Saxon derivation, which surprised even young Cooke.

It was sometime later that the possibility of Doreen Lilly being mixed up in the affair was being mooted abroad with great relish.

Nelly Piggott, unable to keep such richness to herself, mentioned it to little Miss Fogerty when they happened to meet on the green.

'Her mum's real upset,' said Nelly, with evident satisfaction. 'That Doreen'll do anything that fellow tells her, despite the way he's treated her. So Mrs Lilly tells me. She reckons he's behind this, and one or two people have said they've seen this Gordon around here recently.'

'What does he look like?'

'Tall chap. Red hair, what there is of it. He's a skin head, or was. Then he was in jail, you know, so his hair would still be short. Rosa, down The Fuchsia Bush, reckons he came in earlier this summer.'

Agnes remembered the young man screened by the trunk of a lime tree in Lulling High Street. Perhaps not an architectural student after all? Perhaps something far worse?

'He left her with that baby, you know,' continued Nelly. 'Treated her awful, but it never made no difference to Her Love. When he called her back, she just come. There's nothing so wonderful as Love, is there, Miss Fogerty?'

Agnes tried to recall who it was who had said that she felt that a sound bank balance and good teeth were really more important, but refrained from uttering these sensible sentiments, in the face of Nelly's maudlin expression.

She bade her farewell as calmly as she could, but hurried back to Dorothy, seriously perturbed.

'But, Agnes dear, I really see no need to rush to the police,' said Dorothy. 'Should this young man *happen* to be the burglar, and Rosa's tale needs corroboration, then perhaps your evidence – very slight evidence too – might be needed. After all, he didn't look particularly felonious, you say?'

'No, indeed,' replied Agnes, although she did not like to tell Dorothy that somehow she still imagined criminals with shaven heads, attired in suits with broad arrows all over them, and shackles round their ankles attached to heavy weights. Perhaps a subconscious memory from her comic-reading days?

'In fact,' volunteered Agnes, beginning to feel calmer, 'he looked rather like a student of some sort. Rather scruffy, of course, but most young men do these days, don't they?'

'They do indeed,' agreed Dorothy. 'Now we must get on. We have the PTA meeting tomorrow night, and we must look respectable for the presentation. I shall go up and wash my hair.'

She made her way towards the door, checked by the window, and said, 'There's dear little Tim, waiting for his supper. Shall I give him something, or will you?'

'I'll do that,' said Agnes, bustling towards the kitchen. 'You carry on with your hairwash.'

She went, humming happily, to cut up Tim's supper, all fears of suppressing vital evidence now forgotten.

The hot spell of weather began to show signs of ending. During the next day clouds began to gather in the west, and little breezes shivered the leaves.

By the time Agnes and Dorothy were dressing in their best for the great occasion, there were distant rumbles of thunder to be heard.

'It seems much cooler,' commented Agnes, as she followed Dorothy down the stairs. 'I wonder if I should bring my cardigan.'

'You look so nice as you are,' said Dorothy, 'that a cardigan dragged over it would quite spoil the effect.'

Grateful though Agnes was to be told that she looked nice, she was a trifle put out at the suggestion that her cardigans were usually 'dragged on'. However, this was no time to take offence at such a small matter, and she gave Dorothy a smile.

'Well, I must admit my new cardigan doesn't quite go with this blue dress. I try to tell myself it *tones*, but I know really that it *clashes*.'

'Blue is always difficult to match,' said Dorothy. 'Now how do I look?'

She turned around slowly on the front door mat.

'Superb!' announced Agnes. 'Every inch a headmistress!'

'Then in that case,' said Dorothy, head held high, 'we will go over.'

The partition had been pushed back, throwing Miss Robinson's and Dorothy's room into one. Already the place was crowded and to the ladies' discomfiture a round of clapping greeted their entrance.

The rector ushered them to the seats of honour, beside himself and Mrs Gibbons, facing the throng. Gauleiter Gibbons, looking very spruce in a Prince of Wales check suit, was flanked by the other members of the PTA committee, the school governors and Mrs Cooke, the formidable matriarch of the Cooke family, who had joined the party uninvited and whom nobody dared to move away.

Agnes, much embarrassed by all this publicity, tried to shut her ears to the eulogies which Mrs Gibbons and the rector poured forth.

Dorothy, on the other hand, appeared to be relishing the list of her virtues which was now being given to an attentive audience. Agnes envied her aplomb. She herself was trembling with fright, and praying that she did not burst into tears at the crucial moment.

'And we hope,' concluded Mrs Gibbons, proffering a large and obviously heavy parcel, 'that you will both think of us when you use it.'

Dorothy rose, and gave a small jerk of the head, summoning Agnes to join her, and the two ladies held the package between them.

'Undo it now!' hissed Mrs Gibbons. 'Everyone wants to see it.'

Obediently, Dorothy put it on her own desk, now in command of Mrs Gibbons, and began to unwrap the clouds of tissue paper. Agnes stood at one side, excited at the sight.

There was a murmur in the hall, as the final swathings were unfolded, and a cut glass fruit bowl was displayed.

'Ah!' sighed the audience rapturously. Dorothy held the beautiful object aloft, and Agnes gave a genuine smile of delight.

'Madam Chairman, Mr Henstock, ladies and gentlemen,' began Dorothy, swinging gracefully into her prepared speech. 'What can I say? Except to give you our heartfelt thanks.'

She continued, mentioning the happy years both had spent at the school, the kindness and generosity of the parents and governors, and the wrench that it would be for both of them to leave Thrush Green.

The rector looked a little bewildered, as well he might, for it had been planned that he should hand over the governors' present of a clock as soon as the fruit bowl had been unwrapped.

However, Dorothy's prompt, and somewhat lengthy, reply had taken him by surprise, and short of halting her peroration which would have been uncivil, and anyway pretty well impossible, the rector was obliged to await the lady's conclusion with as much grace as he could muster in the face of his fellow-governors' agitation in the front row.

At last, Dorothy came to the end of her speech of thanks amidst polite applause. The rector arose and lifted the governors' package from beside his feet.

'And I have the great privilege,' he said, bowing politely to the two ladies, 'to present you with a small token of esteem and thanks from the governors of Thrush Green school.'

He held out the parcel, not sure which lady should take it. But Dorothy, now realising that she had leapt in rather too prematurely with her thanks, motioned to Agnes to accept the second present.

Agnes went forward diffidently, and a storm of clapping and some cheers broke out, completely dumbfounding that modest lady. There was no doubting the affection which prompted this spontaneous tribute, and Agnes's eyes filled with tears. Dorothy too, joined in the clapping, obviously delighted on her friend's behalf.

'Speech!' yelled someone at the back, and little Miss Fogerty raised a trembling hand for silence.

'Ladies and gentlemen,' she quavered. 'Dorothy has said all I want to say, but I am just going to add a heartfelt "thank you" for many happy years, and to let you see me unwrap this exciting parcel.'

The applause grew again, accompanied by some energetic stamping at the back by old pupils, as Agnes undid the paper and held up a charming brass carriage clock for all to see.

Taking heart from the obvious show of affection, Agnes added, 'This lovely present from the governors will be a memento of our friends at Thrush Green for many years.'

At which, she sat down, smiled across at Dorothy, and thanked heaven that her tears had not actually run down her cheeks throughout her ordeal.

'You were absolutely splendid,' Dorothy told her later that evening, when they had regained the peace of the school house.

'And so were you,' Agnes said loyally. 'I could never have made such a wonderful speech.'

'I didn't find it easy,' admitted Dorothy. 'Thank goodness it's over. But you know what I shall always remember?'

'Mrs Cooke among the governors?'

'No, dear. The well-deserved tribute to you that came from every heart.'

Before midnight, as Dorothy and Agnes were seeking sleep, the storm broke. The thunder had become louder as the evening had worn on, but it was past eleven o'clock before the rain began.

It fell in a heavy deluge. Great drops spun like silver coins as they hit the parched earth. Within minutes, it seemed, little rivulets gushed along the gutters and down the steep hill to Lulling.

Agnes stood by her bedroom window to watch the transformation. The roofs of Thrush Green glistened. Rain dripped from Nathaniel Patten's shoulders, and from the heavy foliage of the chestnut avenue.

The playground was already awash, and the tombstones ranged round St Andrew's churchyard stood wet and shiny like so many old men in mackintoshes.

There was little wind, just this ferocious cascade from the heavens, and Agnes felt the overpowering relief which the plants and trees, and the thirsty earth itself, must be experiencing.

The scent of water on stone, grass and soil, filled her with joy. The hot weeks, so warmly welcomed at first, had held Thrush Green, men, animals, trees and all living things, in a relentless grip of drought for too long.

Now release had come. Agnes held out her hands to catch the raindrops, patted them on to her hot forehead, and went contentedly to bed.

The Misses Lovelock were still without their silver, and still without help in the house.

They took these reverses remarkably well, and looked out a canteen of cutlery of somewhat inferior calibre, which had been in use by the domestic staff in the old days, and trusted that their usual tableware would reappear before long.

The police gave them little hope as the days passed. There was a rapid and well-organised turnover of such objects, the Lovelock ladies were told. The young man probably passed on his haul within an hour or two of collecting it, and there was no sign of his whereabouts.

The only development was a grubby postcard from Doreen

to her mother. The postmark was so faint and smudged that it was quite illegible, but the message was clear:

Me and the boy are all right. Don't worry. I will write again.
  Love,
    Doreen

'You see,' said Gladys to Nelly, 'there's not a word about this Gordon, or about coming back. But she's with him all right. I don't doubt that, and I suppose I'd better take this card to the police.'

Nelly agreed that it would be the proper thing to do. She felt very sorry for Gladys, and for the Lovelock sisters, blaming herself partly for furthering the introduction of the truant to the three old ladies.

Charles Henstock was equally concerned, and had rung his friend Anthony Bull several times to ask if he had heard anything at his end. But nothing occurred to give him comfort. Wherever Gordon, Doreen and the child were, was a mystery, and all that could be done was to wait and hope.

The thunderstorm which had ended the drought, also seemed to have ended the summer as well, for it was followed by a period of cool rainy weather during which Agnes had recourse to her cardigan again.

Most of the residents of Thrush Green greeted this return to semi-winter philosophically, grateful for the refreshment of their gardens, and freed from the bondage of those exhorting them to save water.

Albert Piggott and Dotty Harmer took pleasure in the new pool, admiring their handiwork. Dotty wondered if another six or so ducks would give added glory, but Albert was less enthusiastic.

'They makes a mort of mess,' he observed dourly, watching a dozen webbed feet transferring water, pondweed and general slime from the pool to the freshly-laid stones.

'No, no, Albert!' protested Dotty. 'They are simply behaving naturally. You can see the dear things are really happy. I should like to give a few more ducks the chance to enjoy it. There must be a lot of *deprived* ducks about.'

Albert thought of the few weedy specimens kept in a pen at Perce Hodge's farm, but forbore to tell Dotty of their plight. She'd have them down before you could turn round, he thought, surveying the muddy stones around the pool. His labours were already being spoilt. No point in hastening the process.

Winnie Bailey was another person who was busy in her garden now that it was cooler.

She was pulling up groundsel and some obstinate weeds from the flower border, whilst picking a summer nosegay for the house, when Jenny hailed her from the kitchen window.

'Telephone, Mrs Bailey! It's Richard.'

Winnie hurried indoors, and sank thankfully into the chair by the telephone.

'May I call to see you tomorrow morning?'

'Of course. Can you stay to lunch?'

'I'd love to.'

'And Fenella?'

'Afraid not. She's not up to travelling. Rather poorly at the moment.'

At once, Winnie saw Fenella in hospital, probably in the intensive care department, with some fatal disease which would leave Richard without a wife, and the two children motherless. She was already trying to decide on a boarding-school, a reliable housekeeper, or possibly a second wife for Richard, when she heard herself say, quite calmly, 'I do hope it's not serious, Richard?'

'No, no! Just that she's feeling rotten first thing now. Morning sickness, you know. We're having a baby after Christmas.'

'Well, I'm delighted,' cried Winnie, much relieved. 'What good news! Now, would she like me to do some knitting for her, or does she bring her babies up in those gro-bag things?'

'I'll ask her,' said Richard. 'Yes, we are very pleased. Puts the kibosh on Roger, I hope.'

Richard sounded unpleasantly smug, Winnie felt, and slangy with it. However, she was so pleased to hear the news, that she forgave her nephew, said that she looked forward to seeing him, and then went to break the news to Jenny.

'Good thing we had that chicken from Perce,' said Jenny. 'With plenty of stuffing and a pound of chipolatas, it should do us a treat.'

With great plans of knitting and cooking to engage them, the two friends resumed their tasks.

'It's high time,' said Dorothy one evening, 'that Tim came in to sleep. What about bringing his basket into the kitchen tonight, and shutting the shed door?'

'But it's so wet everywhere,' protested Agnes. 'And it seems to rain every night.'

'Exactly. If he can't get into the shed, he'll look for his basket elsewhere. Let's put the cat flap wide open, and put his basket just inside where he can see it. I'm sure it would work.'

Agnes looked unhappy. Already she had a vision of her

beloved cat, shivering in a rain storm, coat spiky with wetness, eyes half-closed in anguish.

'Perhaps we could leave a folded sack in the shed as well,' she suggested, 'and leave the door ajar as usual. Then he has the choice.'

'We don't want to give him any choice,' said Dorothy firmly. 'Let him find his basket and use it.'

There was no gainsaying Dorothy in this headmistressy mood, and Agnes gave in.

She went up to bed in a very unhappy state. A steady rain pattered against the windows and cars swished through the puddles bordering Thrush Green.

The cat flap had been propped open to its widest extent, with a cork firmly wedged at the top of the join, and Tim's basket, with its blanket plumply folded, stood just inside.

Dorothy had left these little arrangements to Agnes, and had volunteered to go down the garden to shut the shed door. She was half-afraid that Agnes would be tempted to leave it ajar as usual, and Dorothy was intent on cat-discipline tonight.

She fell asleep within ten minutes of climbing into bed, but poor Agnes next door lay listening to the rain and grieving for her pet. At about two o'clock she could bear it no longer, and sliding out of bed, she crept downstairs.

The house was still and quiet. Only the whispering of the rain outside stirred the silence. Agnes tip-toed to the kitchen door, and gently turned the handle.

There was no flurried movement of a cat making his escape, or the creaking of a wicker cat basket. Timidly, fearing the worst, Agnes pushed the door farther open, so that she had a clear view of the cat basket.

There, curled up in deep sleep, one paw protectively over his nose, lay Tim, oblivious to all about him.

A great surge of happiness engulfed little Miss Fogerty. He had come in of his own accord! He had used the cat flap, and found his old familiar bed! There was no doubt about it. He was a highly intelligent cat.

And what was more, thought Agnes, creeping back to bed, he now looked upon this house as his rightful home.

She slept as soundly as the cat below.

20. LAST DAYS

The last day of term was as cool and damp as those which had preceded it, but for young Miss Robinson, in a bustle of responsibility over the presentation of two bouquets and two boxes of chocolates, the atmosphere seemed feverishly hot.

Directions to the Lulling florist had been explicit and much repeated. The flowers were to be delivered *not later than two-thirty* to Miss Robinson herself, who would be waiting in the lobby to receive and then secrete them.

One small girl had been coached *ad nauseam* to present Dorothy's bouquet, and another who was in charge of Agnes's, was equally well primed.

Two little boys, with extra clean hands, and comparatively polite manners, had been detailed to present a box of chocolates apiece. It all sounded simple, but as any teacher will know, such apparently spontaneous gestures need a week or two of anxious preparation, and then they can easily go wrong. Poor Miss Robinson suffered.

It was open house at Thrush Green school that afternoon, so that parents, governors, representatives from the local education authority, friends and neighbours crowded into the classroom in a much more informal manner than at the PTA presentations earlier.

Dorothy and Agnes knew

217

exactly what was going on for a number of children had informed them of the proposed tributes, adding for good measure, the sum which they themselves had contributed to the general largesse. It was a good thing that Miss Robinson, in her innocence, knew nothing of this.

It was a happy party, and the children did their duties admirably. Dorothy and Agnes expressed their surprised delight, and thanked everyone – particularly Miss Robinson – for such beautiful flowers and delicious chocolates.

There were no other speeches, but Dorothy informed the throng that cups of tea were available in Miss Fogerty's terrapin, as Mrs Betty Bell and Mrs Isobel Shoosmith had kindly arranged this. At this juncture, Agnes whispered in her ear, and she added that the Thrush Green Women's Institute had most kindly lent their cups and saucers, and this courtesy was very much appreciated.

In the mêlée that followed, she and Agnes mingled with the guests, accepting good wishes and sometimes a personal present, and it was past four o'clock before the school emptied and the two ladies bore their tributes to the school house. The flowers were deposited in a bucket of water to await later arrangement, and the friends sank thankfully into their armchairs.

'It all went beautifully, didn't it? Do you know,' confessed Dorothy, 'I wondered if I should find this parting too much for me. But it was such a jolly afternoon, wasn't it? I shall telephone Miss Robinson this evening to thank her particularly. I think she's going to be a tower of strength to the new head.'

Agnes agreed, still amazed that Dorothy should admit to the frailties from which she herself suffered. Somehow it made the bond between them even stronger. She too had dreaded the last afternoon, and had been relieved to find it a wholly cheerful occasion.

'And of course,' continued Dorothy, 'we shan't really be saying goodbye for some time yet. It's a comforting thought.'

'Anyway,' added Agnes, 'we can always come back to visit Thrush Green from Barton.'

Dorothy began to tear away the cellophane from her box of chocolates.

'I don't see why we shouldn't celebrate, Agnes. The square ones are hard, I warn you.'

Nelly Piggott had kept her word and accompanied Gladys Lilly to Lulling police station with the postcard from the errant Doreen.

'Well, thanks very much,' said the sergeant on duty. 'You did right to bring this in, Mrs Lilly. I'll pass it on to the officer in charge of the enquiries. Might be a Vital Clue.'

The ladies departed feeling much comforted by this encounter, and Gladys was already making plans to welcome her daughter and grandchild to her home again.

Nelly was not so sanguine, but said little about her doubts to the hopeful mother. However, later that day she met her good friend Mrs Jenner who was walking across the green to see her daughter Jane, the warden at Rectory Cottages.

To her, she admitted her reservations about bringing the culprit to justice, and Mrs Jenner nodded her head in agreement.

'If you ask me,' said that lady, 'poor Gladys won't see her Doreen, nor Gordon and the boy, for a very long time. And the Lovelock ladies won't ever set eyes on their missing silver either.'

And Mrs Jenner was quite right.

It had been Dorothy's idea that they should spend a few days at Barton, staying at their favourite guest-house, as soon as they broke up.

'Now that the business side is settled,' said Dorothy, 'we can chivvy the electrician and decorator if we are down there.'

Dorothy, thought Agnes, seemed to think that her presence would hasten the completion of the work in hand, and maybe she was right. In any case, Agnes looked forward to a few days by the sea, and to visiting the new house again.

They set off on the Saturday morning, planning to stop for a pub lunch near Andover. Isobel had been given minute instructions about the feeding and general care of Tim the cat.

'It's such a relief to know that you are looking after him,' said Agnes. 'He half-knows you already, and he won't be scared away if he sees you about. I'm so anxious that he keeps up the habit of sleeping indoors, and gets thoroughly used to the cat flap.'

Isobel assured her that she would undertake her duties with every care, secretly rather amused at Agnes's earnestness.

'Good thing,' was Harold's comment, when she related this matter to him. 'All the devotion she's put into looking after scores of infants is going to be funnelled into that lucky cat's welfare. I hope the animal knows when it's well off!'

One of the first things that Agnes wanted to see to was the installation of a similar cat flap at the Barton house. Dorothy was more concerned with measuring for carpets and curtains. As always, it seemed, not one pair of the latter could be transferred to Barton, a common disappointment to all who move house.

They arrived at the guest-house soon after two, and then set out on foot to visit their new home. As it was a Saturday, no one was at work there, and the house was very still. Their footsteps echoed on the bare boards as they went from room to room.

The biggest job to be done was the rewiring of the whole place, and as this was a messy job, involving cutting channels in the walls, Dorothy had decided that the decorating might just as well follow this upheaval.

'One thing I have insisted on,' said Dorothy, surveying the work, 'is that the plugs should be half-way up the wall. I don't see why we should grovel about bent double to find switches on the skirting board. They can site them just behind the curtains. Perfectly simple when you think about it.'

Agnes, mindful of her arthritis, applauded this sensible suggestion.

'And we'll have a telephone extension beside each bed,' went on Dorothy, 'and good rails by the bath. I'm afraid we shall have to replace the present bath sometime. It's got badly stained. But we will have time to choose something really pretty.'

They wandered into the garden, but rain began to fall, and they left the few late roses and clematis, the tussocky lawn and weedy borders, and returned to the shelter of the house.

'What a pity we didn't bring a couple of deckchairs with us,' said Agnes. 'I could do with a rest.'

Dorothy surveyed the empty kitchen.

'Nothing simpler,' she announced. She went to the kitchen sink, and pulled out two of the drawers below it. Turning them over, she put them near the wall. 'Try that, my dear,' she said, with understandable pride.

Agnes lowered herself cautiously and rested her back against the wall. Dorothy sat on the other upturned drawer beside her. There was a protesting squeak from the wood, but the temporary seating held well.

'How very clever!' commented Agnes.

The two friends sat side by side, legs stretched out above the dusty kitchen floor, and saw in their minds' eye a fully-furnished, warm and comfortable haven.

To Agnes suddenly came comfort. Her thoughts had been sad ones when she had had time to consider them. She hated change, and her natural timidity made her apprehensive of the unknown. She grieved at leaving her friends, her home and the loved surroundings of Thrush Green.

But, for the first time, sitting inelegantly on the kitchen floor, she began to look ahead with stirring excitement. This was going to be her home! Here she would have the company of Dorothy and dear little Tim. There would be new friends in her life, new interests, new countryside to explore.

'And we can always go back,' she said, thinking aloud.

Dorothy seemed to know what was in her mind.

'Of course we can,' she said cheerfully, 'and the Thrush Green people will come and see us here. We're certainly not losing friends by this move, Agnes, but simply finding a lot of new ones.'

Agnes sighed happily. Dorothy consulted her watch.

'Well, I think we should be getting back. If you could manage to stand up first, I should appreciate what the children used to term "a good lug-up".'

And little Miss Fogerty, much refreshed in body and spirit, obliged.

Back at Thrush Green, the future of the two ladies was a prime point of conversation, and the fate of the school house one of pleasurable speculation.

Betty Bell told the Shoosmiths that she had received an official letter asking her to continue to look after the school until further notice.

'And that's a real relief, I can tell you,' she informed Isobel and Harold. 'I mean the money's regular, which is more than you can say about some.'

She must have noticed the bewilderment on her hearers' faces for she added hastily, 'Not but what you do pay me pronto – always ready done up in a clean envelope as soon as the work's done. But poor old Dotty – Miss Harmer, I should say – she don't know if she's coming or going, and sometimes it's weeks before she remembers.'

'But, Betty,' protested Isobel, much shocked by this disclosure, 'surely Mrs Armitage sees to that?'

'Well, no. You see, Dotty wanted to do it, and of course Mrs Armitage thinks she does, but she don't, if you follow me.'

'Then you must mention it to her,' advised Isobel, mentally making a note to do it herself as well. 'Things can't go on like that.'

'Lor' bless you,' laughed Betty, 'they've been going on like that for years down Dotty's!'

*

Albert Piggott was doing his best to persuade Mr Jones of The
Two Pheasants that he should put in a bid for the school house
and turn it into a small hotel.

'And where would I get the cash for that?' appealed the
landlord. 'Don't get very fat on your and Percy's half-pints of
bitter, I can tell you.'

Even Ella Bembridge, across the green, flirted with the idea of
changing her residence for one short afternoon.

Dimity was horrified. 'You aren't serious? You've been quite
happy in the cottage, haven't you?'

'Well, yes, of course I have,' replied Ella, blowing a cloud of
acrid cigarette smoke towards the ceiling. 'But it would make a
change. Besides there are twice the number of cupboards over
there, and mine are uncomfortably full.'

'Then have a good clear-out for the next Jumble Sale,' advised Dimity, 'and go on enjoying this place.'

The folk at Rectory Cottages were perhaps the most keenly
interested in the future of the school house. Some were positive
that it would be razed to the ground, and eight or ten houses
would be built on the site. Tom Hardy maintained that it would
be turned into offices, and Muriel Fuller surmised that the
education authority would incorporate it into the school itself,
possibly as a store and school kitchen.

'Well, at least,' said Winnie Bailey, summing up the general
feeling, 'that's all in the future. We shall have Agnes and
Dorothy with us for some time yet, thank heaven.'

The two schoolmistresses returned from their break feeling that
much had been accomplished. Dorothy had enjoyed urging the
electrician and decorator to brisker efforts, and had purchased
some particularly attractive cretonne, at sale prices, for curtains
and chair covers.

Agnes had given a local handyman minute instructions about
the cat flap. They had attended the local church and met the
vicar of whom they both approved. The post-mistress seemed
welcoming and helpful, and the owner of the guest-house had

recommended a jobbing gardener. All in all, the ladies were well content.

They were now in a relaxed enough frame of mind to enjoy the spate of informal invitations which came along from old friends and well-wishers. It was a joy to be free during the day to accept coffee in the morning with Ella and Dimity, or afternoon tea with Isobel and Harold next door. With no worries about the term ahead to daunt them, life took on a wonderfully relaxed air, and Agnes and Dorothy blossomed in these first early days of their retirement.

The cat, by this time, now kept them company, though always showing a preference for Agnes, rubbing round her legs, purring loudly, and even jumping on to her meagre lap, much to her delight. Dorothy was large-hearted enough to approve, and only hoped that she too, in time, would be so honoured.

The relaxation of her responsibilities seemed to mellow Dorothy. She even offered the school house curtains and carpets to Ray and Kathleen, when they moved to Barton, and for good measure threw in the nest of coffee tables, much coveted by her sister-in-law, as there was really nowhere to put them in the new house.

'I only hope,' said Isobel to Harold, 'that this general good-will prevails. They are so happy at the moment. I wonder if they will start having pangs when term begins? I wouldn't put it past Dorothy to drop in on the new head to tell him where he is going wrong.'

'Never fear,' said her husband. 'The sound of infant voices raised in battle in the playground will simply bring home to them how marvellous it is not to have to cope. Anyone with any sense welcomes retirement, and those two have plenty of that between them.'

And time proved that Harold Shoosmith was right.

Term began at the end of August, and the two ladies were far too engrossed by then in plans for the move to take much interest in the activity so close to them.

But they did invite the three staff to tea during the first week of term and were much impressed by the good sense and deference of the new headmaster. He was a pastmaster in diplomacy, and congratulated Dorothy on the ship-shape way everything had been left, and the ex-headmistress beamed with pleasure.

As always the jobs at the Barton house took twice as long as estimated, and two days after term began Dorothy issued her ultimatum.

'We shall be moving in,' she told the estate agent, the electrician, the plumber and the decorator, 'in a fortnight's time. The removal men have been engaged this end, and we expect to be in and settled before nightfall on Tuesday, September the sixteenth.'

All protestations, explanations and excuses were swept aside, and Agnes, yet again, was filled with awe and admiration at Dorothy's command of the situation.

Promptly at eight-thirty the removal van arrived and loading began.

In between supervising the bestowal of their household belongings, Dorothy prepared a substantial picnic lunch, and Agnes superintended the arrangements of Tim's travelling basket.

The greatest worry, of course, was the strong possibility that he would keep well away from all the unaccustomed activity, and Agnes had opened a tin of sardines as a particular bribe. Amazingly, it worked, and Agnes secured the cat in the basket just as the removal men were about to move off.

The two ladies were to follow in the car, and to meet the van at Barton at two-thirty. The time now had come to say goodbye to Isobel and Harold who had been helping them.

But not only Isobel and Harold, it seemed, for although the children of Thrush Green school were supposed to be at school dinner, they were instead all at the railings of the playground, with the three staff standing behind them, smiling and waving.

'What a wonderful send-off!' said Agnes, as they drove off towards Lulling. 'What a nice idea of the headmaster's!'

'Yes, a kindly thought,' agreed Dorothy, negotiating the traffic in Lulling High Street. 'I think the school should do *quite well* under him.'

Greatly content, the two friends drove southward to their future.

Friends at
Thrush Green

To Chris
with love

CONTENTS

* * *

1. FRIENDS RETURN

'It is an extraordinary thing,' said Harold Shoosmith one breakfast time, 'but I seem to have lost my reading glasses.'

'I shouldn't call that "an extraordinary thing",' replied his wife Isobel. 'You lose your glasses six times a day on average.'

There was a commotion at the front door.

'Ah! That's Willie Marchant with the post,' said Harold, hurrying into the hall to escape his wife's censure. He returned with a handful of envelopes and began to sort them at the table, holding each at arm's length the better to see.

'Yours, mine, junk. Junk, junk, yours, mine, junk, yours.'

'Junk always gets the biggest pile,' commented Isobel, beginning to slit open her own three envelopes. 'When you think of all the trees that are cut down to end up as junk mail which nobody bothers to open, it really makes one livid.'

She glanced at her husband who was now peering with screwed-up eyes at a lengthy form.

'Do go and get your glasses. Try the bathroom window-sill.'

'Why on earth should they be there?'

'Because I saw you put on your glasses in the bedroom to see the time, and you then went straight to the bathroom, and I haven't seen you wearing them since.'

'Want to bet on it?' said Harold smiling.

'No. I'd hate to see you lose.'

She heard him overhead, and he soon reappeared wearing his spectacles.

'You were spot on, my love. Bathroom window-sill it was.'

They applied themselves to their respective letters, and coffee cups, in silence.

It was broken by Isobel's cry of delight.

'Now here's some good news. Dorothy and Agnes hope to visit Thrush Green next month. "We can easily put up in Lulling or at The Two Pheasants, and we shouldn't dream of imposing ourselves on you and Harold as you so kindly suggest, but of course we hope to see a great deal of you both and our other Thrush Green friends." What a pair of poppets they are! Won't it be lovely to see them again?'

'It will indeed,' agreed Harold, still studying his form. 'I can't make head nor tail of this bally thing. It says at the beginning "Consult your solicitor if in any doubt", and I think that's exactly what I shall do.' He folded it up and thrust it back into its envelope. 'I wonder why you always get the nice letters and I get the dreary ones,' he remarked.

But Isobel was too immersed in her letter to reply.

Later that morning, she dwelt upon the future visit of her old friends as she went about her household tasks.

Miss Dorothy Watson and Miss Agnes Fogerty had been their neighbours at Thrush Green ever since she had married Harold. Dorothy was headmistress of the junior and infant school next door, and Agnes was her loyal assistant.

In fact, it was through little Agnes Fogerty that Isobel had met Harold. She and Agnes had been at a teachers' training college many years earlier, and the two had always kept in touch. When Isobel's first husband died, she had visited Agnes and decided to look for a small house somewhere near her old friend, and in that part of the Cotswolds which she had known all her life.

The two friends, though much the same age, were poles apart in looks and temperament. Little Agnes Fogerty was only an inch or so over five feet. Her soft hair was smoothed back into a bun on the nape of her neck. Spectacles covered her kind weak eyes, and the clothes she wore were in the gentle hues of fawn and brown, as inconspicuous as her retiring nature. She had spent many years in the infants' class of Thrush Green school, and was held in great affection and respect by pupils and parents.

Isobel had always been pretty: her blue eyes sparkled, her fair hair curled, and even now in her fifties, she remained trim of figure and youthfully energetic.

In the months after the death of her first husband, her manner was subdued as she struggled to get over her loss. Agnes's quiet sympathy did a great deal to help her, and the kindness of her Thrush Green friends was an added support.

But it was Harold Shoosmith, a relative newcomer himself to Thrush Green, who proved such a staunch friend. He insisted on accompanying her on many of her house-hunting forays, knowing only too well from his own recent experiences how depressing and exhausting such undertakings can be.

Over the months the friendship grew deeper, and when Harold asked her to marry him, it was, as Isobel mischievously put it, 'the answer to all that house-hunting'; the two had settled down in Harold's house on Thrush Green, to their own delight and that of their friends.

When the two schoolteachers had decided to retire together, the Shoosmiths knew that not only would they miss them sorely but that they would have new neighbours in the school house next door. Until that time, the headteacher of the school had always lived in the school house, but now the education authority had decided to sell the property.

The new headmaster owned a house some twenty miles away, and was quite prepared to make the journey daily. He had two young children who were doing well at their present school, and his wife was happy in their house. It seemed pointless to uproot the whole family to live in a house which needed to have a great deal done to it. In any case, the thought of finding the money for Thrush Green's school house was a daunting one. He decided to let things remain as they were while he tackled his new job.

The travelling did not worry him, nor did the challenge of fresh problems at the school. But he was a little anxious about his wife's health, and hoped that the length of time he would have to spend away from her each day would not depress her.

She had been left rather frail after the birth of their second child, now aged six, and relied – rather too heavily, some of their friends thought privately – upon the cheerful willingness of her husband. She could do no wrong in his eyes, and he was blind to the fact that, like so many apparently gentle and fragile wives, she had an inner core of selfishness which relished dominating her very kind-hearted partner.

Harold and Isobel had invited them to supper soon after Alan Lester had taken up his duties at the school, and agreed that they were a 'nice couple' as they waved them goodbye. They did not see Mrs Lester again but often spoke to Alan, and liked him more and more as the weeks passed.

The school house remained empty throughout the winter, but just before Easter it was bought by a young and obviously prosperous couple called Angela and Piers Finch.

They were an exuberant pair and had great plans for enlarging the house. All through the summer they appeared at odd times in an old but dashing scarlet MG car which scandalized Thrush Green with its noise. They spent several weekends at the house, 'slumming' as they called it, while they pored over detailed plans, tidied the garden, lunched at The Two Pheasants, and visited Harold and Isobel next door.

Isobel found them exhilarating, enjoyed their chatter, and was much touched by the expensive flowers and chocolates with which they showered her.

Harold found them excessively tiring. It seemed to him that they always descended upon them just as he was settling down to read or to listen to music. He viewed their future proximity with some misgiving, especially as their plans to enlarge the modest house were being drawn up with a family in view.

But no actual building began, as it happened, and in the autumn the Finch couple arrived on the Shoosmiths' doorstep with surprising news: he had been posted overseas by his export firm at a salary which staggered Harold, and they were to fly out in a month's time to take up the appointment.

The school house at Thrush Green was on the market again.

Its fate, of course, was a constant source of speculation and surmise among the inhabitants of Thrush Green.

Mr Jones of The Two Pheasants hoped that it would be made into offices so that the staff would visit his establishment for lunch. Albert Piggott, the morose sexton of St Andrew's church on the green and one of Mr Jones's regular customers, was of the opinion that a decent, quiet couple would be best there.

'None of these 'ere yuppies, like that jazzy pair as bought it. Thrush Green don't want that sort.'

'Well, they was free with their money,' pointed out his old crony Percy Hodge, over their half pints. 'Give me three quid for a load of farm muck.'

'More fool them,' growled Albert.

Winnie Bailey, the doctor's widow who lived across the green, wondered if her nephew Richard would like to try his luck again.

'Not a hope,' he told her on the telephone. 'I'd love to live on Thrush Green, as you know, but I can't prise Fenella from London and the art gallery.'

The Reverend Charles Henstock who had the church of St Andrew's in his care, hoped that whoever took the house would support the church he knew so well, and his wife Dimity added her hope that children might live at the old school house, as it was so handy for the school next door.

And so the speculation continued, while the little house stood empty.

It was Betty Bell, the exuberant woman who kept the school clean and also charged round the Shoosmiths' house twice a week, bringing them up to date with village gossip, who came nearest to the mark.

'It'd never surprise me,' she said, unwinding the flex of the vacuum cleaner from the figure-of-eight pattern which so irked Harold, 'to hear as Mr Lester came to live next door. Real handy for the school it would be, wouldn't it?'

'He prefers to stay in his present place, I gather,' said Harold. Was it worth trying, yet again, to get Betty to wind the flex straight up and down to withstand the strain of these contortions? He decided it would be a waste of time. She liked a good tight figure-of-eight finish to her vaccuming labours, and that was that.

'It would be nice to have the Lesters next door,' conceded Isobel, 'but I should think it most unlikely. He thought about it all when he took on the post. I shouldn't think he would change his mind.'

'Ah well,' agreed Betty, crashing the vaccum cleaner against the skirting board and bending to pick up a flake or two of paint with a licked finger, 'time will tell, won't it?'

Meanwhile, news of the approaching visit of Dorothy Watson and Agnes Fogerty to their old haunts overshadowed the problematical future of the school house, which had once been the home of the two retired ladies.

Charles Henstock and his wife Dimity discussed the matter as they pottered about the lovely garden at their vicarage in the Cotswold town of Lulling, only a mile away from Thrush Green, where they had started their married life.

Dimity had shared a cottage for many years with her friend Ella Bembridge, and was still a frequent visitor. Charles Henstock had been a widower for a number of years, and lived opposite Ella and Dimity's cottage in a bleak and hideous rectory, grudgingly looked after by a formidable housekeeper.

On her marriage, Dimity had forsaken her snug quarters with Ella to share the rigours of life at Thrush Green rectory with her adored Charles; the housekeeper had returned to her native Scotland, to the relief of everyone at Thrush Green.

A year or two later, whilst Charles and Dimity were on holiday, a fire broke out at the empty rectory and it was gutted. No one mourned its loss except Charles, who had never really noticed its ugliness, its discomforts and its incongruity amongst so many lovely Thrush Green buildings.

On its site, 'arising like a phoenix from the ashes', as someone said dramatically, appeared a pleasant group of homes for old people, designed by the local architect Edward Young. He himself lived, with his wife Joan, in the most handsome house on the green, and the view of the Victorian rectory had annoyed him for years. The sight of the smoking remains after the night of the fire had given him acute satisfaction.

The Henstocks had spent several months in lodgings nearby but moved into the lovely Queen Anne vicarage at Lulling within the year. It was a great joy to Charles to find that he would still be looking after his old parishioners at Thrush Green, Lulling Woods and Nidden, as well as the more important and larger parish of Lulling in which he and Dimity now lived.

It was a morning in early May when they first heard that their old friends Dorothy and Agnes were coming back to Thrush Green for a week's visit.

The lawn was wet with a heavy dew. A pair of blackbirds ran about collecting food for their family nearby; a lark was greeting the sun with an ecstasy of song, and the great copper beech tree at the end of the garden was turning auburn with young leaves.

'They couldn't come at a lovelier time,' said Dimity. 'May is the best month in the year.'

Her husband straightened up from his weeding, a bunch of chickweed in his hand. His plump, pink face was thoughtful.

'I think I prefer April. Nearly always get Easter then. All those daffodils, and life renewed, and such a *festival of hope*, I always feel.'

Not for the first time Dimity was reminded of how closely woven into his life was her husband's religion.

'But May is *warmer*,' she pointed out, 'and the evenings are longer, and there are far more varieties of flowers to pick.'

'Do you think Dorothy and Agnes will go picking flowers?'

'They'll probably be visiting local gardens open to the public. I know that's the sort of thing they promised themselves when they retired to Barton-on-Sea.'

'Well, we can't compete with Hidcote or Stourhead,' commented Charles, 'but I hope they will visit Lulling Vicarage garden while they're here.'

It was Ella Bembridge, Dimity's old friend, who first mentioned the approaching visit to the Misses Lovelock. These three ancient sisters lived in a fine house in Lulling High Street, and from it they kept their sharp eyes upon the affairs of the town in which they had been born.

Ella had entered the local tea-room, known as The Fuchsia Bush, in search of a much-needed cup of coffee after carrying a heavy box of petunia plants the length of the High Street. She found the three sisters debating the merits of a fruit cake, which would last for several teatimes if the slices were cut thinly, or three scones, one apiece, slit and buttered sparingly, for that day's repast.

'I should take both,' advised Ella robustly. 'The fruit cake will last for days. Save you hunting about tomorrow.'

The sisters looked at each other. Bertha and Ada were obviously shocked by such wanton extravagance but before the protestations could flow, Violet, who was the youngest of the three and still in her seventies, nodded her approval.

'Such a good idea, Ella. Let's do that.'

She called across to one of The Fuchsia Bush's lethargic assistants who was picking little pieces of fluff from the mauve and red overall in which all the staff were arrayed, in deference to the flower named over the establishment's bow window.

The girl came across unhurriedly, looking extremely bored.

'Three scones, please,' said Violet briskly, 'with plenty of sultanas in them, and that small fruit cake. Now, how much is that?'

As she fumbled in her purse, surveyed by her two sisters, Ella broke in.

'I'm in here for coffee,' she said, heaving the petunias on to a chair. 'Come and join me.'

'We really should be getting back,' murmured Ada.

'My treat,' said Ella. 'You gave me coffee the other day, remember?'

'Well,' said Bertha graciously, 'that is most kind of you. Coffee would be very welcome, wouldn't it?'

The four settled themselves at the somewhat wobbly table and Rosa, the languid waitress, exerted herself enough to make her way into the kitchen with their order.

It was then that Ella mentioned the visit of Dorothy Watson and Agnes Fogerty.

'How nice,' said Ada. 'I know that Charles and Dimity know them well, but somehow we never came across them.'

'Not *socially*,' added Bertha.

'But of course we know them *by sight*,' said Violet.

'And heard what excellent women they were,' agreed Ada.

9

'Well then,' said Ella – she began to roll one of her deplorable cigarettes, but thought better of it in present company, and returned the tin containing papers and tobacco to her pocket – 'you *do* know them.'

'By *sight* and *hearsay*,' explained Bertha. 'They never came to the house.'

Ella's face must have expressed the astonishment she felt, for Violet, rather more in touch with life than her venerable sisters, spoke hastily.

'You see, the two teachers were working so much of the time.'

'But *I'm* working,' protested Ella, 'at my handiwork, of one sort and another, and you invite me to your house.'

'You are in *The Arts*,' said Bertha kindly. 'Father always encouraged artistic people. He was devoted to William Morris's principles.'

'And some of the professional people came too,' put in Bertha. 'We often had the vicar to tea, and that nice doctor whose cousin was Lord Somebody-or-other. Father was very broad-minded.'

'What about your dentist?' asked Ella, now thoroughly intrigued by these bygone niceties of social distinction.

Bertha drew herself up. 'One did not meet one's dentist *socially* in those days.'

'The very idea!' said Ada, scandalized.

'Good! Here's the coffee,' said Violet, as Rosa emerged from the kitchen. She sounded relieved.

'I think I could do with a biscuit,' said Ella, looking somewhat shaken at her friends' disclosures of times past. 'Will you join me?'

The ladies accepted with smiles and Rosa, sighing, returned to the kitchen.

'That lot in there,' she said to Nelly Piggott, who was in charge of The Fuchsia Bush kitchen, 'wants a plate of biscuits now. Fair livin' it up today them Lovelocks. I bet Miss Bembridge foots the bill.'

'It's no business of yours who foots the bill, my girl,' responded Nelly. 'It's all money in the till, and that's where your wages comes from, don't forget.'

She watched Rosa rummage in the large biscuit tin to find suitable provender for the four ladies.

'Them custard creams and bourbons are all right, and a few little wafer biscuits, but have a heart, girl, who's going to crunch gingernuts at their age?'

She whisked away the offending gingernuts, added two slender chocolate sticks, inspected the completed plate, and pushed Rosa towards the door.

'There you are! Look lively!' she exhorted.

She watched the door swing back.

'Might as well save my breath,' said Nelly, returning to the sink.

2. LOOKING AHEAD

Nelly Piggott was the wife of Albert Piggott, who was the official sexton of St Andrew's church. She had been a buxom widow when she married Albert some years earlier. If anything, she was now even more buxom, with her passion for cooking both at her place of work and in her small kitchen at their Thrush Green house.

She had little encouragement from Albert when she presented him with succulent pork pies, steak-and-kidney puddings and rich trifles, for Albert's digestive system had been ruined by the steady imbibement of alcohol over the years. Dr Lovell had forbidden a rich diet, as well as the alcohol, but Nelly was incapable of curbing her hand when it came to butter, cream and eggs in her delicious concoctions.

The kitchen at The Fuchsia Bush gave her more scope. She had started as a temporary help when Mrs Peters, the owner of the establishment, pleaded with her 'to help out for a week or two'.

So successfully had she helped that she was soon working there permanently and Mrs Peters, seeing her value, later made her a partner. It was Nelly's salary which kept the Piggotts' establishment going, for Albert worked less and less, partly through natural idleness, but also because of failing health.

Their household arrangements suited Albert perfectly. Nelly left home soon after eight and was back some time between five and six. She had her lunch at the kitchen table at The Fuchsia Bush with the rest of the staff, and Albert was left with a meal for midday. Usually he did not bother to eat the food provided, but went next door for a pint of beer, some bread and cheese with pickled eggs or onions, and a good gossip with his cronies.

On this particular May morning he found Percy Hodge already ensconced in the window seat with half a pint of bitter before him on the table. He went to join him, lowering his ancient limbs carefully.

'Ah, Perce! How's things?' he asked, when he had got his breath back.

'Rotten! I'm thinkin' of sellin' up the farm.'

'What again?'

'Two of me heifers gone lame this mornin'. The pony's kicked a gate flat, an' a fox bin and got 'alf a dozen hens in the night.'

'You don't say!'

'What's more, Willie Marchant brought me up a 'alf 'undred of forms from the Min of Ag in today's post. Don't understand one word in ten, an' that's the truth.'

Mr Jones, the landlord, put Albert's usual before him without a word. The two customers sipped noisily, and with much smacking of lips.

'You needs somethin' to cheer you up,' said Albert lugubriously. He replaced his glass carefully exactly upon the wet ring which it had made on the table. 'Take that girl of yours out,' he continued.

Percy grunted. 'Thought you didn't take to the Cooke family.'

'Nor I don't, but if you're fool enough to take up with one of 'em you may as well enjoy it,' said Albert.

Silence fell. The distant sound of children playing at the school next door could be heard above the rumble of beer barrels being rolled down into Mr Jones's cellar from a lorry outside.

'I hear as that new headmaster is thinkin' of livin' at Miss Watson's,' said Percy, changing the subject from his unsatisfactory love-life. The school house was destined to remain 'Miss Watson's' for a long time to come: at Thrush Green, as in most country places, houses are not known by the names on their gates, but by the owners who live, or once lived, in them.

'I heard as he was all set to stay in his own place,' said Albert. 'He'd have bought Miss Watson's when he took over the school, surely. I bet the price has gone up since them young flibbettigibits bought it.'

The thought appeared to give both men some satisfaction.

'Well, now his wife's bad,' said Percy, 'so I was told.'

'Is she now?' Albert became quite animated. 'What's she got? Nothing serious, I hope, with two young children to leave.'

The afflictions of other people were almost as interesting as Albert's own, but never, of course, so severe.

'I dunno,' said Percy, losing interest. He picked up the two empty glasses, wiped his mouth on his coat cuff, and made for the bar.

Albert waited hopefully for a possible refill. He was unlucky.

Percy made for the door. 'Best be gettin' back. Plenty of trouble up the farm today.'

'Sooner you sells it the better,' rejoined Albert nastily, watching his companion vanishing through the door.

When Nelly came home that evening, Albert told her about Percy's disclosure.

'Funny you should say that,' commented Nelly, busily turning liver about in a sizzling frying-pan. 'Rosa at the shop said her auntie had heard the same. Wonder if it's true?'

'No smoke without fire,' quoted Albert. He was rather proud of his erudition, and repeated the adage rather louder. Nelly took no notice.

'I could do with a rasher with that,' he said, changing his tactics.

'A rasher you won't get,' responded Nelly, 'but I'll pop an egg in for you.'

Over their meal at the kitchen table Nelly reverted again to the news they had both heard.

'You can't believe all Perce Hodge says,' said Nelly, 'but

Rosa's auntie now, she's a different kettle of fish. Strict Baptist, teetotal, and not given to tittle-tattle. I'll lay there's something in this rumour.'

'Be handy for you if they wanted a bit of charring done if his wife's poorly,' observed Albert. 'Practically next door, ain't it?'

Nelly surveyed him coldly. 'I've got more than enough down The Fuchsia Bush,' she pointed out, mopping up the liver gravy with a piece of bread, 'but there's no reason why you shouldn't take on a bit of gardening at Miss Watson's. Lord knows you've plenty of time to spare, and it might keep you out of The Two Pheasants now and again.'

She began to clear the table, bustling about the kitchen with renewed energy.

Albert sat himself morosely in the wooden arm chair, and picked up the newspaper.

'FIGHTING BREAKS OUT AGAIN' said the headline.

It seemed fair comment.

On that same evening, across the green, Ella and her friend Dimity Henstock were busy packing pots of young geraniums into a cardboard box.

'I don't care what people say,' declared Ella, through a haze of blue smoke rising from the dishevelled cigarette in the corner of her mouth, 'but I like scarlet geraniums better than any.'

'Very cheerful,' agreed Dimity.

'I've only lost two cuttings this year,' went on Ella, 'and they were some wishy-washy pink things Muriel Fuller gave me. These are much hardier. How many can you do with, Dim?'

'Twelve would be fine. Fifteen if you can spare them.'

'More than welcome. Glad to get 'em off the window-sills. We'll put the box in the porch then Charles can pick 'em up tomorrow. I've got to go to the dentist, but remind Charles where the spare key is. I still put it under the flint with the hole in it by the front step.'

'I should think all Thrush Green knows that hiding place,'

commented Dimity as they settled themselves in the sitting-room.

'Never thought of that,' said Ella. 'Not that I mind Thrush Green knowing, just the bad lots from elsewhere. Perhaps I should move it?'

'I shouldn't bother. You'd probably forget yourself.'

'True enough. By the way, I saw the Lovelock girls this morning. They get odder than ever.'

She told Dimity the tale of those who were acceptable and unacceptable at the Lovelocks' establishment in the past.

'Of course, they still live a century ago,' commented Dimity. 'All those occasional tables and whatnots, laden with silver. Who would bother with so much work these days, let alone facing the strong possibility of burglars? It has happened, after all.'

'Violet is about the only one now capable of sensible conversation,' commented Ella. 'It's my belief that Bertha and Ada are fast becoming gaga.'

Dimity looked sad. 'Charles is of the same opinion. It's Bertha's behaviour that's perturbing him. She's taken to storing some of those silver knick-knacks in her bedroom, and insisting on some of the most valuable pieces of furniture being taken up there too. The drawing-room is fast being denuded.'

'Good thing!' said Ella robustly. 'You couldn't move in there without knocking something to the ground. I should tell Charles not to worry on the Lovelocks' behalf. They've always been on the make, cadging bits and pieces from all and sundry. Come to think of it, I've not seen my Victorian sugar tongs since they came to tea in the winter. I bet they're somewhere in the Lovelocks' place.'

'If that clock's right,' said Dimity, 'it's time I went. I've promised to call at Dotty's, and there's no getting away quickly when dear old Dotty gets going.'

Dotty Harmer was an eccentric spinster who had lived alone in a cottage between Thrush Green and Lulling Woods for many years. Poor health and advancing age had made it necessary for her to have someone living with her, and she was very fortunate to have her sensible niece Connie and her husband Kit as companions.

She still insisted on tending her garden and the innumerable animals she had acquired over the years, but Connie saw to it that she was clad in warm clothing and stout shoes when she ventured forth. In the old days, Dotty had been quite content to wander about at times in her dressing-gown and slippers, much to the dismay and censure of the local inhabitants and Betty Bell in particular who did her best to keep the place in order once or twice a week.

There was a chilly wind blowing through the narrow path which led from Thrush Green, beside the Piggotts' cottage, to the open fields beyond. The sun was beginning to sink behind the trees of Lulling Woods, dark against a pale sky.

Dimity found Dotty in her kitchen, busy chopping onions with an enormous knife.

'It's good to get into the warm,' she commented, seating herself at the clear end of the kitchen table, and watching Dotty at her dangerous task. 'It's more like February than May this evening.'

'Not surprising since it's the time of the Ice Saints,' explained Dotty, ceasing her labours for a moment. 'May eleven, twelve and thirteen belong to three saints, and it is often perishing cold then. You should never shear your sheep around that time, you know.'

'I don't,' Dimity assured her.

She watched Dotty scrape the chopped onions on to a plate, and then tip them into a large saucepan which was bubbling on the stove.

'That smells delicious,' she said.

'For the hens, dear. I always add some onions at this time of year. They contain so much iron, you know, so needed at the end of the winter. Purifies the blood. My father used to eat his raw. Wonderfully refreshing, and so good for the bowels and bladder.'

Dimity reflected, not for the first time, how naturally Dotty referred to the parts of the body and their functions with no coyness. There was something appealingly eighteenth-century about her old friend, her archaic turn of phrase, her knowledge and use of herbs, and her unshaken belief that all things English were naturally best. Dotty was refreshingly free from doubts; they seemed to have come in during Victoria's reign and had become more and more potent ever since, Dimity surmised.

'Heard about Dorothy Watson's old place? Betty Bell tells me that that new man at the school may live there after all.'

'I heard something about it too.'

'Wonder why? Perhaps Dorothy and Agnes will find out when they come to stay. Have some coffee. It's dandelion – excellent stuff, I drink pints of it – but Connie and Kit still stick to Nescafé.'

'I like that too.'

'Well, I *could* make you a cup I suppose,' said Dotty. She sounded disappointed.

'No, no! Don't bother, please. I only came to give you the parish magazine and to see how you were. Are Connie and Kit out?'

'Yes. At a parish meeting. Somebody wants to buy the field at the back here. Lots of silly plans for houses. Who wants a lot of *people* living in that field? Besides, I need it for the goats.'

'Well, people do need houses, of course,' said Dimity mildly.

'And my goats need grass,' said Dotty. She began to look very obstinate, and Dimity decided that it was time to depart. If the demands of people and animals were in debate, she knew on whose side Dotty would be.

What with the approaching visit of the two retired teachers, the speculation about the headmaster Alan Lester's plans, and now this disturbing news about Bertha Lovelock's oddness, the inhabitants of Lulling and Thrush Green had plenty to engage their interests. They could be seen chatting on every corner.

The cold spell passed, and May began to show itself in all its traditional warm beauty. The lilac bushes tossed their mauve and white plumes in cottage gardens, filling the air with heady scent. Stately tulips followed the dying daffodils, their satin cups in every shade known to man.

Lulling Woods were hazy blue and fragrant with carpets of bluebells, and the last of the wood anemones and primroses starred the leaf mould. Along the road to Nidden the ancient pond teemed with tadpoles. Young birds sat bemused on the grass verges, or hopped behind their busy parents clamouring for food, all fluttering wings and gaping beaks, oblivious of the dangers around them from traffic, callous boys, or the hovering shapes of sparrow hawks which cast their sinister shadows in the May sunlight.

The cuckoo's cry, at first so welcome at the beginning of the month, now annoyed its listeners with its monotonous persistence. The rooks chattered and squabbled in the tall trees overshadowing Percy Hodge's farm, and he was already making plans for a rook shoot with a few of his cronies. Percy was partial to rook pie.

Prudent housewives were spring-cleaning and hanging out quilts and blankets to air on their clothes-lines. Those who ran to winter curtains, as well as summer ones, were folding the former and storing them away, and admiring the crisp freshness of the summer alternatives at their windows.

Paint brushes were at work, inside and out, and wallpaper patterns, bed covers, curtain materials and floor coverings were being earnestly studied in many a home. It was not surprising that amid this hopeful bustle another topic arose to engage Thrush Green's attention.

It seemed that the small communal room at the old people's homes, Rectory Cottages, would have to be enlarged. Edward Young, the architect, had had the foresight to see that this might happen, and luckily had put the room at one end of the buildings where it could be extended if need be.

There had been some doubt as to whether the old people would use this communal sitting-room to any great extent. Jane and Bill Cartwright, the wardens, had been of the opinion that the residents might well prefer to stay in their own comfortable quarters most of the time. But, as it happened, the general sitting-room was a popular feature of the complex, and it was decided to enlarge it by adding a good-sized conservatory-type of building at one end. This would give not only more room, but added light, facilities for growing plants, and a pleasant sunny spot when the Cotswold winds made it too blustery and chilly to sit outside.

The trustees had met, and had gone through the usual preliminaries of discussion, argument and anxious perusal of their finances. With everyone's consent, Edward Young had been given the task of designing the extension and he was now busy preparing plans for approval.

It was a job he relished. It was generally felt that his original plans had worked well, and that Rectory Cottages were an enormous improvement on the former rectory which had been such an eyesore on the green.

He had been given plenty of gratuitous advice by the inhabitants of Thrush Green whilst his original buildings had been in the making. For an impatient man he had been remarkably forbearing, although he grew quite heated with his brother-in-law Dr John Lovell when the latter pointed out that some outdoor steps were a hazard to old people, particularly in slippery weather. As it happened, it was poor Jane Cartwright who was the first to come a cropper, and she had been unable to attend to her duties as warden until the broken leg had mended. John Lovell, to give him his due, nobly refrained from saying: 'I told you so!'

It was quite apparent that funds would have to be raised for this new venture, and already plans were afoot for the usual Mammoth Jumble Sale, a Mammoth Summer Fête, a Mammoth Bazaar nearer Christmas and innumerable sponsored activities such as walks, swimming contests, and even an hour's silence to be kept at Thrush Green school, all in this good cause.

Ella Bembridge had been entrusted with the job of buying and making the necessary curtains and soft furnishings, and was busy co-opting various like-minded ladies to form a working party when the time came.

As the birds flew back and forth in the trees and hedgerows, building their nests and making plans for the future, so did the residents of Lulling and Thrush Green plan their own affairs, in this May world bright with hope and new life.

On the last Wednesday of the month, Isobel Shoosmith finished her domestic preparations for Dorothy's and Agnes's visit. Despite their protestations, she had persuaded the two ladies to stay at her house for a week, and the spare-room stood ready for them, complete with a vase of lilies of the valley, and a selection of reading matter on the bedside table.

She and Harold went to check the room during the

afternoon. The two friends were due at four o'clock, and Isobel still had the cucumber sandwiches to prepare.

'It all looks splendid,' said Harold heartily, surveying the twin beds, smooth and glossy in their matching bedspreads.

'I think they would enjoy Ellis Peters' latest, and Dick Francis's, wouldn't you?' asked Isobel anxiously.

'Be mad if they didn't,' Harold assured her. 'And what about a magazine or two?'

Isobel nodded agreement, tweaked a lily of the valley into place, and decided it really all looked extremely peaceful.

They made their way downstairs, and Isobel set off to the kitchen. There was a cheerful hooting from the front of the house, and there was the well-polished Metro on the drive, with hands fluttering from its windows.

'They're here! They're here!' cried Isobel, and hurried out to greet them in the greatest excitement.

3 · NEWS OF OLD FRIENDS

Naturally, the arrival of the two ladies had been noticed by most of the Thrush Green residents long before the last of Isobel's cucumber sandwiches had been eaten.

The first to see the car draw up was Muriel Fuller, who lived at Rectory Cottages and immediately had taken up a strategic position on one of the seats on Thrush Green. It had an excellent view of the Shoosmiths' house, and as Muriel wore dark glasses and held a newspaper, the casual passerby would assume that she was simply enjoying the sunshine.

For most of her working life Muriel had been headteacher at the little school at Nidden, a mile or two north along the road from Thrush Green. When the school had closed, she was fortunate enough to be allotted one of the seven homes under the care of Bill and Jane Cartwright.

She had continued to give part-time teaching help with Miss Watson and Miss Fogerty, and so looked forward more keenly than most to seeing her friends again. She also intended to tell them how disappointed she was by the new headmaster's attitude: he had *not required* her part-time services, and Miss Fuller was indignant.

A close second in the race to see the visitors was Ella Bembridge. She was clipping a few early shoots from the front hedge and had forgotten about the Shoosmiths' visitors, her mind still busy on the Lovelock sisters' odd ways, as she snipped away.

Mr Jones at the public house saw them through the window of the bar, as they drew up at Harold's. Across the green Winnie Bailey, widow of Dr Donald Bailey who had attended to Thrush Green's illnesses for many years, noticed the Metro standing in Harold's drive as she washed her hands before tea. By five o'clock, eighty per cent of the local residents were happy in the knowledge that the two respected ladies had arrived safely.

But it was Ella who stumped across the green as soon as the six o'clock news had finished. Genuinely anxious to see her old friends and having no qualms about the possibility of being *de trop*, she put her head into the open front door, and gave a cheerful shout.

'Anyone home? Welcome back!'

Albert Piggott, who expected to be one of the first to see anything of note occurring at Thrush Green, was rather annoyed to miss the arrival of the retired schoolteachers. He had spent an hour or two weeding Dotty Harmer's garden and, as usual, had been held up by Dotty's scatter-brained suggestions.

'What about a bird-box in that walnut tree?' was one of her proposals. 'I'm quite sure I saw a green woodpecker there the other evening.'

As the walnut tree was about forty feet in height, and Albert suffered from vertigo, he quashed this suggestion.

'Come and see my rhubarb,' urged Dotty. 'A splendid second crop coming. Do help yourself.'

With such things had Albert been delayed, but he arrived back at the cottage a few minutes before Nelly and had exerted himself enough to put on the kettle.

'Them teachers come?' enquired Nelly, flinging a cloth over the kitchen table and whizzing plates upon it.

'Dunno. Never saw 'em. I was workin'.'

'Makes a nice change,' commented Nelly, briskly setting cutlery round the table as if she were dealing cards.

'No need to be sarky,' growled Albert. 'I was down Dotty's. Got better things to do than to poke my nose into other folks' affairs.'

This lofty attitude was greeted by a snort from his wife.

'Well, I bet you're the only person on Thrush Green who don't know if they've arrived. I saw a few curtains twitching as I come along just now.'

She set about poaching a piece of smoked haddock with her usual dexterity, and after it was consumed went to the sink to wash up, while Albert sank exhausted into his chair with the newspaper.

'I knew a woman,' said Nelly conversationally, 'who *never* washed a frying-pan after using it for fish. Couldn't face the job.' She studied her own wet frying-pan critically.

'What she do with it then?' enquired Albert, rousing himself.

'Chucked it out.'

'You'd better not start that sort of lark, my girl,' warned Albert, asserting himself as a householder.

'I might yet,' replied Nelly.

Albert returned to his paper, and Nelly to her thoughts.

She was perturbed about an incident in the shop that morning, involving Bertha Lovelock. That ancient lady had come in on her own to purchase a small currant loaf, a commodity for which The Fuchsia Bush was justly renowned.

Nelly had turned to the tray to fetch the loaf, and thought she saw, from the corner of her eye, a scone being transferred from the basket on the counter to Miss Lovelock's coat pocket.

She said nothing. She could have been mistaken, and she had no idea how many scones should have been in the basket. Some had already been sold by the assistants, and it was impossible to check. In any case, Miss Bertha Lovelock was an old customer and not to be upset.

She swathed the currant loaf in snowy tissue paper, took the money, wished the old lady a civil good morning and watched her depart. She returned to the kitchen and her pastry-making. Should she question the girls to see if such a thing had happened before? Should she tell Mrs Peters of the incident? Had there *really been* an incident?

Flouring the pastry board and wielding her rolling pin, Nelly began to grow calmer. Let the old dear have the benefit of the doubt this time. It might never happen again, and least said soonest mended. No point in alarming Mrs Peters and the girls over one scone. Nevertheless, Nelly determined to keep a sharp eye on the Lovelock sisters, and Miss Bertha in particular.

Meanwhile at the Shoosmiths, Ella Bembridge had wished the visitors goodbye, invited them to call at any time, and stumped homeward.

'Would you mind very much if we stretched our legs after our drive?' enquired Dorothy. 'That is, after we've helped you wash up these tea things.'

Isobel refused to countenance their presence in the kitchen, and gave her blessing to the proposed walk.

The two ladies naturally looked first at their old school: the playground was empty, the doors and windows shut, but all looked neat and clean, and geraniums had been planted in new window boxes.

'It looks very well cared for,' said Agnes. 'I wish we could go in. I wonder if the fish tank is still kept in my room.'

'Most probably,' said Dorothy, moving along to study the outside of the empty school house.

'I must say,' she continued, 'that it is very sad to see the state of our garden. Those roses should have been pruned, and I can't see any mower getting over the lawn if it is left much longer.'

Agnes could hardly bear to look at her old home. Here she had been so happy; here she had spent years of companionship with Dorothy, and had met so many pupils, parents and friends.

'Let's stroll along the road towards Nidden,' she suggested. 'The evening's so lovely.'

'I must say,' said Dorothy a little later, 'that the air here is better than at Barton. I know we have the *sea* now, but there is something so *pure* and *exhilarating* about the Cotswolds, and of course the trees and flowers are more abundant.'

She stopped by a magnificent elder bush, its creamy flower-heads forming a mass of luminous fragrance. Nearby, a spray of early dog roses cascaded from the hedgetop towards the roadside ditch, and buttercups brightened the grass verge.

Agnes shared her delight, and remembered countless walks with her infants class along this leafy lane. Somehow, in every season it had supplied them all with treasures. In spring, the first small violets appeared under the hedgerows, and in summer the children would return with sprays of honeysuckle or mauve pincushions of wild scabious in their hands. In the autumn, there were hazelnuts, blackberries, hips and haws and all manner of bright berries to adorn the nature table, and even in the depths of winter some treasures could be gleaned; a glossy rook's feather, a bleached snail's shell, or a sprig of frost-rimed yew or holly.

The children's joy in these discoveries was echoed by little Miss Fogerty, reflecting as it did her own childhood memories of the Cotswold village not many miles from Thrush Green.

'Good to be back,' said Dorothy.

'Good to be back,' replied Agnes.

The days passed all too quickly for the visitors. There were so many friends to see, so much news to exchange.

Winnie Bailey, Ella Bembridge, Dotty Harmer and other Thrush Green friends invited the two ladies to their homes. Charles and Dimity Henstock gave a celebratory lunch party at Lulling Vicarage, and the Shoosmiths took them out to the neighbouring villages which their visitors had known so well.

Everything went smoothly until the day before the ladies were due to return, when Agnes started a feverish cold.

'I'm sure I shall be quite well tomorrow,' she assured her anxious hostess.

'In any case, you are to stay in bed,' said Isobel, 'and if you are still groggy in the morning you are staying here until you have recovered.'

Agnes became much agitated. 'Oh, I couldn't *possibly*! There are several things we must get back to do, and I don't want to impose on you any longer, Isobel dear.'

'The longer you can stay the better I shall like it,' Isobel assured her. 'Now lie down, and try to have a nap.'

Downstairs Dorothy was reading the paper, and looked up anxiously when Isobel reappeared.

'What do you think? Should we get Dr Lovell to have a look at her?'

'Let's see how she is in the morning before we do that. Is it absolutely necessary for you to return tomorrow? We'd love to have you another day or so.'

'*Absolutely* necessary,' said Dorothy, with a return of her headmistressy manner. 'I have an old college friend coming to stay on Saturday, and must get things ready. She has been looking after her aged mother for years, and this is a rare break for her. I can't possibly put her off.'

'I can see that.'

'And then there's Teddy,' added Dorothy. 'I usually call in to see him after tea on Fridays.'

Teddy had been mentioned once or twice during the ladies' stay, but apart from the fact that he was a neighbour at Barton, Isobel knew little about him.

'Surely he would understand?' she said.

'Oh, he would *understand*,' replied Dorothy with vigour. 'There never was a more *understanding* man, but I should hate to disappoint him.'

'Well,' said Isobel briskly, 'I don't think we need to make any plans until we see how Agnes is in the morning. Would you like to come down to the greenhouse with me? I'm just going to do some watering.'

As it happened, the greenhouse was a very pleasant place to be, for although the sun still shone, as it had on most days of the ladies' visit to Thrush Green, the wind had veered to the north, and was already stripping some of the young leaves and blossom from the trees.

Agnes slept fitfully that night. Her throat was on fire, the glands behind her ears swollen, and she was feverishly hot. It was quite apparent, when morning came, that she was in no fit state to travel, even downstairs.

John Lovell called before he opened his surgery. Dorothy and Isobel awaited his verdict as they stood at the foot of the patient's bed.

The doctor was reassuring as he replaced his thermometer in its case. 'Keep her here,' he said, 'with plenty of liquids to drink. I don't think it is anything more than a heavy cold, but there's mumps about, and the wind can slice you in two this morning.'

He knew Agnes Fogerty well, and realized how physically frail she was with no spare flesh anywhere. But her spirit, of course, was indomitable, and had often kept her at school when she should have been in bed. This time, the doctor was going to see that she was properly looked after, and he was relieved that she was in the Shoosmiths' care.

'I'll pop in at the same time tomorrow,' he said, as he scribbled a prescription. 'This should take her temperature down, and the more she can sleep the better.'

He patted the invalid's bony shoulder, accompanied the two ladies downstairs, and departed across the green to his surgery.

'What is to be done?' cried Dorothy. She appeared to be extremely upset, quite unlike her usual competent self, and Isobel took charge.

'If you can get in touch with your friend and your neighbour, I suggest that you both stay on here. You are more than welcome, as I'm sure you know.'

'Dear Isobel, you are so kind,' said Dorothy, pacing the room distractedly, 'but I really must get back.'

'Then in that case,' said Isobel, 'you know we shall look after Agnes, and I will bring her back to Barton when she is fit to travel.'

'What nuisances we are!' cried Dorothy. 'I wouldn't have had this happen for the world!'

'Now stop worrying,' said Isobel. 'You drive back as arranged, and we'll enjoy Agnes's company. We can keep in touch by telephone.'

'I will go and tell Agnes about our plans,' agreed Dorothy.

'And I will obey doctor's orders,' answered Isobel, 'and go and make a jug of lemonade.'

Dorothy departed the next afternoon after an affectionate farewell to Agnes and her hosts, and many promises to keep in touch by telephone.

Luckily, Agnes made steady progress and the dreaded mumps did not appear, but John Lovell noted that the cold had left a painful cough, so forbade his patient to venture out whilst the north wind held sway.

It was during this time that Harold heard someone in the school house garden which ran alongside his own. It was almost six o'clock and he knew that the children and staff of the school should have gone long ago. Who could be trespassing?

He moved along on his side of the hedge until he came to a gap. Peering over he could see a figure, and was surprised to find that it was the headmaster, Alan Lester.

'Hello!' he called. 'Are you doing overtime?'

Alan laughed, and came to the gap.

'To tell the truth, I'm just having a recce. I'm wondering if I shall buy this place after all.'

'We'd be delighted to have you as neighbours,' said Harold. 'Are you getting fed up with the car journey every day?'

'Well, no,' said Alan. He seemed slightly embarrassed. 'That's one point, of course, but the fact is I've been offered a very good price by a friend of ours for my present house, and I'm wondering if we should be better off here.'

'Awful lot of hassle selling a place though,' observed Harold.

'That's one of the attractions with this transaction if it comes off. It could be done with the minimum of fuss and delay. Our friends are handing over to his son who has just got married, and they would be free to take over from us whenever we wanted to move.'

'Would your wife like to move here?' asked Harold, and thought he saw an expression of pain pass over Alan's face.

'I'm sure she would,' he replied.

'By the way, we have Agnes Fogerty with us at the moment. Would you like to come in and see her?'

Alan excused himself, saying that he was overdue at home, but that he hoped she would call at the school if she felt up to it.

'Actually, Betty Bell told us that she had been taken ill,' he went on. 'I do hope she will soon be better.'

'And I hope you will decide to take the school house,' replied Harold.

He returned to his own, ruminating on the rapidity with which all news circulated in Thrush Green, and with a valuable nugget of his own to share with his wife and Agnes.

As it happened, the two ladies were in Agnes's bedroom and so engrossed in conversation that Harold did not have a chance to impart his news; he returned to the sitting-room and settled down with a drink and the racing pages of the *Daily Telegraph*.

Dorothy had rung to enquire after Agnes's progress, and to give an account of her own. It was this which the patient and Isobel were discussing so earnestly. Phyllis, Dorothy's college friend, had arrived safely and Teddy was delighted to have his neighbour home again.

'Tell me,' said Isobel, 'who is this Teddy?'

Agnes turned rather pink, and plucked agitatedly at the counterpane.

'Oh, a very nice person,' she replied hastily. 'Very nice indeed.' There was a pause. 'A man,' she added.

'So I gathered,' said Isobel patiently. 'Does he live nearby?'

'Just along the road from us,' said Agnes. 'His wife died a year or so ago.'

'Has he got some help in the house?'

'Oh yes! He has to have help as he is practically blind. It's quite amazing how much he can do, but he misses his reading. That's why Dorothy goes regularly to read to him. He appreciates it so much.'

'I'm sure Dorothy enjoys it too,' said Isobel, with some cunning.

'She does indeed,' Agnes agreed enthusiastically. 'They have become great friends.'

Isobel detected a wistful note in this last comment. Could Agnes resent Dorothy's new interest? It seemed unlike her.

'I just hope,' went on Agnes, 'that Dorothy doesn't take on too much with Teddy. She used to go once a week, but lately it has been twice, and she is already on the WI committee, and helping with church affairs. She is so good-hearted,' cried her loyal friend, 'that I don't think she gets the rest she needs.'

'Hasn't Teddy got other friends to help him?'

'Yes, indeed. He has a wonderful woman who comes every morning to clear up and get his lunch, and then there is Eileen.'

'And who is Eileen?'

'A friend of his who lives across the road. She and her husband used to go on holiday regularly with Teddy and his wife. She visits Teddy quite a bit – pops in with a jam sandwich, and that sort of thing.'

'It sounds as though he gets lots of kind attention,' commented Isobel.

'Dorothy thinks he finds Eileen a little *too* attentive,' said Agnes. 'She is very effusive, talks a lot, and is always laughing. "*Guffawing*", Dorothy says. I must confess she is rather noisy. But then, Dorothy and I enjoy being quiet, just sitting with our books and knitting, and looking at nature programmes on the telly.'

'Perhaps Teddy finds her cheering,' suggested Isobel.

'Oh, I'm sure he does,' agreed Agnes earnestly, 'and she really is most generous with her time there. I think she may be lonely. She nursed her husband for months before he succumbed.'

'Succumbed?'

'To cancer, poor man. They were a devoted couple, Teddy told Dorothy. He says he has a great regard for Eileen.'

'It's good to know he has such good neighbours,' said Isobel, rising to go. 'I'm sure Dorothy will not have to do too much. It's not as though she were the only one to lend a hand.'

'No indeed,' agreed Agnes.

She sounded rather husky, and began to blow her nose energetically.

'But you see, she so *enjoys* lending a hand with Teddy,' she continued, still busy with her handkerchief. 'And, Isobel dear, I know you will understand, I can't help looking ahead and wondering if she is getting *too* fond of him. I mean, people do get married again, and he is a very attractive man, and dear Dorothy might feel . . .'

She faltered to a halt and the handkerchief went to work again.

'Now, now,' said Isobel soothingly, 'you mustn't upset yourself with needless worries. Dorothy has plenty of sense, and I'm sure she knows exactly what she is doing. Try and have a little doze.'

Agnes nodded. She looked wretched, Isobel thought. Surely these fears were groundless?

But then, she thought, as she went downstairs, love can be the very devil, and can strike one at any age. What a muddle!

Later that night in the privacy of their bedroom, she told Harold about Agnes's worries.

'It sounds to me,' said Harold, with rare male perspicacity, 'that Agnes may be a little in love with this Teddy herself.'

'Good heavens!' cried his wife, deeply shocked. 'Of course she isn't! She has the *cat*, after all!'

Harold pondered on this as he lay awaiting sleep.

Should men really have to compete with cats?

4. BERTHA LOVELOCK CAUSES CONCERN

It was some days later that Harold remembered his news about the headmaster's interest in the school house. Agnes had returned to Barton and seemed to have recovered her composure, much to Isobel's relief. She said as much to Harold, on her return from delivering her friend.

'I think she was just a little feverish, you know,' she told Harold. 'Naturally, it upset her to think of Dorothy perhaps making a fool of herself at her age. And in any case, they have planned their retirement together, and where on earth would Agnes go if Dorothy and this Teddy-man made a match of it?'

'Don't *you* start,' begged Harold. 'Nothing will happen, you'll see. Agnes and Dorothy will be happily together for years. I can't see any man coming between them.'

He was too chivalrous to add that he thought neither lady could really inspire passion, worthy though they both were, but privately that was what he felt.

'By the way,' he said, glad to change the subject, 'I forgot to tell you that Alan Lester is considering taking on the school house.'

'Yes, I did hear that,' replied Isobel. 'Betty said something about it, and Ella seemed to think he's worried about his wife's health. Charles said he thought it might be the journey over here in the winter that was making him think again.'

Not for the first time, Harold realized that he was well behind with the local news.

'I'll never get used to the *speed* with which gossip flies around here,' he commented. 'In Africa the natives' drums were

35

reckoned pretty efficient, but Thrush Green's tongues can beat them hollow.'

Down at The Fuchsia Bush in Lulling High Street, Nelly Piggott had other things to worry about.

Bertha Lovelock had appeared less than an hour before to purchase a currant loaf. Rosa had served her.

On the counter stood a tray of rolls filled with ham and lettuce. Each was wrapped in hygienic clingfilm. Nelly herself had prepared these snacks which had become increasingly popular with drivers and delivery men in the early part of the morning. A second batch was prepared later for the local office workers and shop assistants who hurried in to fetch a quick lunch to take back to their place of work.

It so happened that Nelly pushed open the door from the kitchen at the precise moment when Bertha was surreptitiously sliding one of the shiny packets into her shopping bag. Rosa had her back to Miss Lovelock as she was dealing with the till.

Nelly's first impulse was to rush towards the old lady and demand back the goods, but prudence won. In the first place, there were several customers taking morning coffee, and she did not want a scene in public. Secondly, she wished to check with Rosa that none of the rolls had been sold: there should be ten in the tray, as she knew, having brought them through herself only ten minutes or so earlier. Thirdly, she wanted to consult Mrs Peters, the owner, about the best way of dealing with this awkward situation. Lurid headlines in the local paper would not do The Fuchsia Bush any good, and the Lovelocks were an old respected family.

As soon as Bertha had gone, Nelly counted the packets; there were nine left.

'Haven't sold any yet?' she asked the girl.

'Give us a chance,' replied Rosa grumpily. 'You only brought them through ten minutes ago.'

'Just check them,' commanded Nelly.

Rosa obeyed.

'Nine,' she said, stopped, and stared at Nelly. 'Surely, she never . . .' she began, awe-struck.

'Never you mind,' said Nelly. 'It's me and Mrs Peters' problem. You just hold your tongue.'

The girl nodded, looking shocked, and Nelly bustled back into the kitchen.

Mrs Peters was in the storeroom alone, and Nelly told her the news.

'And it's not the first time,' continued Nelly. 'That's to my knowledge, so Lord knows how long it's been going on.'

Mrs Peters sat down heavily on the step-stool. 'Gosh! What a pickle! I'm not getting the police in for this one. I think one of us had better have a word with Miss Violet. She's the only one with a ha'porth of sense.'

She looked at Nelly, who shook her head.

'Don't ask me, love. I know we're partners now, but you're better able to do it than I am. I've got the courage to face them old dears, but you'd do it more tactful, and that's the truth.'

'I don't mind doing it, if you think that's the right step.'

'Dead right. But how are you going to get Miss Violet on her own?'

'I'll ask her to call here about a private matter, and see her in the office. Meanwhile, not a word to anyone.'

'Our Rosa knows.'

'I'll deal with Rosa,' said Mrs Peters grimly. 'One squeak out of her, and she goes.'

She got up from the step-stool and patted Nelly's fat arm.

'Don't worry, Nelly. We've faced worse than this before.'

And, somewhat comforted, Nelly went back to making her gingerbread.

While his wife was coping with the affair of Bertha Lovelock, Albert was plying a broom in the churchyard.

There had been a wedding at the weekend. There had also been a high wind, which had not only played havoc with the bride's veil and the ornate coiffures of the bridesmaids, not to

37

mention the wedding guests' hats, but had sent confetti in every direction.

Albert pottered about morosely, jabbing under shrubs, along the edges of the paths, and attempting to free the grass of its scattered finery.

It was while he was thus engaged, and counting the minutes to opening time at The Two Pheasants, that Percy Hodge appeared.

He rested his arms upon the gate top and watched the labourer.

'You busy then?'

'Whatjer think?' replied Albert, nastily. 'It's time the rector stopped all this confetti lark. Look at the mess.'

He paused and leant upon his broom.

'Ah well!' replied Percy indulgently. 'You can't blame young folks wantin' a pretty weddin'.'

'These wasn't young folks,' said Albert. 'That old fool Digby this was. Got spliced to that gel as works at Boots. A case of have to, they say.'

'Not so much of "that old fool Digby",' said Percy. 'We was at school together. Besides . . .' He halted and began to look sheepish.

'What's up?' asked Albert, coming nearer.

'Well, the fact is, I'm thinkin' of getting' married again myself.'

'You ain't!' cried Albert, dropping his broom. 'You silly juggins! What on earth do you want to clutter yourself up with a woman for?'

'There's reasons,' said Percy primly.

'Not the same as old Digby's?'

'Not the same at all, Albert. And I don't like your nasty way of thinkin'. I just want a bit of company, and the house cleaned up, and a decent dinner to come home to, same as any other man.'

'If it's that flighty Emily Cooke you've got in mind,' said Albert, bending to retrieve his broom, 'you ain't likely to get any home comforts. She's nothin' but a slattern, and got that boy Nigel as a by-blow, too. You'll be takin' on two of them. Not to mention her 'orrible old mother. You must be out of yer mind, Perce.'

The farmer's face was scarlet. 'You mind your own business! I knows what I'm doin' and when I needs your advice – which is never – I'll ask for it. That poor girl has learnt her lesson, and she'll make a good wife, you'll see. Anyway I'm fond of young Nigel.'

'More than anyone else is,' responded Albert. 'Well, they say there's no fool like an old one, and it looks as though that's right. You'll regret it, Perce. You'll regret it.'

At that moment Mr Jones opened the doors of The Two Pheasants, and Albert propped his broom against the church porch.

'Comin' over?' he queried.

'Not with you I ain't,' replied Percy coldly, and made his way towards Lulling.

Far away at Barton-on-Sea, thoughts of matrimony for the elderly were also tormenting poor little Agnes Fogerty.

She was scraping new potatoes at the sink, and wondering whether it would not be better to throw in the sponge and take to the potato peeler, so refractory were the vegetables.

Dorothy had gone to see Teddy, taking with her a cutting from the *Daily Telegraph* about pesticides which she thought might interest him.

Any excuse is better than none, thought Agnes with unusual tartness, but remained silent.

Really, she mused, as she struggled with the potatoes, there is far too much of this marrying, and giving in marriage, about. One could get on perfectly well without it, and she and Dorothy were good examples.

Nothing had been said between the two friends, but Dorothy had seemed to make a point of visiting their nearly-blind neighbour every day since she had been back. It was not only the *unsuitability* of the relationship which worried Agnes; there were also serious and practical aspects to consider.

In the first place, would Dorothy really be happy as Teddy's wife? Or anyone else's, for that matter? Dorothy was used to having her own way. She was also singularly undomesticated, able to ignore dust, spots on the carpet and windows which needed cleaning. She disliked cooking, although she was quite capable of roasting a joint and preparing a straightforward meal, but she got no pleasure from doing it. Those regular household chores such as spring-cleaning, ordering the fuel, having the chimney swept and so on, had been arranged by Agnes.

It was not that Dorothy was inefficient, Agnes told herself loyally. The household accounts, the business letters, the interminable forms for taxes, registration of this, that and the like, were all competently managed. But no doubt Teddy, or any other man, would already be coping with such things, and Dorothy's skills in this direction would not be needed. Would she find this frustrating? Would she be critical? Dorothy's patience was easily exhausted, and she would not hesitate to state her feelings. Men, so Agnes believed, very much disliked interference in their methods and habits, particularly as they grew older.

And there was an even more pressing problem for Agnes. Where could she go? There was no question of the three of them living under one roof, which meant of course she would have to find other accommodation.

Her savings were far too inadequate to contemplate buying a small house, no matter how modest. She would have to look about for a bed-sitter like the one she had had years ago at Thrush Green before she shared the school house with Dorothy. It was a bleak prospect.

Or perhaps she ought to start collecting brochures from those excellent societies who care for indigent gentlewomen. She believed that there were several connected with the church, as well as those advertising themselves as 'Homes From Homes', with photographs of stately houses with white-haired old ladies in the foreground, looking bemused in wheelchairs under an ancient cedar tree.

But even more distressing than the thought of Dorothy regretting such a step and her own financial difficulties, was the overriding misery of having to leave Dorothy and their new little home to which she was now deeply attached. She had never been so content.

How would it all end?

She gazed out of the window over the sink, the view somewhat blurred by incipient tears. The cat came and rubbed round her legs, and she bent to fondle it with a wet hand.

'Timmy, we are in a pickle! What is to become of us both?'

Would cats be allowed in these homes for gentlefolk? Come to think of it, she hadn't seen hair nor hide of an animal in those photographs. Whatever happened, Tim should stay with her.

She blew her nose, tucked the handkerchief in her apron pocket, and surveyed her handiwork. She seemed to have scraped seventeen potatoes altogether, and only six were needed.

'Well, they will just have to do for the next two days as well,' she told Tim briskly.

And putting her fears from her, she set about cleaning the sink.

The day after the unfortunate affair at The Fuchsia Bush, Miss Violet Lovelock, gloved and hatted, called next door at the shop. She was ushered in by Miss Peters, who led the way to her office at the rear of the premises.

'Do sit down,' said Mrs Peters, pushing forward the only comfortable chair in the room.

'Thank you,' said Violet sitting bolt upright, and removing her gloves.

Through the window behind the desk at which Mrs Peters was sitting, she could see the brick wall, rosy with age, which divided this garden from the Lovelocks'. At one time, a retired admiral had lived here, and this office had probably been his study, she surmised. Her father had taken a dislike to this neighbour, and threats of writs, solicitors' letters and the like had been tossed verbally across this self-same wall when she and her sisters were toddlers. It was a strange feeling to be sitting here now, awaiting Mrs Peters' pleasure.

Mrs Peters approached the matter with great tact and sympathy. She suspected that the culprit's sister, now busily folding her gloves together, had some idea of what was afoot, and in this she was right.

When at last she ceased to speak, Violet sighed heavily. 'My dear Mrs Peters, I can only apologize and hope that you will allow me to reimburse you.'

'That won't be necessary, I assure you.'

'The fact is,' said Violet, 'my sister is getting very old. Well, I suppose we all are – but dear Bertha is becoming rather eccentric with it. I suppose that one could say that this is a mild form of kleptomania, and I should tell you that she has taken to removing quite a number of objects to hoard in her bedroom. It is all most distressing, but a common symptom of senility, I believe.'

'So I have heard,' said Mrs Peters. 'The thing is, what can we do? Sooner or later, one of our customers will notice, and probably tell the police. This is why I felt it best to have a word with you.'

'You are quite right,' replied Violet. She sat very upright and dry-eyed, but Mrs Peters watched the thin hands, dappled with age-spots quivering, as she played with her gloves.

'We had absolutely no idea that this was going on,' went on the old lady. 'I mean, the scones or buns, or whatever she purloined, must have been eaten in secret. It seems such an odd thing to do. I shall have to speak to her about this at once.'

'Thank you,' said Mrs Peters, glad to see the end of this painful interview in sight. 'I wondered if you might think of consulting your doctor? He might be able to help.'

'I shall have a word with her first myself and, believe me, we shall not let her come in here again on her own.'

She rose to go, back as straight as a ramrod and hand extended in farewell, but her papery wrinkled cheeks were flushed with embarrassment.

Mrs Peters' heart was touched. What a bully one felt, but it had to be done.

'You can be quite sure that this will go no further, Miss Lovelock,' she said. 'We are all much too fond of you and your sisters to wish to see you troubled in any way.'

The old lady inclined her head graciously. 'I very much appreciate the kind way in which you have dealt with this unhappy incident,' she replied. 'I shall do my best to put things right.'

She preceded Mrs Peters through the tea-room, bowing slightly to an acquaintance in the corner. Mrs Peters opened the door for her and watched her depart next door.

The old lady mounted the three steps to the Georgian front door, steadying herself by the iron handrail. To Mrs Peters' anxious eyes, she seemed to cling rather more heavily than usual to this support, suddenly looking particularly frail.

Feeling sad, Mrs Peters returned to the office. She found that she was trembling.

'Rosa,' she called. 'Bring me a cup of coffee. Black today, please.'

Violet went straight up to her bedroom and sat down in an old sagging wicker chair by the window. Outside, in the garden which ran alongside that of The Fuchsia Bush, a blackbird piped merrily. The scent of pinks floated through the window, and some yellow Mermaid roses nodded from the wall which divided the two properties.

The scene was tranquil, but the watcher was not. Violet's heart was thumping in a most alarming manner, and she was quite unable to control the tremors which shook her frame.

The thought of confronting her sister Bertha was devastating. As the youngest of the three, Violet had always felt slightly subservient to her older sisters' demands, although recently she had come to realize that they relied upon her more and more as their own strength receded.

But this was a different matter. This was a question of being dishonoured, of inviting ridicule, of personal shame.

Violet rose from the chair, which gave out protesting squeaks, and rested her hot forehead against the cold window pane.

What should she do? How best to approach this dreadful problem? What would be Bertha's reaction? Would she deny the charge? Would she break down, and confess to even further guilty secrets?

Violet decided that it would be best to tackle Bertha after they had all had their morning coffee. She herself should be calmer by that time, and more able to face her unpleasant task.

She went downstairs to the kitchen and began to set the tray with three large cups of exquisite Limoges china and three silver teaspoons. In the Lovelock household, such plebeian objects as mugs were not used, even for morning coffee.

Going about this simple task made her feel more settled. If only they had had a brother, she thought wistfully. This was the sort of thing a man could cope with so much better.

As she waited for the kettle to boil, she toyed with Mrs Peters' suggestion that it might be a good idea to speak to Bertha's doctor, but she rejected it at once. Dr Lovell was much too young, and there might be disagreeable consequences, such as further consultations with psychiatrists and other horrors.

And then she thought of Charles Henstock, and a warm glow suffused her. Dear Charles! The complete answer! If Bertha should prove even the tiniest scrap difficult, then Violet would seek help from their old and wise friend.

The kettle boiled. Water poured on to the coffee grounds and Violet stood savouring the rich aroma, now mistress of herself.

5 · TROUBLE AT THE LOVELOCKS

July arrived, and gardeners were picking broad beans and raspberries and admiring their swelling onions. They were also, of course, spraying their roses for blackspot and mildew, and trying to cope with ground elder, couch grass, chickweed and groundsel, all of which rioted in their flower borders.

'But,' as Muriel Fuller observed to Ella Bembridge, 'there is no pleasure without pain.'

She was inclined to trot out these little sayings as though she had just thought of them, which Ella found distinctly trying.

The two ladies were meeting rather more often these days, as they were sharing the responsibility of coping with the soft furnishings for the extension to the sitting-room at Rectory Cottages.

The footings were already dug and, like all footings everywhere, looked ludicrously small, as though the room would be hard put to it to accommodate two chairs, let alone the dozen or so envisaged.

The question of curtains awaited further discussion for Edward Young, the architect, was strongly in favour of pull-down blinds being fitted to the windows inside for easy adjustment, and for an awning which could be pulled down on the outside of the glass building facing south.

The two ladies were quite content to shelve the matter of the curtains until such things as expense and necessity, should blinds be considered adequate, were settled; but they decided to go ahead with cushions and other small objects, and had prudently chosen a William Morris pattern which they were assured 'was always in stock'.

'Though that's not to say that the manufacturers may not discontinue some colour or other,' said Ella morosely to her companion. 'Still, we can't do more, and as far as I can see this pattern should tone in pretty well with most colours. The Cartwrights are having a plain hair-cord carpet, so that's a help.'

Those ignorant of the art of cushion-making might have thought that it was a simple process of stuffing soft material into an attractive bag, but Ella and Muriel were artists, and the problems were formidable. Should they be square or oblong? Should they sport a frill, or be left plain? Should they be piped, and if so, inside or out? What about silk edgings, fringes, tassels?

The discussions went on, each lady clinging tenaciously to her own ideas, but in the meantime quite a lot of local gossip was exchanged in Ella's sitting-room.

'You are lucky to be farther from the school than I am,' said Muriel. 'The noise at playtimes is quite horrendous, and I don't think the teachers are on playground duty as promptly as they were in Miss Watson's time.'

This, Ella realized, was a side-swipe at the new headmaster, whom Muriel had never forgiven for spurning her services as a part-time remedial reading teacher.

'All children get excited at playtime,' she commented diplomatically.

'But that's when accidents happen. I well remember at Nidden once . . .'

Ella let her ramble on about her old village school which was now closed, where Muriel had spent the greater part of her working life in comparative obscurity. Her attention returned, however, on hearing Muriel say that she was quite sure that Alan Lester would be coming to live in the school house.

'I doubt it,' responded Ella robustly. 'After all, he had the chance when he took over the job. Prices have gone up since then, for one thing.'

'Maybe,' said Muriel, stooping to pick up a thread from the floor, 'but Betty Bell heard it from his own lips. He was measuring the windows, and saying that he doubted if any of their existing curtains would fit.'

'That's a law of nature,' said Ella. 'Nothing ever fits the next house. That's partly why I don't contemplate moving, and I'm surprised he is.'

'They say,' went on Muriel, 'that it's because of his wife – ailing, in some way. I suppose he worries about her while he's at work.'

'Well, he'll be away at his duties in school anyway,' replied Ella, 'and if she's ailing, I should think the noise of the children would upset her even more. What's the trouble?'

'Betty Bell didn't say.' She held up an embryo cushion cover, surveying it critically. 'I wonder if a frilled ruche of toning satin ribbon would look well round the edge?'

Ella winced. 'No, it wouldn't,' she told her.

It was Harold Shoosmith who next heard more, and it was Alan Lester who enlightened him.

The children were making their way home, loitering in the dusty summer lanes, playing idly on the swings at the corner of Thrush Green, too indolent in the heat to make much noise.

Harold was clipping the privet hedge for the second time that season and thinking how remarkably unpleasant the smell of the little white conical flower-heads was, when he became conscious of the headmaster pacing at the rear of the school house.

He was accompanied by a man whom Harold felt he ought to know. Was he one of the Lulling shopkeepers? A plumber? An electrician? Someone he had met at a party?

Harold contented himself with a wave to both men and continued clipping. A pity the chap who put in this hedge had not settled for yew, thought Harold; it would only need cutting once a year. But then, he supposed, when this privet was planted it was clipped by the full-time gardener who had been kept at Quetta, as his house was once called, along with a resident cook and housemaid.

Intent on his work, he was scarcely conscious of the departure of the two men next door, until he heard a car drive away. He straightened his aching back, and saw Alan Lester emerging from the school house gate, presumably on his way to fetch his own car from the corner of the playground, where it had stood all day in the shade of an elder bush which was so rampant that it could almost be called a tree.

Seeing Harold he came over to speak to him. Harold lowered his shears with relief.

'That's a job that's waiting for me at home,' he observed to Harold. 'I keep putting it off. I'm not all that fond of privet, it grows too fast.'

'My view entirely,' agreed Harold. 'Here, come in and have a drink before you go home. I'm stopping for a bit anyway.'

'Thank you,' said Alan, following his host to the open front door. 'It's hellishly hot today. The children have been drooping all over the place, and I don't blame them.'

Isobel was out, so the two men sat alone in the cool sitting-room. They both settled for Isobel's homemade lemonade, and the ice chinked comfortably in the misted glasses.

'That was a friend of mine who was with me,' announced Alan. 'He's a local builder, Johnson by name. I came across him at Rotary, and he's having a look to see if we can enlarge one of the rooms without too much hassle and expense.'

So that's why I felt I knew him, Harold thought.

'So you really are going ahead – with buying the place next door?'

'Definitely. I should like to have everything signed and sealed before next term. I had great hopes of getting things done during the summer holidays, but I can see that's out of the question.'

'It's no good getting impatient in these affairs,' agreed Harold. 'Simply asking for a heart attack. I've yet to meet anyone who has got into his house at the date first given.'

They sipped their cool drinks in companionable silence. Outside, a blackbird scolded furiously. A child called to another. Someone was mowing a lawn across the green, and the curtains stirred in the light summer breeze.

'It's a very good place to live,' said Harold, at last. 'I'm sure you won't regret the move. The natives are friendly – I know from experience!'

'I've discovered that myself.'

'Will your wife mind uprooting herself? I always think the women have to do so much more in adapting to a different house.'

'I think a change is just what she needs at the moment. She's not been too well, and I shall be able to keep an eye on her more easily.'

'Nothing serious, I hope?'

'No, no. Nothing like that. But both children are at school all day, and I'm away from soon after eight until getting on for six some days. She gets rather lonely, I feel, and she's never been one to make a lot of friends.'

His voice trailed away. He turned his empty glass round and round, his eyes upon it. He looked very tired.

'Let me get you another,' said Harold rising.

Alan Lester came to with a start. 'No, many thanks. I must get back to my own privet hedge. I've held you up long enough.' He put his glass on the tray. 'And thank you again for that life-saver.'

Harold went to the gate with him. The scent from the lime trees filled the warm air. The statue of Nathaniel Patten hard by was throwing a sharp shadow across the grass. Some sparrows were busy in a dust bath at the edge of the road.

'Well, I'm sure you will find Thrush Green very welcoming,' he assured the headmaster. 'And it will be good to see the school house occupied again. We all miss Dorothy and Agnes. You and your wife should be very happy here.'

'I sincerely hope so,' replied Alan.

He was smiling as he said this, but Harold had the feeling that, despite the brave words and the bright smile, some small doubt was lingering.

What was it, Harold wondered, picking up his shears, that was worrying the poor chap?

At the Lovelocks' house, Violet had made little headway with her problem. She had expected either fierce denials and a frightening display of temper from her sister Bertha, or a complete collapse and confession accompanied by a storm of tears.

Either would be quite dreadful, but had to be faced, and she had confronted the culprit when Ada was safely out of the way. It was a shock to find that Bertha neither denied nor confessed. Instead, she gazed at Violet with a look of utter stupefaction on her face.

'What on earth are you trying to tell me, Violet?' she said coldly. 'You seem very distressed about something.'

Violet explained all over again, only to be met with shrugs and shakes of the head.

'I don't think you are quite yourself,' said Bertha. 'I refuse to listen to any more of these silly remarks. You are giving me a headache. I shall take two aspirins and lie down, and I advise you to do the same.'

Thus dismissed, Violet was thrown into even greater confusion. Should she tell Ada? She doubted if she would get any further help from that source. Ada had always hated trouble, and would probably be as scathing as Bertha in dealing with the problem.

She went to the telephone and rang the Henstocks' number.

'Come whenever you like,' said Charles's reassuring voice. 'I shall be here all day, and shall look forward to seeing you.'

At half past two, Violet emerged from the front door of her home and made her way up the High Street towards the vicarage. The lime trees cast pools of welcome shade on the hot pavements. Bees murmured among the lime-flowers, and Violet thought how much pleasanter it would be sitting in a deck-chair in the garden at home than embarking on this worrying project. She had left her two sisters dozing there, as she crept away, feeling like a conspirator.

She crossed the large green at the southern end of Lulling; the great parish church of St John's dominated the scene, its benevolent presence comforting the distraught woman.

She found Charles in the vicarage garden, his hands full of groundsel, his shirt sleeves rolled up. He waved her towards a rustic seat beneath the cedar tree, and sat on another opposite her.

'We shall be quite undisturbed here,' he told her. 'Dimity has gone shopping with Ella. Something to do with cushions. Lots of talk about *ruching* and *piping* on the telephone. It had rather a Highland Games' flavour, I thought.'

He beamed at her, his spectacles glinting in the sunlight. He put the bunch of weeded groundsel on the ground, dusted his hands, and put them on his plump knees.

'Now, what's the trouble?' he enquired.

His voice was so kind and gentle that Violet was afraid she might weep, but Lovelocks did not show emotion under pressure, and she forced herself to remain calm.

'It's about Bertha,' she began, and told him the whole sad tale.

He listened without interruption, noting Violet's fluttering hands, and her voice husky with emotion. Certainly this old friend of his had suffered much, and needed all the help he hoped that he might be able to give her.

'And I still don't know if I should have consulted John Lovell first, but really, Charles, he might have felt that she should be sent to some mental specialist, or one of those clinics dealing with kleptomaniacs. I know so little about these things, but I do know that Bertha would absolutely refuse to have medical advice in this case.'

She paused for a moment, her eyes downcast, and her fingers plucking at the silk of her skirt.

'So I came to you,' she added.

Charles leant across and put his pink (and rather dirty from the groundsel) hand upon her own agitated ones. It was like holding a bird, he thought; there was the same fragility, the panic, the brittle feel of small bones.

'My dear,' he said, 'you should not have to suffer like this. I'm glad you came to me first. We may have to consult Lovell at some time, but not yet.'

'But what can we do?' cried Violet. 'I mean, we simply can't watch her behaving like this! It's not only a case of "what-will-the-neighbours-say?" It is *fundamentally dishonest*, and I can't let Mrs Peters and heaven knows how many other tradesmen be at the mercy of Bertha.'

'It is that which is the main problem,' agreed Charles.

Violet went on to tell him of Bertha's strange ways of moving objects of value from all over the house into her own bedroom.

'She's always been excessively possessive,' Violet told him. 'She would never lend Ada or me any of her things, not even a belt or a pair of gloves for some particular occasion.'

'And did she borrow yours?'

'Oh, frequently! We rather treated it as a joke when we were girls. "Go and look in Bertha's room", we used to say to each other, if we missed a brooch or some other trifle.'

Charles nodded. 'It sounds as though it has simply grown more obsessive as the years have passed,' he said. 'Do you think she has any inkling of what she is doing?'

'I can't say. Somehow I think she *does* know that she is at fault, but she is so clever at evading the issue that I simply can't tell. It is as if she shuts her mind to the consequences of her actions. And I'm quite sure this isn't just forgetfulness, as it would be in dear Ada's case. Bertha is a much more ruthless person, I'm afraid, as I know to my own cost after all these years.'

They sat in silence for a time. Bumblebees tumbled about in the border nearby. A thrush stood, still and statuesque, at the edge of the lawn, before running purposefully to a spot which he jabbed energetically with his beak. There was a distant cackle of laughter from the almshouses nearby, where two ancient neighbours, it seemed, were sharing a joke.

Charles sighed. 'Leave this to me, Violet. You have done all you can, and I can only suggest that you make sure that Bertha is accompanied wherever she goes, so that nothing is taken. Mrs Peters, I imagine, will see that nothing is said?'

'Mrs Peters is the soul of loyalty and discretion,' replied Violet. 'I trust her absolutely. If others have been robbed I only hope they will tell *me*, and not the police.'

'If you have heard nothing, then I should assume that nothing has happened.'

'But will you speak to her, Charles, or just wait to see if this is her only slip?'

Charles looked thoughtful. 'I rather think I shall have a word with her. It will follow up your own efforts, and also make her realize that her actions are being noted.'

'She'll certainly take more notice of you than she does of me,' said Violet, getting up from the seat.

They began to walk towards the gate. Violet stopped suddenly and faced the clergyman.

'Charles, I can't begin to thank you. You are a tower of strength, and I feel so very much better for talking to you.'

'I've done very little,' said Charles. 'You have done most of the work. Mine lies ahead.'

He watched her as she retraced her steps across the green. She looked old and frail, but the Lovelock back was as straight as ever, Charles noted with admiration.

It grew hotter and more humid as the month of July went on. The grass at Thrush Green became brittle and brown, and the gardens of the houses around it needed watering every evening. Hoses, sprinklers and watering cans went into action as soon as the sun began to sink behind Lulling Woods, but all house-holders awaited the grim warning from the council banning the use of the life-saving liquid for the crops and flowers.

'It's the same every year,' grumbled Percy Hodge to Albert in The Two Pheasants. 'We gets fair flooded out in February and March – water butts overflowin', puddles up to your hocks, gumboots on day in and day out – and then comes three weeks dry, and we're told we've got a drought!'

'Gets in your chest, too,' said Albert, fingering an empty glass.

'What! The drought?'

'That's right. The dust like. Brings on me cough.' He essayed a short spell of somewhat unconvincing hacking.

'You best have another 'alf,' said Percy, not moving. His own glass was half full.

Seeing that there was no possibility of being treated to his drink, Albert shuffled to the bar to get a refill.

'Got two weddin's this Saturday,' he said on his return. 'What with the dust, and them old lime trees shedding their muck, not to mention rice and confetti, I'll be at it all Saturday evenin' clearin' up for Sunday.'

'Well, it's your job, ain't it? What you gets paid for? Weddin's is to be expected.'

'And when's yours to be expected?' asked Albert sharply. 'You havin' it here? White, and all that? I'll look forward to seein' you all dolled up in a mornin' suit and topper.'

Percy looked at him coldly. 'Ah! Very funny, Albert Piggott! I hope I knows how to behave at the right time.'

He pushed aside his glass and made for the door, slamming it behind him.

'You shouldn't have said that,' said Mr Jones, mopping down the counter. 'It's his own business, after all.'

Albert looked faintly embarrassed. 'Well, we all knows he's makin' a fool of himself if he takes up with that Cooke girl. Don't do any harm to twit him now and again.'

'There's such a thing as playing with fire,' the landlord told him, wringing out his cloth. 'How would you feel if some chap made nasty remarks about your Nelly?'

Albert stared stolidly at him across his empty glass. 'I'd join him,' he said.

6. Charles Henstock Does His Best

Percy Hodge's courtship had been common gossip, in a somewhat desultory way, to all Thrush Green and Lulling. The death of his first wife some years earlier, followed by the departure of his second and their subsequent divorce, had left Percy lonely and on the lookout for a new wife.

At one time he had paid unwelcome attention to Winnie Bailey's companion, Jenny. He had been repulsed, and Jenny was one of those most relieved to hear that Percy's hopes of matrimony might come to fruition in the near future.

She and Mrs Bailey were discussing the matter as they washed up the breakfast things together, for Jenny lived in, in a comfortable flat upstairs in Dr Bailey's old home. It was a happy arrangement. Winnie had found, to her shame, that she was nervous alone at night after her husband's death, despite the many friends around her. When Jenny's parents went into a retirement home, she was offered her present quarters, and the two women had settled together with the utmost satisfaction.

'I must say,' said Jenny, rinsing cups under the hot tap, 'that it'll be a relief to see Perce settled.'

'Nothing like the relief I felt when you turned him down,' replied Winnie. 'What should I have done without you?'

'There was never any chance of me taking on that fellow,' said Jenny briskly, 'and Emily Cooke's a fool if she does.'

'Well, she does have her little boy to consider,' replied Winnie tolerantly. 'I suppose she feels it is best for Nigel to have a father – or stepfather, I should say.'

'It won't be Nigel she'll be thinking about if she takes on

Percy,' said Jenny. 'It's her own comforts that'll be on her mind.'

'Percy is certainly what my husband's people used to call "a warm man", with that big house and quite a bit of land.'

'It'd take more than that to persuade most women to saddle themselves with Percy Hodge,' said Jenny.

At that moment they heard a thud in the hall, and Winnie went to collect the post from the door-mat. Willie Marchant, the postman, was making his way back to the bicycle which was propped up by the gate.

Winnie took the letters back to the kitchen, and sat at the table.

'Two for you, Jenny, and one enormous packet for me. What can it be?'

It turned out to be a book, most carefully swathed in tissue paper and then stiff brown paper, with a label addressed in what Winnie suddenly realized was Agnes Fogerty's clear print.

There was a letter enclosed which Winnie read attentively.

'It's a book I lent Miss Fogerty when she was laid up at the Shoosmiths. I wish she hadn't bothered to return it. The postage is so expensive, and they are bound to be coming up again.'

'How are they?' enquired Jenny, propping her two postcards on the dresser.

'They sound busy, and seem to have made quite a few friends. Dorothy is doing good works, including reading to a blind man called Teddy.'

'Poor chap!' said Jenny. 'I reckon being blind is the worst of the lot. My old people were both stone deaf towards the end, and that was bad enough.'

'Losing any of your five senses is dreadful,' agreed Winnie, stuffing Agnes's letter back into its envelope.

'Have you ever thought,' commented Jenny, busily swabbing the draining board, 'that if you can't see you're called *blind*, and if you can't hear you're called *deaf*, but if you can't smell anything, like Bill Cartwright, there's no word for it?'

'Oh, but there is,' Winnie informed her. 'My old uncle always said he was *snoof*!'

A little later that morning, Winnie was pegging out some washing when she was hailed by her neighbour Phyllida Hurst who lived next door. Winnie approached the useful gap in their common hedge, where one of the hawthorn bushes had expired and never been adequately replaced.

'I've promised to do the flowers for the church this week,' said the younger woman, 'and I wondered if you could spare some of your copper beech twigs.'

'Of course, Phil. Come round whenever you like. Is there anything else of use here?'

'Can I come and see? All I appear to have here are dwarf begonias and nasturtiums. Not quite the stuff for church decorations really.'

She squeezed through the gap, and the two women paced round the garden, assessing Winnie's floral produce.

It was perfectly true, Winnie thought, that the next door garden never did as well as her own. Something to do with the soil, no doubt, but also the several years of complete neglect before the Hursts had taken it over.

The former occupants of Tullivers had been an elderly couple, Admiral Josiah Trigg and his sister, Lucy. To be sure, Josiah had tended his flower border assiduously, and a jobbing gardener had cut the grass and hedges in his time, but when the admiral had died Lucy had done nothing to the garden.

Hedges became spinneys, lawns became meadows, and the seeds of thistle, dandelion, and willow herb floated into neighbouring gardens. Brambles and nettles invaded the place, and the inhabitants of Thrush Green grieved over Tullivers' sad condition.

Nothing had been done to the house either for that matter, Winnie remembered. She had been perturbed by the condition of her neighbour's house; the grimy windows, paths and steps, and the utter neglect of all that was inside.

It was not as if Lucy Trigg were senile, far from it. Winnie knew her as a formidable bridge player and solver of crossword puzzles, and she had trenchant views on current events. But her surroundings meant nothing to her, and her meals were as erratic as dear old Dotty Harmer's at Lulling Woods: an apple crunched as she read the newspaper, or a doorstep of brown bread spread with honey, as she filled in the crossword, sufficed Lucy.

It had been a relief to everyone when a young woman, then Phyllida Prior, had taken over the house and set about tidying up, with the help of her little boy and a succession of local amateur part-time gardeners. It was Harold Shoosmith who had really done most of the reclamation in the early days, and although the garden was much improved, it was not until Phil married again, an older man called Frank Hurst, that the place became trim, although it was never as fruitful as some of the other much-loved gardens at Thrush Green.

Winnie and Phil collected an armful of beech sprays, some roses, lupins and Canterbury bells.

'It seems a motley lot,' observed Winnie, surveying their harvest. 'I suppose you really want some trailing stuff for the pedestals. You can quite see why the Victorians liked smilax to drape everywhere.'

'This is splendid,' Phil assured her. 'I'm only in charge of the humbler efforts at the foot of the lectern and the font. The real high-fliers like Muriel Fuller are the only people let loose on things like pedestals.'

'That reminds me,' said Winnie, sitting on the garden seat and patting the space beside her. 'I heard from Dorothy and Agnes today. They do seem to have settled very happily at Barton.'

'They'd make friends wherever they went,' replied Phil. 'You get good training at Thrush Green in the art of sociability.'

'I think you are right. I only hope that Alan Lester's wife will think so too. As the headmaster's wife, she'll be scrutinized pretty thoroughly, I'm afraid. It's not easy, you know, living on top of the job like that.'

'Agnes and Dorothy managed it,' said Phil.

'Agnes and Dorothy,' responded Winnie, 'were two remarkable women, whose lives were outstandingly exemplary and virtually an open book.'

'Well, let's hope the Lesters will prove the same,' said Phil, rising to return next door.

'Let's hope so indeed,' echoed Winnie.

While the two ladies were conversing in the garden at Thrush Green, the subjects of their discussion were studying a Trust House Hotels' brochure with much interest. It had been Dorothy's idea that another short break would do them both good.

'After all, Agnes,' she said, 'you had to spend quite some time in bed when we were at Thrush Green. The visit really didn't do you the *benefit* it should have done. What about somewhere further north?'

'Scotland, do you mean?'

'No, no, no! There's no need to go somewhere as extreme as that, all mist and murk.' She turned the pages briskly.

'I'm really quite content to stay here,' ventured Agnes.

'I'm sure you are,' said Dorothy, 'but the fact remains that in this humid weather Barton seems as hot and sticky as most places. I should like somewhere more wooded, and with a few nice hills.'

'What about Wales? Are there any Welsh hotels in that brochure?'

'Quite a few.' She browsed in silence for a time. 'What I like about these Trust House places is that they have a kettle in the bedroom.'

Agnes looked bewildered.

'For tea, dear, or coffee,' explained Dorothy in the tone she used to address somewhat dim-witted children in her teaching days. 'It does mean that one can have a cuppa in the privacy of

61

one's room rather than having to be civil to strangers in the lounge.'

It was quite clear to Agnes that they would certainly be setting off for another few days' holiday within the next few weeks, and she adapted herself to the idea, though with some remaining misgivings.

'What about your meetings? And Teddy?' she added.

'We can pick a time when we haven't any commitments; and I have no doubt that Eileen would be only too pleased to read to Teddy.'

She sounded a little waspish, Agnes thought. She disliked Eileen's noisy ways as much as Dorothy did, but recognized the fact that Eileen was a lonely woman, and also extremely kind-hearted. In fact, Agnes remembered, with a wave of gratitude, she had offered to look after dear Timmy if they were away.

'There's Timmy—' she began.

'Well, we know all about Tim,' said Dorothy, shaking out the brochure impatiently to find the map. 'We faced the problem of Tim when we took him on. No doubt one of the neighbours will feed him.'

'I was just going to say so,' said Agnes. 'Eileen mentioned it only the other day. Anytime, she said, she would look after him, and I'm sure she meant it.'

'I'm sure she did,' agreed Dorothy, spreading the map on the table. 'There's nothing Eileen likes more than seeing inside other people's houses.'

Agnes fell silent. It was the only thing to do when Dorothy was in this mood.

'There seem to be some nice hotels in the Derbyshire area,' said Dorothy.

'Isn't that rather a long way to drive? Isn't Birmingham in the way?'

'Well, Birmingham doesn't stretch *right the way across*! We could drive to the left or right of it, if you see what I mean.'

Agnes joined her friend and studied the map too.

'There are certainly some lovely old houses to see,' she

agreed. 'Kedleston Hall and Hardwick, and lots of others. And, of course, we should get the hills, shouldn't we?'

At that moment the telephone rang, and Dorothy hastened into the hall to answer it. She was smiling when she returned.

'It was that nice Terry Burns,' she told Agnes, naming one of the churchwardens. 'He's bringing round some gardening books at about six. I wonder if we've any sherry? He likes it dry, I seem to remember.'

'There's some of the Tio Pepe left that Isobel gave us,' Agnes reminded her, relieved to see how much happier Dorothy seemed now that Eileen was forgotten.

'Perfect,' replied Dorothy, folding up the map. 'What should we do without our friends?'

A few days after Violet's visit to the vicarage, Charles Henstock made his way down the High Street to call upon the Misses Lovelock, and Bertha in particular. His heart was heavy. This was one of those duties which had to be undertaken, but it filled him with foreboding. However, he had promised Violet that he would have a word with her sister, and so it must be done.

Violet opened the door to him; her expression of joy and relief as she greeted him was more than compensation for the good rector's endeavours.

'Ada is shopping,' said Violet, 'and Bertha is in bed, not too well. I will lead the way.'

Charles followed Violet's bony legs upstairs and along a dark landing to a bedroom overlooking Lulling High Street.

'I've brought you a visitor, Bertha,' said Violet.

'Well, what a nice surprise,' replied Bertha, removing a pair of steel-rimmed spectacles. 'How kind of you to call, Charles.'

She extended a fragile hand. It felt almost like a bird's claw as Charles held it in his own plump one.

'Would you like coffee?' enquired Violet.

'Not for me,' said Bertha.

'Not for me, many thanks,' smiled Charles.

He was aware of Violet's agitation by the unusual flush

which now suffused her face and neck, but he could not help admiring the aplomb with which she was carrying out her duties as hostess.

'Then I shall leave you to talk,' she said. 'If you will excuse me, I will go back to my kitchen affairs.'

She closed the door, and Charles had a chance to look about the room as Bertha busily folded up the newspaper she had been perusing. It certainly was uncomfortably crowded, and Charles recognized one or two pieces of furniture which had once had their place in the drawing-room downstairs.

A glass-fronted china cabinet was squashed between the dressing-table and wardrobe. It appeared to be crammed with exquisite porcelain, and on top stood a heavy silver rose-bowl which Charles knew had once been presented to the sisters' father.

More silver pieces were lodged on top of the mahogany wardrobe: Charles could see mugs, salvers, wine coasters, jugs and at least three silver teapots. A little Sheraton sofa table, another exile from the drawing-room, stood by Bertha's bed, and this too carried a host of miniature silverware. Charles recognized a dolls' tea-set, a miniature coach-and-four, and a windmill.

There was certainly something very odd happening in this house, and Charles felt a shiver of apprehension. Here, he knew, was madness – madness of a mild kind, no doubt, but something strange, sad and ominous.

'And how is dear Dimity?' enquired Bertha.

'Very well, thank you, and sends her love.'

Bertha inclined her head graciously. She seemed to be completely in charge of herself, but Charles noticed that the bony hands which smoothed her bed-covers were quivering.

He decided to broach his painful duty. 'I see you have had some things transferred from downstairs.'

'I like to have pretty things around me.'

'But don't your sisters miss them?'

Bertha looked at him sharply. 'They are not their property. And in any case, they can see them when they come up here.'

Charles decided on another approach. 'But don't you find they get in the way? It must be quite difficult to move around with so much in here.'

'I can manage,' she snapped.

Silence fell. A car hooted in the street below, a baby wailed, and a dog barked. The life of Lulling continued as usual outside in the fresh air, and Charles became aware of the stuffiness of this cluttered bedroom.

'I *want* the things here,' said Bertha at last. 'Ada and Violet don't appreciate them, and never have. I've taken them into my care, and I intend to see Justin Venables about changing my will.'

'Changing your will?' echoed Charles, much bewildered.

'Everything in this room is to go to St John's church in gratitude for Anthony Bull's ministrations.'

Charles was stunned. He felt as if he had been struck with a hard and heavy object, and was conscious of his head throbbing and his heart behaving in a most unusual fashion.

'Would you mind if I opened the window a little, Bertha?' he asked.

'Please do. Violet is inclined to keep the windows closed.'

Charles struggled from his chair, and heaved at the large sash window furthest from Bertha's bed. It was a relief to see the normality of Lulling outside, and the cool air revived him. He took several deep breaths and returned to his chair.

'My dear Bertha,' he began, 'it is a most generous gesture of yours, but before you do anything about the will, please consult your sisters and tell them what is in your mind.'

'I shall do nothing of the sort,' Bertha rapped out. She looked at him suspiciously. 'You are on their side! They've put you up to this!'

'I'm on nobody's side,' protested poor Charles, 'and no one has "put me up", as you say, to anything.'

'I shall tell Justin to call here,' replied Bertha. She was now very flushed and breathless. Charles knew that it was useless to try to reason with her. He had failed in his mission, and it was time to depart. It was obviously going to be impossible to go into the matter of taking things from The Fuchsia Bush at this stage.

He got up from the chair and approached the bed. He took Bertha's hand and patted it.

'I am sorry to have upset you, Bertha, and I'm going to leave you to rest now. But please think about my suggestion. I hope you will decide to talk to Ada and Violet.'

'I told you – I shall certainly *not* consult them.'

Charles released the hand. 'Then I beg of you,' he said earnestly, 'to consult your conscience instead.'

And with that he left.

Violet was fluttering about in the hall as he descended the stairs.

'Come into the drawing-room,' she whispered.

They sat down facing each other.

'Well?' queried Violet.

'Not well at all, I fear,' said Charles. 'I haven't really helped much.'

He told her, as gently as he could, about her sister's plan to alter her will, virtually laying claim to all that was in her bedroom. However, he purposely did not tell Violet about Bertha's idea of leaving all the treasures to St John's church. There was no point in burdening her with this extra problem, and he disliked the idea of this crazy plan of Bertha's being discussed in the parish.

'And she intends to see Justin?' gasped Violet. 'What shall we do?'

'I should do nothing while she is safely in bed,' replied Charles. 'I gather that the only telephone is in the hall down here, and any letters will pass through your hands. If she does propose getting in touch with him, then I think you must speak to him first and explain matters. If need be, I will have a word with him whenever you give me permission.'

'Charles! I hope it won't come to that.'

'So do I. In any case, I am sure that Justin will know exactly what to do in this sort of situation. I seem to recall something at the beginning of a will to the effect that: "I, being of sound body and mind etc." and I'm sure it is now sadly plain that Bertha is *not* of sound mind at the moment.'

'I fear not,' agreed Violet, much agitated.

'I must go,' said Charles. 'I'll come again in a day or two to see how things are going. Get in touch at once if you are worried, but I'm sure we can only wait and hope that she will realize how foolish she is being.'

'Thank you, Charles, for everything. I shall take your advice.'

As Charles returned to the vicarage he felt a great sense of failure. He also turned over in his mind Bertha's strange intention to leave everything to the church. The fact that the gift was to be a tribute to his predecessor Anthony Bull, who now had a parish in London, did not perturb or surprise him. Anthony was an old friend, and Charles was the first to recognize and appreciate his dynamic qualities.

Anthony Bull's outstanding good looks, his charm of manner, and his almost theatrical delivery of his sermons, had won the hearts of all who met him. It was not surprising that Bertha Lovelock had felt such burning affection for him. She was only one of many in his congregation to whom he had brought colour and comfort.

It was also quite logical that she should wish to repay the inspiration he had given her, and to do it through the church she had always attended rather than as a direct bequest to the man himself, showed a certain delicacy of feeling, and a sense of propriety quite consistent with the attitude of the Lovelocks.

But Charles hoped sincerely that nothing would come of Bertha's alarming plans. Rumours of her incipient kleptomania were already rife in Lulling, and Dimity knew that he had made today's errand in the hope of being able to help. He would have to tell her that he had failed in his mission, but that he hoped to try again.

The business of the will, he decided, should remain secret.

7 . Preparing to Move

It came as no surprise to anyone to find that the school house at Thrush Green had little to show in the way of additions when the school holidays began. To be sure, there was an area at the back of the house which had been marked out with pegs, and one morning in early August a lorry had backed in and deposited a load of sand.

Betty Bell remarked on it when she was at the Shoosmiths one morning, giving them what she termed 'a good turn out'.

'I'll bet my bottom dollar them poor Lesters won't be in that place before next Christmas. I thought the old people's place was taking its time; but this lot haven't even got started.'

'Well, I believe the Lesters are on holiday for a week or so,' said Isobel. 'I expect they'll chivvy things up when they return.'

'Gone to the seaside, have they?' asked Betty, turning a dining-room chair upside down and tackling the legs with a generous dab of polish.

'No. The Peak District, I think. They're touring, and Mr Lester hoped to go to the opera at Buxton.'

Betty's ministrations were arrested. 'I went to the opera once,' she said. The tone was of one recollecting a nasty session at the dentist's.

'Didn't you enjoy it, Betty?'

'No, I didn't! The *noise*! What with all that screeching, and the band on top of that, I had a splitting headache. I really prefer the telly – you can switch it off.'

She resumed her polishing with renewed vigour.

'So when's he hoping to move in?' she enquired somewhat breathlessly.

'I believe he hoped to move in during August,' said Harold, who was looking out of the window to the house next door.

'He'll be lucky,' commented Betty.

And Harold was inclined to agree.

But a week later, Alan Lester's car drew up outside the property and out tumbled two little girls followed, more decorously, by their parents.

Interested inhabitants of Thrush Green watched the schoolmaster unlock the front door to allow his family some folding-chairs, several large baskets and assorted packages into the empty house.

'That looks more hopeful,' commented Harold to Isobel. He watched Alan Lester return to the car to retrieve an unwieldy bundle of brooms, a bucket and a vacuum-cleaner.

'Don't be such a busybody,' said Isobel. 'You are as bad as the Lovelocks, peeking behind curtains.'

Harold laughed, and went into his study to write some letters. They could hear the children playing next door, exploring the playground and peering in the hedge for abandoned nests.

When it became time for mid-morning coffee, Isobel suggested that Harold might call next door to invite them over. The Lesters seemed delighted to down tools, and the four of them joined the Shoosmiths in the garden.

'I must say,' said Harold, 'that we didn't dare hope to see you quite so soon. You really have bought it, then?'

'It was a case of moving quickly,' said Alan. 'The fellow who bought my house had the ready money and was anxious to move in quickly as his wife is expecting their first baby shortly. It suited us, too.'

'It's good news for us,' Isobel said. 'We've hated seeing the place standing empty. Is there much to do?'

'Basically, no. The extension will simply have to be done while we are in residence, but in some ways that will be a good thing. We can keep an eye on affairs.'

'What we *would* like,' said Alan's wife, 'is somebody to give the place a good scrub out. Can you suggest anyone?'

'Domestic help is pretty thin on the ground at Thrush Green,' replied Isobel. She told her about Betty Bell, but Margaret Lester was adamant that she would not employ someone who was already heavily engaged.

'It's the quickest way to make enemies,' she said smiling, 'but perhaps she might know of someone? We want to move in in about ten days' time, and it would only be this one occasion. I don't think I shall need regular help.'

Isobel promised to make enquiries, and the conversation turned to such matters as milk deliveries, reliable grocers and butchers, the rarity of jobbing gardeners and the everlasting boon of The Two Pheasants.

The two men, followed by the little girls, then went on a tour of the Shoosmiths' garden, while Isobel and Margaret sat talking.

'I do so hope it will all work out,' said the latter. 'It's all been done in such a hurry, but Alan was worried about me, I know.'

'Do you have health problems?'

Margaret sighed. 'I've really not been quite as fit since Kate was born. There's nothing that the doctors can do, so they say, but I get the most appalling headaches, and they leave me terribly low and depressed.'

Isobel made sympathetic noises. Privately, she wondered if Margaret Lester was something of a hypochondriac; she seemed almost pleased to be discussing her symptoms.

'In that case,' said Isobel, 'I'm sure Alan is doing the right thing by moving here where you can be together so much more. And you will find Thrush Green people are very friendly. As for the air here, it's absolutely a tonic in itself. I'm sure you will all feel the benefit.'

'Well, I certainly hope so,' said Margaret wanly. 'I really can't face feeling like this for the rest of my life!'

'You won't have to,' replied Isobel sturdily. 'Come round here if you need anything while you are working next door; the telephone is here, and a couch if you feel like a rest.'

'You are so kind. We are having lunch at The Two Pheasants and Mr Jones has said exactly the same. I think we are going to settle in nicely.'

'I'm sure of it,' said Isobel, and watched the woman making her way towards the family, and then next door to resume her labours.

Later that day, Isobel voiced her fears about Margaret Lester's possible hypochondria, but Harold was dismissive of such conjectures.

'I thought she was a very nice little woman. And after all, they are obviously having quite a lot of worry at the moment, with all the upheaval of moving, and getting the little girls used to the idea of going to the same school as their father. It's not surprising that she seems a little low at the moment.'

Isobel said no more, but reserved her judgement.

＊

True to her word, Isobel spoke to Betty Bell about the cleaning of the school house.

'Well, now,' said Betty, 'I'd dearly like to take it on myself, but I've got my old auntie coming for a bit, and I shall be tied up with her.'

'Don't worry, Betty. Mrs Lester didn't really expect you to do it, just to suggest someone, if possible.'

Betty Bell ruminated, picking automatically at what appeared to be congealed marmalade on the edge of the kitchen table.

'Tell you what,' she said at last, 'have a word with Nelly Piggott. She might do it, and if not she'd know of someone, I don't doubt.'

That evening Nelly Piggott was busy frying what she termed 'a nice bit of rump' when Isobel called to make her request.

'Come in, come in,' cried Nelly, shifting the sizzling pan to one side of the stove, but Isobel made her request from the doorstep, not wishing to disturb Nelly's labours.

'I'd do it myself if I'd the time,' Nelly told her. 'Nothing I like more than a bit of steady scrubbing, but we're a bit short-handed at the shop, what with holidays and that. I'll have a word with a friend of mine, Mrs Lilly. I know she might be glad to earn something.'

This was good news, and Isobel explained that Nelly's friend should get in touch with the Lesters, if she were interested, and gave Nelly their telephone number. She returned home feeling that she had done her duty.

The evening was hot and humid. Tiny black thunder-flies were everywhere, speckling the white paint and crawling over bare skin in the most irritating manner.

Isobel sank thankfully into a chair and brushed her tickly arms. 'Heavens, I'm tired!'

'What have you been up to?' queried Harold.

Isobel told him.

'Now for pity's sake, don't go rushing about on the Lesters' behalf,' he said crossly. 'They are quite capable of coping with their own affairs, and there's no need to wear yourself out.'

'I haven't done much,' protested Isobel. 'Only tried to find someone to clean the house for them before they move in.'

'Well, don't let them impose on you,' said Harold, who could not bear to see Isobel worried in any way.

'You sound like my mother,' laughed Isobel, 'who used to say: "Start as you mean to go on!" '

'And quite right too,' agreed Harold. 'Now stay there, and I'll get you a drink.'

Meanwhile, replete with rump steak, fried potatoes, onions and baked beans, Nelly took herself down the hill to the road where Gladys Lilly lived.

It was one of the smaller, older terraced houses in the street, a 'two-up-two-down' cottage where Gladys had lived alone since the death of her husband.

A year or so earlier, in the last few months of Miss Watson and Miss Fogerty's reign at Thrush Green school, a daughter Doreen had kept her mother company. The girl had a young son, and had worked for a time at the Lovelocks, leaving the child with his grandmother. It was not a happy arrangement. Doreen had hated her job, and to give the girl her due it was hardly surprising, for the Lovelocks' house was large, over-furnished and difficult to keep clean. The three sisters were demanding and paid a poor wage. Gladys got used to listening to a string of complaints about life in Lulling when Doreen came home from work each day.

But it was a considerable shock to Gladys when the girl sneaked away with the child one day, leaving no message and no address. It was soon apparent that she had run away with the young man who was her little boy's father. Apart from a sparsely-worded postcard, on which the postmark was so blurred that it was indecipherable, Gladys had heard no more, and had resumed her solitary existence with both resentment and relief.

She was delighted now to see Nelly, and the kettle was put on at once for a cup of coffee. While it boiled, Nelly broached the purpose of her visit, and handed over the slip of paper bearing the Lesters' telephone number.

'What are they like?' asked Gladys.

'To tell the truth, I've never clapped eyes on *her*,' replied Nelly, 'but *he's* a nice enough chap. Good with the kids. I haven't heard anyone criticizing him yet, and that's saying something after all those years Miss Watson and Miss Fogerty were there.'

Gladys nodded ruminatively. 'Well, I'm game,' she said at last. 'I keep the chapel clean these days, but I don't do much else. The money would come in handy, too. I'll give them a ring later on.'

The two ladies then turned their attention to other matters.

'What's all this I hear about the Lovelocks pinching things?' enquired Gladys.

Nelly, for all her love of a good gossip, had no intention of discussing this matter which so intimately concerned The Fuchsia Bush.

'Don't know much about that,' she asserted, 'but is there any news of Doreen?'

Thus diverted, Gladys imparted exciting news. Doreen, it seemed, had rung the next door neighbour and left a message.

'And what was it?' asked Nelly, equally agog.

'Just to say she was all right. Might be coming down sometime.'

'But where is she? And who with? And is the little boy all right? Is she still with that fellow of hers?'

Gladys responded to this spate of questions, with a sad shaking of the head.

'She never said no more. Makes me wish I'd got the telephone myself. I could have found out more. The money run out evidently, and she just rang off.'

'Well, that was bad luck,' said Nelly, with genuine sympathy.

'Still, you do know she's all right. Be nice to see her again, won't it?'

'A mixed blessing, I expect,' replied Gladys. 'She's not turned out as I'd have hoped, brought up chapel too, and kept respectable. Makes you think, don't it?'

The ladies sighed in unison.

'Must be off,' said Nelly, getting up.

'I'll come as far as the phone box with you,' said Gladys, picking up the slip of paper.

'Can't you ring from next door?'

'I *could*,' replied Gladys, 'but I don't want everyone knowing my business.'

Nelly nodded her approval, and the two friends walked to the foot of the hill to Thrush Green and parted there by the telephone box.

'Well,' murmured Nelly, as she puffed homeward, 'I suppose I've done my good deed for the day. And now for the washing-up.'

It so happened that Charles Henstock saw the two women in the distance as he returned from a stroll by the River Pleshey. It was one of his favourite walks, and one which he always found himself undertaking when particularly perplexed in mind.

There was something about running water which healed the spirit as surely as sleep did. For Charles Henstock, the company of the river was indeed: 'Balm of hurt minds, great nature's second course,' and he usually returned from it calmed and comforted.

He sat by its side on a grassy bank, watching the secret life of the water creatures: a dragonfly alternately darted and hovered above the surface; while a water vole emerged from a hole on the opposite bank, fearless of the still figure so close, and paddled across, its hairy muzzle and bright eyes just clear of the water, leaving a wake behind it as neat as an arrow.

Flies studded the glistening mud at the edge of the bank, and a trio of butterflies played among a patch of nettles. An ancient willow tree stretched a gnarled arm over the water, and a flycatcher sat, still and erect in between its rapid darts, to secure an unwary insect.

Purple loosestrife and wild mint stirred in the light breeze, setting free the river smell, 'unforgettable, unforgotten' which brought back to the watcher on the bank a hundred memories of other loved rivers. Charles sat there for almost half an hour, letting the magic work its spell, and then he rose to return home.

The sun was beginning to sink behind Lulling Woods, and midges hovered in gauzy clouds over the river. In an hour or so the owls would be out, and the bats and moths, all busy above the glimmering water in their search for food. The river creatures of day and night might be different, thought Charles, setting off for home, but the river was unchanged in its steady progress eastward and the music of its voice.

Charles strode along the footpath until it emerged into the most westerly road of Lulling within a mile or two of the vicarage. He was calmer and more refreshed than when he had set out, but his mind was not entirely at ease.

It was the plight of Violet Lovelock which worried him. He had kept his word and returned to see Bertha again, hoping that she might have faced the fact that she had been at fault, and determined to overcome her weakness.

But his visit had been in vain, as he suspected it would be. Bertha was as evasive as ever, admitted nothing, was even more autocratic than was usual, and now that she was up and about appeared to be determined to go out as soon as possible.

Violet had been unable to get Charles alone on that occasion, but cast him appealing looks which rent poor Charles's kind heart. Later, he had spoken to her on the telephone, urging her to call at the vicarage whenever she felt the need. She had sounded resigned and exhausted, which Charles found even harder to bear than her earlier agitation, but there seemed little more that he could do.

As he walked up the High Street of Lulling in the failing light, he came to the Lovelocks' house and paused. There were lights in the drawing-room. They were not very bright lights, to be sure, probably just one or two table lamps containing low-watt bulbs, just enough to give adequate light to the sisters' knitting or crossword puzzle.

On impulse, Charles mounted the steps and knocked. Footsteps approached, and there was a rattle as the chain on the door was removed. Bolts were shot back, the door opened, and Violet stood silhouetted against the dim light of the hall.

'Oh Charles!' she cried. 'How lovely to see you. Do come in.'

Her two sisters fluttered to their feet as Charles came into the drawing-room, expressing delight and offering sherry or coffee.

Charles declined and apologized for disturbing them.

'The fact is,' he explained, 'I simply saw your lights on and couldn't resist calling to see you.'

'How very kind,' said Ada.

'Very kind,' echoed Bertha.

The room seemed stuffy and chilly at the same time, but Charles told himself that it was probably his own walk in the fresh air that made this present situation so enervating in contrast.

The usual polite enquiries were exchanged about health, gardens and the like, until Bertha announced with some pride: 'Tomorrow I am taking Ada and Violet to lunch at The Fuchsia Bush.'

There was a gasp from Violet, and a puzzled look from Ada; it was quite apparent that this was the first they had heard of it.

'Are you sure, dear?' enquired Ada.

'I had prepared a little chicken in a casserole,' said Violet.

'No, no!' said Bertha, with some vehemence. 'I *particularly* want to go next door tomorrow.'

There was a pause.

'Very well,' said Violet at last. 'I'm sure we should all enjoy it.'

'I must be off,' said Charles. 'Dimity will wonder where I am. So good to see you looking so well.'

Violet accompanied him to the front door. 'One moment,' she whispered. 'I will walk part of the way with you.'

She returned to the drawing-room briefly, and then joined Charles. He was surprised to see that she did not put on a hat or gloves, as was her wont, but simply drew on a jacket which was hanging in the hall. Charles helped to arrange it round her skinny shoulders, and they descended the steps into the deserted street.

'I felt I must have a word with you,' began Violet, as they set off towards the vicarage. 'You have been *such* a support through this awful time, and I just wanted you to know that I am feeling so much better about the whole affair.'

'Is she over it? Faced things? Or has John Lovell seen her?'

'No, no, nothing like that. She still refuses to admit anything, but I have made up my mind that we can only do so much and no more. It's I who have faced things, Charles.'

She slowed to a stop. It was now almost dark. Moths fluttered around one of the street lamps which were beginning to come into light along the High Street. A black-and-white cat trotted purposefully under the shadow of the shop fronts, intent on its nightly business. In a nearby front garden, the night-scented stocks sent out a heady perfume.

'I shall keep a sharp eye on Bertha, and accompany her whenever she goes out. Luckily, I don't think she is able to slip away unnoticed. And if she transfers any more things to her bedroom, I shall simply ignore it.'

'Has she said any more about the will?'

'Not a thing. But I am quite prepared to have a private word with Justin if she broaches the subject again.'

'I don't think you can do more at this stage,' agreed Charles, 'and I must say I am so relieved to hear that you feel that you can cope with her.'

'What else can we do? She is my sister, and I am devoted to her, infuriating though she is at the moment. I know I can ask you for help, and if need be I can speak to Justin and John Lovell. Meanwhile, I live in hope that she will come to her senses.'

She gave a sudden shiver.

'You are getting cold,' said Charles anxiously. 'The wind is quite chilly. I think you should go back, and I will come with you to the door.'

'No, no, indeed! It is only a few steps, and I shall hurry back. But I wanted to tell you how things are. No better really for Bertha, but much more settled for me.'

'Call on me if ever you are worried,' replied Charles, and watched her scurry back to her home.

Later that evening he told Dimity about his visit to the Love-locks' establishment.

'You are not still worrying about Bertha's little weakness?' said his wife. 'It is general knowledge, you know, and most people are very understanding about it.'

'I hadn't quite realized,' replied Charles, somewhat taken aback, 'that the Lovelocks' affairs were generally known.'

'Good heavens, Charles,' cried Dimity, 'you've lived in Lulling long enough to know how news gets about! All that I bother about is seeing you so worried. I suppose poor Violet has been unburdening herself to you!'

'I'm truly sorry I've been a worry to you,' said Charles. 'I should have realized that you are ever-watchful. But I really think that things will be easier now in that unhappy household.'

He told her a little of Violet's attitude, and of her reaction to Bertha's strange ways.

'It certainly sounds more hopeful,' said Dimity, folding up her sewing in preparation for bed time. 'Now I shall get a hot drink. You look tired and cold, as well you might with the Lovelocks' burdens upon you.'

She kissed the top of his shiny bald head as she passed his chair on the way to the vicarage kitchen, and wondered if his parishioners really knew how completely he lived for them.

8. TERM BEGINS

Gladys Lilly had performed her cleaning task at the school house with exceptional zeal and speed, and Thrush Green was pleased to see a large removal van draw up at the Lesters' gate one morning.

'They've got a lovely sofa,' Jenny told Winnie Bailey as they made the beds together. She was standing at the window, plumping up a pillow as she gazed across the green. 'Like my old folks had, only their springs had gone. And I wonder what's in them crates?'

'Jenny, do come on! I've left the gammon boiling, and it will be all over the stove.'

Jenny wrenched her attention from the Lesters' affairs, and returned to the bed-making reluctantly.

'I wonder what they'll find missing at the end of the day,' she remarked, as she tucked in sheets in an efficient hospital corners' way. 'It's usually something small like the tea strainer, or the washing-up brush.'

'Bound to be something vital,' agreed Winnie.

Of course, the rest of Thrush Green was equally enthralled by the Lesters' arrival. Joan Young and her husband Edward reminded each other of the upheaval they had experienced when settling Joan's parents into their new abode.

Muriel Fuller, sorting out material with Ella Bembridge, told her of the horrors she had endured when it came to packing up her old school's property, and her own personal belongings as well.

'It's not so much what you want to *keep*,' she said, 'as what you simply *have* to throw away. I nearly had a nervous break-down. Dr Lovell was so understanding. He said I'd been living with my nerves for years.'

'You wouldn't be much use without them,' said Ella bluntly, and Muriel withdrew into affronted silence.

Isobel Shoosmith, the soul of hospitality, would have liked to ask the Lesters for morning coffee, but in view of Harold's earlier remarks about doing too much for their new neighbours decided to leave any invitations until later in the day. It was possible, she thought, that Harold himself might make overtures over the hedge.

But the most concentrated attention came from Albert Pig-gott who had taken up a strategic position in the churchyard. Ostensibly, he was weeding round the edges of the plot, and had a bucket beside him in which he occasionally deposited a handful of grass, chickweed or groundsel. The more virulent intruders such as young brambles, stinging nettles and the like, Albert ignored. Young Cooke could get on with those – what was he paid for?

Albert noted a nice plain green carpet going in, followed by a set of book cases and two upholstered arm chairs. Getting the sitting-room done first, thought Albert with approval. They'd need a good rest this evening. A number of tea chests were carried in next; they clanked rather noisily, and Albert surmised that they held kitchen equipment.

He moved round inside the churchyard wall to get a better view, just in time to see a single divan bed being hoisted from the pantechnicon. Now would that be for one of the children or for the master or his wife? Albert watched closely from behind a tombstone erected to 'Ezekiel West 1798–1860, Beloved By All' (an assertion which Albert had always considered unduly optimistic) and watched as one more single divan followed the first.

Albert hoped these would be for the parents. He and Nelly

had separate beds, in fact, they had separate rooms, and Albert appreciated it. Nelly snored, although she hotly denied it.

Having satisfied himself about the sleeping arrangements, Albert left Ezekiel West's resting place, and shifted to 'Patience Wellworth, Devoted Wife and Mother' whose dates of birth and death were obscured by some tendrils of ivy which Albert had no intention of removing. Resting his arms on the top of Patience's granite cross, he observed with pleasure that the landlord of The Two Pheasants was opening his doors.

At the same moment, he became conscious of a large object being manhandled through the school house's front door, to the accompaniment of warning shouts. It was a large double bed, and Albert's hopes were thrown to the wind.

He put down his half-empty bucket and sought solace in the pub.

Betty Bell, returning from her labours at the Shoosmiths that morning, called to see Dotty Harmer on her way home. As well as her regular visits to that house, Betty often 'popped in', as she said, to keep an eye on the old lady, although this was not so vital now that Kit and Connie were there to look after their eccentric relation.

Dotty was busy trying to rake dead leaves from the surface of her little pond. She was not being very successful, and the half-dozen displaced ducks were squatting moodily nearby, occasionally giving a protesting quack.

She abandoned her task and motioned Betty to the garden seat, taking her place beside her. Betty was not surprised to see that Dotty's shoes and stockings were soaking wet, and that she had a streak of mud on one cheek.

'I'd let Mr Kit do that job,' said Betty. 'It's too much for you. And you ought to get your shoes off. Catch your death, you will.'

'Don't fuss, Betty,' responded Dotty. 'You're as bad as Connie. A little dampness never hurt anyone. After all, we are three parts water I believe, and originally evolved from water creatures.'

'Some time ago,' Betty pointed out reasonably. 'You on your own?'

'Kit and Connie are getting back for lunch,' said Dotty. 'Which reminds me, I'm supposed to turn on the oven.'

'Well, let's go and see to it,' said Betty, used to Dotty's vague ways, 'and I'm going to see you take off them wet shoes, and give you a cup of coffee. I don't suppose you've had any?'

'Well, no,' admitted Dotty, 'I've been rather busy.'

Betty shepherded the old lady into the kitchen, peered into the oven, turned it on, and then filled the kettle. Within ten minutes, Dotty's stockings and shoes were removed and replaced with dry ones, and the coffee was made.

'Is this the milk?' queried Betty, sniffing at a small jug. 'Smells a bit off to me.'

'Oh, that will do, dear. I really don't mind it slightly cheesy.

After all, the Tibetans always use rancid milk in their tea – and *yak's* milk at that.'

'I think I'll have mine black,' said Betty, and the two settled happily at the kitchen table for ten minutes' gossip about the newcomers to Thrush Green.

It so happened that Isobel saw nothing of her neighbours for several days as she and Harold had an unexpected invitation to have a few days with friends in Wales. On their return, Isobel rang the Lesters to enquire how things were going. Alan answered the telephone.

'We're settling in nicely,' he said cheerfully. 'We shall be pretty straight indoors before term starts next week.'

'That's good,' replied Isobel, 'and how's the building getting on?'

'Far too slowly, but I'm not sorry really as poor Margaret is under the weather again.'

'Oh dear! Can we help?'

'No, no, it's just this wretched migraine. She gets an attack now and again, and bed's the only place until it passes.'

'I expect she's been doing too much,' said Isobel. 'Let us know if there's anything we can do.'

'You are kind. She'll soon be over it, I'm sure. We're quite geared to this sort of thing.'

'I wonder,' said Isobel to Harold some time later, 'if they've decided to move here because of these migraine attacks?'

'Maybe,' said Harold engrossed in the crossword. 'Have you ever heard of "Taxonomy"?'

'Never.'

'Nor me. These crossword setters must be born in the knife-drawer, as my mother used to say. Far too sharp for me.'

Term began at Thrush Green school and Alison and Kate Lester were enrolled as new pupils, along with half a dozen new five-year-olds who were escorted to the classroom which had once been the domain of little Miss Fogerty.

On the same day, far away at Barton-on-Sea, Agnes was watching a little knot of children making their way to school. She was moved to see the small ones, obviously new entrants, clutching their pristine school bags and wearing school blazers which were rather too large, 'to allow for growth'.

'Do you ever wish you were back at Thrush Green, Dorothy?' she asked.

Dorothy was poring over a form which had just come in the post. 'Well, of course I do,' she replied. 'But not at the school.'

She had heard children's voices, and knew from neighbours that this was the first day of term. She also knew, from her long association with Agnes, exactly what was going on in that kind lady's heart.

'Not at the school?' echoed Agnes, somewhat surprised.

Dorothy put down the form. 'Pure gobbledegook this is! Why these so-called communications can't be expressed in plain English I cannot understand.' She surveyed Agnes with sympathy. 'No, I can assure you, I would not want to return to teaching. I did over forty years, as you did too, and I am very happy to have retired.'

'Yes, of course,' agreed Agnes. 'It's just that seeing the new babies going along just now, so trusting and *clean*, you know, it brought it all back.'

'It should also bring back the memories of tears and tantrums and puddles on the floor, which marked the first morning of term,' said Dorothy briskly. 'And do you remember that terrible boy who bolted home? We caught him half a mile up the Nidden road. Wretched child!'

'He was a Cooke,' said Agnes.

'That,' replied Dorothy, 'does not surprise me. Now, about this form. I think you have to sign it, too, but I'll slip along to Teddy later on and read it to him. He's bound to know what it means.'

She was as good as her word, and in her absence Agnes busied herself in the garden. The dahlias were making a fine show of scarlet and gold, and the roses still showed a few late blooms, but there were signs of autumn already. The new pyracantha, pushing its way valiantly up the wall by the porch, was a mass of berries just beginning to turn orange. The birds would be grateful, thought Agnes, watching some blue-tits squabbling over the peanut-holder nearby.

She sat down on the seat to enjoy the sunshine, and hoped that Dorothy would not be too long with Teddy. It was so difficult to time the potatoes exactly when she went out in the morning. She ruminated again about Dorothy's attitude to this new friend. He certainly seemed to take up a great deal of her time, but she remembered Isobel's sensible words. Dorothy was a wise person, and would not be likely to do anything rash. It would be quite dreadful if she let her kind heart rule her head though, and succumbed to Teddy's pleas to marry him.

At this alarming thought Agnes pulled herself together. Now, who on earth had said anything about Teddy proposing marriage? Or about Dorothy accepting him? It really was unfair to either of them to think this way. Teddy, after all, was a good, decent, well-educated man, with beautiful manners and a voice not unlike dear Anthony Bull's of Lulling. Perhaps, thought Agnes, with a return of the flutters, that was what made him all the more dangerous! Anthony Bull had often been called a charmer; was Teddy equally irresistible?

What rubbish! Agnes rose from the seat and set about deadheading pansies with unusual violence. And one really must trust Dorothy's judgement in this situation. She was simply being kind to an afflicted neighbour. The fact that he was *male* was beside the point. *Any* neighbour, Eileen say, who had been blind, would have been treated by Dorothy with the same selfless kindness which was one of her great qualities.

But Eileen? The ubiquitous, noisy, laughing Eileen, who also called so frequently upon Teddy? *Would* Dorothy do as much for Eileen?

Agnes dismissed the doubt from her mind and deadheaded an innocent yellow pansy with such violence that the whole plant came up in her hand. She decided it was high time to put on the potatoes.

At Lulling that same morning, Ella Bembridge and her old friend Dimity Henstock were enjoying coffee together at The Fuchsia Bush.

'And how goes the new extension at Rectory Cottages?' asked Dimity. 'I keep meaning to come up and have a look, but Charles keeps me informed about its progress.'

'It's taking shape well,' responded Ella. 'It didn't take the men long to erect the glass part, and it will be marvellous for the old folk when it's done. I've just been to see about the curtains.'

'So it is to be curtains after all?'

'Yes. Muriel and I had a word about it with the committee. It would have been rather bleak, we thought, just with those blinds Edward wanted. Sometimes I find Edward's ideas a trifle *Scandinavian*.'

'Scandinavian, Ella? Well, what's wrong with that?'

'Cheerless,' asserted Ella, helping herself to a piece of Nelly Piggott's gingerbread. 'Angular, cold – not right for us anyway.'

'What did Edward say?'

'Nothing. We told him that old people living in the chilly Cotswolds would want something cosier than just glass all round them in the winter.'

'I expect he wanted the blinds because he was thinking of the heat in the summer,' said Dimity, feeling rather sorry for Edward Young who had obviously met his match in Ella and Muriel.

'More fool him,' pronounced Ella rather indistinctly through the gingerbread. 'We have far more cold days than hot ones. Anyway, top and bottom of it is that Muriel and I are coping with the small curtains at the side, and the main ones, which are enormous, are being made by Prouts. I've just been over there to check the headings and fixtures.'

She went on to such technical matters as pulleys and

pinch-pleating which meant nothing to Dimity, but she was brought back to earth by hearing Ella say that Muriel had called on the headmaster's wife.

'She was looking very poorly,' Ella said. 'Red-eyed and rather snuffly. Probably getting a cold, Muriel didn't stay long in case she caught it.'

She dived into her handbag, producing several keys, a man's handkerchief of red-and-white spotted cotton, and a large sheaf of booklets which she deposited on the table.

'Raffle books,' she announced.

'What for?' enquired Dimity, feeling for her purse and about to do a vicar's wife's familiar duty.

'The extension, of course. The money's coming in quite well, but the autumn is going to be a mad whirl of whist drives, concerts, jumble sales and the usual things. How many can you manage, Dim?'

'Ten, I think,' said Dimity. 'I'm still coping with RSPB, Save The Whales, RSPCA and Blue Cross raffle books.'

'But they are all *animals*,' protested Ella.

'I prefer them,' replied Dimity simply.

When Dimity returned home that morning she found Charles searching for a box of tissues.

'I think I have a cold hanging about,' he said. 'I'll go and gargle. Such a nuisance so near to Sunday.'

Dimity remembered Ella's remarks about Mrs Lester's cold, and became extra solicitous.

At eight o'clock that evening Charles confessed that his head ached, and he thought that he should go to bed. He slept in fits and starts, and Dimity heard him tossing and turning in the other bed, occasionally mumbling incoherently.

At first light he awoke to find Dimity standing beside him, thermometer in hand.

'It's John Lovell for you,' she said firmly on reading the result.

'But I have to take a funeral,' protested Charles.

'It will be your own,' Dimity told him, 'if you don't do as you are told.'

Charles knowing when he was beaten, put his aching head back on the pillow.

Within three hours, of course, it was known that the rector was seriously ill, with complaints ranging from a heart attack, a fall downstairs, appendicitis and pneumonia to tonsilitis and influenza.

John Lovell's diagnosis was a combination of the two latter afflictions, but knowing how easily Charles contracted severe and painful chest troubles, he pumped a good measure of antibiotics into his victim, left a list of medicaments with Dimity, and strict instructions to see that his patient remained in bed.

'And as for that funeral he is fretting about, it will have to wait,' said the doctor, his mind naturally full of his duties towards the living rather than the dead.

Dimity, secretly shocked, said that she had already been in touch with the clergyman at the neighbouring town, who had kindly offered to stand in.

She closed the front door behind John, and made her way into the kitchen before going upstairs to assure her husband that everything was arranged, and that he could now relax and concentrate on his own affairs for a change.

But John Lovell's single-minded attitude still troubled her. Fancy saying that the funeral could wait! What about the relatives' unhappiness, and such practical matters as the catering for all those people who might have come from a distance? And think of all the flowers being made into beautiful sheaves and wreaths, and all the cards and letters? Really, men were so thoughtless, so inconsiderate!

Putting off a funeral, indeed!

Full of righteous wrath, Dimity set about making a jug of lemon barley water for the invalid. Thank goodness Charles was such an exceptional person, so unlike the usual run of men.

Thus dwelling on her good fortune, Dimity's rage gradually

simmered down, and she was able to bear aloft the soothing drink in her usual gentle frame of mind.

Harold Shoosmith was one of Charles's first visitors.

'Well, I must say you look pretty comfortable up here,' he remarked, looking down at the sunny garden and his old friend propped up on the plump pillows enjoying the view. 'Far better than the first time I visited you as an invalid, when you were in the clutches of that ghastly housekeeper at Thrush Green rectory.'

'Oh, really,' protested Charles, 'poor Mrs Butler did her best.'

'Well, it wasn't good enough,' maintained Harold. 'I remember her martyred expression as she puffed into your bedroom with a couple of water biscuits and a wizened apple for your lunch. I wonder you didn't succumb with malnutrition as well as bronchitis.'

'I must say Dimity is a first-class nurse, and I'm being thoroughly spoilt.'

'Now, what can I do? Any errands to run? Messages to deliver? Parish magazines to take round? Just say.'

'I think Dimity has most things in hand, but I am supposed to be introducing things at Joan and Edward's coffee morning later this week. It's for the old people's extension. Could you do that?'

'Of course.'

'Otherwise I'm just having to put things aside until I'm out and about again. It's the visiting which worries me. I have met Alan Lester, of course, but when I called to see his wife she was upstairs with a severe headache.'

'That's often the way,' Harold told him. 'I feel very sorry for Alan.'

'Indeed, yes,' said Charles, his face puckered with concern. 'It must be dreadful to have an invalid wife.'

'I'm not sure myself,' said Harold slowly, 'that she is an invalid in the sense you mean.'

Charles looked mystified. 'Not an invalid? But if she is so often prostrate upstairs what else can it be?'

But at that moment, Dimity came in with a tea tray, and Harold was spared the necessity of answering.

9. FAMILY AFFAIRS

Charles Henstock was confined to his bed for over a week. Both Dimity and John Lovell saw to that, despite protests from their patient who kept remembering parish duties of the most urgent nature which, so he maintained, could only be undertaken by himself.

His pleas fell on deaf ears.

'Do you want me to send you to hospital?' threatened the doctor.

'Do think of yourself for a change,' pleaded Dimity.

In the end it was simpler to give way, and the good rector had to admit to himself that it was really pleasant, apart from some aches, to loll back among the pillows and look forward to appetizing meals being brought at regular intervals and, even better, the visits of old friends.

Among them, to Charles's delight, was his predecessor Anthony Bull, who blew into the bedroom like a breath of sea air, and laughed to see Charles's astonishment.

'I'm on my way to Bath for a conference,' he explained, after enquiries about the patient's progress, 'and I couldn't pass so near without calling. Dimity has kept me in touch. Tell me the news.'

Charles rattled away, and was sorely tempted to tell him about Bertha Lovelock's alarming intentions concerning her will. But one of his favourite precepts was: 'Least said, soonest mended', and with that in mind he simply gave a brief account of Bertha's growing eccentricity and poor Violet's worries.

'And I've news for you,' said Anthony. 'Gladys Lilly's

daughter Doreen turned up the other day, and I very much hope that she will decide to come back to Lulling.'

'What has been happening to her? And why didn't she go back to her employers? Didn't they live near you?'

'Indeed they did – and still do. But I don't think she had the pluck to go back after deserting them. She seems to have left the so-called husband, but she looked pretty pathetic, so did the child. I did my best to persuade her to go back to her mother, but all she would promise was to get in touch by telephone.'

'I believe Dimity heard that she had,' said Charles.

'At the moment she says she is staying "with friends". I only hope they are female,' commented Anthony. 'I have promised to give her her fare home, and she says she will be in touch. We fitted her out with some clothes from the church box, and the boy too, but she wouldn't give us the "friends'" address. Do you know if her mother is on the telephone?'

'I can find out, but I doubt it. Maybe a neighbour is.'

Anthony looked at his watch, then rose and went to the window to survey the garden which had once been his.

Charles looked at his handsome back in its well-tailored dark suit. His silver hair was as abundant as ever, his bearing youthful and his face unlined. How soon, Charles wondered hopefully, would he be made a bishop? Somehow it seemed inevitable, and how well Anthony's elegant legs would look in gaiters!

'The garden looks better than ever,' said Anthony. 'Do you know, I think we were happier here in Lulling than in any other living. We loved everybody here.'

'It was reciprocated,' Charles assured him, as they made their farewells.

Harold Shoosmith carried out his duties at the coffee morning with the general approval of Thrush Green.

'Well, if it couldn't be the rector,' one of the inmates of Rectory Cottages was heard to remark to her neighbour, 'then you couldn't do better than Mr Shoosmith.'

And this, Harold reckoned when told the tale, was high praise indeed.

Although the morning was overcast, and the Youngs' garden was already showing signs of autumn, it stayed dry and pleas-

antly warm. Butterflies rested on the Michaelmas daisies, opening and shutting their dappled wings. A pair of collared doves strutted about among the visitors, alert to any crumb which might fall.

Mrs Curdle's old gipsy caravan, which now had a permanent resting place in the Youngs' small orchard, was being used as a bring-and-buy shop that morning. Ben, Mrs Curdle's grandson, and his wife Molly were in charge, and pots of jam and marmalade, lavender bags, handkerchiefs, homemade fudge and all the other familiar bring-and-buy objects were changing hands at a brisk pace, while the small drawer, where old Mrs Curdle had kept her takings for so many years, was in use again and chinked steadily with a stream of coins.

Winnie Bailey had suggested to Margaret Lester that they should go together since it would be a good opportunity for the headmaster's wife to meet people. She was then going to Winnie's for lunch.

Certainly the newcomer seemed to be enjoying herself, and talked animatedly to those she met. She was quite pretty, Winnie decided, when she forgot her troubles and joined in the general activities. It was important, Winnie felt, that Alan's wife should be seen to be pleasant and approachable, for a man in his position would be very much in the public eye, and his family under scrutiny. As the widow of the local doctor, Winnie knew that the wife of a leading resident played a part as vital as the man himself.

It was a relief to her to see the pleasure with which her friends greeted Margaret. She had been so much of a recluse since moving in, suffering from those mysterious headaches, that very few people had met her. Now everyone was anxious to welcome her to the small world of Thrush Green.

Muriel Fuller seemed particularly effusive in her greetings, and went to some length to say that she had called at the school house on several occasions and had been perturbed to hear of Mrs Lester's indisposition.

Winnie, seeing that the two were getting on so well, excused herself and went across to Ella and Dimity.

'And what news of Charles?'

'Getting on steadily, and dying to get out and about again.'

'Sure sign that he's on the mend,' commented Winnie.

'And far more difficult to control,' added his wife, 'than when he was really too groggy to go far. With luck, he should be back on light duties next week.'

They had both met Margaret Lester, and agreed that it was splendid to see that she was fit again.

At that moment, Winnie noticed that a car had stopped outside her gate, and a man was walking to her front door. Even at that distance, Winnie could see that it was her nephew Richard who had the disconcerting habit of turning up without warning.

'Oh dear,' cried Winnie, 'I'd better go across and see what's going on. I'll just let Margaret know where I'm going.'

She spoke to the headmaster's wife, and then hurried across

the grass. Trust Richard to arrive when there was only one trout apiece for lunch! Why couldn't it have been steak and kidney, or something equally *stretchable*, a casserole perhaps?

Richard was in the kitchen with Jenny sipping coffee, and he greeted his aunt affectionately.

'I'm on my way to pick up Fenella and the children. They've been staying with an old cousin of hers. I must say, I'll be glad to have them back. The place has been like a morgue without them.'

Winnie thought this sounded most satisfactory. Richard's marriage had had its ups and downs, and sometimes Winnie had wondered if Fenella might leave him. She was a strong-minded young woman who ran a picture gallery in London where the family lived. Sometimes Winnie suspected that it was the main reason for keeping the family together, and wished that Richard would provide the home as most husbands did. Fenella definitely called the tune, but Winnie was the first to admit that Richard was a difficult fellow to live with, and perhaps it was as well that Fenella could hold her own.

When the school house had been on the market, Richard had made an attempt to buy it, but Fenella had refused point-blank to leave London and her livelihood.

'Do stay for lunch,' said Winnie.

'No, I'm due at the cousin's at twelve-thirty,' replied Richard. Immediately Winnie ceased trying to think of how to stretch the three trout so it would not have looked too contrived, and relaxed at once.

'Call in on your way back if you can.'

'We'll have to stop for tea with the old lady,' said Richard. 'Fenella says she's very proud of a fatless sponge she makes, and we are in duty bound to sample it and congratulate her. Damn dry it is, too,' he added.

'It's all right if it's eaten the same day,' Jenny said stoutly, defending a fellow cook.

'Old Cora must make hers a week before,' said Richard.

'I must go back to Margaret,' said Winnie, kissing her nephew. 'Nice to have had a glimpse of you.'

He had gone when the two ladies returned from the Youngs' garden shortly before lunch.

'Sherry?' asked Winnie, in the sitting-room before lunch.

'Do you happen to have some gin?' asked Margaret. 'I find I can take a little gin,' she explained, 'without getting an attack of migraine. Sherry seems to bring it on.'

Winnie poured her a generous tot, and they sat back to enjoy their drinks. Winnie was a little surprised to see her visitor's glass empty so quickly – and even more so when her offer of 'the other half' was accepted.

Quite soon, Jenny appeared to tell them that lunch was ready, and the three sat down together.

Normally, Winnie and Jenny were content with a glass of water apiece with their meal, but today they had provided a bottle of white wine in honour of their guest. It was empty by the end of the meal.

Jenny brought them coffee in the sitting-room, but would not join them.

Margaret, now rather flushed, rattled away about her new kitchen cupboards, and the pleasure she was getting from her new oven. It was two-thirty by the time she rose to go. She seemed unsteady on her feet, and Winnie said that she would walk across the green with her.

People were clearing up in the Youngs' garden; Winnie could see Ben and Edward carrying trestle-table tops to the shelter of the garden shed, and Molly Curdle and Joan Young seemed to be stacking crockery on trays. They waved to them as they passed.

Winnie left Margaret at the gate of the school house. Children were playing in the playground, and Winnie thought, with a pang, how often she had seen Dorothy and Agnes among their charges. She missed them sorely.

The sun had come through and as she made her way back,

Winnie sat down on one of the seats on the green. She felt very tired. The lunch had gone well, and it had been good to see Richard, but there was no doubt that entertaining, even with Jenny's incomparable efficiency, was getting increasingly burdensome. It was old age, she supposed, looking across at Rectory Cottages where even more aged friends lived.

Her thoughts turned to the new one she had just accompanied home on the other side of the green. There was definitely something wrong there. Winnie, as a doctor's wife for many years, was quite accustomed to seeing patients who were over-fond of alcohol, and knew the misery that it could bring to a family.

She roused herself from the bench and returned home. Jenny was on her knees putting away the best china, and looked up from the low cupboard with a welcoming smile.

'Nice party,' she said. 'But my word, she can put it away, can't she?'

It would not be long, Winnie realized, before a great many people would be of Jenny's opinion, and what might that augur for the happiness of the Lester family?

The former occupants of the school house were in the throes of packing for a few days away in Wales. It was Dorothy who took longer over this chore than Agnes. Possibly it was because Agnes owned far fewer clothes, and was not distracted by having to make a choice between six or eight different cardigans, say, or four or five frocks suitable to wear in the evening.

Dorothy too was more clothes-conscious altogether and, as a headmistress, had always made sure that she looked well turned out. Agnes, much less perturbed by her appearance, aimed to be neat, clean and unobtrusive. So when it came to packing, she was at a distinct advantage.

'Now, if I take my black,' Dorothy said, 'it means putting in my black patent shoes which are most uncomfortable and will take up far too much room.'

'I shouldn't take the black,' advised Agnes. 'I think the green, and that pretty new fawn dress should be ample for evenings. Then your brown shoes would look right with both.'

Dorothy looked undecided. 'It means wearing each one twice,' she said.

'I don't suppose anyone will have the vapours if you do,' retorted Agnes with unusual tartness. 'I'm only taking one skirt for evening with two dressy blouses, and people will have to put up with it.'

Dorothy nodded abstractedly.

'In any case,' continued Agnes, 'they will be worrying about their own appearance, not ours.'

'I'm sure you are right,' responded Dorothy, putting the black dress back in the cupboard.

'I'll just go down and check Timmy's provisions,' said Agnes. 'It's so good of Eileen to take him on. He's becoming quite devoted to her.'

When Dorothy appeared downstairs, case in hand, she found that Agnes was about to fill a flask with coffee for their picnic lunch.

'I'm popping along to say goodbye to Teddy,' she announced.

'But I thought Eileen was going in this morning,' replied Agnes, jug poised.

'She is,' agreed Dorothy, 'but I thought it would look more friendly to say we were just off, and leave our telephone number with him.'

'But I left it with Eileen!' protested Agnes.

'No harm in letting them both know where we are,' said Dorothy. 'I shall only be a minute.'

She vanished, to leave Agnes sitting on the kitchen chair watching Tim cleaning his handsome whiskers.

'Teddy this, and Teddy that,' sighed Agnes. 'Where will it all end?'

The coffee morning brought in almost three hundred pounds, a record sum at Thrush Green for such an event. Much cheered, the inhabitants braced themselves for further efforts during autumn, and watched the progress of the new extension with renewed proprietorial interest.

The topic was discussed by Nelly Piggott and her friend Mrs Jenner as they made their way down the hill to Lulling one evening, bound for an evening's diversion at Bingo. Nelly thoroughly enjoyed her regular outings, not only for the possible thrill of winning some money, but also for the more practical pleasure in sitting down after a day on her feet at The Fuchsia Bush.

Mrs Jenner was one of the oldest residents of Thrush Green, and sister to Percy Hodge the farmer. She lived a short distance along the road to Nidden, had once been a nurse, and was mother to Jane Cartwright, one of the wardens at Rectory Cottages. In any emergency it was ten chances to one that Mrs Jenner was called first, before the doctor or the vet, or the police or the fire brigade. She was indeed, as the rector often said: 'A very present help in trouble.'

Both Charles and Dimity knew this from first-hand, for when the rectory had gone up in a blaze that fateful night, it was Mrs Jenner who had offered them a home for several months and given them comfort as well as shelter after their shock.

She and Nelly had met at Bingo, and struck up a friendship. Mrs Jenner appreciated Nelly's good sense, her industry and cheerful disposition. She felt some pity, too, for her role as Albert Piggott's wife. She had known Albert since their school days, and knew also that he was incapable of changing his curmudgeonly ways.

The evening was fine, the two ladies agreed, but there was a definite nip in the air. At the bottom of the hill they saw Gladys Lilly hurrying towards them. Occasionally she joined the Bingo-players, but as a devout chapel-goer she sometimes had qualms about games of chance which her old father had roundly condemned as 'the devil's work'. Tonight, it seemed, she was about to put aside her doubts and was going to enjoy an evening out.

'Such news!' she gasped, as she approached the two friends. 'My Doreen's back!'

Nelly and Mrs Jenner said how pleased they were and they expressed their gratification as the three made their way up Lulling High Street together.

'She just turned up at midday. Some fellow she'd met, a window-cleaner in London, was off to see his mother in Cirencester, and he gave her a lift.'

'Is she staying long?'

'That I couldn't say.'

'And the little boy?'

'Into everything. Had my dripping bowl over before he'd been in the house five minutes. I'm going to have my hands full, I can see.' By now they had reached the hall where more people were going in. Gladys Lilly lowered her voice. 'There's one snag about all this. Glad though I am to see the girl, she's expecting again, and I've no doubt she'll reckon to stay with me till it arrives.'

Mrs Jenner had gone ahead and was talking to a friend.

'Oh lor!' said Nelly. 'The same fellow, is it?'

'Who's to tell?' replied Gladys despairingly. 'She won't, that's for sure. And to think I brought her up strict chapel.'

The chilly spell of weather which had been blamed for Charles Henstock's illness and a host of other people's ailments, now changed to warm sunshine.

Harold Shoosmith, who was at the end of his garden surveying the view across to Lulling Woods, wondered if anything could beat a sunny, dewy early September morning.

The harvest was now in, and most of the fields sloping away to the Pleshey valley had already been ploughed or drilled, ready for planting. The one immediately adjoining Harold's was still bristling with stubble, and Harold was pleased about that. For one thing, at night it had a strange luminosity which had a beauty of its own. More practically, it provided food for a covey of six partridges which sometimes wandered through the hedge and delighted Harold and Isobel as they sat at breakfast.

This morning they were not to be seen, but Harold became conscious of noises coming from next door in the school house garden. The children were in school and Thrush Green lay peacefully in the morning sunlight; gradually, Harold became aware that Margaret Lester was pottering about at the end of her garden, just as he was.

'Hello!' he called. 'Lovely morning.'

'Oh, you made me jump,' gasped Margaret. She came towards the hedge, and Harold approached her.

'Enjoying the sunshine?'

'It is rather nice,' she said vaguely. 'I've really been too busy to notice.'

There was a sound which Harold surmised was a hiccup.

At that moment, Isobel appeared to say that he was wanted on the telephone. She waved to Margaret, and the Shoosmiths excused themselves to hurry indoors.

'Margaret Lester doesn't look well,' commented Isobel as they traversed the garden.

'Margaret Lester,' said her husband shortly, 'is drunk.'

10. Crisis for Violet Lovelock

On that same bright September morning, Violet Lovelock was busy in the garden, too. Girded in a hessian apron and wearing leather gardening gloves, she was cutting a few late roses for the drawing-room's silver trumpet-shaped vases, and deadheading the dead ones at the same time.

Violet liked gardening, unlike Ada whose arthritis hindered her from stooping. She limited her gardening activities to watering geraniums in pots at waist level, while her younger sister bent and stretched, trundled the wheelbarrow, and enjoyed comparative agility.

Among the roses, Violet thought about Bertha; so far, nothing untoward had happened. John Lovell had had to be called when Bertha had developed pains in the chest after the ubiquitous cold germ had done its worst in Lulling, and Violet, finding herself alone with him downstairs, had told him, somewhat guardedly, about Bertha's eccentricities.

John Lovell, who had heard the rumours anyway, was reassuring, simply saying that it would be best to accompany Bertha everywhere in her present state, and that if her symptoms gave cause for anxiety she was to get in touch at once.

On these carefully ambiguous phrases they had parted company, and since then Violet had been comforted by the thought that both Charles and John would now be at hand for support if needed. Meanwhile, it seemed that Bertha, who had soon recovered, was behaving in a normal manner although her bedroom still remained crammed with articles from all over the house, and every now and again some fresh piece of china or silver was added surreptitiously to the collection upstairs.

After Violet's gardening session, the three sisters partook of their usual sparse lunch, took a rest, and spent the remainder of the day in various domestic pursuits. The roses were much admired in the drawing-room that evening as Violet did the crossword, with equal help and hindrance from her sisters, and Ada and Bertha knitted.

At ten o'clock, as the grandfather clock in the hall was striking, the three ladies retired to bed.

Violet remained wakeful. A large moth, pattering against the window pane, obliged her to get out of bed and rescue it. No sooner had she settled again, when she found that the moon, as large and round as could be, was sending brilliant beams across her pillow. She stirred herself again to adjust a curtain, and returned to bed.

This time it seemed she was about to find rest, and was in that pleasant state of drifting between conscious thought and the dreams awaiting her when she was startled to hear loud cries emerging from Bertha's room across the landing.

She struggled once more from her bed, envisaging a dozen emergencies from a severe stroke to a bat which had lost its way during its night-time pursuits, and hurriedly put on her dressing-gown. She heard Ada's door bang along the passage and her voice raised. Within half a minute, the three sisters had met in Bertha's room.

Bertha herself was sitting bolt upright in bed, and a very alarming sight she posed for her two agitated sisters. She was wearing what was known to her as 'my boudoir cap', a confection of pink net decorated with a rosette over each ear, and fastened with pink ribbons under her wrinkled chin. Under the pink net were a dozen or so bumps denoting hair-rollers.

But it was not the boudoir cap which so alarmed Ada and Violet, for they were quite accustomed to Bertha's night-time appearance. What made this particular night's costume remarkable was the cascade of necklaces around their sister's neck.

Gold chains, ropes of pearls, and an Edwardian opal pendant which had been one of their mother's favourites jangled, together with strands of glass beads of every colour, two amber necklaces and one of jet.

Pinned to Bertha's pink bed jacket were over a dozen brooches ranging from regimental marcasite-and-silver badges to gold horseshoe tie pins with seed pearls for nail-heads. Gold jostled silver, agate vied with lapis lazuli, and an outsize Italian cameo brooch dwarfed the diamond cluster and the solitary ruby beneath it.

Bertha's bony fingers were ablaze with rings, and there was even a man's signet ring adorning one thumb. Overturned jewel boxes of every shape and size lay on the bedspread, and she was busy scrabbling in another which seemed to hold earings.

'What's the matter, Bertha dear?' enquired Ada, intent on

ignoring her sister's bizarre appearance, and rather hoping that what she saw before her was a mirage.

Violet, strengthened with the indignation of one snatched from sleep all too often, was more positive in her approach. 'What on earth are you doing with all the jewellery? It ought to be in the bank anyway.'

'Rubbish!' retorted Bertha. 'It's far better off here where it belongs, and I can keep my eye on it.'

'It is simply inviting a burglar,' pronounced Violet, 'and in any case, why were you shouting for us in the middle of the night?'

'I simply wanted to find out where the watches and bracelets are,' said Bertha, with a dignity which did not match her bedizened appearance. 'Have you girls moved them from the bottom of the wardrobe drawer?'

'Indeed no,' quavered Ada, now beginning to sound tearful. She had always been the timid one.

'I had no idea all this stuff was here,' responded Violet with spirit, 'and the best thing would be to put it all back.'

She advanced upon the bed, but Bertha began a shrill screaming which made the two sisters recoil. At the same time she began to tug at the ribbon which secured the boudoir cap, her scrawny neck twisting this way and that in her struggles. The multi-jewelled collection of necklaces tinkled and jangled, sending out gleams from gold and flashes of fire from precious stones, and all the time the high-pitched screams continued.

When at last she had flung the cap to the floor, she tore out the plastic rollers which it had concealed, hurling them one by one after the cap. Her hair stood out from her scalp in wild spikes, her breathing came in noisy gasps and her eyes rolled in an alarming way.

With considerable courage, Violet strode towards her and slapped one withered cheek smartly. The screaming stopped and Bertha fell back upon her pillows.

For a moment there was a dreadful silence in the room, then

Ada began to cry, the pathetic frightened snivellings of a scared child.

'Go back to bed,' said Violet to her sister. 'I can cope now.'

She kept her gaze upon Bertha, but was conscious of Ada's retreat and the sound of her bedroom door closing.

Violet could hear her heart drumming in the most alarming way, and longed to be able to telephone for help, to get John Lovell with his panoply of remedies, injections, pills, inhalants, and the overall comfort of his authority.

She was afraid of madness. She was afraid of violence. She was mortally afraid of doing something, in her terror, which would seriously damage her sister. But something had to be done to restore some sort of order, and at least the appalling screaming had ceased.

'Sit up,' she commanded. 'We're going to put all this stuff back.'

Bertha struggled from her pillows. She was trembling and looked shocked.

'You *struck* me, Violet,' she whispered. 'How dare you *strike* me?'

'I shall do it again,' Violet said stoutly, 'if you don't help me to take off all this jewellery.'

With shaking fingers, she began to unravel the tangle of necklaces, undoing clasps, hooks and complicated fastenings. Bertha slowly began to slide off the rings, fumbling with various ring-boxes on the counterpane, and watching vaguely as one or two of the trinkets rolled to the floor.

'I thought all this was in the bank,' fumed Violet. 'You know we agreed that you would send it there years ago.'

'I changed my mind,' said Bertha. 'And you are pulling my hair.'

Violet scooped a handful of released necklaces into one of the largest jewel boxes. It was a faded green leather one which had come from Siena on their mother's return from her honeymoon. What would that sweet gentle soul think if she could see her daughters now? Violet pushed this thought away, and concentrated on disentangling a fine silver chain.

'What possessed you to try and keep all this?' demanded Violet, freeing the last of the necklaces. 'It's asking for trouble. Heaven knows what this lot is worth now. It hasn't been valued for years.'

'I want it here,' replied Bertha, with a return of her dominating manner. 'Everything in this room is mine. Possession is nine-tenths of the law.'

'Rubbish,' said Violet, bundling the boxes into a drawer. 'You know quite well that everything in the house, *including* everything in this room, is divided equally between the three of us. Justin has Father's will, and it is perfectly plain.'

She stooped to pick up two rings from the carpet, and realized how dizzy she was with exhaustion. It had been a long day.

'I shall get Justin to change it,' said Bertha, with some spirit.

'You will do no such thing,' responded Violet. 'Tomorrow I shall get John Lovell to call to see you.'

'I shan't see him.'

'We'll see about that in the morning. Meanwhile, lie down and sleep. Even if you don't want to, at least let Ada and me have a few hours rest.'

She tucked in the bedclothes, found a stray brooch which she recognized as one of her own, and left her sister in comparative peace.

Ada's door opened a crack as Violet returned to her bed. 'Is she all right?'

'As right as she'll ever be,' responded Violet despairingly. 'We'll talk in the morning.'

And that won't be long in coming thought poor Violet, climbing once again into her crumpled bed.

The news of Doreen Lilly's return and, of course, her interesting condition, was soon spread about Lulling and Thrush

Green. Speculation upon the possible paternity of the expected child also gave considerable pleasure to the gossips.

Charles Henstock rang his friend Anthony Bull to let him know the whereabouts of the girl he had befriended. Anthony had heard nothing since his earlier encounter, but was glad to hear that she had returned to her mother.

'What are her plans, do you know?' he enquired.

Charles admitted that he had no idea, but intended to call at the Lilly household, and would keep him informed of any developments.

They rang off after suitable messages to their families, and Charles decided to put aside his weekly sermon-in-the-making, and call on Doreen and her mother that afternoon.

Already the lime trees in Lulling High Street were dropping a few crumpled leaves. There was an autumn freshness in the air, and the sky was of that pellucid blue particular to early autumn. Great cumulus clouds towered in the north, lit brilliantly by the sunshine. It was a day when cares were cast aside and the world of nature offered refreshment of spirit.

Charles was admitted by Mrs Lilly who told him that Doreen had gone shopping, taking the little boy with her.

'I've called because I let my friend Anthony Bull know that she was here. As you know, she turned to him when she was worried in London. He has been anxious.'

Mrs Lilly expressed surprise. 'I thought she'd written to him,' she told Charles. 'She said she was going to. He was very good to her.'

Charles brushed aside her apologies with a smile. 'The thing is, what is she going to do now?' asked the rector.

'She'll stay here for a bit,' said Mrs Lilly. 'Maybe you know she's expecting again?'

'I had heard so.'

'She'll have to get a little job – part-time, say, to bring in a bit. The boy can go two mornings a week to play-school down the road. I found that out yesterday.'

'An excellent idea.'

'Doreen was with the Lovelock ladies before, but I don't think she'd fancy going back.'

Charles's private opinion was that the Lovelock ladies would certainly not have her back. She had previously left them in the lurch, and it was generally thought that she had helped the burglar who had broken into that house some time before, Doreen Lilly would certainly not be welcome there.

'Well, we'll keep in touch,' said Charles rising, 'and if I hear of any work which might suit Doreen I will send a message. I'm sure Mr Bull would be very glad to have a letter from her.'

'I'll see she sends one,' promised Gladys, opening the door. 'And it's very nice of you to call.'

She did not actually say the words, 'as you are church and I'm chapel', but Charles felt that they hovered somewhere in the air as he made his farewells.

Harold Shoosmith's blunt assessment of Margaret Lester's condition had shocked his wife. Isobel had not said a great deal about it, but naturally it was very much in her mind. Did the two little girls have any inkling? What misery it must be for her husband! Was that, she wondered, why the family had moved, so that Alan could keep a closer eye on Margaret?

At breakfast the next morning Isobel said to Harold, 'Surely Margaret couldn't be drunk so early in the morning? I can't believe it, you know.'

'Habitual drinkers,' replied Harold, reaching for the marmalade, 'are pretty well sozzled all the time. We had a fair number in Africa. Not a lot you can do for them.'

'But we must do something,' protested Isobel. 'Can't we help?'

'We can help her best by keeping quiet about it, and being at hand if Alan and the children want some first-hand support,' said Harold.

At that moment, Willie Marchant arrived with the letters, and Harold and Isobel examined their post.

'A lovely card from Agnes and Dorothy,' said Isobel. 'What a stupendous Welsh waterfall!'

'Where is it?' asked Harold.

Isobel studied the card more closely. 'It's a place with a long name, which has no vowels in it, beginning with two Ls,' she said.

'You surprise me,' said Harold.

On the morning after the Lovelocks' disturbed night, Violet rang the surgery to ask if Dr Lovell would call to see her sister.

'Dr Lovell,' said the new young receptionist, 'is out on an emergency case.'

'When will he be back?'

'In emergency cases,' said the voice with hauteur, 'we have no way of assessing the time needed.'

'Naturally,' replied Violet, with equal frigidity.

'Dr Lovell's assistant *could* call, of course.' She made it sound as if, despite innumerable difficulties, such as physical paralysis, overwhelming commitments to urgent cases and extreme exhaustion, the new doctor might possibly martyr himself to the extent of struggling into his car to drive half a mile to see the patient.

Violet, holding the receiver, knew that it would be hard enough to persuade Bertha to see John Lovell – the new doctor would not have a chance of being admitted.

'Don't bother him,' said Violet, 'I will ring another time.'

'That would be best,' conceded the receptionist graciously, and rang off.

Bertha, the cause of Violet and Ada's exhaustion, was in considerably better shape than her sisters. She received her breakfast tray happily, commented on the sunshine with pleasure, and seemed oblivious to the night's mayhem.

Violet was not amused, and was determined to get at least some of her problems solved.

'John Lovell is engaged at the moment,' she told Bertha, 'but I intend to consult him.'

'A lot of fuss about nothing,' commented Bertha.

'And I am getting in touch with Jenkins to revalue the jewellery. Then it is going to the safe-deposit at the bank.'

'Jenkins died last Easter,' said Bertha.

'Jenkins' son is running the shop,' responded Violet quickly, 'and very competently too.'

'I can't see why you make such a to-do about the stuff,' said Bertha.

'It's too valuable to have lying about. Those gold chains alone are worth a great deal of money, and there are several diamond and sapphire rings.'

'But we may want to wear some of it,' cried Bertha, dropping a piece of toast, butter-side down, on the top sheet.

'We can keep back a few favourite things,' replied Violet, 'but the rest goes to the bank.'

'I think you are being *quite* unreasonable,' stated Bertha, attending to the buttery patch with an even more buttery knife.

Violet, who had suffered much, was stung into action.

'*You* are the unreasonable one, and well you know it! Any more of these tantrums and Dr Lovell will be obliged to refer you to a *mental specialist*, and you know where he might well send you!'

At this, Bertha really did look a little shaken. She pushed aside her tray, and was temporarily deprived of speech. She suddenly looked very old and very frail, and for a brief moment Violet felt compunction.

But this weakness did not last long. Picking up the tray she made her way to the bedroom door. 'The best thing you can do, Bertha, is to lie there, think things over, and decide to mend your ways.'

And with this patting shot she made for the stairs.

The fact that Doreen Lilly was back in Lulling soon reached the ears of Violet and her sisters. As Charles surmised, they were determined never to let her into their house again.

It was at the next Bingo session that Doreen's future employment was settled, and that was through the practical good sense of Mrs Jenner.

Nelly Piggott, Gladys Lilly and Mrs Jenner were enjoying a cup of coffee and bourbon biscuits during the interval in the Bingo hall, discussing Doreen's plight.

'At least,' said Gladys, 'she's got the child enrolled at the play-school: Tuesdays and Thursdays from nine-thirty to twelve, so at least I'll have a few hours to myself.'

'If we had a vacancy at The Fuchsia Bush,' said Nelly, 'I'd give her some work there and could keep an eye on her for you, but the fact is we're fully staffed just now.'

'Would you like me to have a word with Jane?' enquired Mrs Jenner, putting down her cup. 'She sometimes likes some extra help with the old people. It might not be much, general cleaning probably, but it wouldn't be far for her to go, and she would be earning something.'

'That would be ideal,' said Gladys warmly, 'and she could pick up Bobby on the way home.'

'Well, I can't promise, of course,' said Mrs Jenner, 'but I'll speak to Jane, and she'll get in touch with Doreen, one way or the other, and your girl can decide if she likes the idea.'

'She'd better,' said Doreen's mother grimly, stacking the cups and saucers in readiness for the next half of the Bingo session.

11. WHERE IS EMILY COOKE?

It was Mrs Jenner's intention the next morning to go to visit her daughter Jane at Rectory Cottages, as soon as she had finished her breakfast. She always rose early, a legacy from her nursing days, and knew that she would find Jane, who had also trained as a nurse, well on the way with her morning duties among her elderly charges.

Mrs Jenner was putting away the last of the breakfast washing-up when there was a thumping noise at the back door. On opening it, she was not unduly surprised to find Mrs Cooke who lived some quarter of a mile away on the road to Nidden.

Mrs Cooke was a byword in Thrush Green and Lulling. Her large family was known to most of the residents, the rector, the probation officers and the local police force. Very few months passed without a mention of one or another of the Cooke family in the local paper, usually concerning a hearing at the Lulling Magistrates' Court.

Mrs Jenner, as midwife, had attended several of Mrs Cooke's lying-ins, and later had been called into the house for various crises such as a broken arm, beads stuffed into infant Cookes' ears and noses, sudden rashes on Cooke chests, or lacerations on rather grubby Cooke feet.

She let in her agitated visitor and offered her the kitchen chair. What did she want now, wondered Mrs Jenner? Medical advice? Help with an official form? Money 'for the meter'? A cupful of sugar?

All these things and many more had been asked for over the

years, but today her visitor produced a crumpled piece of paper, and thrust it towards her.

She read:

'Gone of for a bit back by Satday
Nigel's
shoos need mending
Emily.'

'Oh dear!' said Mrs Jenner.

'Oh lor!' howled Mrs Cooke, throwing her apron up over her face and head, like someone at a wake in an Irish film. She began to sway back and forth emitting harsh cries of grief.

Mrs Jenner put on the kettle.

After a minute it began to hum comfortingly, and Mrs Cooke replaced her apron. The yells changed to sobs and hiccups, and Mrs Jenner reached for the recently emptied teapot.

'What she want to go and do this for?' sniffed the bereaved mother. 'Leaving me with all yesterday's washing up. *And Nigel.*'

'What's happened to Nigel?' asked Mrs Jenner, making the tea. 'Is he alone at your house?'

She knew from experience that any young Cooke left alone in a house could create havoc, and Nigel was no exception.

'I pushed him off to school,' said Mrs Cooke, 'afore I come up here.'

She accepted the cup of tea and spooned in three teaspoonfuls of sugar.

'Well, have you any idea why she's gone?'

'I blame St Giles for this,' said Mrs Cooke, stirring her tea morosely.

'What's he got to do with it?'

'Who?'

'St Giles.'

'St Giles' *Fair*, up Oxford. She *would* go. Took young Nigel too, and they never got back till past midnight. That's where she met this chap. He's at Oxford.'

'You mean he's one of the college boys?'

'No, no! He *works*! Up Cowley, I think.' She sipped noisily at her tea cup, the hiccups subsiding.

Mrs Jenner studied the note again. 'I don't think there is much to worry about,' she told her visitor. 'She says she'll be back on Saturday. If she doesn't turn up then, you could tell the police.'

'*Tell the police?*' echoed Mrs Cooke indignantly. 'I don't want that lot scratting around! We're respectable folk.'

Mrs Jenner, with remarkable self-control, refrained from comment.

'I come up here really,' went on Mrs Cooke, 'to see if you'd heard anythin' about my girl. I knows your brother Perce takes an interest in her.'

Mrs Jenner realized with some shock that she had completely failed to link Emily with Percy. He had made so many attempts, over the past months, to find a companion that she had dismissed the rumours out of hand. In truth, she had little in common with her brother, and the two rarely met, although their gardens adjoined.

A terrible thought struck her: if Percy ever married Emily Cooke (heaven forbid), she would be related by marriage to this dreadful old woman before her.

'I know nothing of that,' she said as calmly as she could. 'If I were you I should leave things alone. Emily's old enough to know what she's doing, and ten chances to one she'll be back on Saturday as she says.'

Mrs Cooke gulped down the last of her tea, and stood up.

'Well that's that. Maybe you're right. Best wait and see.'

Mrs Jenner opened the back door for her.

'Oh, by the way,' said Mrs Cooke on the doorstep, 'you couldn't give me a lend of half a loaf? I was that upset about Emily I forgot the baker.'

Mrs Jenner returned to the kitchen, cut a loaf in half, put the bread into a paper bag and handed it, without a word, to the waiting woman.

'Ta ever so,' said Mrs Cooke, walking briskly to the gate.

Somewhat later than she had intended, Mrs Jenner arrived at Rectory Cottages. As she had expected, Jane was there sorting out a first aid kit which was an important part of her warden's equipment.

'You remember Doreen Lilly,' began Mrs Jenner.

'I should hope so. She was in my Brownie pack years ago. What's happened? I thought she'd left home.'

'She's back,' said her mother, and proceeded to tell her about Doreen, her present condition, the problem of Bobby, and the concern of Gladys Lilly.

'If she's not too proud to do a bit of cleaning, windows, hoovering, that sort of thing, I'd find her a job here for two mornings a week. She could give a hand with the vegetables too. One or two of the old dears are poorly, and I get them a midday meal while they're under the weather.'

'Then shall I tell her to call?'

'Yes do, Mum. It won't be permanent, but it should help her out.'

That matter settled, Mrs Jenner told Jane about Emily Cooke and her mother's visit.

Jane looked unusually perturbed. 'It'll upset Uncle Percy, won't it?'

'Oh, there's nothing in that,' replied her mother dismissively. 'You know what a silly old thing he is.'

'But I think he's quite serious about this one,' said Jane, rolling up a loose bandage and securing it neatly with a safety pin. 'He ought to be married, you know.'

Mrs Jenner got to her feet. She found all this very unsettling. Perhaps she should have kept a closer eye on Percy's philanderings.

'I can't see any woman with a ha'porth of sense taking on your Uncle Percy,' she said flatly. She kissed her daughter's cheek. 'Thank you for helping out with Doreen, I'll tell her to get in touch. Now, I must get back. I've a nice little chicken to put in the oven, and dear knows when that'll get dished up, with all this to-ing and fro-ing.'

She waved cheerfully to several of the residents who were watching her departure, and made her way briskly along the road to Nidden. To passersby, she appeared her normal self – calm and capable. But Mrs Jenner's emotions were in turmoil. Surely Percy, stupid though he was, and always had been, could not seriously be thinking of making an alliance with a *Cooke*?

Tongues wagged, of course. They began to wag even more busily when Saturday was over and the girl had not returned. Mrs Jenner kept her worries to herself, and even felt a slight gleam of hope. Did this mean that Percy was out of the running altogether?

Percy, on the other hand, seemed to want to tell all and sundry about his blighted hopes. Albert Piggott, who had managed to evade him, was finally button-holed on Monday morning when he was defenceless in the churchyard, sweeping up the shower of autumn leaves which rustled round and round the church paths and porch.

'You heard about my Emily?' queried Percy lugubriously.

'Yes,' said Albert, flicking his broom along the edge of a flowerbed with unwonted energy.

'It's a terrible thing,' sighed the rejected lover. 'She could be anywhere.'

'That's right,' agreed Albert.

'With anyone.'

'Right. She could.' He negotiated a tricky corner by one of the drains with a twist of the broom.

'Could be abroad even.'

'Probably is,' said Albert.

'Not that I think she is,' said Percy. 'Len Matthews said he saw her in Oxford.'

'Well then,' said Albert, activity arrested at this mention of an old acquaintance, 'what you fussin' about?'

He looked searchingly at his companion. He did look pretty

rough, come to think of it. Even Albert's flinty heart was moved.

'Here, come and sit in the porch out of this pesky wind. Jones hasn't opened yet. Well go over when he does.'

They sat together on one of the stone benches which lined the venerable porch. It was a chilly seat on a misty October morning, and Albert hoped that Percy's confidences would not take long, as gloomy thoughts of piles and other unpleasant afflictions went through his head.

'So what did Len say?' he urged, hoping to hurry along the proceedings.

Percy gave a gusty sigh. 'Not much. Just said he saw her in Cornmarket with this young chap. Laughin', she was.'

'Not one of them young chaps at college? She don't want to get mixed up with them. There's Deans and Masters and that, they gets proper shirty with any of their blokes as gets girls into trouble. Send 'em somewhere, they do, or sack 'em, or somethin'.'

'It wasn't one of that lot,' said Percy, dismissing all university men in one sentence. 'I heard it's some fellow up Morris's.'

'Oh well,' replied Albert, 'he ought to know better, workin' up Morris's.'

The conversation lapsed. Only the rustle of the leaves around their feet broke the silence. Albert began to find the cold more than he could bear. He rose from his chilly seat and surveyed his sorrowful companion.

'If you wants my opinion, Perce—' he began.

'I don't,' said the sufferer.

'Well, you're goin' to get it,' replied Albert with spirit. 'You wants to snap out of this 'ere mood you've got yourself in. No girl's worth it, and that Emily Cooke—'

He broke off as Percy leapt to his feet, red in the face with rage. 'You shut up about my Emily!' he shouted. 'Ain't I got enough to bear without you bein' insultin'?'

Albert picked up his broom defensively. 'All right, all right! Keep your hair on! No fool like an old one, they say, and that's true enough!'

He skipped dexterously out of the porch, and began to sweep again at a safe distance.

Muttering under his breath, Percy shuffled through the leaves to the church gate. At that moment, the welcome sound of the doors of The Two Pheasants being flung open could be heard. Without altering his pace, Percy made for the inn. Albert, judging discretion to be the better part of valour, decided to wait until a glass of beer had quenched Percy's ardour.

But it was really very annoying.

Autumn seemed to arrive particularly early that year. Albert Piggott was not alone in cursing the volume of dead leaves which created a major problem for all gardeners, as well as the Lulling Council leaf-sweeping vehicles that plied up and down Lulling High Street, doing their best to cope with the prodigal vegetation from the lime trees.

Against the golden stone of the Cotswold buildings, pyracantha berries glowed, and the palmate leaves of Virginia creeper clad many a house with vivid colour ranging from wine to cream. Variegated ivies and winter jasmine, as well as dying clematis and wisteria clothed the walls, and in the country hedges wild bryony threaded its necklaces of bright beads.

There were elderberries, late blackberries and sloes in plenty that year, and families were busy collecting this natural harvest. In Lulling Woods the bracken was turning crisp and auburn, providing shelter and bedding for the small animals which were already thinking of hibernation.

It was the season when redoubled activity in fund-raising reared its head, and Ella was just utilizing some of the remnants left over from the soft furnishings of Rectory Cottages' extension when her door bell rang.

Winnie Bailey stood on the step, a basket of apples at her feet. 'Are these coals to Newcastle, Ella?' she enquired.

'Far from it. Come in,' replied Ella, lifting the basket, and leading the way to the kitchen. 'I'll make some apple jelly. It always goes like hot cakes at produce stalls, and I'm getting stuff ready for the Mammoth Harvest Bazaar.'

'I wonder why everything is "Mammoth" in Thrush Green?' mused Winnie.

'Just a local habit,' said Ella. 'Coffee?'

Coffee being declined, the two ladies went into the sitting-room, and Ella picked up her smouldering cigarette and gave a grateful puff at it. The air was blue and acrid with the smoke, and Winnie hoped that her eyes would not water too noticeably.

As if reading her thoughts, Ella stubbed out the remains of the cigarette. 'Sorry about this filthy habit. I keep meaning to give it up. Tell myself about cancer of the lungs, and other people's revulsion, and how much I should save if I packed it in.'

'So you have tried?'

'Lord, yes! Time and time again. I can get through twenty-four hours, and then I crack.'

'It could be worse, I suppose.'

'How come? Drink, do you mean?'

Winnie was silent. Margaret Lester had come suddenly into her mind. She picked up some of the remnants of chintz which littered the sofa. 'And what are you going to make with these?' she asked.

'Well, I'm keeping some to make oven gloves, and Muriel is dead keen to make egg cosies and those rather sissy clothes' hangers. Does anyone *want* egg cosies anyway? My boiled egg doesn't have time to get cold, I can tell you, and all my coat hangers are those nice functional wire ones the cleaners give you free.'

'As a matter of fact,' said Winnie, 'I like a few padded hangers for special silk blouses and other delicate things. I'm sure Muriel's efforts will be snapped up.'

She was just congratulating herself on evading the dangerous topic of alcoholism when Ella spoke again.

'We thought it might be an idea to ask Margaret Lester to make things for the bazaar. I hear she's a good needle-woman. Tapestry rugs and all that. Besides, Muriel says she thinks she needs company. Gets depressed evidently.'

Winnie wondered how much Ella knew. Not much escaped those shrewd eyes behind their usual veil of cigarette smoke.

'It's a kind thought,' said Winnie. 'She doesn't seem to have made many friends, but of course it's early days. I know the Youngs have invited them to play cards once or twice.'

'And I bet those useful migraine attacks have cropped up,' commented Ella. 'Tell me, Winnie, what's your opinion?'

'Well, I hardly know—' began Winnie, feeling cornered.

'I do,' said Ella. 'She's on the bottle, and most people in Thrush Green know it.'

At Barton-on-Sea, Agnes and Dorothy were busy clearing the garden ready for winter and going through all the decision-making which gardeners face at this time of the year.

'Shall we try and keep some of these geraniums?' asked Agnes. 'They could stand in the porch.'

'No room. Better put them on the compost heap.'

'But Dorothy, they cost a great deal of money.'

'And they'll cost us a great deal of inconvenience stuck in the porch all through the winter.'

Agnes, brought up much more thriftily than her friend, put the dying geraniums into the wheelbarrow with some reluctance.

'We'll split these penstemon,' said Dorothy, struggling with a small hand fork. 'They make a good show, and we could do with some more in the front garden.'

She heaved at the plant, becoming red in the face with effort.

'Please, Dorothy,' begged Agnes, 'please leave it for Peter to do.'

They were fortunate in having the help of a young man now and again who 'obliged' when he needed extra money.

'It's certainly tough!' puffed Dorothy, straightening up.

'You have to have two large forks back to back, and sort of *ease* them apart,' explained Agnes. 'It's really a man's job.'

'Well, Peter's welcome to this one. Now what about a new shrub to climb up by the shed? Now's the time, I believe, to plant one.'

'Certainly that clematis has been most unsatisfactory,' agreed Agnes. 'What shall we have instead?'

'I'll ask Teddy,' replied Dorothy, and Agnes's heart sank. Why must Teddy – charming fellow though he was – be brought into everything? Even a little autumn clearing up seemed to need his assistance.

'I promised some of our pink Michaelmas daisies to the flower ladies for Harvest Festival,' continued Dorothy, unaware of Agnes's feelings. 'Miss Jones asked particularly, and I said we could spare some.'

Agnes, pulling up handfuls of chickweed, did not reply.

'I really think they make too much of Harvest Festival here,' went on Dorothy. 'Apparently they are having an *anthem*. Something about the corn.'

'I hope it's "The valleys stand so thick with corn that they laugh and sing",' said Agnes.

'I believe it is. Rather far-fetched, I think. Have you ever seen a *valley* laughing and singing?'

'Poetic licence,' said Agnes.

'And Eileen is singing a solo.'

'Oh good! She has such a lovely voice.'

'I find it rather shrill,' replied Dorothy. 'And I'm not sure she is quite true on her top notes. I think she needs some of her solos transposing to a lower key. But then she wouldn't be able to boast about her high Cs.'

'Oh come, Dorothy! She doesn't *boast*!'

'She does to Teddy,' answered Dorothy.

Agnes threw a handful of chickweed into the wheelbarrow.

'Let's go indoors for a cup of coffee,' she said, with unusual firmness. 'I've had enough of this.'

And enough of Teddy too, was her private comment, as she went back into the house.

At Rectory Cottages, Doreen Lilly was proving surprisingly useful. Whether it was the fact that she was working for her former Brownies' leader and felt obliged to do her utmost to please Brown Owl, nobody could say, but she seemed to enjoy spending two mornings a week with Jane Cartwright, while young Bobby was at play-school, and the old people liked her.

Jane, who had really only given Doreen some work out of the kindness of her heart, was pleasantly surprised at the girl's competence. She had always thought that Mrs Lilly's brisk efficiency had meant that her daughter did little in the house and, like so many daughters of bustling mothers, was content to drift about keeping out of the whirlwind's way.

Evidently, when allowed to, Doreen could tackle a household chore as well as her mother, and Jane found her invaluable. She cleaned brass, copper and silver, she scoured baths and washbasins, polished and dusted, and even coped with such recalcitrant objects as faulty cisterns and clogged-up drains. She was in the early months of her pregnancy and Jane, knowing much about such things from her nursing experience, watched her carefully and made sure that she did not overdo things.

She told her own mother how pleased she was with Doreen's work one morning.

'Well,' said Mrs Jenner, 'don't sound so surprised. Gladys Lilly's renowned for hard work, and Doreen's dad worked at the baker's all his life. He used to go along there at four-thirty every morning. Could set your clock by him, people said. Doreen may have been a silly girl over that young man of hers, but she comes of good stock. Does she ever talk of Bobby's father?'

'Never a word, and I don't question her. But it's going to be hard for her when the baby arrives. There's mighty little room in her mother's house, and neither of them want to live together anyway.'

'They'll have to sort out that problem when the time comes,' said Mrs Jenner.

12. An Accident in Lulling

The whereabouts of Emily Cooke, which was still the subject of much conjecture, was settled by the arrival of a letter to the girl's mother. Miss Watson and Miss Fogerty would have been appalled at the grammar, spelling and general grubbiness of their former pupil's literary effort had they been in a position to see it, but Mrs Cooke seemed surprisingly thrilled.

'She's bin and got married!' she shouted to Mrs Jenner, who was tidying her front garden.

Mrs Jenner went to the gate. A less diplomatic woman might have commented: 'And about time too!', but Mrs Jenner was more circumspect. 'You must be relieved,' she said kindly. As I am too, she thought, remembering the narrow escape she and Percy had had from an alliance with this deplorable family.

'Oh, I'm over the moon!' cried Mrs Cooke, beaming broadly. 'Just think of it! Our Emily married at last! I never thought to see her with a wedding ring.'

'Where is she now?' enquired Mrs Jenner.

'Up Oxford. Headington way, she says, and I'm to go over next Sunday to tea.'

'And what about Nigel? Will he be going to Oxford to live?'

'I expect so. Emily don't say anything much about that in her letter, but I'll take him with me on Sunday.'

Mrs Jenner wondered if Emily would want to be reunited with her young son; she had left him without a qualm. Would Mrs Cooke be left 'holding the baby' yet again? It would not be the first time she had been the unwilling minder of her grandchildren.

'Well, I'm sure it will all work out for the best,' she said. 'You must excuse me. I've left some washing out, and it looks like rain.'

She made her escape from Mrs Cooke, and went round the house into the back garden where a line of washing billowed in the autumn wind.

She was struggling with the sheets when she was hailed from the hedge which divided her property from her brother Percy's. With some vexation, she deposited her bundle on the garden seat, and went to their common boundary. Percy's face, pink and lugubrious, loomed above the clipped hawthorn hedge.

'Saw you with Mrs Cooke. She tell you about my Emily?'

'Percy, she's not "your Emily". Why do you make such a fool of yourself? Yes, she did tell me. Something you probably know already. Emily's married and living in Oxford.'

'No need to be snappy,' responded Percy. 'A bit of sympathy wouldn't come amiss at a time like this.'

'Well, you won't get it from me, Perce. All Lulling's laughing at you. Keep your grizzling to yourself, and stop feeling sorry for yourself too. A day's work is the best medicine.'

'You always was a hard 'un,' moaned Percy. 'Don't my broken heart mean nothin' to you?'

'Nothing at all,' said she briskly. 'And I reckon you've had a lucky escape. Don't get caught again now, Percy. Pull yourself together. What about a few days' steady gardening? Your thistle seeds have been blowing over here for weeks now.'

She bustled back to her washing line before Percy could think of a retort.

Later that morning, Percy told his sad story to Albert Piggott as they sat in The Two Pheasants. Albert's reaction was much the same as Percy's sister's, and it soon became apparent that sympathy was not going to be offered.

'Best thing that could've happened,' maintained Albert. 'She was always a bit of no good. That Oxford chap don't know what he's taken on. You forget her, Perce.'

Even Mr Jones, the soul of propriety, added his contribution.

'Albert's right, you know. You put her out of your mind, Percy. Plenty of good fish in the sea.'

'But they don't seem to swim my way,' said the disconsolate suitor, with a sigh.

'Here, have another half on me,' said Albert, with unwonted generosity. 'Nothin' like a drop of beer to put new heart in a man.'

'That's right,' agreed Mr Jones.

One bright October morning, soon after the news of Emily's wedding had rustled round Thrush Green, Winnie Bailey saw Margaret Lester emerge from her gate and set off towards Lulling. She carried a shopping bag, and Winnie guessed correctly that she would come back on the bus that left Lulling High Street at eleven-thirty with the shopping bag full.

She herself, and most of the Thrush Green shoppers, were grateful for that particular bus. It was a pleasure to trot down the hill with an empty bag in the cool of the morning, when one was fresh; it was quite another thing to struggle uphill from Lulling with a bag heavy with potatoes, celery, carrots and groceries an hour or so later.

Margaret had told her one day that Alan did not like her driving alone. He was afraid that she might be overcome by a sudden migraine attack, she said. Knowing a little more now, Winnie guessed that Alan dreaded a mishap when Margaret was at the wheel, and a breathalyser being produced. Poor fellow, thought Winnie, he must live under the most appalling strain.

Other eyes had also noted Margaret passing.

Replenishing the stocks, thought Ella Bembridge.

Wonder what she's off to buy? thought Albert Piggott, unlocking the church door.

She's looking better this morning, thought Jane Cartwright. But all three had bottles in mind.

Nelly Piggott, putting a basket of croissants in the window of The Fuchsia Bush, watched her neighbour going purposefully into one of Lulling's three supermarkets. The thought of bottles crossed her mind too, but the appearance of Bertha Lovelock, with Violet in close attendance, put all conjecture about Margaret Lester from her mind.

She opened the door for the two ladies, and noted with approval that Violet steered her sister to a table farthest from the display of cakes, scones and other delightfully tempting titbits on the counter.

'Now what can I get you?' she asked. 'Coffee as usual, I suppose? And I'm just bringing through some Eccles cakes. Would you like to try 'em?'

Violet agreed to all these suggestions, and Nelly hurried away.

She and Mrs Peters had been relieved to see the Lovelocks again. They had wondered if the unfortunate affair of Bertha's pilfering would mean the end of their visits, but Violet had been as good as her word, and Bertha was now never seen unaccompanied on their shopping expeditions.

The Fuchsia Bush was exceptionally busy that morning. A number of people who intended to catch the popular eleven-thirty bus which made its way north, passing through Thrush Green as it went, had called in for refreshment, their heavy bags and baskets littering the floor.

As the time grew near, half a dozen or so paid their bills and departed to join the little knot of waiting travellers at the bus stop immediately outside the tea-room.

Nelly Piggott, replenishing the basket of croissants in the window, saw the bus pull up, and the queue mounting the step.

At that moment she saw Margaret Lester, with a laden bag in each hand, hastening awkwardly across the road. The bus began to pull away when she was halfway across Lulling High Street, but it stopped abruptly as presumably someone had pointed out Margaret's plight to the conductor.

Obviously quite breathless and flustered, she hurried forward – and tripped over the kerb, her bags flying forward on to the pavement.

The conductor leapt down to the sprawled figure, two passersby set about rescuing the shopping, and Nelly Piggott hurried out to help.

'I'm all right,' gasped Margaret. 'Quite all right.'

But it was immediately apparent that she was not. Blood was beginning to ooze from a badly grazed knee, and her hands were covered in dirt.

'You come into the shop,' said Nelly, taking command. 'You can't get on the bus like that. You come and rest for a bit.'

'You going to be all right?' asked the conductor solicitously. A row of concerned faces in the bus window watched anxiously.

'I'll see to her,' said Nelly, collecting the bags. 'You get on. You've got your bus to look after.'

'I'm a bit late now,' confessed the conductor. 'Righto, missus. Hope you'll soon be all right.'

One of the bags seemed to be intact, but it was plain that the other had a broken bottle in it, as a trickle of liquid was running freely across the pavement. Nelly investigated, and found one bottle of gin with its neck shattered. Ruthlessly she poured the remaining liquid into the gutter, tested what appeared to be a second bottle in the bag, and found that intact.

Margaret was leaning against the bus stop post, shaking visibly and near to tears. A little knot of spectators were offering sympathy and advice, but all, Nelly noticed, were quite aware of the broken bottle and its contents. The smell of spirit alone was enough to give it away.

One of the men carried the bags into The Fuchsia Bush, and Nelly supported Margaret through the tea-room and into a chair in the privacy of the office. Rosa was dispatched for a bowl of warm water and the first aid kit, and Nelly set to work on her patient.

Margaret was in a state of great agitation. 'I must get in touch with Alan,' she cried. 'I must ring him. He'll be so worried if I'm not home.'

'As soon as I've done this,' said Nelly, 'I'll ring him, and tell him to fetch you home in the car.'

But at that moment Mrs Peters appeared, offered sympathy, and said she would do the telephoning.

Meanwhile, Rosa and Gloria had gone through the shopping bags. One held a few groceries, some toiletries from Boots, and one bottle of gin wrapped in a carrier bag from one of the supermarkets. Nothing appeared to be damaged.

The second bag held the remains of the broken gin bottle, which had been wrapped in another carrier bag from a second supermarket. The third bottle, luckily undamaged, was wrapped in a bag from yet another of Lulling's supermarkets.

The girls said little, but exchanged meaningful glances as they settled the undamaged bottle in the grocery bag. The dripping carrier with its shattered glass was put into the café's dustbin.

'Well, if that's sorted out,' said Mrs Peters, bustling in and out, 'for pity's sake get back to the tables. I can see to things here.'

Alan Lester had sounded remarkably agitated on the telephone, she thought. She had done her best to minimize his wife's injuries, but he sounded quite distracted.

'I'll be down immediately,' he told her. 'I wouldn't have had this happen for the world.'

He had the car outside within ten minutes and Margaret, now calmer, and sporting a neat bandage on her knee, was helped into it by Nelly.

Alan was full of gratitude towards the two good Samaritans when he went back to the tea-room for the bag of shopping. Rosa handed it over, obviously full of excitement at this unexpected fillip to the day.

'One bottle was broke,' she said brightly, 'but me and Gloria put the good one in with the other.'

Alan Lester looked startled, but simply thanked her before making his way to the car.

Mrs Peters surveyed her assistant coldly. 'There was no need to say anything about the breakages,' she pointed out. 'Mrs Lester is quite capable of explaining things to her husband, even if she has got a cut knee.'

'Well, I just thought he ought to know,' replied Rosa sulkily.

'It's not your place to tell him,' said Mrs Peters. And in any case, she thought to herself, no doubt the poor fellow knows well enough, without anyone telling him.

The news of the accident was soon the subject of local interest. The fact that it had occurred in Lulling High Street, amidst so many spectators, meant that there were varied accounts of the incident, and plenty of confirmation about the contents of the publicly shattered gin bottle.

To be fair to the inhabitants of Thrush Green and Lulling, it was concern for Margaret and her family rather than censure which was paramount. There was widespread sympathy for the headmaster in his domestic difficulties, and there was great care in keeping the matter as quiet as possible.

Even Betty Bell, who had summed up the situation early on, checked her ebullient tongue, although Dotty Harmer was less restrained when they met.

'I hear that Mrs Lester is a drunkard,' she remarked brightly to Betty one morning. 'Fell down in the High Street, they tell me.'

'She tripped,' began Betty.

'Such a nuisance when drink gets the better of anyone,' continued Dotty. 'The best thing is to have a drink constantly at hand.'

'But that's just what—' protested Betty, but was cut short again.

'An *innocuous* one, of course. A really strong herb tea, cold preferably. I used to make up a bottle for our old cook when I was a girl; she couldn't resist the cooking sherry, I remember. We soon weaned her on to my nettle beer, and later to a light apple juice.'

'I expect Mr Lester knows how to deal with things,' said Betty.

'I wonder if he does. I might get Connie to run me up there with a bottle or two of my own medicinal brew, and explain how to use it. He must be a very worried man.'

Betty privately thought he would be far more worried if Dotty appeared, jangling bottles and advising on the methods of tackling alcoholism. At any time Dotty was alarming; in the rôle of witch doctor she would frighten the life out of anyone.

And yet, thought Betty, one could not help admiring the direct and outspoken way that Dotty encountered trouble. It was a change from the muted remarks being passed around when the Lesters were mentioned. Here was Dotty, talking frankly of drunkenness, and offering practical help with honest sympathy.

'We had quite a bit of drink trouble in our family,' she went on with the utmost cheerfulness. 'One of my uncles was so bad when in his cups – violent and most abusive – that he couldn't keep a job. In the end, my grandfather was obliged to ship him to Australia.'

'But would anyone want him there?' asked Betty, feeling that it was hardly fair to the Australians to have to put up with such a reprobate.

'Oh, he went out to a *job* there,' said Dotty airily. 'Rounding up sheep, I think. Or kangaroos perhaps.'

'And how did he get on?'

'I've no idea. When one went to Australia in those days, one hardly ever came back.'

'My cousin,' said Betty, trying to guide the conversation away from alcohol, 'had a holiday there last year. He took a month off. Said it was lovely, when he got back. His photos took us all evening to get through.'

'That's what I mean,' said Dotty. 'In my uncle's time, when people were sent off to Australia you could be quite sure that you wouldn't see them again. Now it seems they hop up and down over the Equator like so many yo-yos. Very disconcerting.'

'Well, isn't that a good thing?' asked Betty.

'My grandfather wouldn't have thought so,' said Dotty firmly.

The new extension to Rectory Cottages was officially opened one wet and windy day at the end of October.

The local member of Parliament had been invited to declare it open, but at the last minute was unable to come as he had been obliged to attend to government business overseas.

Charles Henstock feared that yet again he would have to deputize for a guest of honour at short notice. It was Dimity who suggested that he should ring Anthony Bull to see if he could come.

'When? Wednesday? Fine, I should thoroughly enjoy a trip to see you all,' said Anthony.

He promised to arrive in time for lunch, and everyone, particularly the rector, looked forward to seeing him again.

As many friends as possible had been crammed into the premises. As well as the new room, all the residents had thrown open their own accommodation, and there was a general air of festivity. Flowers were everywhere, windows shone, furniture gleamed and on the table in the forefront of the extension stood a magnificent iced cake, and some bottles of champagne.

The only disappointment was the fact that Prouts had failed to deliver the large curtains in time. Agitated messages had been sent throughout the week prior to the party, and Prouts had surpassed themselves with excuses ranging from shortage of staff to a change in the dye of the lining material.

Ella and Muriel were in rare unity over the affair. Their own smaller side curtains hung proudly in place, and their strictures on the firm of Prout were severe.

Edward Young who, as architect, was among those present, would have liked to have said how much more satisfactory it would have been if his suggestion of *blinds* at the windows had been adopted. However he was magnanimous enough, and mellowed by the champagne, to keep these thoughts to himself.

Anthony Bull, of course, was welcomed rapturously, and seemed genuinely delighted to be among some of his former parishioners.

Through the windows overlooking the green, the bonfire could be seen awaiting November the fifth. It was a noble pile already, and everyone knew that the schoolchildren would be hard at work making the guy that would rest on the top.

Anthony looked at it with pleasure. 'And does Percy Hodge still supply potatoes to bake in the ashes?' he asked Jane Cartwright.

'Indeed he does! My Uncle Percy gets as much fun out of Guy Fawkes' night as the children do.'

'Delicious cake,' mumbled Anthony, through a mouthful. He spotted Doreen Lilly across the room. She had been invited to lend a hand, not only with preparing for the party, but to help with the waiting.

'I must go and speak to Doreen,' he said, wiping his fingers on a snow-white handkerchief. 'Does she work here regularly?'

Jane explained the position, and added how well she had fitted in. 'And she's so good with the old people,' she added.

'She certainly looks a lot happier than when I saw her last,' commented Anthony.

'It's good for her to be back in Thrush Green,' said Jane. 'She's a country girl at heart, and I hope she decides to stay here.'

'She couldn't do better,' agreed Anthony.

It was dark when the party ended. The wind was almost at gale force, and as Anthony Bull and his friend Charles drove through Lulling to the vicarage, the rain lashed across the windscreen, giving the wipers a hard task to keep pace with it.

Leaves from the lime trees whipped across the High Street. Lights from The Fuchsia Bush gleamed across the dark wet pavements, and the street lamps were reflected in murky puddles which were ruffled by the wind.

'You're going to have a rough ride back to town, I'm afraid,' said Charles. 'Are you sure you won't change your mind, and stay the night?'

'I wish I could, but I've two meetings tomorrow morning. Don't worry, Charles. I've been much refreshed by my visit. It's so good to see old friends.'

He went on to comment on the improvement he had seen in Doreen Lilly.

'She certainly seems to have found her feet,' agreed Charles. 'Who knows? She may marry again. I think that is what her mother would like above all things.'

'Maybe,' agreed Anthony, turning into the vicarage drive, but he sounded doubtful. 'She may not relish matrimony after all that has happened to her,' he went on.

'Well, we must live in hope,' said the rector, trying to open the door against the howling gale. 'One thing, she looks remarkably bonny. Let's hope fortune continues to smile upon her.'

13. PERCY HODGE'S BUSY DAY

For the past several years Percy Hodge, now middle-aged, had lived alone, but he did not enjoy his solitary state. Now that Emily Cooke had finally deserted him for another, his loneliness was even more acute.

He woke, on this particular November morning, to the usual sad contemplation of his single life. It was still dark, for the luminous bedside clock showed ten to six, and the bedroom was chilly.

'Been a frost, I don't doubt,' said Percy aloud, swinging his legs out of bed. He made his way across the landing to the bathroom to perform his brief ablutions. Ten minutes later he went downstairs to the kitchen which was warm and welcoming. The Aga stove made this the most comfortable room in the house, and Percy spent most of his time there.

His dog Gyp leapt from his basket near the stove to greet his master. It was this animal that had collided with Dorothy Watson's car some time ago, causing that lady considerable anguish. Luckily, the dog's injuries had been slight and he bore no scars.

Percy had kept a dog, and sometimes two or three, throughout his life. Normally they had slept in one of the barns or outhouses on the farm, but Gyp had been more privileged since Percy allowed him to sleep indoors. The truth was that Percy enjoyed his company since the death of Gertie, his first wife, and then the disappearance of his second, whom he had later divorced. He chatted to Gyp as he would have done to a human companion and the dog, a particularly affectionate animal, responded in the most satisfactory manner.

This morning he gambolled about his master's legs as the Aga was filled with a scuttle of solid fuel, and only desisted when Percy put down a dish full of dog biscuit and meat scraps.

Percy set about getting his own breakfast: he lifted down a large, heavy frying-pan from a hook on the wall, and placed it on the hob. He put in four large rashers and two sausages, for Percy believed in a substantial meal at the beginning of the day. He cut two thick slices of bread ready to put in when the bacon and sausages were done, and set the basket of eggs handy for the last addition to his meal.

Meanwhile, the kettle had been moved to the hottest part of the stove and was singing cheerfully. The large enamel teapot, which he and Gertie had bought in the early days of their happy marriage, was warming nearby.

Percy did not bother with such niceties as a tablecloth, but set out his knife and fork on the bare wooden table, and stood the milk bottle nearby. By now the bacon was sizzling, and Gyp had finished his breakfast, clattering the dish about the floor as he licked the last crumbs.

'Now out you go, old man,' said Percy fondly, opening the back door into the yard, and the dog ran out.

Percy adjusted the old wooden calendar which stood on the mantelpiece above the appetizing smells wreathing from the stove. As he turned the small knob showing the date, November the fourth, he remembered that the scoutmaster had promised to pick up the sack of potatoes ready for the morrow's celebration of Guy Fawkes' night. Percy had already sorted out some large beauties, and they awaited collection in the back scullery.

He was just shifting the rashers in the frying pan when Gyp's furious barking disturbed him. Dropping the fork, he hurried to the back door. It was beginning to get light and, with a countryman's eye, he automatically noticed the heavy frost on the nearby cabbages and the ice on a shallow puddle.

Gyp was growling and sniffing at the crack of the door of Percy's shed which stood close to the back door. Here were kept such useful things as the paraffin can, garden tools, a hand mower, two bins of chicken food and a pile of useful sacks.

On opening the door and bidding Gyp to 'Sit!', it was on this pile that Percy discovered a startled man. He was fully dressed, if dressed you could call it, in a long dirty overcoat tied at the waist with binder twine, with a tattered scarf round his neck, and a pair of broken boots inadequately covering bare feet. Blue rheumy eyes gazed at Percy from a stubble-decorated face.

'What you doin' here?' growled Percy. He was not unduly alarmed, or even surprised at this encounter. Over the years he must have come across a dozen or more travellers who had used his buildings for a free night's accommodation. He had been lucky, he knew, that not one of them had done damage, though he suspected that a few turnips and stored apples and carrots had been carried away in the usual capacious pockets. Some of his farmer friends had suffered arson at the hands of these gentlemen of the road, and Percy was thankful it had never happened to him.

Gyp kept up a menacing growl as the two men surveyed each other.

'I never done no 'arm,' pleaded the tramp, rising to his feet. 'Just 'ad a kip overnight.'

He sniffed noisily, and wiped his rheumy eyes with dirty knuckles. It was a child's gesture which Percy found strangely moving. He moved aside to let the tramp out.

From the kitchen, the neglected rashers and sausages sent out delicious smells.

'Cor!' said the tramp. 'I'm that 'ungry I could h'eat a h'ox.'

Percy looked at him. He was a most unsavoury fellow to have at the breakfast table, but there was no reason why he should not have some victuals in the shed.

'I could set the dog on you,' Percy told him sternly. 'You bin trespassing! For all I know you've filled your pockets with my stuff.'

'Ain't got no pockets,' protested the tramp, pulling some filthy rags from the side of the dilapidated overcoat. 'See 'ere, mister.'

Gyp growled afresh, longing to rush at the interloper. A distinct smell of burning now began to waft towards the group, and Percy started towards the house.

'You can wait at the door,' he told his visitor. 'I'll give you a bite, and then you're on your way.'

He hurried in and was just in time to rescue the rashers and turn the sausages. He scooped them to one side, and put in the bread.

Gyp remained in the scullery facing his foe at the back door, but ready to hurry to his master's side if needed. He welcomed this diversion at the beginning of the day, and the unusual smells emanating from their visitor were most exciting, almost fox-like.

Percy made the tea, looked out an enamel plate and mug which had been used for just such emergencies before, and set out some of his own breakfast portion for the tramp. Plate in one hand and steaming mug in the other, he pushed past Gyp and handed them to the waiting figure.

'Cor! Mister!' cried the man.

'Eat it in the shed,' ordered Percy, 'and don't forget to bring the plate back. And the mug.'

He shut the door sharply and returned to his own food. Gyp sighed contentedly, and stretched himself in front of the stove.

It was very quiet in the kitchen. Only the ticking of the great wall clock and the humming of the kettle broke the silence as Percy mopped his plate with a piece of bread. It was at times like this that sadness pervaded him. Breakfast time with Gertie had been a busy occasion when they discussed the day's plans and then washed up together, for Percy had always been more domesticated than most farmers, and his sister, Mrs Jenner, had made sure that he did his fair share of the chores when they were young together in this very same kitchen.

He thought about the fellow outside. Had he ever had a home, he wondered? A poor life for a man, everlasting roaming the country. Worse than his own. At least he had a roof over his head, a fire and victuals in plenty. It was just company that he missed.

He was about to take his plate to the sink when he heard the knocking at the back door, and found the tramp proffering the empty plate and mug.

'Thanks, mate. That went down good,' he said.

Percy put the plate and mug on the battered scullery table, and surveyed his visitor. He was certainly a sorry sight. It was the pink flesh showing through the gaping boots that struck Percy as the most pathetic part of the general air of destitution.

'You goin' far?' he asked.

'Makin' to Banbury way. Got a mate there. Do a bit of beatin' for the toffs' shoots.'

'You won't get far in those boots,' commented Percy, eyeing

a pair of his old gardening boots standing hardby. They looked, though Percy would not have known it, very like the famous lace-up pair belonging to Gertrude Jekyll, well-worn but serviceable.

'Take them,' he said, 'and chuck those wrecks in the dustbin.'

He left the man on the floor coping with his new acquisitions, and went back to the kitchen. An ancient pullover, knitted years before by his sister, lay on one of the chairs awaiting washing. Well, it would save him doing that chore, thought Percy, taking it to the scullery.

The man was busy lacing up one boot. Percy suddenly remembered Gertie on just such an occasion, asking one long-past traveller anxiously what size he took. He had teased her when the man had gone. Didn't she know he could stuff newspaper round the gaps, or cut a slit if they pinched?

But Gertie, child of a Lulling shopkeeper, had not had much first-hand knowledge of tramps and her ignorance had amused Percy enormously.

The sudden remembrance softened Percy now. He handed him the pullover. 'Keep out the cold,' he said gruffly. 'Want a hunk of bread to take with you?'

The man stood up, stamping in his new boots.

'They're great, mate, and you're a real gent.'

'Well, don't tell your friends,' warned Percy. 'I ain't usually so generous.'

He went back to the kitchen. He had no intention of inviting the man farther into his domain for he would be as verminous, he had no doubt, as a stray dog.

He rolled up the end of the loaf in a page from the *Radio Times*, adding a lump of cheese from the nearby cheese-dish on the dresser.

His visitor stood, still admiring his boots.

'Right! There you are, and now be off with you,' said Percy, opening the back door.

'God bless you, guv,' said the tramp fervently, and Percy

watched him striding away, in his old boots, into the frosty morning.

'Sometimes,' remarked Percy to Gyp, as he poured another cup of tea, 'I reckon I'm too soft.'

An hour later the scoutmaster called for the sack of potatoes, and Percy helped him load it into the boot of his car. He was on his way to work at the bank in Lulling High Street, and Percy thought how nice it must be to have a job which started halfway through the morning, as it seemed to him.

He himself had already seen to the cattle, mended a fence, rung the corn chandler, prepared a mash for the chickens, filled in a form for some ministry or other which meant nothing to him, looked out another pair of boots, demoted now from everyday to gardening, and left his dishes and the tramp's in the sink to soak.

Just before ten he decided to take the shabby Land Rover down to Lulling to get the tyres looked at, praying that he need not go to the expense of a new one on the off-side which was definitely suspect. Then he would seek refreshment and a little company at The Two Pheasants. Tuesday today, he thought, as he trundled down the hill; might be a lardy cake at The Fuchsia Bush, and that was just the thing on a frosty day.

He trod on the accelerator. You never knew – that Lulling lot might have cleared out all the lardy cakes if he didn't look lively.

At Rectory Cottages Doreen Lilly was busy at work. She had left Bobby safely corralled in the nursery school with a pair of blunt-nosed scissors and some coloured paper.

Today she had been asked by Jane to tidy the store cupboard and clean the shelves. It was a pleasantly straightforward job, stacking packets and tins in a small room with deep shelves on three sides, which was lit by a large window at the end.

All went well until Doreen noticed how dirty the hopper of the window had become. It was a small slanting pane, always ajar to air the place, and was liable to catch any dust and debris which the main part of the window missed.

She went to fetch the short pair of steps, which only stood hip-high and had a useful padded top which could be used as a stool. Doreen was fond of these steps: Jane had warned her about too much stretching at the present stage of her pregnancy, and they were a great help to her.

She opened them now and made her way up them, a damp cloth in her hand. The shelf was wide, and stacked with innumerable tins. Doreen found it difficult to reach across them to her target.

'Drat it all,' she muttered, and stepped on to the padded top to give her better access to the window.

It was at this point that the steps skidded away. They fell with a hideous clatter, and Doreen ended up lying awkwardly across them still clutching the cloth in her hand. Half a dozen tins, dislodged in the upset, dropped painfully upon her, and she cried out.

Jane came running, took in the situation at a glance, and soon had the girl sitting in the kitchen. She had the sense not to scold her. It was apparent from the girl's ashen face that she was upset enough already. She was bent double, and holding her stomach.

'Got an awful griping,' she gasped, and Jane's heart sank.

'You'd better come and lie down,' she said, helping the girl to her feet.

As soon as she had the girl flat on the bed she rang the surgery to explain the situation. John Lovell answered the telephone himself and, having faith in Jane Cartwright's nursing knowledge, said he would be over immediately.

'I've just finished surgery,' he said. 'In fact I was on my way to the car. I'll be with you in a couple of minutes.'

By the time the doctor arrived, Doreen was tearful and in great pain. John Lovell gave a brief examination, and straightened up.

'I want her in hospital,' he said quietly to Jane. 'May I use your telephone?'

Some ten minutes later the inhabitants of Thrush Green were greatly intrigued to see an ambulance drawing up outside Rectory Cottages, and a stretcher being carried in.

One of the poor old dears, thought Ella, surveying the scene from her landing window.

'Someone's been took ill,' Jenny told Winnie Bailey, as they made the bed together.

'I hope that's not poor Muriel Fuller,' said Isobel to Harold, catching sight of the ambulance as she put out the milk bottles. 'She was very shaky in church last week.'

Not one of the interested viewers guessed that the youngest person in the place was the victim.

Albert Piggott and Percy Hodge had just emerged from The Two Pheasants, Albert to continue his desultory tidying-up, and Percy to drive the Land Rover back to the farm.

'Wonder who that is?' said Percy, watching the laden stretcher being returned to the ambulance, accompanied by his niece Jane Cartwright and Dr Lovell.

'One of them old 'uns, no doubt,' responded Albert. 'You has to expect it at their age.'

His tone was dismissive, and he was already turning away towards the church. But Percy, whose sight was clearer than his companion's, still watched attentively.

'That's the Lilly girl!' he exclaimed. 'Doreen, or somethin'.'

The ambulance doors clanged shut. Dr Lovell raised his hand to Jane as he departed, and she, to Percy's surprise, came hurrying towards him.

'Uncle Percy, do me a favour.' She seemed unusually agitated.

'What's that?'

'Young Doreen Lilly's had a fall. She might have a miscarriage. What's worrying her is that her little boy's at play-school and she usually fetches him at twelve. Could you take a message to her mother? She'll be able to collect him, I'm sure. Do you know the house?'

'Lord, yes! Where the baker lived. I'll drive down now.'

'Thanks very much. I dare not leave my old folk. And tell her to ring the hospital direct. Visiting hours are six to seven-thirty. The hospital will tell her if the girl's up to seeing her.'

Percy clambered back into the Land Rover, and turned to drive down the hill. He was somewhat perturbed at the delicate task before him, and sorry for the young woman whom he had always considered unusually pretty. Percy, particularly now that he was alone, was susceptible to female attractions.

He found Gladys Lilly busy with a mound of ironing; there was a pleasant scent of clean linen, and a clothes' horse bearing innumerable small garments, presumably belonging to her grandson.

'Oh my!' cried Gladys, on hearing the news. 'What a thing to happen! It was all going so well too. What a blessing it was that your Jane was there to look after her.'

Percy added the message about telephoning the hospital and the visiting hours.

'I'll pop in next door and ring from there as soon as I've fetched Bobby,' promised Gladys. 'If you'll excuse me a moment, I'll go and get a coat.'

Percy was left alone in the kitchen. It was warm and tidy. A pile of newly-ironed pillow cases and sheets stood nearby, and something delicious sizzled in the oven. On the hob stood a freshly cooked rice pudding, with a nice brown crinkled top smelling of cinnamon. It reminded Percy sharply of the dinners his mother had cooked for them years ago, in that same kitchen along the Nidden road where his breakfast dishes still awaited attention in a scummy sink. It was a good thing, he thought, that his mother could not see it now.

Mrs Lilly, somewhat calmer, reappeared, and Percy offered to give her a lift to the school, but she refused.

'It's no distance, thanks all the same. You've done enough, Mr Hodge.'

Percy was touched by the rather formal address.

'Well, let me take you up to the hospital this evenin',' he said. 'It's a good step, and they've promised us rain after dark. Shall I pop down, say at half past six, and see how things are?'

'That's uncommon kind of you,' said Gladys. 'I'd really be glad of a lift.'

They left the house together, Gladys hurrying along to the school, and Percy making his way back to his midday bread and cheese. That rice pudding, he thought wistfully, would have gone down a treat.

At half past six he reappeared at Gladys Lilly's door. He had exchanged his working jacket for a somewhat cleaner one, wore a tie and had brushed his hair.

Mrs Lilly, who was already in her outdoor coat, climbed into the Land Rover. She looked tearful, and Percy was at a loss to know what to say.

'All right to visit then?' he said at last.

'Yes. Hospital folk said it was OK. Sad though. She's lost it.'

'Lost what?'

'The baby. Didn't you know? She was having her second.'

Percy did know now that he came to think of it, but his apparent ignorance was easier in the circumstances.

'Is she all right?'

'Will be, they say, but she's got to stay in a day or two.'

'She's a nice lookin' girl,' ventured Percy, driving circumspectly up Lulling High Street.

'Takes after her dad,' said Gladys. 'I was never no beauty.'

She sounded quite matter-of-fact, and was certainly not angling for compliments, which Percy approved.

'Yes, he was a handsome chap,' he agreed. 'You must miss him.'

'Thirty-three years we was married, and him in the same job up at Carters in Grain Street all that time. He was a baker, you know.'

'I did know,' said Percy, turning into the hospital gates. 'Used to make first-class lardy cakes. I had one from The Fuchsia Bush today, but it's not a patch on Carters!'

He stopped the Land Rover, and watched his passenger clamber down.

'You coming in? There's a kiosk where they sell coffee and tea.'

'No. I'll wait here for you. Don't hurry yourself,' replied Percy.

He had parked at the side of the hospital, and sat looking at the row of lighted windows before him. The glass was frosted, and he could only discern human shapes passing to and fro about their business.

A little nocturnal animal scrabbled under the laurel bushes in front of him, and somewhere a child was wailing inconsolably, probably missing his mother and the warm security of his own bed.

Poor little devil, thought Percy. He knew how he felt, lost and alone, and away from all the comforts of home. It was getting unpleasantly cold with the engine turned off, and Percy decided to take a brisk walk around the car park.

There were very few cars there, but a steady stream passed on the road outside, lighting up the leafless trees in the grounds, and turning the window panes of the hospital into silver squares.

A man came hurrying out, and Percy recognized him as a neighbour from Nidden.

'What you doin' here?' he called.

'Why, Perce, it's you, is it? My boy's broke a leg. Nothin' serious. Blasted motorbike of his. Who you waitin' for?'

Percy told him.

'Young Doreen, eh? Pretty girl, but no better'n she should be, so I hear.'

'You don't want to believe all you hear,' said Percy snappily.

'No, that's right,' agreed the other, sounding somewhat startled. 'Well, I'd best be off. Gettin' chilly again, isn't it?'

Percy did not answer, but watched him get into his Ford car and drive away.

'Everlastin' gossip,' he commented to the unseen animal which was still scrabbling among the laurels. 'Makes you sick.'

And at that moment, Mrs Lilly reappeared and Percy opened the door of the Land Rover for her.

'How is she?' asked Percy when they had joined the stream of traffic outside the hospital.

'Like a little ghost,' replied Gladys. 'Got a drip thing stuck in her. She looks terrible, but the nurse says she's OK.'

'Good. Want a lift up there tomorrow?'

'Oh, I couldn't bother you, Mr Hodge.'

'No trouble. And call me Percy.'

'Well then, thank you, Percy.'

They drew up outside the house, and Percy secretly hoped to be invited into that comfortable kitchen for a drink, but he was to be disappointed.

'I won't keep you now,' said Gladys, as she climbed down to the pavement. 'I've got young Bobby to fetch from my neighbour, but I hope you'll have a bit of supper with me tomorrow.'

'I'll look forward to that,' said Percy heartily. 'See you same time tomorrow then.'

As he trundled home towards Nidden, he felt uncommonly happy. The bonfire awaited tomorrow's lighting on the green, and he remembered how he himself had enjoyed the yearly frolic as a boy. He was glad he had provided the potatoes for tomorrow's celebrations; his father had done so for years, and it was good to keep up the tradition.

What a day! How far, he wondered, had the tramp got on his way towards Banbury in his old gardening boots, and how was poor young Doreen getting on in her hospital bed? You never knew what the day would bring you.

He turned into the farm yard and was greeted by ecstatic barking from Gyp.

'Time we was both fed,' Percy told him, reaching for the dog biscuits with one hand, and the frying-pan with the other.

14. MIXED PROBLEMS

At Barton-on-Sea, Agnes and Dorothy were busy with Christmas cards and parcels bound for friends overseas.

'We really should have sent to Freda Potts in Australia last month,' said Dorothy, studying a pamphlet from the Post Office.

Freda Potts had taught with Dorothy in her first school, and had been a frequent visitor to Thrush Green before making her home abroad.

'So soon?' queried Agnes. 'I should have thought it would have got there far too early.'

'I'm inclined to put a handkerchief in with our Christmas card, and send it air mail,' said Dorothy. 'Really, Christmas seems to get earlier every year; here we are on November the fifth, and still behind time.'

'I wonder how the bonfire will go tonight?' mused Agnes, pen arrested.

'I don't intend to light it,' said Dorothy, 'the leaves are much too wet.'

'I meant at Thrush Green.'

'Ah!' sighed Dorothy. '*That* bonfire! What fun we had with the guy!'

'I wish we were nearer, then we could be there to see it.'

Dorothy looked at Agnes's wistful face. 'We'll bear it in mind for next year,' she promised. 'Perhaps we'll have a day or two up in the Cotswolds, and have a last fling before we hibernate.'

'Lovely!' cried Agnes.

'And I'll ring Isobel tomorrow to hear all about it,' continued Dorothy, reaching for another Christmas card.

'And the rest of the Thrush Green news,' added Agnes. 'It seems a long time since we saw them. Would you like me to do the telephoning?'

'No, no. I can do it when I come back from Teddy's,' replied Dorothy, banging on a stamp energetically.

Teddy, thought Agnes rebelliously, *would* have to come into things! Even a telephone call to dear Thrush Green, it seemed, had to be tailored to fit in with Teddy's requirements.

She banged on a stamp of her own, with some vehemence.

Thrush Green's bonfire was set alight just after six o'clock, and a goodly crowd was there to watch. It was flaming vigorously when Percy made his way towards Mrs Lilly's house. A crowd of people held up his Land Rover for a few moments as they crossed the road from The Two Pheasants. He was hailed by a woman as he waited, and he saw that it was Nelly Piggott.

'Coming over, Percy?' she called, one hand on the van window.

'Can't tonight. Just off to the hospital.'

'Oh dear! Who's bad then?'

'Doreen Lilly.'

He attempted to edge away, not wanting to go into details, but he was obliged to linger as the new schoolmaster, his wife and the two little girls went across towards the bonfire.

'I'm sorry,' said Nelly. 'I hadn't heard.'

At last he got away and Nelly, following the excited Lester children across the grass, had much to think about.

Later, she told Albert of this encounter. 'D'you think he's got his eye on young Doreen, now that Emily Cooke's turned him down?' she enquired.

'Wouldn't be surprised,' grunted Albert. 'Perce is fool enough for anythin', and always had an eye for the girls.'

Mrs Lilly was waiting on the pavement when Percy arrived, and he did not have the opportunity of presenting her with the dozen brown eggs he had brought as a small offering to his hostess.

They made their way to Lulling High Street. The sky on their left was bright with reflection from the bonfire, and Mrs Lilly chattered brightly about the times she had taken Doreen to see it over the years.

'Bobby wanted to go but I promised I'd take him next year. He had a late night yesterday, what with all this upset, and my neighbour Mrs Brown is sitting with him. I got him to bed early tonight. One thing, he's not much bother about going to bed. Doreen was a real handful over that when she was little.'

As before Percy waited while she went in to see her daughter. If anything, it was colder than ever, and a myriad stars sparkled over a world already frosty.

Percy found himself looking forward eagerly to Gladys Lilly's supper, and hoped it would be a cooked one. A chap didn't fancy cold meat and salad on a night like this, and Percy fell to envisaging steak-and-kidney pudding, with good thick gravy oozing out when the knife went in, or perhaps a steaming Lancashire hot-pot like his dear Gertie used to make, with brown potato slices sizzling on top.

The waiting time seemed longer than yesterday's, hungry as he was, and the church clock was striking seven when Gladys came from the door.

'I'm to ring tomorrow morning, and they may let her out after the doctor's done his rounds. She looks more herself today.'

'Want me to fetch her?' asked Percy.

'I don't think you need to trouble,' said Gladys. 'Someone from the hospital car service will bring her, they said. If it's daytime you'll be out on the farm, and you've done more than most would already.'

'Only too pleased to help,' responded Percy. 'Let's leave it that you'll get in touch sometime tomorrow. I'd like to know how she's doin'.'

He left the Land Rover in the street, and followed Mrs Lilly into the house. A delicious smell of cooking greeted them, and Percy realized that he was even more ravenous than he had first thought.

'Now come in, Mr Hodge – I mean, Percy. It's set in the kitchen, and Mrs Brown is having a bite with us.'

Percy felt unduly annoyed at hearing that this was not to be the tête-à-tête he had envisaged. However, it was Gladys's affair, and obviously a nice way of showing appreciation of her neighbour's help during these worrying two days.

Gladys took his jacket and cap, and led him through to the kitchen. Mrs Brown was a small wizened old lady with hair of a startling orange hue. Percy knew her by sight, and remembered that her husband, who was now dead, had been a gamekeeper on one of the Hampshire estates to the south of Lulling.

Introductions were made, Mrs Brown and Percy were invited to sit at the table, and Gladys took the supper from the oven.

It proved to be just the sort of meal that Percy liked best, steak-and-kidney simmered in a casserole with a large dish of potatoes baked in their jackets and another of carrots.

Percy, like most men, enjoyed plenty of meat with brown gravy. When he had married Gertie, an accomplished and imaginative cook, he had stipulated 'no damn stuff in white sauce'.

Gertie soon weaned him by way of cauliflower cheese and fish fillets in white sauce, but he still thought that the predominant colour on a fellow's dinner plate should be brown with a touch of home-grown green – say runner beans, peas or sprouts – on the side.

'Well, this looks wholly good,' he told Gladys. 'I don't get real home-cooking these days.'

'Nothing like it,' agreed Mrs Brown, who seemed to eat at an alarming pace despite the regular clicking of ill-fitting false teeth. 'When I was in service at Marchleaze we had a wonderful cook. Mind you, she was temperamental. Blew hot and cold. One minute all smiles, the next as black as thunder. Being an artist in her own line, you see.'

'Ah!' agreed Percy. Gladys passed him the pepper pot, and was about to speak, but Mrs Brown forestalled her.

'My lady understood her funny little ways,' continued Mrs Brown. 'Never turned a hair when cook sulked. A wonderful woman she was. Heiress in her own right, but would sit down with anyone. Brought up the children the same, but it didn't stop Master John taking to the bottle. And worse! But a lovely boy. Used to have beautiful hair before he went bald. And nice manners too, even when he was half-seas over.'

It soon became apparent to Percy that Mrs Brown was one of those people, all too common, who regaled their listeners with lengthy tales about people who were entirely unknown and, after an hour or so of increasing boredom, thoroughly disliked.

He and Gladys were subjected to a monologue about Mrs Brown's lady, her looks, disposition and extensive wardrobe. The doings of Master John, Miss Adela and the three younger siblings were also described in minutest detail, while Mrs Brown's two companions ate in silence.

The main course was followed by a magnificent trifle, and then by biscuits and a noble hunk of Cheddar cheese. Percy did full justice to everything put before him, and attempted to turn a deaf ear to his neighbour who was now describing the grandeur of her lady's drawing-room.

'And over the mantelpiece there was a great picture of her mother – ever so big – as big as that door there. No! I tell a lie! Perhaps about three-quarters of that door, but with a gold frame that took a bit of dusting, I can tell you. It didn't have no glass over it, it was done in oils, you see, and that could catch the dust too, specially as they liked log fires, and you know what wood ash is if you get a draught. The gardener used to bring in the logs. Why, some of them would be as long as this table here, and as thick as a man's leg. Burn for hours, they would.'

The fireplace and portrait were followed by descriptions of the chairs, cabinets and their contents, the soft furnishing, both for winter and summer, and how the staff set about spring-cleaning when the lady of the house ordered it.

By nine-fifteen Percy was beginning to get restive. He was more than grateful to Gladys for this wonderful meal, but disappointed in having so little opportunity to express his appreciation, or to express anything else, for that matter, with the relentless outpourings of Mrs Brown in full spate.

At last she stopped, looked at her watch, and rose in a flurry.

'So late! I had no idea! I must get back, Gladys. My programme's on, and I want to see if Kevin and Mandy have made it up.'

She waved goodbye to Percy, and Gladys escorted her to the front door, thanking her profusely against Mrs Brown's monologue which still continued.

Gladys returned and smiled at Percy. 'Runs on a bit, doesn't she?'

Percy thought that this was the understatement of the year, but was too polite to comment.

'Have a cup of coffee,' urged Gladys. 'We might have a chat, now she's gone. But this I will say, despite all the gab, her heart's in the right place.'

*

It was not long, of course, before the news flew round the neighbourhood that Percy Hodge was now paying his attentions to young Doreen Lilly. Well, hadn't he visited the hospital twice while the girl was there? And hadn't he been seen visiting the house several times since Doreen was home again?

The general opinion was that Percy simply could not keep away from these young girls like Doreen and Emily Cooke, and all foresaw another disappointment in store for the amorous wooer.

But other topics soon crowded out speculation about Percy's adventures. For one thing, the spate of fund-raising continued, and the Fur-and-Feather whist drive, Lulling's Mammoth Nearly-New Sale, and the flutter of raffle books which these activities aroused, turned attention from Percy's plight.

Nelly Piggott had troubles of her own, for one morning Bertha Lovelock had entered The Fuchsia Bush alone, and taken a table dangerously near to the counter where such tempting titbits as home-made shortbread fingers and delicious scones, warm from the oven, gave forth their fragrance.

Nelly, who happened to be in the shop when the lady appeared, was confronted with a number of options to protect the shop's property.

It would look offensive to remove the goods from the counter and to put them out of Bertha's reach. She could, of course, pretend that she wanted to re-arrange them in the kitchen and whisk the lot outside.

She could stand guard over the array, or post one of the girls to stand on duty. She could, at a pinch, telephone Violet Lovelock and tell her that Bertha was at large on her own, and did she know?

All these unpleasant possibilities flashed through Nelly's head, until she came across a more acceptable solution.

She approached Bertha with a smile. 'Good morning, Miss Lovelock. Chilly today, isn't it?'

Bertha inclined her head graciously.

'Can I bring you some coffee?' asked Nelly.

'Yes, please. Nothing to eat.'

Nelly looked around with affected solicitude. 'I think you are going to be in a draught here, Miss Lovelock,' she said anxiously. 'Every time the door opens, you know. Wind's easterly this morning. Let me put you over here. You'll be more comfortable.'

Bertha seemed remarkably obliging, and began to gather gloves, purse, two letters awaiting posting, and an ancient fur stole which she had hung on the back of the chair.

At that moment, however, there was a crash from the kitchen, and Nelly went to see what was the matter, and to order Bertha's coffee.

Her back was turned for approximately twenty seconds, and Bertha was still collecting her belongings when Nelly reached her side. Before long, the old lady was settled by the wall, out of harm's way, and Gloria was approaching with a steaming cup of coffee.

Nelly carried the basket of scones into the kitchen to count them. As she feared, one was missing. One really could not help but admire Bertha's sleight-of-hand manoeuvres, embarrassing though they were, thought Nelly.

Gloria had been left on duty, having been primed beforehand about the action to take should Bertha ever appear alone, and Nelly made a quick decision.

She would do nothing on this occasion; poor old Violet had enough to cope with. But she intended to see that Bertha paid her bill for the coffee, and she would watch to see that she went straight home. Both these things happened, and Nelly was left to wonder if she should mention the matter to Mrs Peters and the girls. Or was it right to turn a blind eye, as she had decided to do?

Being a partner in the firm certainly complicated life, thought Nelly, returning to her domain in the kitchen after she had seen Bertha disappear through her own front door. If Nelly had been a mere assistant, like Rosa or Gloria, she would have reported the matter to Mrs Peters and left it at that. But now she had more important obligations. 'Rank imposes responsibilities' someone had once told her, and Nelly, somewhat ruefully, realized that she must face that fact.

This time no action, she told herself, shaking flour on to a pastry board, but if it happened again she would harden her heart and send for Miss Violet to cope with her sister.

Winnie Bailey was also having private worries. As a doctor's wife for many years, in a small community, she had frequently known of the complaints and conditions of many of her husband's patients. Obviously she had been discreet, and had not interfered in her husband's affairs, but the fact remained that she was often privy to confidences disclosed by Donald's patients almost before she could direct them to his surgery.

The case of Margaret Lester and her family worried her considerably. Her kind heart went out to the man who was doing his best to carry on the sound tradition of good schooling which his predecessors had maintained, whilst instigating some more modern methods of his own.

She was even more concerned about the two little girls. She came across them occasionally, and was impressed by their good manners and friendliness. The children played frequently with John Lovell's two children who were much the same age, and one morning Winnie ventured to broach the painful subject of Margaret's addiction to alcohol with the doctor.

He listened with his usual sympathy. He was devoted to Winnie, recognizing her sterling virtues and unfailing common sense. But on this occasion, he was obliged to be firm.

'There is nothing I can do, Winnie, as you know, until I am approached either by the patient herself or by someone directly responsible for her, like Alan. I am as upset as you are by the problem, and I can only hope that Alan can persuade her to seek help.'

'Have you ever been called to the house?'

'Not for Margaret. I have had occasion to visit the children once or twice, but the migraine attacks about which we hear so much are dealt with by Alan and Margaret herself.'

'But those poor little girls!' cried Winnie. 'What can we do about them?'

'Mighty little, I fear, until we are asked to help. We can only stand by in readiness, and rush to the rescue if necessary.'

'I just dread the possibility of something unpleasant happening in that house,' said Winnie sadly. 'It could so easily.'

How prophetic her words were!

15. FRIENDS AT THRUSH GREEN

November grew gloomier as the days passed. It was not cold, but dark and oppressive. Mist hung in the valleys and the sun was nowhere to be seen. The trees dripped, the hedges were spangled with droplets, and the roads and grass were permanently wet.

Lights were on in the houses, shops and offices from morning until dusk. It was a depressing period for all. Everyone was lethargic, from the young school children to the venerable inhabitants of Rectory Cottages.

Even Betty Bell's exuberance seemed diminished as she went about her duties, first at the school and then at the Shoosmiths' house.

'Fair gets on your wick,' she said, collecting her tin of polish from under the stairs. 'I mean, what's the good of polishing in this weather? "Love's labour's lost", as my mum used to say.'

'Well, perhaps you'd better leave it,' said Isobel. 'The windows could do with a wash instead.'

'No, no. It's polishing today, and that I'll do,' said Betty firmly. 'Can't let the weather have the best of it. By the way, old Dotty – Miss Harmer, I should say – is in bed with a chill. At least, she should be, but she keeps getting out and she's driving Miss Connie up the wall.'

'Oh dear! I'm sorry, I'll ring Connie this morning.'

'It's this weather,' went on Betty, taking up the tin of polish. 'No end of the kids are away from school, and Mrs Lester's taken to her bed again.'

'Dear, dear!'

'And not only to her *bed*,' said Betty ominously, and made her way upstairs, leaving Isobel much disturbed.

Later that day she and Harold roused themselves enough to tackle the task of sweeping up leaves. It was heavy going, for the ground was sticky and the leaves sodden. They wheeled a few barrow loads to the compost heap, and surveyed the hundreds which still adhered obstinately to the lawn.

'I don't know about you,' remarked Harold, 'but I've had enough. It's so damn warm, too. Let's call it a day. We'll tackle this lot when it's dried out.'

'It suits me,' agreed Isobel, who had already shed her coat which lay over the hedge.

'What we want is a good brisk wind,' said Harold. 'Or some frost. Preferably both.'

'Better still,' said Isobel, 'an early cup of tea.'

They went indoors to get it.

It had never been really light all day, but by five o'clock it was truly dark, and the inhabitants of Thrush Green and Lulling were thankful to draw their curtains against the miserable world outside, and turn to indoor pursuits.

Soon after six o'clock the first rumbles of thunder began, and Thrush Green was lit, every so often, by flickering lightning.

Harold, returning from the front porch, was cheerful. 'This should clear the air,' he said. 'No rain yet. I suppose it'll come. Alan Lester's just driven off, by the way.'

'Is Margaret with him?'

'I couldn't see. I just waved, and he hooted. Off to a meeting I expect, poor devil. Thank God, I'm retired and don't have to face meetings any more.'

'What rubbish!' cried Isobel. 'You are often out at committee meetings of the Parish Council and other Church matters, not to mention Scouts and Guides and British Legion and Uncle Tom Cobley and all.'

'I don't count those,' said Harold equably. 'They aren't Business!'

They settled down with their books, while the thunder rumbled. The electric lights flickered ominously, but it was an hour later when there was an almighty crash of thunder overhead and all the lights went out.

'Damn!' said Harold. 'And I've just dropped my glasses.'

'Then don't move your feet,' begged Isobel. 'Where do you think they are?'

'If I knew that,' replied Harold patiently, 'they wouldn't be lost. I'll just grope about. Can you find a torch?'

Isobel felt her way into the hall where a large torch stood permanently. On returning, she picked up the gleam of Harold's spectacles on the hearthrug, and restored them to their owner.

'Good girl! I'll go and light the oil lamp. Hope our neighbours have some auxiliary lighting.'

'Oh, it shouldn't take long,' said Isobel hopefully. 'Don't we get switched to another grid when this happens? Last time it was only a few minutes before the electricity came back.'

She followed Harold into the kitchen and directed the beam of the torch while he lit the ancient oil lamp and carefully replaced the glass and shade.

'It really is a lovely soft light,' commented Isobel when it was installed on the table between their chairs. The fire gave out some light, and a few small logs which Harold added soon leapt into flame.

'It's really quite snug,' went on Isobel. 'Not really bright enough to read. A wonderful excuse to lie back and doze.'

But such hopes were not to be realized, for at that moment the front door bell rang shrilly, and there was a sound of frightened voices. Harold grabbed the torch and went into the dark hall, followed by Isobel.

A flash of lightning illuminated Thrush Green as he opened the door. Huddled together and crying were the two little Lester girls, their shoulders spattered with the rain which was now beginning to fall.

'Come in quickly!' cried Isobel, leading them to the fire. She was shocked to see that they were in their night-clothes –

pyjamas under their dressing-gowns, and their feet were clad only in soft slippers.

'It's Mummy,' said Alison, 'we can't wake her, and I can't reach the candles in the cupboard.'

She was calmer than her younger sister Kate, who was still in tears, but both children were trembling, and not only with the cold, Isobel surmised.

'I found the matches,' went on Alison, 'but I was afraid to go upstairs to find the little paraffin lamp Daddy keeps on the landing. I didn't like the thunder, you see, and the matches kept going out.'

Harold and Isobel exchanged glances.

'I'll take the hurricane lamp and go over,' he said.

'I think I ought to come too,' replied Isobel, much troubled. What on earth would he find? Margaret unconscious? The house in flames?

Harold took command. 'I'll come back for you, if need be. But these two could do with a hot drink. Use the old saucepan. That fire should be good enough to heat some milk.'

Isobel heard the front door bang as Harold departed, and then began to do her best to comfort the children. The thought of matches, candles, and a paraffin lamp in the darkness next door, and the frightened young children's pathetic attempts to find a light amidst the terrors of the storm, made Isobel feel positively sick with horror.

She fetched the milk and set it to heat at the front of the fire, and the two little girls, with a biscuit apiece, sat on the hearthrug and began to calm down.

'Do you know where Daddy is?' she asked, pouring out the milk into two mugs.

'At a meeting,' said Kate.

'Near Oxford,' added Alison. 'At a school with a funny name.'

'An animal,' volunteered Kate. 'A white animal, "White Lion", I think.'

'No, no, it's not,' said Alison firmly. 'It's "White Hart".'

'It's more than that,' maintained Kate defensively, 'like "White Hart Road School".'

At least, thought Isobel, they appeared to be getting back to a more normal sisterly exchange of communication, and there was a slight chance of being able to ring the school where the meeting was taking place.

She was relieved when Harold returned.

'Is Mummy all right?' asked Alison.

'She's fine. Just resting. I told her we'd look after you until your daddy came back.'

He exchanged glances with Isobel, shaking his head slightly.

'I'll try and phone Alan,' he said. 'Any idea of the place?'

'It's a school called "White Something",' said Alison.

'An animal,' added Kate.

Harold found the telephone directory, put it on the table in the light of the oil lamp, and settled his glasses.

'Schools!' he was muttering to himself as he leafed through the pages.

'Ah, here we are! The only "White Something" is "White Rose School".'

'That's it,' said Kate.

'But that's a *flower*,' protested Alison.

'It's a *deer*,' proclaimed Kate fiercely. 'A *rose* deer!'

'That's *roe*, stupid,' shouted Alison, pink with fury.

'Now, now,' said Isobel, 'that's enough! Just be quiet while Harold telephones.'

The children subsided, and Isobel followed Harold into the hall where he was dialling the number by torchlight. She was careful to close the sitting-room door.

'How is she?'

'Flat out, but safe where she is. She's on the bed. I covered her up.'

'Should we get the doctor?'

'That's Alan's job. All I can do is tell him the position. Is that White Rose School? Is Alan Lester there? It's rather urgent.'

'He left about ten minutes ago,' said a deep voice, which Isobel could hear clearly. 'I'm just off myself. I'm the head here, and we've just finished the meeting. Lester should be home in about twenty minutes or so.'

'Have you had a power cut over there? We're groping about in darkness.'

'No. We're still all right, I'm glad to say. Do you want me to get in touch with Lester?'

'No, no. We'll do that. We live next door to the school house. Many thanks, anyway.'

He put down the telephone, and looked at Isobel. 'I think the best thing to do is to put the little girls to bed in their own house, and we'll wait there until Alan gets back. Some home-coming for the poor chap, I'm afraid!'

A quarter of an hour later the children were in bed. The emergency lamp on the landing had been lit, and their bedroom door left ajar.

Isobel crept upstairs to look at them a few minutes later, and was relieved to see that they were asleep.

She opened the door of Margaret's room, heard regular snoring, and closed the door again quietly. If only Alan could get back quickly and take over! She went downstairs, and she and Harold sat in the chilly sitting-room which was lit only by the light of two candles which Harold had discovered in the kitchen cupboard.

How sad this little house seemed now, thought Isobel. In this room, so often, she had gossiped with dear old Agnes and Dorothy about the fun and foibles of Thrush Green parents and their children. Upstairs in Dorothy's old bedroom, which had always been restful and scented with lavender, there now lay poor unhappy Margaret in a room reeking of stale alcohol, while across the landing in Agnes's always-neat bedroom, two defenceless little girls lay in uneasy sleep.

Again Isobel's thoughts reverted to their pathetic efforts to find a light when darkness had suddenly enveloped them. She thought of matches being struck with the little girls' hair hanging dangerously over the flames. She thought of a heavy oil lamp being carried in a child's hands, of spilt paraffin, of leaping flames, of nightdresses on fire, of terror and panic. How easily there could have been a tragedy involving an unconscious mother and her young children! Something would have to be done about Margaret.

She shivered with horror and chill, and thought longingly of the bright fire they had left next door. At that moment a car drew up, the lights of the headlamps sweeping the room, and Harold went to the front door to greet Alan.

'Hello! What's happened? Where are the lights?' Isobel heard Alan say.

She could not hear Harold's reply, just the sound of his voice explaining things.

'My God! I must go upstairs to Margaret,' Alan said, in a shocked voice. 'I'll be down in a second.'

Harold returned, and they sat in silence, listening to the

footsteps in the room above. Within minutes Alan returned, and dropped exhaustedly into a chair, his head in his hands.

'I think,' began Isobel tentatively, 'I should get you a drink, if you can tell me where things are.'

Alan gave a great shuddering sigh, and looked up. 'You are both so kind. I can't begin to thank you.' He stood up. 'I'll take a candle and go and light the Primus. We'll have some coffee.'

'And we'll help you,' said Harold. 'This damn power cut makes you realize how much we depend on switches, doesn't it?'

They all three went into the kitchen, and set about their preparations. It was only ten minutes later, when they had returned to the sitting-room with steaming mugs of instant coffee, that Alan asked for more details.

Harold told him, keeping nothing back. The sudden darkness, the frightened children, the matches, the attempt to light an oil lamp, all were related, while Alan listened with an expression of such horror on his face that Isobel's heart went out to him.

'If you hadn't been there,' he said at last, when the story ended, 'I could have come home to a burnt-out house, and no family! I blame myself. The meeting went on far longer than expected and—'

'It's a way meetings have,' interjected Harold.

'I'd seen that the girls were ready for bed. Margaret was not too bad, but said she would go to bed too as she was tired. As you see, we have no open fires here now, just the night storage heaters, for safety's sake. But of course I never envisaged a power cut, and all it entails.'

'You've got a problem,' said Harold.

'I know that well enough,' said Alan bitterly, 'and this evening has brought it to a head. Tomorrow I shall get Margaret to see John Lovell. We're desperately in need of help, and we must tackle this immediately.'

'Yes, you *must* do that,' said Isobel, 'for everyone's sake.'

Alan sat, turning the empty mug round and round in his hands. At last he broke the silence.

'I'm sure that you both guessed poor Margaret's trouble long ago. After her mishap in Lulling High Street, I don't think anyone had any doubts about things here.'

'I'm afraid people have known for some time,' said Harold, 'but, believe me, the general feeling is of great sympathy. I haven't heard a word of criticism. After all, this is just as much an illness as, say, pneumonia.'

'Not so simply dealt with though,' replied Alan, with a sigh. 'It all began when Margaret had what the medicos call post-natal blues. She never really got over them, and that's when the drinking began.'

'Did you get help then?'

'To some extent. The doctor we had then was very under-standing, and for a time she seemed better. Then I got this job, and she was alone all day, and it began again. It was the main reason for deciding to buy this place, where I felt I could keep an eye on her and she would not feel so lonely. But, as you see, it just hasn't worked out.'

'But why,' asked Isobel gently, 'didn't you get help from the doctor again?'

'Our old doctor has now retired, and frankly Margaret was so ashamed of herself she simply refused to see John Lovell.'

'Well, I'm sure he will be of enormous support to you,' said Harold rising. 'I suspect that he will be mightily relieved to be asked to help. And now we'll be getting back.'

At that moment, the lights came on again, bathing the room in unusually bright light after the mellow illumination from the oil lamp.

'Thank heaven!' cried Isobel. 'Now you will be all right.'

'Not quite "*all right*",' said Alan with a wry smile, 'but better able to cope.'

He put an arm around Harold's shoulders, and thanked him again. To Isobel's surprise he kissed her cheek. He was obviously deeply moved by all that had transpired.

'I shall never be able to thank you adequately,' he said, opening the door, 'but thank heaven for good friends at Thrush Green.'

Two days later Alan arrived at the Shoosmiths' house bearing a magnificent dark red azalea which he presented to Isobel.

'Come in,' cried Harold. 'How are things going?'

'Margaret's coming to see you herself later on. She's with John Lovell at the moment, at the surgery, picking up some tablets.'

'Can he help?'

'Indeed he can. He's been absolutely marvellous, and has fixed up an appointment at a clinic he knows well and thoroughly recommends. With any luck, Margaret will be able to go there within the week.'

'So she is really being co-operative?'

'Absolutely. I know it's early days, and she knows herself it's a long hard road to go, but she was so shattered about events the other night that she said at once we must get the doctor to help.'

'You must let us help too,' said Isobel. 'How long will she be away?'

'Difficult to say, but a few weeks probably.'

'And how will you manage?'

'I rang my mother, and she is coming down to stay for as long as she's needed.'

'She sounds a trump.'

'She certainly is! She's known about this from the start, and helped a lot when we were in the old house. She's lived alone since my father died, and she says she will shut up the house, and come as soon as I ring her.'

'Do the children know?'

'I've simply told them that their mother is ill and needs treatment, and have left it at that. Alison knows what it is, I'm quite sure, but she doesn't speak about it. Kate doesn't seem to have twigged, thank heaven. They both adore my mother, so they'll be happy with her.'

'Well,' said Harold, 'things certainly look more hopeful, and we are so relieved to know that Margaret is getting medical help.'

'It certainly takes some of the burden from my back,' confessed Alan. 'I fear poor Margaret is in for a tough time, but at the moment she is absolutely determined to be cured. She wants to come and thank you herself for all you did.'

'Oh please,' begged Isobel, 'don't let her worry about that. She may find it painful, and she's enough to think about as it is.'

Alan looked grave. 'She wants to do it,' he said soberly, 'and I think it will do her good to tell you about this trouble. Look upon it as one of the first steps towards rehabilitation. That's how I see it, and I think Margaret feels that way too.'

They watched him stride across the green to meet his wife at the surgery.

'I feel desperately sorry for that fellow,' said Harold, as they closed the front door.

'And I feel desperately sorry for the whole family,' replied Isobel. 'It makes you feel that you will never touch alcohol again, doesn't it?'

'Speak for yourself,' said Harold.

16. Christmas and After

December had hardly begun before all the frenzy of Christmas began to break out.

At the village school the windows were dotted with blobs of cotton wool representing snow flakes; paper chains hung across the class rooms and frequently collapsed upon the children beneath, much to their delight.

Every time a door opened a powdering of imitation frost, Christmas cards in the making, and pieces of embryo calendars fluttered to the floor, followed by excited children attempting to retrieve their property. The usual pre-Christmas chaos prevailed.

The ladies of Lulling and Thrush Green were busy preparing to raid local hedges and gardens for holly and ivy to decorate St John's and St Andrew's churches, as well as making wreaths for front doors and the graves of those departed and at rest in the churchyards.

The Lulling shops were filled with anxious customers wondering if elderly aunts would appreciate tea-cosies fashioned as sitting hens, or whether it would be better to play safe with yet another bed-jacket.

Husbands were busy buying enormous flasks of fabulously expensive scent, with names such as 'Transport' or 'Vive', destined to end either down the bath drain or as a raffle prize at a future bazaar.

In the electricity showroom, the annual display of a snow-white cooker decked with tinsel stood in front of the window, and the somewhat battered plaster turkey stood on top of it. The inhabitants of Lulling looked with affection upon this old friend. It really would not be Christmas without its reappear-ance, although it was beginning to look uncommonly dark – almost burnt – with advancing age.

At The Fuchsia Bush the results of Nelly's art filled the window: iced cakes clad in gold and scarlet frills, Dundee beauties topped with almonds, and pyramids of mince-pies brought in admiring customers.

In the few days before Christmas, activity rose to fever pitch, and when the ladies of Lulling, having their pre-Christmas shampoo and set, were offered a glass of Cyprus sherry as they sweltered under the driers, it was quite apparent that the festive season, in all its fury, was upon them.

Christmas Day was its usual mild and green self. The children's hopes of heavy snow, tobogganing, making snowmen, and sliding on the ice, were dashed yet again, but their spirits were greatly restored by the plethora of presents, the rich food and the indulgence of their parents.

Out in the country the necessities of work went on un-changed: Percy Hodge attended to his cattle, fed the hens, and moved his small flock of sheep to an adjacent field. As the daylight began to fade he went indoors, followed by the faithful Gyp, fed the dog, made up the stove, and went to his bedroom to change into his best blue serge suit.

Mr Jones, looking out from the window of The Two Pheas-ants, caught a glimpse of Percy's Land Rover as the farmer drove towards Lulling.

'And I wonder what he's got as a present for Doreen,' he commented to Mrs Jones, who was resplendent in a new scarlet cardigan, her husband's Christmas present.

'Might be an engagement ring,' surmised Mrs Jones.

'That wouldn't surprise anyone,' said Mr Jones. 'It's the *wedding* ring that's going to be Percy's problem.'

There was general but nicely-concealed relief when January arrived.

'Good to get back to normal,' said one to the other. 'We had a lovely meal of lamb chops today, and the turkey carcase is simmering for stock.'

'Won't be long before the children are back to school,' the mothers comforted each other.

Dotty Harmer, with her usual forthrightness, summed it up when talking to Betty Bell. 'I love Christmas, always will. But what a lot of fuss! I feel convalescent until mid-January.'

'That's only because you are getting on,' Betty told her, reaching up to unpin Christmas cards from the banisters. She stopped her endeavours to study one of them.

'This is pretty, but I can't make out the message.'

Dotty took it from her. 'It's Latin, dear. "Celebrating the birth of our Saviour", it says. Did you learn Latin at school?'

'What, down the Secondary? Not likely! Us girls was lucky to get a half-hour's Domestic Science as it was called then, and that was only about washing your hands before making pastry, which we all knew anyway from our mums.'

'You really didn't miss much,' observed Dotty. 'It's a tiresome language. How the Romans ever managed to converse I can't imagine. They had the verb at the end of the sentence, you see, Betty.'

'Can't say I do,' puffed Betty, retrieving a drawing pin from the floor.

'For instance, they might say: "Caesar, seeing that the day would be fine and clear, summoned his centurions and their assembled cohorts, with their weapons and a vast array of horses and" – well, what do you think, Betty? "Had breakfast"? "Changed his socks"? "Sang a ditty"? "Faced the enemy"? You see what I mean? *Such suspense* for the listener!'

'I must say,' agreed Betty, 'it seems a bit silly. Perhaps Domestic Science was more my mark after all.'

By this time Margaret Lester was away from the school house, and Alan's mother was in charge. She was a small brisk

Yorkshire woman, and the house was spick and span within twenty-four hours of her arrival.

Margaret had gone to the hospital recommended by John Lovell a few days before Christmas, and she remained there while the festivities were going on, at her own request. So far, Alan told the Shoosmiths, she was making a determined effort to overcome her problem, and the treatment she was getting was excellent.

Alan and his mother did everything possible to ensure that the little girls enjoyed their motherless Christmas. They were invited to several children's parties, including John and Ruth Lovell's and, as is the way with children, did not appear unduly cast down by their mother's absence.

Certainly, Mrs Lester senior was soon welcomed into the world of Thrush Green, and as she was an accomplished bridge player, she spent several happy afternoons at neighbouring houses once the school term started.

Isobel Shoosmith grew very fond of this near neighbour as the weeks passed. She admired her energy, her practical ability and her shrewd appraisal of people. Spotless washing billowed on the school house clothes-line on Monday morning and Thursday morning, and the old-fashioned baking day took place on Fridays when the school house was fragrant with the scent of freshly-baked pies, sausage rolls and jam tarts, as well as such traditional north country delicacies as parkin for the cake tin.

Alison and Kate looked relaxed and cheerful under this new regime. Undoubtedly they had sensed the tension in the household earlier, and were aware of their father's anxiety whenever their mother had immured herself in the bedroom.

They appeared to have forgotten the terrors of that black night which had taken them trembling to the Shoosmiths' door, and everyone tried to make the little girls' path as easy as possible while their mother fought her lone battle away from home.

*

One of the first people to call on Alan's mother was the rector, Charles Henstock. He had heard the rumours of Margaret Lester's trouble as had many other people in Lulling and Thrush Green, and had visited the house as soon as the Lesters had moved there. Now, months later when the news was out, he took to calling at the school house more often, and found a warm ally in Alan's mother, as well as Alan himself.

Alan and his mother seemed glad to discuss Margaret's condition, and the rector seemed remarkably well-acquainted with drink problems, much to Alan's surprise.

'Parsons aren't quite as unworldly as we may appear,' Charles told him, with a smile. 'We get our share of drunkards in country parishes, you know.'

'I haven't noticed a great many reeling out of The Two Pheasants,' commented Alan.

'Jones keeps a respectable house,' responded Charles. 'And so do most of the Lulling publicans. I'm afraid the trouble occurs when too much is taken in the home, as was case with your poor wife. At least she was never violent with it. I know at least four cases in my parishes where the men absolutely terrify their families.'

'What do you do?'

'Remonstrate, of course. Usually to little effect. Then I try to get them to Alcoholics Anonymous who do wonders. My good friend Anthony Bull told me about them. He gets far more problems in his town living, and is far better at coping with them than I am, I fear. But I do try to comfort the families.'

'And that,' Alan assured him, 'you do superbly.'

'I agree,' said his mother. 'Now I'm going to mash the tea, and you must try some of my Grasmere gingerbread.'

News of Margaret Lester's absence from Thrush Green had reached as far as Barton-on-Sea, for Isobel and Agnes had kept in touch by telephone ever since the two schoolteachers had retired.

Dorothy and Agnes discussed the situation as they sat by

the fire one grey January afternoon. Dorothy's attitude was inclined to be censorious. Agnes, less worldly, was more sympathetic.

'It must make a difference to the school,' commented Dorothy, lowering the crossword to her lap. 'I'm sure the parents must be unhappy at the thought of all that going on behind the scenes.'

'Isobel says that she has only heard sympathy for the poor man,' said Agnes. She was nursing Tim, fondling his ears which he particularly enjoyed.

'But it must mean that he is unable to give complete attention to the running of the school, Agnes. And as you well know, that is a *full-time* job.'

'He seems to be doing very well.'

'I'm not sure,' said Dorothy meditatively, 'that he shouldn't consider giving up the post in the circumstances. What an example to the children!'

Agnes ceased stroking Tim's ears. 'But surely, he's setting a very *good* example to the children! He's behaving bravely, carrying on his job, caring for his poor wife and children—'

At this moment Timmy, offended by the neglect of his ears, leapt to the floor, in a state of umbrage. Agnes bent to apologize.

'It doesn't alter the fact,' said Dorothy severely, 'that he has rather more to cope with than a normal headmaster should. I was never too sure that he was the right man to take over from me. It now seems my forebodings were justified.'

Agnes knew better than to argue when Dorothy was in this trenchant mood. Silently she attempted to lift the cat back to her lap. But Tim was not to be mollified, and stalked to the door.

'That cat,' remarked Dorothy, 'is getting too big for its boots. Teddy says he thinks we overfeed it.'

Sometimes, thought poor Agnes, I should like to scream when Teddy's name is mentioned, which seems to be every ten minutes.

'I don't think that Teddy knows very much about cats,' she ventured.

'He's never had one,' conceded Dorothy, 'but he really is most knowledgeable about *dogs*. In his time he has had two corgis, three cocker spaniels, and a Norfolk terrier. All devoted to him, of course.'

'Eileen told me that he doesn't seem to like her dog.'

'Well, naturally. You know how badly-behaved it is. Eileen is quite incapable of training anything. Far too indulgent. All young things need a little discipline now and again. Teddy says that he and his brothers were very strictly brought up, and you see how well it has stood him in good stead in his affliction. Never a complaint passes his lips. An example to us all.'

The maudlin expression on Dorothy's face as she pronounced this eulogy was almost more than Agnes could bear. She rose to let the ungrateful cat make his exit, then returned to her armchair.

'How's the crossword?' she said brightly, intent on diverting the subject from Teddy.

Dorothy rose to the bait. 'Well, I really can't see what DAIRY CATS have to do with architecture, but according to the clue, which may be erroneous of course, there is some connection.'

'CARYATIDS,' pronounced Agnes, and took up her knitting.

January grew steadily colder as the month progressed. The newspapers displayed chilling photographs of Scottish shepherds on skis searching for their flocks, and trains marooned in snowy wastes awaiting help from helicopters.

Further south, rescuers and rescued were shown taking shelter in the Izaak Walton Hotel at Dovedale in Derbyshire, and intrepid skaters at Cambridge were depicted attempting to reach Ely on the ice.

Even as far south as Barton-on-Sea the snow fell, and freezing fog and icy roads kept Agnes and Dorothy indoors for several days.

Dorothy began to get restive one Friday afternoon. 'I really think I should make the effort to call on Teddy. He so enjoys my reading to him, and I'm sure he must find this weather as depressing as we do.'

But within five minutes, while she was still resisting Agnes's attempts to dissuade her, the telephone rang and Eileen was in conversation.

'I really don't think you should venture out, Dorothy,' Agnes heard her say. 'It's not just that the roads are so slippery, but Teddy has an appalling cold, and I've forbidden him to move from the fire.'

'In that case,' said Dorothy who had become rather pink in the face, much to Agnes's alarm, 'I feel I should come and see him.'

'He says he would rather you didn't.'

'Oh, really?'

'He's so anxious that you might pick up the infection. You see you haven't had any flu jabs. I'm so glad I did, it gives me much more confidence in a case like this. No *please*, Dorothy, put off your visit until I let you know how my patient is.'

'Very well,' said Dorothy, in a tone as icy as the outside world. 'Give him our love, and I hope he will soon be better.'

She put down the receiver with unnecessary force, and turned to Agnes. 'I expect you heard all that – Eileen's voice is exceptionally loud. Obviously, I am not wanted there at the moment.'

'Perhaps it's as well,' said Agnes.

'What I *cannot abide*,' said Dorothy ferociously, 'is the perfectly dreadful proprietorial attitude that Eileen takes over Teddy! Anyone would think she *owns* the man! He will have to put her in her place one day. Her behaviour is outrageous!'

Agnes remained silent.

The cold spell was particularly severe in the Cotswolds: the stone houses crouched like sheep in the snow drifts, and many of the dry stone walls had vanished completely beneath the blanket of snow. The birds, fluffed out with the cold, sat motionless in the black hedges or lined the rafters in barns and out-houses, seeking what shelter they could from the bitter weather. The smallest birds, such as the wrens and tits, sought comfort in garden nesting-boxes, and huddled together for warmth.

Flocks of rooks swept the sky, searching the inhospitable fields beneath them for food and cawing mournfully. The farmers had rounded up their cattle and brought them down to fields and yards nearer the farm. Water was a problem: field pumps had frozen, water pipes burst and everyday living was a constant battle in these cruel surroundings.

People struggled on foot to the shops for such essentials as meat and bread, and one enterprising baker drew a sledge through the streets of Lulling to deliver his loaves.

Cars had been abandoned on many of the more exposed hills, and at one stage it was only possible to get through the lanes around Thrush Green in high vehicles such as Land Rovers.

The sky remained grey and fresh snow fell frequently,

smoothing over the black ribbons made by tyres and the inky footsteps of each day's activity. Old people and young children were kept indoors, all longing for a return of sun and freedom.

At the village school the numbers were almost halved, for children living at any distance could not make the journey, and coughs and colds kept others in their beds. Simply keeping warm was as much as most people could undertake.

It was in this inhospitable period that Margaret Lester was driven home in an ambulance, the only safe vehicle to manage the main roads from the clinic to her house. She emerged, looking like a ghost, pale and dark-eyed, to be enveloped by her husband's arms and the happy greetings of her family.

The door closed behind her. The ambulance started on its return journey, and Margaret was left to continue on the long hard road to recovery.

17. CHANGES FOR THE BETTER

The thaw came at the beginning of February. It brought with it fog, filthy roads and influenza. The last remnants of snow lay along the roadside in dwindling heaps, discoloured by dirt thrown up by the passing traffic.

Under the hedges, beneath the dripping leaves, more snow lingered, fretted with the claw marks of innumerable foraging small birds. Mist floated in the valleys with no wind to disturb it, and the River Pleshey moved sluggishly between the bleached dead grass of its banks.

It was a dispiriting time, and the only comfort was that life could begin again, in a torpid manner, as the icy roads cleared and people began to move about their daily business.

It was a great pleasure to Nelly Piggott when the Bingo sessions began again. The hall had been shut through the worst of the weather, for few people left their firesides after dark, and the practical difficulties of keeping the large hall heated and cleaned proved impossible.

Mrs Jenner called for Nelly and the two women made their way down the hill to their evening's amusement. Gladys Lilly did not appear.

'She may well be down with this flu,' surmised Mrs Jenner. 'I know Doreen's been off work this week with it.'

Nelly, who had been consumed with curiosity for months about the possible romance between Mrs Jenner's brother Percy and the young girl, felt that she could do a little circumspect investigation.

'A nice girl. Your Jane thinks the world of her. Your brother was very good to her too, when she was took bad that day. Does he still keep in touch?'

Mrs Jenner, who was no fool, realized that Nelly was avid for information. Normally she would have been somewhat terse in reply for she disliked gossip and, as a nurse, had been trained to be discreet. But she was fond of Nelly, and would not wish to snub her.

'To tell the truth, I don't take much interest in Percy's affairs. He's never been the same since his Gertie died, and made a fool of himself over a lot of silly young things, as everyone knows.'

'It's understandable,' said Nelly tolerantly, 'men being what they are. Poor tools really, compared with us.'

'Exactly!' agreed Mrs Jenner. 'But I know no more than you do, Nelly, about Percy and Doreen. I did have a quiet word with Jane, but she says the girl hardly ever says very much, and in any case she'd be extra careful when speaking to Jane, her being Percy's niece, you see.'

'Well, who knows?' said Nelly cheerfully. 'It might turn out very nicely. Gladys has brought her up proper, good at cleaning and cooking, and that little Bobby is as nice a child as you could meet in a month of Sundays. Percy could do a lot worse, I reckon.'

By this time they had reached the hall. It was noisier than usual, as people greeted each other after their enforced absence and compared notes on burst pipes, leaking roofs, coughs, colds and all the other ills of a hard winter.

'Good to have a bit of company,' cried Nelly to her friend, as they settled down to a convivial evening. To be sure, she had not learned anything about the Percy–Doreen affair from Mrs Jenner, but no doubt time would tell.

At Thrush Green, Margaret Lester was slowly coming to terms with life. The spring term was now in its stride, and with the worst of the weather over, attendances became more normal.

Alan Lester watched his wife with acute anxiety. She was still as adamant as she was on her return that no alcohol should be allowed into the house. Some medical men, she told Alan, were of the opinion that a tiny amount now and again could do no harm to those trying to break the habit, but Margaret, in her zealous mood, would have none of it, and Alan thought that she was right.

He thought that it was right too that she talked freely about the dangers to their children. She could not forgive herself for what might have happened on the night of the power cut, and was filled with such horror and remorse that Alan sometimes wondered if this bitter self-torture might be holding back her full recovery.

His tough old mother was more realistic. 'She's working things out in her own way, and in her own time,' she told him when Margaret was out of the room. 'It is one way of keeping her off the bottle, which is the main thing, and she is getting it out of her system with this suffering. I know it's distressing for you to watch, when you've been laid open to all these wishy-washy ideas that things should be easy for everybody, but I was brought up to fight the good fight, and to recognize the devil as well as the angels. And it's fighting that's going to be poor Margaret's salvation.'

Old Mrs Lester certainly was a tower of strength to the family during these first weeks of Margaret's return. It was planned that the whole family would go to Yorkshire at half-term, to take Alan's mother back and to give them all a change of scene.

Meanwhile, Isobel and Harold, in company with other friends nearby, gave as much attention as they could to the family. The little girls were invited out frequently. The Shoosmiths took Margaret out with them on their afternoon strolls. Winnie Bailey and Ella Bembridge had pleasant hen-parties which included both Mrs Lesters. There was no doubt about it; what with her own determination, fears of what-might-have-been, and the support of family and friends, it was apparent that Margaret had every hope of winning her battle.

When the first pale rays of spring sunshine emerged, life started to look more hopeful. The snowdrops, aconites and crocuses began to bring colour to the gardens, and along the road to Nidden yellow tassels of catkins waved from the hazel bushes.

Seed catalogues were studied, and orders sent for stocking the kitchen and flower gardens. Travel brochures, adorned with sun-bronzed men and maidens with enviable teeth, hair and figures, were browsed over in the homes at Thrush Green and Lulling. Should it be Greece this year? Or Spain perhaps, or even Turkey? What about taking some savings out of the Lulling Building Society and having a real splash somewhere in the Bahamas?

Most of these day-dreams were shattered by programmes on the television of fractious infants, exhausted mothers and bad-tempered fathers, jammed together in airport lounges for hours on end, awaiting flights which failed to materialize.

The brochures were thrown away. What was wrong with dear old Ilfracombe anyway?

Hardy souls such as Ella Bembridge took their first long walks of the year, striding along enjoying the exercise and the heady smell of spring in the air.

Those who were just over bouts of the widespread influenza tottered out for a few turns in the lanes, well-muffled up against any chill in the air, and felt greatly relieved to get back to the comfort of their armchairs after ten minutes or so.

Among this last category came Doreen Lilly and Gladys, each holding the hand of young Bobby. They came slowly up the hill and stopped to speak to Albert Piggott who was picking up litter by the church gate and depositing it in his bucket. Most of it came from careless customers at The Two Pheasants, for although Mr Jones provided a conspicuous litter-bin, there were always a few untidy consumers who preferred to fling their litter to the ground.

When the wind was from the west, a certain amount ended up by the churchyard, much to Albert's fury.

He was glad, as always, to stop work.

'Say "Good morning" to Mr Piggott,' prompted Gladys.

'I've 'ad the flu,' said Bobby with pride.

'Oh-ah!' said Albert.

'*And* my mummy. She 'ad the flu.'

'Oh-ah!' said Albert again, looking at Doreen. She smiled but said nothing.

'But my Granny never,' continued the child.

'I was the lucky one,' said Gladys briskly. 'We thought a little fresh air would do us good.'

'We're goin' to Uncle Percy's to see the lambs,' volunteered Bobby.

Albert became more alert. 'Better watch they don't bite you,' he said.

The child looked at his mother with alarm, but she remained silent.

It was Gladys who answered. 'Mr Piggott's making a joke,' she explained. 'Lambs don't bite. Now, come along or we'll be late.'

They nodded farewell and continued their journey towards the farm.

Albert crossed the road to The Two Pheasants.

'That girl don't say much, do she?' he said to Mr Jones. 'Cat had her tongue, I shouldn't wonder.'

'I like a quiet woman myself,' said Mr Jones diplomatically. 'Maybe she's shy.'

'Not shy enough, to my way of thinking,' commented Albert censoriously. 'Anyway, old Perce is "*Uncle* Percy" now. I suppose he'll be "*Daddy* Percy" before long.'

'I shouldn't count on it,' advised the landlord. 'Not with Percy's record.'

It was on one of these early spring mornings that an extraordinary event took place in the house of the three Misses Lovelock.

It was the custom each morning for Violet to make a pot of Earl Grey tea in her bedroom, and to take a cup to each of her sisters.

Years before, of course, there had been a resident maid who would mount the stairs with a jingling tray and distribute the tea. She would also pull back the curtains, and comment on the weather in Lulling High Street.

Those days had disappeared long ago, and Violet, with great initiative, had bought herself a tea-making machine which she installed in her bedroom and learnt to manipulate with commendable speed.

She quite enjoyed the early morning ritual, and Ada and Bertha were grateful for her service. Each sister kept a tin of biscuits in her room. Violet favoured Gingernuts, Ada Rich Tea, and Bertha stuck to Digestive. Sometimes the cup of tea, with a dip into the biscuit tin, was all that was required by way of breakfast as the ladies grew older and frailer.

On this particular morning, Violet carried in Bertha's cup and found her sister sitting bolt upright and looking rather flushed. She nodded her thanks as Violet deposited the steaming cup on the bedside table, and patted the bed, inviting her sister to sit.

'What is it, dear?' asked Violet.

'Spring-cleaning,' said Bertha.

'It's rather early to be thinking of that,' countered Violet.

'We'll start in here,' announced Bertha. 'This room has become most frightfully cluttered. Why have you brought up so much rubbish from downstairs?'

'You brought it up yourself, Bertha.'

'Nonsense! Why should I want all the silver and some of the furniture too! It *hampers* me. It must be cleared away.'

By now, Bertha was becoming much agitated, and Violet decided to humour her.

'Well, we must make some plans, dear. Meanwhile, drink your tea while it's hot, and I'll come in again when I'm dressed.'

By that time, Violet surmised, her sister would have forgotten all about it, and the day would proceed in its usual way.

But she was wrong.

When, some half an hour later, she opened Bertha's door, it was to discover a scene of complete chaos. Wardrobe doors stood open. Every drawer gaped, and the unmade bed was piled with an assorted jumble of silverware, porcelain, photoframes and bric-à-brac of every variety.

'Bertha!' cried Violet aghast. 'What on *earth* are you doing? I've never seen such a mess!'

'Must make a start,' puffed Bertha, now scarlet in the face. She threw a silver tankard, presented years before to their father, on to the bed, dislodging a heap of smaller articles which cascaded to the floor.

Violet took charge. She forcibly pushed Bertha into a wicker chair, and stood over her.

'You will give yourself a stroke, rushing about like this, and then where shall we be? Just leave everything alone, get dressed, and Ada and I will help you to put everything away later this morning.'

Bertha seemed to see reason and shrugged her shoulders. 'Very well,' she replied, with immense dignity. 'We'll spring-clean later on.'

Without speaking, Violet collected Bertha's underwear from beneath a pile of assorted objects, and put the articles by her.

'I'll be back,' she said at last, and went to apprise Ada of this latest domestic upheaval.

Later she returned, meeting Bertha on the stairs. Her sister was carrying a large silver tray piled precariously with small objects.

Violet took it from her and preceded her to the drawing-room, where she deposited the tray on a sofa.

'Now sit down, Bertha, and we may as well sort out this pile now.'

'Such an odd collection,' replied Bertha, who seemed quite calm. 'Do you know, I'm sure we have a silver coaster that is Charles Henstock's. And a pair of sugar tongs that I distinctly remember seeing at Ella's. Why on earth did they give them to us?'

Violet, who knew very well the acquisitive nature of her sister and indeed had been equally guilty on occasions, decided to ignore the question.

The two articles mentioned were on the tray, and she quietly put them aside. She also returned a pair of silver vases, three photoframes and a pair of candlesticks to the mantelpiece.

'It looks better at once,' said Bertha approvingly. 'It was a very silly idea of yours to lumber up to my bedroom with all this stuff. And some of it, you see, not even belonging to us. It looks so dishonest.'

'It does. Shall we go upstairs and fetch some more?'

After an hour or two of sorting out, all three ladies were exhausted and decided to have lunch, which could only be biscuits and cheese with tinned pears to follow, then their usual short rest, before continuing with their labours.

What was really peculiar, thought Violet, as she lay on her bed after lunch resting her aching bones, was the way in which Bertha had put aside all those pretty pieces which had been begged, permanently borrowed, or simply purloined over the years, and those which were legitimate Lovelock property. Could there be some deep-seated guilt which had been suppressed all these years? Was this frenzy of activity a form of remorse? Or was Bertha simply suffering from another mental breakdown, and would she be her usual inconsequent and kleptomaniac self by morning?

It seemed best, thought Violet, to go along with this spring-cleaning urge. At least, it restored Bertha's hoard to their rightful places in the house, and a lot of prized objects to their rightful owners. It was not going to be simple, thought Violet uneasily, explaining the return of such valuables as Ella's tongs and Charles's coaster, but it would just have to be done. Bertha's eccentricity would be a good excuse.

Wearily, she clambered from her resting place and went into Bertha's still cluttered bedroom.

The clearing of the room, and its return to comparative normality, took the three sisters the best part of a week to complete.

Bertha still maintained her air of perplexity about the amount of things collected in her room, and it was apparent to Violet that nothing much could be done about it. Was Bertha genuinely confused, or was she deliberately blaming others for her own behaviour? Violet guessed rightly that no one would ever know.

The only practical thing to be done was to return other people's property, and this unwelcome duty she undertook.

It was humbling to find how kindly friends responded to her apologies. In truth, the Misses Lovelocks' ways were such common knowledge in Lulling and its surroundings, that it was quite a pleasant surprise to see their property again.

'I must admit I had wondered where that coaster had hidden itself,' said Charles. 'It was one of a pair that Anthony Bull gave us one Christmas, with two bottles of exquisite Claret. I am delighted to know it is safe.'

Ella was equally understanding about her purloined Victorian sugar tongs. The Shoosmiths welcomed back a bonbon dish, and also collected a cigarette box which had been Miss Watson's. The Youngs were glad to see an Edwardian dolls' tea-set again, and John Lovell was delighted to receive a silver ash tray which he had never missed.

All in all, Violet had an easier time than she had envisaged as she returned these long-held objects, and was grateful that no recriminations were forthcoming. It was, she felt, really more than she deserved, and said much for the generous spirit of their old friends.

As the days lengthened people's spirits rose. It was good to get out and about again in the light, and to go and come back from an afternoon tea-party without having to remember a torch.

The sun appeared almost every day, and gardeners were already busy. So were the birds, flying with grass and feathers trailing from their beaks, as they set about nest-building. Prudent housewives were already planning dates for the chimney sweep, the window-cleaner and painters and decorators.

The January sales were far behind, and Lulling shops already displayed summer hats and frocks, and even swimsuits for those who had been bold enough to book a holiday abroad.

It was a heady time, and at Barton-on-Sea Dorothy broached the subject of a few days away.

'We both need a change,' she declared. 'You've looked quite peaky ever since that last cold, and my hip is definitely getting arthritic. Somewhere fairly flat, I think, don't you? What about East Anglia? I had a wonderful cycling holiday there as a girl.

Hardly ever needed to get off, you know, the slopes were so gentle.'

'There are some splendid churches,' said Agnes. 'We could go on day-trips by bus perhaps, if we found somewhere central.'

'We should have the car for that,' said Dorothy. 'I'm not so arthritic that I can't drive.'

Agnes fetched the engagement calendar, and the two ladies studied it.

'Very little on in the next few weeks,' commented Dorothy. 'I can swap church flower duties with someone, and we can cancel that Conservative lunch.'

'Good! I was already wondering what to wear. My best suit needs cleaning.'

'There's just Teddy, of course,' mused Dorothy, tapping the calendar with her pencil. 'Still, I should think Eileen could read the newspaper to him quite as well as I do.'

'Not *as well*,' said Agnes, 'but *adequately*, I expect, for such a short time.'

At the end of the month the schools of Lulling and Thrush Green broke up for half-term.

The weather continued to be mild, and the Lesters were ready packed to get off early on the Saturday morning. Alan's mother had said her farewells, and promised to return to the village in the summer.

'Or earlier if I'm needed,' she confided to Isobel, 'but I pray it won't be necessary. So far, so good. I can't tell you how I admire Margaret over this affair. She's doing splendidly.'

'She had your help,' pointed out Isobel, 'and the support of the family.'

'That was very little really. She knew it was a case of self-help, and she's stuck to it.'

Later, Alan came round to leave the key and the Yorkshire telephone number. 'I think I've switched off everything possible,' he told Harold, 'but no doubt I shall remember something vital when we're halfway up the Ml.'

'Then ring us,' smiled Harold. 'Go and enjoy yourselves. See you next week.'

Ten minutes later they saw the Lesters drive away, a bevy of hands fluttering their goodbyes.

18. THE BIRTHDAY PARTY

Miss Bertha Lovelock had been born on February the twenty-eighth in a Leap Year. Her mother had often told her how narrowly she had missed being born on the last day of February in a Leap Year, and the horror of having only one true birthday every four years.

This particular year was Bertha's eightieth birthday, and Violet intended that the occasion should be marked by a party. It would only be a *small* one, all the sisters agreed, just for a few old friends, and after considerable thought and discussion it was decided to have a modest tea party at the house.

Consequently, Violet went next door one morning to The Fuchsia Bush to order a birthday cake, two dozen scones and other small cakes for the celebration.

Mrs Peters attended to her, and was extremely helpful. She was fond of her eccentric neighbours and Bertha's pilfering was now, everyone hoped, a thing of the past.

'Not too rich a mixture,' said Violet. 'We shall all be elderly, and not able to digest anything too heavy.'

'None of our produce is *heavy*,' protested Mrs Peters, stung by this criticism of her wares, 'but I do understand. Would you prefer a madeira cake, suitably iced, of course?'

Violet pondered awhile. 'No. I think a fruit mixture, but without brandy perhaps. I will leave the recipe to you and Mrs Piggott. I feel sure it will be delicious.'

'I wonder,' said Mrs Peters diffidently, 'If you would like one of my girls to come in and wait on you? It is early closing in the town on that day and we are never busy then. I could spare Rosa or Gloria for two or three hours if it would help.'

'That is most kind,' said Violet sincerely. 'We shall be about ten or twelve altogether, and should be glad to have one of the girls.'

So it was left, and Mrs Peters also made a note to order a small bouquet to be taken in as a tribute from all at The Fuchsia Bush. It was a great relief to have things on an even keel again. Keeping the boat upright, she thought, as she bustled about her duties, was a tricky job anywhere. Next door to the dear old Lovelocks, it was doubly so.

The great day was blessedly mild and sunny.

Violet took a suitably celebratory breakfast, the brownest boiled egg, boiled lightly, to her sister, and she and Ada sat sipping their tea as Bertha unwrapped their presents.

Ada had given her a silk scarf which all three recognized as a Christmas present to Ada from a distant cousin. Naturally nothing was said about this, but the three frugal sisters secretly approved.

Violet's gift was a box of Floris soap, and this she had actually bought at the local chemist's. It was much appreciated.

'Now you must take things gently today,' said Violet. 'Ada and I are going to cut a few sandwiches after we've had our afternoon rest, and then we shall dress in readiness for our friends.'

'Are they all coming?'

'Well, no, dear. I think I told you yesterday that the Bulls are abroad, and Ella is staying with a school-friend in Scotland.'

'So who are we expecting?'

'The Henstocks, the Venables, and Winnie Bailey. There's just a chance that Dotty Harmer will come, but she was expecting some wire netting to be delivered, and particularly wanted to see the man as the last lot started disintegrating far too soon, according to Dotty.'

'Oh dear! I wonder how long she had had it?'

'Since Coronation Year, I gather, but Dotty thinks it should have gone on for another ten years or so.'

'Well, we must just hope that we will see her,' said Bertha, putting aside the breakfast tray. 'Anyway, it is going to be a lovely day for me. I suppose *eighty* really is a great age?'

Her sisters assured her that it was indeed an achievement.

It had been decided, when plans for the party had been drawn up, that only the Lovelocks' contemporaries would be invited. Anthony Bull and his wife were the exceptions.

Justin Venables – known locally as 'Young Mr Venables' to distinguish him from his father, now long-dead, and his wife, had grown up with the Lovelocks. They had attended the same dancing classes in Lulling, fox-trotting to 'Tea For Two' and 'She's My Lovely', in the far-off twenties and thirties.

They had shared picnics in ancient open cars, made up parties for the local Hunt Ball, and attended private dances at some of the large houses in the surrounding countryside. They had organized innumerable projects for charity, and had seen Lulling change from a sleepy little Cotswold market town to a busy community in which strangers thronged the streets, and far too much traffic struggled to pass through.

It was an altered world, but their memories of the past held them together with ties which endured.

Dimity and Ella, though a little younger, had also played a close part in the sisters' lives, and Dotty Harmer, who was almost exactly the same age as Bertha, was another friend who had shared in the early Lulling activities. The fact that her father had been a much respected (perhaps 'feared' would be more truthful) headmaster of the local grammar school for many years, strengthened Dotty's position as a pillar of society in the town.

Charles Henstock had appeared in Lulling some time after the war, and although he knew little of the Lovelocks and Venables in their youth, was welcomed as a man of the cloth and, later, as Dimity's husband.

It was the absence of Anthony Bull which caused Bertha the greatest regret. Her admiration for this handsome priest was absolute, and his was the first name she had put on her list.

However, it had to be faced. Anthony and his wife had promised to go to Italy with another couple, and the hotel and flight had been booked for months. Bertha had to be content with a congratulatory cable, and an arrangement of spring flowers from Interflora from the absent Bulls.

By half-past three the ladies were in a flutter of anticipation: Bertha was resplendent in navy silk, Ada in pearl-grey, and Violet, as the youngest, quite dashing in coral-pink.

True to her word, Mrs Peters had sent in Rosa complete with a sheaf of daffodils and irises, and a card saying:

'*From all at The Fuchsia Bush*
Congratulations and Best Wishes'

Bertha was much touched. Violet, watching her, wondered if any trace of guilt added to her sister's high colour, but dismissed the thought as unworthy of this occasion.

Justin and his wife arrived first, bearing a large box of Bendick's mints which they knew Bertha loved. The Henstocks came a few minutes later with a bottle of Bertha's favourite eau-de-cologne, and Winnie arrived with a box of exquisite linen and lace handkerchiefs.

The birthday cake stood on a side-table, and everyone agreed that The Fuchsia Bush had excelled itself. Ada and Violet's sandwiches were sampled, the buttered scones were passed round by Rosa, who was seemingly awed by her surroundings and the venerability of the guests, and all went swimmingly.

The conversation, rather naturally, was of the past.

'And Justin was a demon on the tennis court,' Bertha told Charles. 'A terrible smashing service he had, I remember.'

'So did Winnie,' Violet reminded her. 'She was one of the first Lulling ladies to serve over-arm. We were all greatly impressed.'

'And do you remember your first car, Justin?'

'Only too well. It let me down on Porlock hill which wasn't too awful, but when it practically exploded in Lulling High Street, my father said it was a disgrace to the firm and that clients would be taking their affairs elsewhere.'

Back and forth the reminiscences flowed as Rosa cleared the tea things away. The cake was to be cut a little later, and taken with a glass of champagne. This was Violet's idea, and she had kept the champagne a secret, knowing full well that she would have been chided for gross extravagance if she had told Bertha earlier.

The sun was still shining, and the company took a turn about the garden to admire the crocuses and the budding daffodils. Secretly, Justin grieved over the neglected state it was in. In their young days, a full-time gardener had been employed, and the kitchen garden had produced all that was needed to supply the Lovelock family and staff. Now a young man came once a fortnight to cut the shabby lawns and the weeds in the borders were strangling the perennial pinks and peonies and roses which had once been the pride of the family.

The outside paintwork, he noticed, was also neglected and flaking. Some of the Cotswold roof tiles had slipped, and one or two were missing. It was sad to see such a noble property in disrepair, but he knew that the Lovelocks' parsimony would never let them spend even the smallest amount on repairs, and this project would certainly need several thousands to put it back into its former state.

Well, he thought, as they followed their aged hostesses indoors, maybe it will last the old ladies' time, and then let's hope someone with money, and love, will take it over. On their return to the house, they were met by an untidy figure, who was being divested of her coat by Rosa.

Dotty Harmer had arrived.

'Well, what a lovely surprise!' cried Bertha. They pressed their wrinkled cheeks together. 'We had quite given you up. Tea, Dotty?'

'No, thanks. I've just had a cup with the wire-netting fellow.'

'Then you are in time for a slice of my cake. Do sit down.'

There were general greetings as Dotty handed a small parcel to Bertha who began to unwrap a square jeweller's box with some trepidation. One could never be quite sure of Dotty's offerings; it might well be some rare beetle found in her garden, or a fossil from her father's collection.

Fortunately, the little box contained a brooch, a circle of seed pearls surrounding the letter B in gold.

'But, Dotty,' protested Bertha, suitably touched, 'this is much too valuable to give away. Am I right in thinking it was your mother's?'

'Quite right, Bertha. She was "Beatrix", you know, and I thought it was only right that you should have it.'

'Then thank you *very* much. I shall treasure it.'

She began to pin it on the lapel of the navy silk frock, amidst general admiration.

Rosa now opened the champagne with a suitably celebratory pop and the glasses were filled while Bertha began to cut the cake amid polite cheers. When they were settled, Charles stood up, raised his glass and asked everyone to drink to the health of their good friend Bertha.

'Well,' said that lady when this had been done, 'I suppose I ought to say something.'

'Indeed you should,' said Justin.

'What shall I say? Just how delightful it is to have so many old friends here today. I only wish dear Anthony could have been here, too.'

'We all wish that,' said Charles.

'Why *Italy*?' enquired Dotty waving her glass, and splashing Dimity's best dress. 'The food is so indigestible, and the meat so scarce, and really the way they treat their animals is quite appalling. I read only the other day—'

'Dotty, dear!' said Dimity reprovingly, and Dotty subsided.

'I was going to say,' said Bertha, with some hauteur, 'that I particularly wanted Anthony here today as I have a little project of mine to tell you about.'

'About animals?' asked Dotty animatedly.

Charles Henstock began to look alarmed. What on earth was Bertha about to disclose?

'I think we ought to have a proper memorial in the church to celebrate Anthony's ministry here,' announced Bertha.

'His name has been added to the list of vicars on the chancel wall,' interposed Charles gently.

'That's as maybe,' rapped Bertha, who was now trembling with excitement. Two red spots had appeared on her cheeks, and her eyes flashed. Could the champagne have something to do with it, wondered Rosa?

'I intend to leave all my money to St John's, as some of you may know, with directions about the sort of thing I have in mind as a public tribute to dear Anthony.'

'But, Bertha . . .' protested Justin. He was ignored.

'Something worthy of the man. No piffling little plaque or a pedestal for flowers. I had in mind something in the way of a large stained-glass window, or perhaps a new Organ. The present one wheezes dreadfully at times. Most irreligious.'

'Anthony wouldn't want that,' said Dotty. 'He hated any sort of ostentation. You think again, Bertha dear. Give a nice dollop to some charity he suggests. He was always very generous to the RSPB, I recall.'

This unusually sensible suggestion of Dotty's was met with a murmur of approval from the company. Most of those present were acutely dismayed by Bertha's proposals; Justin, as her solicitor, was frankly appalled, and her two sisters were becoming increasingly distressed as Bertha's agitation grew.

'I shall do exactly as I like,' shouted Bertha, 'with my own money! No one, not even my own sisters, has really appreciated all that Anthony Bull did for Lulling. I am absolutely adamant that he should be remembered!' She pointed a shaking finger at Justin. 'I shall be in your office tomorrow to alter my will, Justin. If it's the last thing I do, I shall honour dear Anthony with some fitting memorial in the church he served so well.'

She pulled a handkerchief from her pocket, and began to dab at the tears which now coursed down her papery old cheeks.

'So *nobly*,' she added, sniffing. 'With such *distinction*! With such *inspiration*!'

'There, there!' said Dimity, putting an arm round Bertha's shaking shoulders. 'You are over-tired. It has been a wonderful party, but I feel we should go now.'

Bertha looked about her in a bewildered manner. 'Please do. I can't think why you are all here anyway. Some idea of Violet's, I suppose.'

'Bertha, *please*!' protested Violet and Ada in unison.

'Now what have I said?' demanded Bertha fiercely. 'All I've done is to tell you what I propose to do. Charles knows all about it anyway. I can't understand why you are all so silly. And why have we got this sticky cake for tea? You know I much prefer madeira or seed, Violet. So extravagant!'

By this time, the Venables and Henstocks had risen, and were making their farewells. Ada and Violet, almost in tears themselves, saw them to the door.

'She's simply over-excited,' said Charles to the two agitated sisters. 'Don't worry about it. We've thoroughly enjoyed the party and if I were you I should see that she goes upstairs to rest.'

'You are so understanding,' quavered Ada. 'Do you think she really will buy a stained-glass window, or a new organ?'

'No, I don't,' said Charles. 'Don't think any more about it.' The last thing the departing guests heard as they descended the steps to Lulling High Street was Dotty's voice advising Bertha.

'You'll have the devil of a job getting anything done in the church, Bertha. Consistory courts, ecclesiastical faculties and I don't know what. You spend it on the animals. I can give you the address—'

The closing of the front door terminated Dotty's harangue.

The four old friends were in a state of shock as they walked together to their homes.

The two women were ahead, and discussing anxiously not only Bertha's extraordinary proposal, but also the possibility of a mental breakdown.

Justin and Charles were having their own less feverish conversation.

'An unhappy end to a jolly party,' said Charles.

'As you say,' agreed Justin.

'Is it possible for her to change her will?'

'It's possible,' said Justin, 'but highly unlikely. As you can see, she is quite unstable.'

'I feel so sorry for the other two.'

They kept step with each other, their breath now showing in the chill of evening.

'Did you really know anything about this crazy idea?' asked Justin at length.

'She mentioned it some weeks ago,' said Charles uneasily, 'but I thought it was just a passing whim.'

'I think it is. I don't propose to do anything about it, and I am quite sure she will not turn up at my office. Ada and Violet will see to that, though it's my belief Bertha will have forgotten all about the business by morning. In any case, I can handle all this.'

'Thank heaven for that,' sighed Charles. 'I only hope that Anthony doesn't come to hear of it. The very idea would horrify him. I tremble to think how he might react.'

By now they had reached the Venables' gate and caught up with their ladies.

'You need never tremble on Anthony Bull's behalf,' laughed Justin. 'He can cope with any situation in the world, which is why Bertha admires him so much.'

And on this cheering note, they parted.

19. SEVERAL SHOCKS

The Lesters returned from Yorkshire looking all the better for their break, but within a week of taking up his teaching duties Alan Lester had been smitten with influenza. Dr Lovell was called to the school house three days later when it was obvious that something more severe than the usual influenza was involved.

'He won't eat or drink,' Margaret told him agitatedly.

John Lovell surveyed his prostrate patient and felt his stomach. 'It's gastro-enteritis as well as the common bug that's been plaguing us all.'

He left two pills, a prescription, and a stern order 'to keep drinking'. 'And see that he does,' he told Margaret as they went downstairs. 'Don't worry, he's going to be all right in a day or two. I'll be in again tomorrow.'

It was certainly a vicious viral attack, and Alan Lester was too weak at the end of five days to return to work. A supply-teacher, well-known in the district, came to hold the fort until he was fit to resume his duties.

Margaret nursed him diligently, administering pills at the appointed times, making up jugs of lemon barley water, washing and ironing innumerable pairs of pyjamas, and changing the bed linen.

'I'm afraid she will exhaust herself,' Isobel said to John Lovell when she enquired about his patient. 'She's not a hundred per cent fit herself.'

John Lovell smiled. 'It may be tough luck on Alan,' he said, 'but it's the best possible luck for Margaret at the moment.

Concentrating on someone else's trouble is a sure way of forgetting your own.'

In her weekly telephone call to Barton-on-Sea, Isobel told the ladies about the stricken headmaster and Mrs Hill who had come to take his place.

Dorothy Watson was far from pleased when she heard this, and said so to Agnes. 'Well, I only hope she doesn't have too much to do with teaching reading to the younger children. You know how pig-headed she was about the "Look-and-Say" method. That, and that alone! The arguments I had with that woman about the need for using *all* methods! I told her, time and time again, that the children knew the red card said "Stand up" and the blue one said "Go to the door", and the one with the corner off said "Hands on heads", so that the children didn't really *read* them at all. I proved it to her one day, as you may remember.'

'Very well indeed,' said Agnes hoping to stem the flood of outraged memories, but in vain.

'I put the same sentences on the blackboard,' Dorothy continued remorselessly, 'and could those children read them?'

'No, they couldn't,' said Agnes dutifully. 'You certainly proved your point there.'

'I only hope that poor fellow gets back to school before she does *irreparable* harm,' said Dorothy. It was plain that she was still very much The Teacher.

'Would you like me to ring that hotel in Bury St Edmunds? It sounded very pleasant, didn't it?' asked Agnes, changing the subject.

'Yes, that would be kind of you. And if they can't have us, I will try Lavenham tonight.'

Having successfully dislodged Dorothy from her hobby-horse, Agnes went to the telephone. Really, one trembled for dear Dorothy's blood-pressure at times like this!

*

It was at about this time that Doreen Lilly was observed in the company of a handsome young man.

Only close neighbours of Gladys and Doreen first noticed him, and he was dismissed as a family friend, a cousin perhaps, or someone breaking his journey from London to the west. As it happened, the last guess was nearest the mark, for the young man was the window cleaner with a mother in Cirencester. He had befriended Doreen in London, where he worked, and had returned her to her mother, with young Bobby, months before. He had called once or twice since then, usually after dark, so that his visits had gone unobserved. Now, it seemed, he was paying the daughter more regular attention.

It was soon common knowledge in Thrush Green, and Jane Cartwright mentioned it to her mother one day.

'Not that Doreen says anything. I never get a squeak out of her, though she is always polite and a very good worker. If anything does come of this, I shall really miss her.'

'I've heard nothing,' said Mrs Jenner, 'but if Gladys Lilly says anything about it, I will let you know.'

'What about Uncle Percy? Do you think he's heard the rumours?'

'I really don't know. Percy's quite old enough to run his own life, and if he's silly enough to imagine a young girl is going to make him a wife, then he should know better. Heaven knows he's been jilted often enough! Look at Emily Cooke! Surely he's learnt his lesson from that affair.'

'I don't think Uncle Percy will ever learn,' said his niece sadly. 'All I know is I'd like to see him settled. He really needs a good wife.'

'Well, that's his problem,' said Mrs Jenner, and the conversation turned to other matters.

The general opinion was that poor old Perce was going to come another cropper, and the situation was observed with some amusement and very little sympathy. Not surprisingly, among the most unfeeling was Albert Piggott. He took it upon himself to find out Percy's reactions to this delicate matter one cold March morning.

The grass of Thrush Green was shivering in an easterly wind, and the rooks above the fields behind The Two Pheasants were being blown about the sky, cawing raucously.

Albert was sipping his half-pint when Percy arrived. The newcomer blew on his fingers and made for the fire.

'Coldest we've had all winter,' he remarked.

Albert nodded. 'Bad weather for lambin',' he rejoined. 'Well, bad for all young things.'

Percy did not respond to this remark, simply ordering a pint from Mr Jones and turning his back to the comfort of the fire.

'I said it was bad weather for *all young things*,' repeated Albert loudly, intent on leading up to the matter he had in mind.

' 'Tis that,' agreed Percy, collecting his tankard. 'There's a new baby at the Cookes', they say.'

'What *another*? Not your Emily's, I hope?'

Percy began to look irritated, just as Albert intended.

'She's not my Emily, as you well know. And no, it ain't her baby. It's the young sister's, if you must know. And they're both pretty poorly, so I gather.'

'That's bad,' commented Mr Jones, a kindly man.

'I expect she asked for it,' said Albert. 'These young girls are all kittle-cattle. They take up with whoever comes along. Look at Doreen Lilly now.'

This did cause some reaction from Percy, who put his tankard down, and turned towards Albert.

'What about Doreen?'

'Got some new young man hangin' round her, they say.'

'Who says?'

'Well, most everybody. Some chap from London she met when she was workin' up there. Nice-lookin' bloke. Quite the film star.'

'She's a pretty girl herself,' said Percy equably. 'You can't wonder she gets a follower or two.'

He drained his glass, wiped his mouth on the back of his hand, and nodded to the landlord.

'Must be off. Got some sheep dip to pick up. Be seein' you, Albert.'

The door slammed behind him, and a gust of chilly air swirled about the room.

'You didn't get much change out of him,' observed Mr Jones, putting another log on the fire. 'And serve you right, Albert Piggott, trying to stir up trouble.'

'Silly old fool asks for it,' growled Albert, but he had the grace to look discomfited.

Meanwhile, at the Lovelocks' house things continued their erratic course.

On the morning after the disastrous birthday party, Violet went into Bertha's bedroom bearing the usual cup of tea. She had had a poor night herself, tortured with remembrances of the humiliating end to the party. The question of the will hung over her. Would Bertha go ahead with this deeply embarrassing plan? Would Justin be able to cope with it? Could Bertha really put in hand such a preposterous plan as the ordering of a stained-glass window, or an organ? Come to that, would Bertha decide on something even more extravagant: a side chapel, say, or a complete reorganization of the interior seating? Really, there was no end to the list of follies which her poor sister might decide to undertake. And would she be stopped? And if so, by whom?

She found Bertha sitting peacefully in bed, brushing her sparse locks with a silver-backed hairbrush. She smiled at Violet.

'Oh, lovely! How I do look forward to this first cup of tea! So sweet of you, dear, to provide it.'

'And how did you sleep?' enquired Violet, remembering her own disturbed night.

'Like a top, dear, after that lovely party. It all went so well, didn't it? I am so grateful to you and Ada for making it such a perfect day.'

Violet stood in silence, looking out of the window at Lulling High Street which was already busy with traffic. It was quite apparent that Bertha was not going to admit to any of the unpleasantness that had occurred. Was this intentional, or did she really forget anything disturbing?

She left Bertha sipping her tea, and returned to her own bedroom. She had come to a conclusion which was to support her throughout the years to come. She must simply take Bertha as she found her, day by day. It had to be faced. Bertha was slightly mad. She was senile, and quite erratic. In the future, she must be cared for as one would care for any patient with mental trouble. It would involve constant supervision, hopefully at home in the house they had shared all their lives, but if need be, in some suitable institution.

Meanwhile, she knew she had the support of John Lovell, Justin Venables, and dear Charles Henstock. With such a powerful trio behind her, Violet felt that she could cope with all that life with Bertha might bring.

After a fortnight away from school, Alan Lester tottered back to his classroom. He felt ten years older, and looked it too. Why was it taking so long to recover, he asked the doctor querulously.

'Because you were thoroughly run down when this hit you,' John told him. 'You've been under appalling strain for years now. I have a theory that those days in bed are nature's way of making you let up.'

'But it's absolutely absurd,' protested Alan. 'I walk across to the school and have to sit down to get over it. Then I try to write on the blackboard, and I can scarcely get my arm up. Can't you give me something to put some spunk into me? I'm a walking zombie.'

'I'll give you a tonic,' promised John. 'Just take things gently, and you'll be yourself again in a few days.'

The doctor was not the only one to supply jollop. When Betty Bell related the fact of Alan Lester's prolonged convalescence to Dotty, that resourceful lady produced a large bottle filled with a murky liquid which had already corroded its metal cap.

'Now, this is just the thing,' Dotty told her. 'You take this to the school house, Betty, and tell the poor fellow to take a tablespoonful three times a day. It's a wonderful pick-me-up. One of my old aunt's recipes. It has rose-hip syrup and black treacle in it.'

'What else?' asked Betty suspiciously.

Dotty looked flummoxed. 'Now what was it? Certainly horehound and a bunch of garlic, so good for the chest. And I am sure there were half a dozen other things, all wholesome of course, I will look at the recipe if you like.'

Betty said she was not to bother, accepted the bottle, and privately determined to warn the patient to leave it sealed. She confided her decision to Harold Shoosmith some days later, and he heartily approved.

'Well, I was afraid it might explode in his face,' said Betty. 'It looked dangerous to me. Do you reckon it might have been any good?'

'As paint-stripper maybe,' replied Harold.

Isobel was able to tell her Barton friends that the headmaster had returned to his duties, and that Mrs Hill had now departed to brush up her 'Look-and-Say' method of reading for her next session as supply-teacher in the district.

Dorothy sounded greatly relieved. 'And I will ring next week, Isobel, for we're setting off in a day or two for our little break. We shall be at The Swan at Lavenham. Such a good centre, and we were very well looked after there last time.'

Isobel sent her best wishes for the jaunt, and asked about Timmy.

'Oh, Eileen is looking after him. And Teddy too,' was the reply.

I wonder, thought Isobel, as she put back the receiver, who will worry most? Agnes about Timmy, or Dorothy about Teddy?

The day before the ladies were due to depart from Barton, they suffered an appalling shock.

The packing was half done, and last-minute duties attended to: the newspapers had been cancelled, the milkman instructed to leave only half a pint each time for Timmy's use, and the spare keys deposited with Eileen. The maps were ready on the hall table, the coffee flask waiting in the kitchen and Agnes had already put out the clothes she intended to wear on the journey.

They were having their after-lunch rest when the telephone rang, and Agnes answered it. Dorothy sat up, alert. It was Eileen's voice at the other end, and it sounded strained.

'Such a dreadful cold. I was coming up to tell you the news, but frankly it wouldn't be fair to you, just as you are going off.'

'What news?' enquired Agnes.

'Well, dear, we both wanted you and Dorothy to be the first to hear – Teddy has asked me to marry him.'

There was a little cry, hastily checked, from Dorothy. Agnes found herself trembling, but kept her voice steady.

'But that is wonderful!' she said. 'Congratulations!'

'It won't be for some time, but no point in waiting about at our age. I only wish I hadn't developed this appalling cold. I think I must have caught it from Teddy.'

There was another choking sound from Dorothy, who now hurried to the bathroom. Agnes heard the bolt slam home. Her heart sank.

'This won't make any difference,' Eileen was saying, 'to my looking after Timmy. I shall be quite fit enough to pop along

tomorrow when you have gone. Is Dorothy there? I should like
to tell her our news.'

'She's not at the moment,' said Agnes truthfully, 'but I
shall pass on the message. I know she'll be as delighted as I
am.'

'Teddy asked me to give you the news. He said women are so
much better at these things.'

The great coward, thought Agnes indignantly!

'Well, our love and congratulations to you both,' said Agnes.
'We'll ring before we go, and if you are not up to it, I will ask
Mrs Berry to see to Timmy, so don't worry about that.'

She hurried to the bathroom door.

'Are you all right, Dorothy? I expect you heard?'

'I heard,' said a muffled voice, 'and I'm quite all right.'

Reluctantly, Agnes returned to her chair. Her heart was
thumping in an alarming way, and her hands trembled as she
picked up her knitting. Poor, poor Dorothy!

She seemed to be a very long time in the bathroom, and
Agnes's anxiety grew. Was she prostrate with grief? Had she
collapsed on the floor, perhaps striking her head on the wash-
basin and now lying stunned? Could she – dreadful thought! –
be contemplating *suicide*?

The bathroom cupboard certainly held medicine, but nothing
much more toxic than aspirin, TCP and calamine lotion. To be
sure, there was a bottle of disinfectant for the lavatory. And
prisoners in cells sometimes *hanged* themselves, but apart from
the belt of the bath-robe there was really nothing to hand in the
bathroom in that line. In any case, Agnes thought wildly, that
hook on the door would scarcely stand the weight.

It was really devastating, decided Agnes, knitting furiously,
how one's mind encompassed a hundred horrors in the space of
a minute. If she did not pull herself together she would be
mentally choosing the hymns for Dorothy's funeral, and wondering if the Distressed Gentlefolks Aid Association could do
with her clothes.

At that moment, Dorothy returned from the bathroom and

stood with her back to Agnes, gazing out into the garden. Her hand clutched the wet ball of her handkerchief, which she was turning round and round.

Agnes dared not speak, and waited with a pounding heart for Dorothy's first words.

'Thank you for coping with that, my dear. I couldn't have spoken. I simply couldn't.'

'I understand. It's been a shock to us both.'

Dorothy went back to her armchair. Her face was blotchy, but the tears had gone. 'I've been a fool, Agnes.'

'That happens to us all,' said Agnes gently. 'It doesn't really matter, you know. Just don't upset yourself. I think Eileen will make Teddy a good wife. After all, they've known each other for many years.'

'Well, I'm not forecasting anything,' said Dorothy with a slight return to normality. 'It's their affair. I shall ring Eileen, and Teddy too, this evening, to congratulate them.'

'That's right,' said Agnes approvingly. 'We must leave things comfortably here before we set off tomorrow. It's a very good thing we are having this break. It will do us both good, and we shall be able to come back and face their wedding.'

'Do you think we'll be invited?' asked Dorothy in alarm. 'I don't think I could face it.'

Agnes was silent for a moment, gazing in dismay at her knitting. 'I've done at least two inches of *moss-stitch* when it should be *rib*,' she cried. 'I shall have to unpick it.'

Dorothy rose. 'I shall make us some tea,' she announced. 'I don't care if it is only three o'clock. We both need it.'

Agnes heard her in the kitchen, filling the kettle for that never-failing help in times of trouble.

To her surprise, Dorothy reappeared within a minute. 'What I cannot *stomach*,' she told Agnes fiercely, 'is the way *Teddy* asked *Eileen* to break the news. So like a man!'

'Just what I felt,' cried Agnes. 'Men are such *cowards*!'

Neither of the ladies slept well that night. Dorothy, though proud of her good behaviour on the telephone that evening to Eileen and the perfidious Teddy, still smarted from self-recrimination over her conduct during the last months. It was hard to accept the fact that one had been foolish and invited ridicule. She thought of Agnes's kind remark about everyone being foolish at some time. It gave her some slight comfort.

In the adjoining bedroom, Agnes's thoughts were more anguished, mainly on her friend's behalf. Certainly Dorothy had appeared calmer as the evening had progressed, and her congratulatory messages to Eileen and Teddy had been done most graciously. Agnes, knowing how much she was suffering, was immensely proud of her. But was it a good thing to suppress her feelings, wondered Agnes, as she lay worrying in the small hours, still unable to sleep.

Those dreadful moments considering Dorothy's possible suicide in the bathroom came back to torment her. Was Dorothy *really* over it? Or would she do something senseless within the next day or two, suddenly distraught? Agnes recalled reading about some unhappy person who had driven deliberately straight into a lamp-post after being crossed in love. And only last week she had read about another poor fellow driving over a precipice to his death.

Well, thought Agnes, trying to find some crumb of comfort,

there were not any precipices between Barton-on-Sea and Lavenham.

And on that somewhat unsatisfactory thought, she fell into an uneasy sleep.

20. WEDDINGS

As if to compensate for the wretched winter, March grew more balmy as the days passed.

At Thrush Green, the sticky buds on the chestnut trees were beginning to sprout tiny green fans, and the stark hedges were softening with young leaves. Daffodils and early tulips brightened the gardens, and at the edge of Lulling Woods the banks were starred with primroses. Beneath the hedges, hidden in dead silky grass, blue and white violets lurked.

Chaffinches, tits and other little garden birds foraged ceaselessly to feed their nestlings, and Percy Hodge's lambs skittered about their field, bleating with the excitement of youth and fair weather.

Altogether it was a heartening time, and people were glad to get outdoors and greet each other without shivering in the wicked east wind which had cut short many a neighbourly conversation earlier.

Alan Lester recovered his strength, and the fact that the schoolchildren could spend their playtimes out of doors, running off their high spirits, greatly helped him through his convalescence.

As John Lovell had predicted, Margaret had thrived on the nursing she had been obliged to undertake. She was now taking a much more active part in the affairs of Thrush Green, and Ella Bembridge and Muriel Fuller were largely responsible for this.

Now that their part in preparing the new room at Rectory Cottages was finished, the two needlewomen were at a loose end, and fairly jumped at Charles Henstock's diffident suggestion that St Andrew's could do with some new hassocks.

With considerable energy, not to say bullying, they had roped in half a dozen helpers, including Margaret Lester, who was an accomplished needle-woman; the choosing of designs, colours and types of wool and canvas engaged all the ladies as spring fever inspired them. This led to other activities, especially for Margaret, who found herself, before the month had ended, not only secretary to the Women's Institute, vice-president of Lulling Brownies and the Red Cross, but also a part-time assistant at the Sue Ryder Charity shop. Alan's relief in her rehabilitation knew no bounds, and Thrush Green rejoiced with him.

Dotty Harmer too was imbued with this spring fever, and decided to supply the ducks with a sloping ramp to ease their access to the pond. She had asked Albert's advice on the project, and he had weaned her from the ambitious plan of a concrete structure to one involving less work for himself. A nice wooden plank, he told her, would be just the thing, and could be lifted out for a good scrub if it grew too slimy.

Dotty saw the sense of this, and once it was installed she had the delight of watching her tiny yellow ducklings waddling up and down the slope. Even Albert's flinty heart was softened by this domestic scene, and felt pride in the result of his suggestion for the ducks' convenience. He told Nelly about it when she returned one evening from The Fuchsia Bush.

But Nelly had news of her own. 'That young chap who's courting Doreen came in today. She was with him, and little Bobby. I bet there's a wedding there before the summer's out. Gladys will be glad, I should think. There's not much room in that place of hers with Doreen and the boy.'

'Maybe they'll all go and live there,' suggested Albert, looking, as usual, on the gloomy side.

'Rubbish!' snorted Nelly, whisking away his empty plate. 'Gladys will see that doesn't happen. She won't want a great useless man under her feet any more than I do.'

Albert took the hint, and made his way over to The Two Pheasants.

The mild weather was widespread, and Agnes and Dorothy enjoyed their change of scene.

Isobel had a call from them in the middle of the week, to say that they had decided to make a detour on their way home and would call to see them if it was convenient.

'Of course!' cried Isobel. 'What a lovely surprise.'

'And we want you to have lunch with us,' continued Dorothy, 'at The Two Pheasants, if you will be kind enough to book a table. Better say one o'clock, or a little after. We intend to make an early start, but it's impossible to guess what hold-ups there will be these days. Even *here*, in *Suffolk*, there is an amazing amount of traffic.'

She spoke as though East Anglia should be in the horse-and-cart stage, and seemed to resent the fact that it was as congested as the rest of England.

Isobel commiserated, thanked her for the lunch invitation, and promised to do as she asked.

She went to tell Harold the news. 'So nice of them,' she commented. 'They really have made themselves a peaceful pleasant life since they moved to Barton. They don't seem to have a care in the world.'

Needless to say, she knew nothing as yet about poor Dorothy's damaged feelings, and Agnes's concern for her companion.

Harold Shoosmith, on his walk to The Two Pheasants to book a table for four, met Mrs Jenner who was on her way to visit her daughter at Rectory Cottages. They agreed that it was good to see the sun, that it made one feel ten years younger, that it was about time they had a decent spell of weather, and after these necessary civilities they parted.

Jane Cartwright was in her little office filling in forms. She rose to greet her mother.

'Doreen's just been in. She's definitely engaged to that young man and, of course, I'm glad for her sake but we'll all miss her.'

'Why? Is she likely to move from Lulling? Can't he get a job here? I could do with a good window cleaner myself.'

'He's evidently got a lucrative round in London, hotels and shops, that sort of thing. And he's got a flat too, so of course they'll set up home there.'

'Gladys will be relieved anyway,' surmised Mrs Jenner. 'Maybe I'll hear more about it tonight at Bingo.'

Gladys Lilly seemed only too pleased to enlarge on the news of Doreen's future as she, Nelly and Mrs Jenner dallied over their coffee during the Bingo interval.

'He's a good fellow,' she enthused, 'and Bobby likes him. It's time that child had a man to deal with him now and again. Our Doreen's too soft with him. Looking back, I can see it was a blessing in disguise when that second little stranger came to nought.'

Her companions sighed, and nodded sadly in agreement.

'One's one thing,' went on Gladys, 'but a chap's going to think twice before taking on two.'

'That's right,' agreed Nelly.

'So when is the wedding?' enquired Mrs Jenner.

'Next month. Just down the registry, and then a quiet buffet lunch at my place.'

'Very suitable,' approved Mrs Jenner.

Gladys Lilly began to fidget with her gloves, and looked unusually coy.

'And that's not all,' she went on. 'I'm thinking of getting married myself.'

'No!' gasped Nelly.

'I'm glad to hear it,' said Mrs Jenner warmly.

Gladys became even more agitated. 'Well, I hope you'll still be glad when I tell you who it is. You see, it's your brother Percy who's asked me.'

'Well, I'm blowed!' cried Nelly. 'And we all thought—'

Mrs Jenner cut in before the sentence could finish. She leant across the table, and kissed Gladys's flushed cheek.

'Of course I'm glad! It's the best day's work Percy ever did, and I couldn't wish for a nicer sister-in-law.'

Nelly imparted the great news to Albert that night when he returned from The Two Pheasants at closing time.

It was gratifying to see his stunned expression.

'Never thought old Perce would have so much sense,' was his comment eventually.

'Mind you,' said Nelly, 'she's getting the worst of the deal, if you ask me. That place of his will want cleaning from top to bottom, and Percy don't like parting with money, like some others I know of not a hundred miles from here.'

Albert ignored this side-swipe, still bemused by Percy's good fortune.

'They say she's a good cook too,' he was muttering to himself. 'D'you reckon she's throwing herself away on old Perce? I mean, he's no great catch, is he?'

'Very true,' agreed Nelly, setting the kitchen table for breakfast with her usual rapidity. 'But then what man is?'

She stopped suddenly, clutching a handful of cutlery to her well-filled cardigan.

'You see, it's *love*,' she told Albert. 'That's what makes people do these silly things. *Percy's* a lucky chap, but I only hope poor *Gladys* don't live to regret the day!'

Such exciting news soon spread like a bush fire through Thrush Green and Lulling; it was generally agreed that this was a most suitable marriage, and that Percy was an extremely lucky fellow. No one, said the gossips, could be more capable of coping with that neglected house and poor lonely Percy than Gladys Lilly, who had always been much respected in the neighbourhood. Why, she might even get Percy to attend chapel, and that would be a real advance!

Charles Henstock told Dimity that he was delighted on Percy's behalf, and had always thought that a marriage made later in life was usually successful. Why, look at his own! It would have been nice if he could have officiated at the wedding ceremony, but he supposed that Gladys would wish to have it at the chapel, or perhaps they would simply have the civil ceremony at the registrar's office.

Dotty Harmer told Albert, when he came to inspect the duck ramp for signs of wear, that Gladys Lilly was one of the most sensible women she knew, and always kept a pot of goose-grease to rub on chests suffering from winter coughs and congestion.

Winnie Bailey and Jenny greeted the news with relief: at last Percy would stop pestering Jenny and all the other young girls who had excited Percy's amorous inclinations in the past.

Mrs Jenner and Jane were much in favour of the union, and the thought of her old home being restored to its former cheerful state gave the older woman great happiness. The neglected garden too, she guessed, would soon be put into good order, and her brother's disreputable appearance would change for the better with Gladys to feed him properly, mend his clothes, and send him regularly to the barber's.

Percy himself went about in a daze of happiness. He had to stand a good deal of banter, but was so pleased and proud that he accepted all the jibes with a smiling countenance, and even stood a round to his cronies at the pub.

Doreen Lilly's forthcoming marriage did not promote quite so much interest. After all, she was young and pretty, bound to marry sometime, and in any case, the chap was a foreigner, wasn't he? Nevertheless, Charles Henstock felt that Anthony Bull should know what was happening to Doreen and her mother, and rang him one evening.

'Splendid news!' said Anthony heartily. 'She was such a pathetic little waif when I saw her last. I hope you'll let me know her address when they come to London eventually. I should like to keep in touch. And as for Gladys, I remember her so well, and her first husband's lardy cakes. Give them all my congratulations.'

The day of Dorothy and Agnes's visit dawned fair and cloudless, and the ladies arrived a little before one o'clock, happy with their successful negotiation of a new route.

'Really no bother!' cried Dorothy. 'Agnes is a first-class navigator. We did find that Milton Keynes kept getting in the way, I must confess, but once we left that behind it was plain sailing.'

They had a celebratory glass of sherry while they exchanged news, and then walked across the grass to The Two Pheasants.

The children were still at play before afternoon school, and Alan Lester, who was on duty, hurried to greet the two teachers.

'Do come in. We'd all love to see you. You haven't met my wife yet, and she would be so pleased.'

But the ladies explained that they had to be off soon after lunch.

'Then next time! I'm sure there will be a next time,' said Alan, looking enquiringly at the Shoosmiths.

'Indeed there will,' cried Isobel. 'We hope they will be here again very soon.'

A Land Rover was parked outside The Two Pheasants, and a black and white collie had its head out of the driver's window.

'Why, it's Percy Hodge's dog,' exclaimed Dorothy, stroking the silky head. 'It's so good to see that it hasn't suffered from that wretched accident.'

'No harm done,' said Percy, who had just emerged from the pub looking unusually spruce, and in the company of a middle-aged lady.

Dorothy was surprised and relieved at Percy's affability. He had remained somewhat surly after she had slightly injured Gyp, and their subsequent encounters had been definitely frosty.

Yet here he was, positively beaming at them!

'This is my wife-to-be,' he announced with pride, and all was revealed to the bemused ladies. There were congratulations all round, and Dorothy patted Gyp with renewed affection before the couple drove off, and the Shoosmiths ushered their visitors into the bar where they were welcomed warmly by Mr Jones and his wife.

They returned to the Shoosmiths after lunch, and Dorothy was taken down the garden by Harold to collect a cutting of winter jasmine which he had kept for her.

It gave Isobel and Agnes a chance to exchange confidences.

'And is Dorothy still attentive to Teddy's needs?' asked Isobel.

The flood-gates opened, and Agnes described the dreadful consequences of Eileen's telephone call, remembering how sympathetic Isobel had been when the matter of Teddy had cropped up earlier when she was staying there.

'She has been so brave,' Agnes said. 'After the first awful shock she pulled herself together, and I hope this little break has given her time to come to terms with things.'

'Poor Dorothy!'

'I just dread meeting Eileen and Teddy face to face. It might well open up the wound for Dorothy, and I really don't think I could bear to see her suffer so again.'

'Dorothy will cope,' said Isobel. 'You see, things will be easier than you imagine. I'm sure that the future will be much as you both planned it when you went to Barton-on-Sea.'

Dorothy returned, farewells were said, and the ladies set off homeward.

Agnes dozed part of the way, and woke with a start to find that they were within a few miles of home. Her fears came flocking back like menacing birds. How would Dorothy react to this return to familiar things? Would she be able to keep up this brave front of calm? Would she be able to face Teddy and Eileen in their new role of those about to be married?

These thoughts, as well as the hope that their house would be free from flood, fire and burglars, kept Agnes in a state of severe agitation.

Dorothy turned the car into their lane. They passed Teddy's house and Eileen's opposite it. All was calm and deserted.

'Two weddings at Thrush Green,' said Dorothy, 'and another to look forward to here.'

And Agnes saw, to her intense relief, that her friend was smiling.

Village School

In a village there are no secrets. As head of Fairacre's two-class school, Miss Read's every deed is subject for speculation, and she is inevitably involved in most of her neighbour's concerns.

Her fist novel recounts the ups and downs of a year in 1950s Fairacre with the clear-sighted tolerance, sharp observation and gentle irony that make her so enduringly popular. From Miss Clare's failing health to the new infant teacher's budding romance and Mrs Pringle's never-ending complaints, from the everyday wonders of nature to the often less wonderful behaviour of the villagers, very little escapes Miss Read's notice . . .

ALSO BY MISS READ

Village Diary

'As I have been given a large and magnificent diary for Christmas – seven by ten and nearly two inches thick – I intend to fill it in as long as my ardour lasts. Further than that I will not go. There are quite enough jobs that a schoolmistress just must do . . .'

Luckily for her readers, Miss Read's ardour lasts all year, encompassing every aspect of Fairacre life. Whether embroiled unwillingly in her friend Amy's marital hiccups, discussing the changing world with Miss Clare or the modern problems of good local education and rural impoverishment with the schools inspector and the doctor, she remains balanced, humorous and wise – and never forgets either her most important charge, the mixed bag of children in her school, or the joys of the changing seasons.

Storm in the Village

Fairacre and the neighbouring village of Beech Green are under siege by planners who want to build a new estate on Harold Miller's Hundred Acre Field, and the inhabitants are vocally divided on the subject. As the schoolmistress, Miss Read is inevitably involved – but she also has more personal problems to deal with.

Her junior Miss Jackson's unwise passion for a very unsuitable man, the niceties of defining categories for the flower show, and the ever-leaking and finally collapsing skylight in the schoolhouse are just a few of the problems Miss Read deals with in the course of another enchanting year as one of the most observant recorders of a rural community.

Tyler's Row

'They closed the broken gate carefully and looked through the archway at the scene which had fascinated so many sight-seers before them. "It would never do, of course," said Diana, at last . . .'

Miss Read heard about the sale of Tyler's Row from Mrs Pringle – and long before Fairacre was alive with rumours. Why were the present owners selling? Was it true that a football pools winner was about to buy it? Had Tyler's Row been condemned – or was it to be restored?

All speculation ends when Peter and Diana Hale arrive in Fairacre to view Tyler's Row, with plans to create their own rural haven. However, the Hales soon discover that Fairacre is no Utopia, but a normal English village, with all the usual ups and downs . . .

ALSO BY MISS READ

Over the Gate

'The story of the village goes back a long, long time, and it still goes on . . . I have listened to my neighbours' accounts of tales of long ago, and with what unfailing curiosity I observe the happenings of today!'

From an unusual recipe for losing weight found in an old notebook (and used with alarming consequences) to the queen of copy-cats who drives her neighbour mad with anger – to say nothing of a touch-and-go romance – Miss Read, the schoolmistress, continues to attract odd stories and village folklore, and retells them with her characteristic compassion and humour.

ALSO BY MISS READ

Christmas at Fairacre

'Winter may not be everyone's favourite season, but of all the year's festivals Christmas takes pride of place, and has lost none of its magic. Outside, the winter landscape has a beauty of its own: bare branches against a clear sky, brilliant stars on a frosty night and perhaps a swathe of untouched snow. But these beauties are best when seen from the comfort of one's home with a good fire crackling and the smell of crumpets toasting for tea . . .'

This charming collection of Christmas tales is packed with unforgettable characters, enchanting stories and festive cheer.

All Orion/Phoenix titles are available at your local bookshop or from the following address:

Mail Order Department
Littlehampton Book Services
FREEPOST BR535
Worthing, West Sussex, BN13 3BR
telephone 01903 828503, *facsimile* 01903 828802
e-mail MailOrders@lbsltd.co.uk
(Please ensure that you include full postal address details)

Payment can be made either by credit/debit card (Visa, Mastercard, Access and Switch accepted) or by sending a £ Sterling cheque or postal order made payable to *Littlehampton Book Services*.
DO NOT SEND CASH OR CURRENCY

Please add the following to cover postage and packing

UK and BFPO:
£1.50 for the first book, and 50p for each additional book to a maximum of £3.50

Overseas and Eire:
£2.50 for the first book plus £1.00 for the second book and 50p for each additional book ordered

---

BLOCK CAPITALS PLEASE

name of cardholder _____

address of cardholder _____

delivery address
(if different from cardholder)
_____
_____

postcode _____   postcode _____

☐ I enclose my remittance for £_____

☐ please debit my Mastercard/Visa/Access/Switch (delete as appropriate)

card number ☐☐☐☐☐☐☐☐☐☐☐☐☐☐☐☐☐☐

expiry date ☐☐☐☐   Switch issue no. ☐☐

signature _____

prices and availability are subject to change without notice